NAMED & SHAMED

A dark and dirty erotic fairy tale

First published in 2017 by Sinful Press.
www.sinfulpress.co.uk
Copyright © 2012 Janine Ashbless
Cover design by Studioenp
The right of Janine Ashbless to be identified as the author
of this work has been asserted in accordance with the
Copyright, Designs and Patents Act, 1988.

A CIP catalogue record for this book is available from the
British Library

ISBN-13: 978-1-910908-19-8
Second Edition
First edition published in 2012 by Sweetmeats Press

NAMED & SHAMED

A dark and dirty erotic fairy tale

Janine Ashbless

SINFUL PRESS

Lizzie met her at the gate
Full of wise upbraidings:
"Dear, you should not stay so late,
Twilight is not good for maidens;
Should not loiter in the glen
In the haunts of goblin men."
- 'Goblin Market,' Christina Rossetti

Contents

Prologue: Tarnished Gold

BOOK ONE: TOWN

BOOK TWO: COUNTRY

BOOK THREE: COURT

Prologue

Tarnished Gold

You appear to be in distress," said the thing that looked like a man, but wasn't even human. "May I help?"

Despite my fear, I forced myself to say, "It's very kind of you to offer." If there's one rule about dealing with Them There that comes close to being universally true, it's *Be Polite.* They hate rudeness. "But no, thank you," I added.

"What's your trouble?"

"Really, thank you, but it's not—"

"Are you looking for something?" He glanced over my shoulder, through the gate I'd been kicking.

"My car's in there... My, um, carriage."

His eyes narrowed. "I know what a car is."

"Sorry."

"You were crying. What is so important that it makes you weep?"

He just wasn't taking *No* for an answer. I shouldn't be having this conversation—but I couldn't refuse to talk. So I said, reluctantly, "It got locked up by mistake. If I don't get it back this evening…" I clenched my jaw. "There's something inside it that I need back, tonight, or a friend of mine will be in terrible trouble."

"Then let me retrieve the thing for you."

"I'm not asking for help."

"But I am offering."

I bit my lip. This was awful. I didn't want to even start negotiating with this creature. But if I didn't, a man could die. Really die. They didn't mess around, that sort. And it'd be my fault.

What choice did I have?

"You'd want something in exchange, I suppose?" I asked.

"Of course. But nothing you'd be unwilling to give."

What was this I was getting myself into, I wondered— some sort of messed up version of *The Princess and the Frog*? Was he going to fetch my golden ball from the bottom of the well in exchange for my promise to marry him? As if in sympathy, my voice came out croaky. "What?"

"Eight warm inches of your flesh, my sweet. Wrapped around eight inches of mine."

Not exactly marriage then. But consummation, anyway.

"I see."

"You look perturbed. Is it an offence to desire such beauty as yours? I promise you will enjoy it, and that I will not hurt you… unless that is your pleasure too."

"Let's get this straight. One fuck, yes?"

"Yes. Exactly."

❧ ❧ ❧

I was wrong though. This story wasn't *The Princess and the Frog*. In that story the proud princess calls the shots and it's the frog who endures all the humiliation and pain. I didn't know it then, but this was an altogether different tale.

If only I'd realised.

BOOK ONE

TOWN

Chapter One

An Early Draft

The E in *E L Blakey: antiques bought and sold* stood for Edmund, of all things. I didn't think *anyone* was called Edmund these days, but it suited him. He was slim and scholarly-looking and had wings of silver hair brushed back over the legs of his wire-rimmed spectacles. He was old enough to be my father and then some. But I didn't let that, or his silly name, stop me falling in with him as he browsed the stalls of the London Antiques Fair, or, ever-so-casually, striking up an enthusiastic conversation with him on the subject of Victorian books. Or going for a drink with him. Or agreeing to his offer to take me back to his shop to see some of his rarer folios. Damn it—I worked *hard* to hook him. I don't think he was used to young women showing that much interest in either him or his work. He still wore a faint air of disbelief as he hailed us a taxi.

I giggled as he held the door for me and made sure he got a good flash up my long legs and under my plaid miniskirt to the lacy whites beneath. I'd picked those clothes especially for such an opportunity.

Hell no, I wasn't being subtle. What would have been the point of that? He was such a repressed sort that he'd never have made the first move without the assistance of my heavy hints. Anyway, I'm not the sort of person who likes to pussy-foot around. Know what you want, take your knocks and grab your chances—that's how I play it.

Everything else went out the window when Them There came back.

Edmund Blakey was a gentleman, though. He didn't try to grope me in the cab, even though I frequently reached to touch his knee and leaned in to give him a view down my deep cleavage. He just bit his lip and cleared his throat and talked with even more determination about folios and palimpsests, though he had to drape both hands over his crotch to hide his growing consternation.

Hey, he was cute. I'd stuck my nose into some pretty dodgy places on behalf of the Home Office, but for once this felt like no hardship.

"You say your thesis is on women poets, Tansy?" he asked as he unlocked his front door.

The shop stood in a block of irregular redbrick facades. I knew it very well, from the veiled muse carved on the lintel to the genteel hand-lettered name painted on the frontage and the iron fire escape at the back. After all, I'd been to scope it out several times. "Oh yes," I said, trying to sound breezy and hoping he wouldn't catch me out. In fact it's been a few years since I was a student. "My theme is sexual subtext in Victorian women's poetry."

"Well, I'm sure I have some volumes you'll find interesting."

"Ooh, I can't wait," I gushed.

Damn right he had things that interested me. I keep an eye on what comes up for auction, and I knew what he'd been buying. Nursery tales, Golden Age books of folk stories… lots of stuff that comes under my remit now. And he'd been selling seventeenth century golden guineas too, according to my contact at the auction house. Treasure trove. We know what that means: somebody had been helping him out with his purchases. Either he was up to something, or he was fronting for the real buyer. Maybe someone who didn't like to appear in public.

As the door opened, a waft of perfumed air rolled out from within and I stiffened involuntarily. Ogres, it had turned out, love patchouli. For a moment I felt a cold misgiving that he'd picked me up for reasons entirely unrelated to my teasing attire and my blatant flirting. My hand tightened around the strap of my handbag; inside were a number of defensive items ranging from a cross of welded horseshoe nails to an illegal flick-knife that I'd never used yet but liked to keep close. I smiled in what I hoped was a relaxed manner, pretending not to notice that musky, bewitching scent as he ushered me within.

"Wow. What an amazing place!" I spun on my heel, looking at the stacked fireplaces and dressers, the blanket chests and grandfather clocks and ornate fly-spotted mirrors. And lots and lots of wardrobes. That didn't surprise me.

People have been getting rid of wardrobes for the same reason they've been sawing the legs off their bed-frames… Some very nasty things can lurk in those dark domestic corners. More clutter sat on the flat surfaces: smoothing irons and oriental plates, porcelain dolls and books with gilt-lettered spines, almost everything looking brown and dusty in the dim light.

"Well, thank you." He looked gratified. "I've been in the business a few years now. There are some very nice pieces here, if I say so myself."

It could be entirely rubbish and I'd be none the wiser, I thought as he led me through the passages between the stacked lumber. I know bugger-all about antiques—which is in fact only slightly less than I know about Victorian women poets. My real M.A. is in anthropology. Comparative folklore, in fact, which had to be the world's least marketable academic subject at the time. Then Them There came back. Suddenly I have a niche. Specialist knowledge pays off. Like, I was one of the few people who knew from the start that it was dangerous to say certain nouns out loud. That it's best to stick to *Them There* and *The Good Folk* and other traditional euphemisms— otherwise they get irritated. And, seriously, nobody wants that.

The government pays me for this. Quietly, under-the-table, on a freelance basis. They don't want it to be known. That suits me just fine. And it's a living.

Edmund, charmingly awkward, showed me his desk, piled high with receipts and invoices. Hanging behind the chair was an art print I recognised. *Beata Beatrix*, with her heavy eyelids and smoky red hair like a cooling lava flow. Cha-ching—I'd struck gold.

I shook out my own long red curls, batted my lashes and

said, "Dante Gabriel Rossetti! Oh, I love that picture—it's so romantic. Just smouldering, don't you think?"

Edmund mumbled, "Quite." He was standing slightly awkwardly, probably self-conscious about that semi he had pushing up against his trousers. I took a step forward right into his personal space, my full breasts almost brushing his shirt, and laid a finger on his chest. In my strappy cork-heeled shoes we were eye to eye, almost exactly the same height.

"Do you like red hair too, Edmund?"

"Very much so," he admitted, his voice all thick. He was handsome, I thought, despite his age. A real silver fox. I gave him a long look.

"You know Rossetti's sister was the most famous female poet of her era, don't you, of course?"

"Um. Yes. Christina Rossetti. You know, I might have something you'd like to take a look at." He'd forgotten how to blink.

"I'm sure I would."

"Something of hers, I mean."

I granted him a slow, dirty grin. "Really? Show me, then."

"If you could… Um… Wait here, please."

I twirled a copper-coloured tress around my finger and grinned, twisting from hip to hip as he backed from the room. Then I gave him thirty seconds before I followed. My shoes looked impractical but they were surprisingly quiet. Edmund couldn't know that my heart was racing as he led me further into the depths of the shop and up a wooden stair.

Sticking my head round yet another doorway, into a room that must have been right at the back of the building, I found Edmund stooped over a giant nest. That's what it looked like to me, though a dragon's hoard might be more accurate. It was a stack of books as high as my waist and about twelve feet across, topped with a brocade mattress. The odd yellowing page protruded from the otherwise neat arrangement. The smell of patchouli was very strong in here, stronger even than the smell of manky old paper.

Bingo. It had the hallmarks of an obsessive collector, which to me fairly screams of the Good Folk. Lots of Them There like to collect things. Jewellery, shiny rocks, cage-birds… teeth… heads. That sort of shit. Actually, I'd met one —Gong-lubber Jakes—who did specifically collect shit. Lived in the sewers and snuck his long hairy arms out through u-bends at night to grab people. Not nice at all.

Anyway, old books—why not? It makes at least as much sense as anything else they're into. I'd been right about Edmund purchasing on another's behalf.

I cast my gaze across the floor, and there in the corner was a bone. Just the one. Someone had been tidying up. A clean hock-bone, like the chew-toy of a big dog. I snorted down my nose. Edmund half-turned, and nearly shot out of his skin to find me behind him.

"Tansy! You shouldn't be in here!"

"It's okay. Don't worry."

"This is… it's private." There was a look of real trepidation on his face.

"But you don't mind showing me your private things, do you Edmund?"

His throat worked. "It's… not mine."

"Heh. Is that a bed?" I asked, indicating the mountain of paper.

"Um. Yes, it is. It's all right," he added, not sounding the least bit confident of that. "She doesn't get home until after midnight."

Almost certainly an ogress, I thought, *given the size of the bed, and the smell.* And the discarded bone. And unlike so many of Them There, ogres get out and about in daylight. Okay, another entry in the Home Office database. Another Good Neighbour for them to keep tabs on.

"I've got a house-hob at home too," I lied, playing dumb. House-hobs are the commonest kind of Good Neighbour in urban areas like this.

His smile was sickly. I couldn't help feeling sorry for him. It wasn't as if he'd have had any choice when the ogress moved in.

"What did you want to show me, Edmund?"

He hesitated, and I saw that his thumbs were clenched inside his balled fists. Time to distract him from thoughts of his tenant. I linked my hands at the small of my back to thrust my breasts out in their white blouse. The cloth strained across my rack.

"Is it very exciting?" I asked with wide-eyed faux-innocence. I was pleased to see his glance drop and fix upon my boobs. "Is it something very few people have got their hands on?"

"Here," he grunted, tearing his gaze away from my body and going back to the mattress. Lifting the edge, he slid out a sheaf of papers from beneath. They were tied in a brown ribbon. "*Goblin Market*, by Christina Rossetti," he breathed, holding out the slim bundle to me. "Published in 1862. This is an early draft, in her own handwriting, dated 1850. It's only very recently come to light. Take a look, if you like."

Oh wow. I didn't have to fake my big, grateful smile or my "Ooh!" of anticipation. I might not know much about poetry, but *Goblin Market* falls right into my area of professional interest. This manuscript coming up for sale had been enough to catch my attention and bring me snooping here. I looked eagerly down at the delicate script in its browning ink.

"May I?"

"Let's go back to my desk, shall we? The light's better there for reading."

Actually there was perfectly good light in here from the tall window, but I wasn't going to quibble. He had every right to feel nervous. I let him steer me out of the room and down the stairs, one hand on my arm.

"This is so exciting! Has it been authenticated?"

"Um. Yes. Well… In a manner of speaking. I've received expert advice."

"Have you read it?"

"No." He looked at me over his glasses. "That is to say, not yet. I don't read all the books I buy, Tansy."

"No." I giggled. "Of course not. This is so sweet of you, Edmund, letting me see this."

He smiled. He seemed more relaxed now that we were away from that great paper nest. "My pleasure."

"Oh," said I, dropping him a sultry wink. "I'm sure it'll be pleasure all round."

He took his glasses off and laid them carefully on the desk among the neat stacks of invoices and catalogues. I saw his hands tremble a little. "Here, my dear," he murmured, clicking the switch of the desk-lamp. "That's a better light to read by."

"Thanks." Standing before the desk, I laid the manuscript down to pick at the knots in the ribbon. He stood very close, right at my side. I felt a hand brush my hair, very gently, and I shot him an encouraging smile over my shoulder. As I turned the first couple of pages I felt his fingertips caress the skin of my neck and I shivered with pleasure.

"Oh, my Penthesilea," he murmured, as my eyes grew used to the handwriting.

Ah, the benefits of a classical education, I thought, somewhat distracted. Most men get no further than some reference to Amazons as they paw at me, because at six feet tall and with a rack like this I can't help but invite the comparison. I'll never be skinny but I keep active, which means I end up with a taut waist, but I'm still plenty curvy in other places. Add to that my red hair—not an insipid ginger but ferociously bright metallic waves—and pale skin that explodes into freckles all over my shoulders and arms at the first touch of summer, and I get a lot of attention from a certain type of guy. Not necessarily the sort of guy I want, to be honest. Pretty much every man who goes for me has this submission fantasy and they want me to wrestle them to the floor or crack a whip over their ass. Goddamn. That's not my preference. I want someone who can look me in the eye and not be intimidated. I want a guy who can make me feel overwhelmed. That's not easy to find— which is why there've been so few real boyfriends in my past.

The last one was Gavin, two years ago. He owned a garden centre where I went to buy herbs for my window box. Tall and weather-beaten, he was all muscle from hefting flagstones and bags of peat, but he had a grin like the sun coming out. We'd only just started seeing each other, still clumsy and uncertain and euphoric at every meeting, when Them There returned. I dropped by one day and he'd gone. The rows of plants were kicked over, the poly-tunnels were slashed, and his employees were wandering around in confusion. He'd just vanished, and he never reappeared. Yes, I looked for him. Desperately. A lot of people disappeared in the early days, before we worked out what was going on. Before we relearned the old wards: iron and rowan, salt and graveyard earth, leaving offerings of milk and blood, and staying indoors after dark. Before we learned our place, once more.

Stop it, Tansy, I told myself, shivering from more than just the tickle of Edmund's fingertips on my nape, as he gathered my hair and pressed his face to it, breathing its scent. I shouldn't be thinking about Gavin. I'd beaten myself up over him enough. I should be thinking about this, now. A first draft of *Goblin Market.* What a prize.

I turned a couple of pages at random, picking up the familiar helter-skelter rhythms as the words sounded in my head. They tumbled along so quickly that it felt like they were falling over their own feet:

> *Laughed every goblin*
> *When they spied her peeping:*
> *Came towards her hobbling,*
> *Flying, running, leaping,*
> *Puffing and blowing*
> *Chuckling, clapping, crowing*

Heh. Like she'd swallowed a thesaurus.

Tentatively, Edmund put one hand on the small of my back. He held his breath, waiting for me to shrug him off. All

I did was arch my spine a little, thrusting my ass in its miniskirt out a bit more, lifting my tits. My eyes never left the page. I felt Edmund's breath, warm against my ear, as he let out a shaky little exhalation. Inside, I smiled.

Then my flitting gaze hit a new patch.

> *Then Laura without more delay*
> *Loosened off her sister's stays*
> *And bared her to the moonlight's rays.*

Hold on. That wasn't familiar at all. I knew *Goblin Market* reasonably well and I was damn sure that wasn't in it.

> *Lizzie, loving Lizzie, let her:*
> *Though Laura seemed to be half-crazed;*
> *Urged her hand where she was wetter:*
> *"This, she cried, "Oh, this is better!"*

And after that it just got more crazy. I mean, it had always read like a coy story of incestuous lesbian lust to me, but this was way out there:

> *Her body, quaking with each tickle,*
> *Heaving at that tongue's hot licking,*
> *Surrendered to those fingers fickle,*
> *Sometimes stroking, sometimes flicking;*
> *One hand on her silken skin*
> *One hand plunging deep within.*

The paper looked old, the handwriting suitably ladylike and formal, but I couldn't imagine the uptight, ultra-religious Rossetti sending *that* to any male publisher. Or was this an early, *early* draft then? One which had never seen the light of day?

Oblivious to my surprise, Edmund ran his palm down

over the curve of my bum. I could feel the pulse thrumming under my breastbone—his importuning and my own discovery combined in one rush of arousal. As he patted the curve of my behind I pushed back into the cup of his hand. He squeezed the rounded flesh gently through my skirt, as if testing its resilience.

There was life in the old dog still, then. My teasing clothes, the flirtation—he couldn't keep his hands off me any longer.

"Would you mind…?" I asked, hearing the hoarse edge in my voice that betrayed my mounting excitement.

"Yes? What?"

"If I read it out loud?"

"Please. Please do. Oh, thou fair Atalanta…"

"Shush," I chided.

Placing my hands flat on the desk I braced myself at an incline, my rump thrust out to offer him maximum access while I got on with my perusal. Edmund shifted round behind me and, as I started on the first lines, he lifted up my skirt and laid it across my back, baring the white panties beneath and the twin swells of my ass cheeks, jutting out over white hold-up stockings. With a tiny grunt of delight he laid claim to those cheeks. His hands were warm and reverent, caressing the rounded curves of my bum as if I were carved of the most precious antique alabaster.

I started reading. The poem was familiar at first, differing from the one I knew by only the odd line, if at all. The story was familiar too: Laura goes to the goblin market-men—despite the warnings of her sensible sister Lizzie—and purchases from them, for the price of a lock of hair, the sumptuous fruits she craves. I read slowly, enjoying the rhythm of the words and the sensuous glut of imagery, just as I was enjoying the movement of Edmund's hands over my bottom; the way he spread my cheeks with sweeping caresses, and the forays—delicate at first, and almost shy—to the territory between. He stroked me through the lace-trimmed fabric, finding the dimple of my rear entrance and the deep split of the fleshy furrow beneath. When he tickled over the hidden nubbin of my clit I squirmed deliciously, my breath catching. I could feel the hot leak of my wetness into a cotton gusset no longer as pristine or innocent as its colour suggested.

"Oh, you good girl," he murmured happily.

I ignored him, concentrating on my reading. Laura gluts herself on the sweet, forbidden fruit—and here was where the poem departed from the version I knew. In the published edition the sexual imagery was implicit—that was the core of the work's appeal and notoriety—but here on the page before me it leapt out without restraint:

> *Sucked the fruit 'tween fingers crushed:*
> *Goblin fingers, goblin lust;*
> *Licked their plums with shameless greed,*
> *Ate their pricks as in they thrust,*
> *Eagerly took all she must,*
> *Swallowing stones and juice and seed.*

Dirty Laura, thought I, half-dazed, my mind running on two parallel tracks of awareness simultaneously. It took all my will-power to keep reading in a low, even voice, as Edmund eased his fingers under the cotton and laved them in my wet cleft. My pussy felt as swollen and juicy as one of Laura's over-ripe fruits, and the touch of his fingertips on my most sensitive tissues sent an aching thrill through my whole body. I broke off mid-verse to squeak softly.

"That's right," gasped Edmund, his breath ragged. "What a good girl you are, Tansy. But I'm going to need to take these knickers off. Otherwise you're going to get them all wet, you see."

I didn't answer. I just took a deep breath and plunged back into the rhymes. Edmund tucked his fingertips under the waist of my panties and tugged them down, over hips and bum-cheeks, sinking to his knees behind me. He lifted first one of my feet and then the other, as if I were some long-legged filly, as he drew them off and laid them aside.

So there I was—knickerless and exposed in a dusty antique shop, being examined at shockingly close quarters by the shopkeeper. From his breathy murmurs of appreciation, he liked what he saw very much. I heard his sigh as he inhaled my bouquet, and a blush rose to my cheek, like the pink ghost of my modesty.

I'd discovered long ago that a little shame excited me. Well this was shameful—the age difference, the lifted skirt, my exposure... the first touch of his fingertip on my uncovered bum-hole and my sex lips and the swollen bud of my clit. Like Laura in the poem, I was selling my dignity for a taste of the market-man's wares.

And like Laura, I was revelling in it.

Laura, poor dirty Laura, has one orgiastic feast of goblin fruit but wakes the next day yearning for more. Her hunger becomes obsessive and then crippling. Life drains from her. But she can't find the goblin men again for a second fix; virtuous Lizzie is the only one who can still hear their mocking calls to "Come buy."

And all the time I read, Edmund knelt behind me, stroking my ass and patting the swell of my sex below. It wasn't the least unpleasant. He was the soul of courtesy, if you can call a man running his fingers through your labia courteous. Certainly my body responded to his ministrations, my pussy-lips swelling and my honey leaking out. He licked his fingertips and then, growing bolder, pressed his face up into the moist cleft. I felt the hot gust of his breath and then the stroke of his tongue over my clit, and it made me stammer. Spreading my thighs further apart, I pushed my rump back into his face and folded at the hips, bracing my elbows on the desk.

Edmund gripped my bare thighs precisely above the tops of my stockings. Glancing down, I saw how dark his hands looked on the luminous pallor of my skin. But it was only a glance. I went back to my task straight away, not precisely trying to ignore the tongue burrowing into my open sex, but to carry on regardless, surfing the waves of pleasure rising in me and riding the words over each crest and trough.

Oh, he ate well. He ate me like I was a juicy, over-ripe mango, nuzzling deep into my wet folds and sucking and lapping, just as Laura had slurped and sucked at the goblin fruit. My body seemed to open up to him, and as his licking became fiercer and more extravagant I could picture my sex like a split honeydew melon that he was hungrily guzzling down.

As her junkie sister draws close to death, Lizzie finally decides to go purchase another dose of the deadly wares and bring it home for her. The goblin men abuse the wiser sister quite horribly, smearing her all over with pulped fruit—that's in the original too:

> *Scratched her, pinched her black as ink,*
> *Kicked and knocked her,*
> *Mauled and mocked her,*
> *Lizzie uttered not a word;*
> *Would not open lip from lip*
> *Lest they should cram a mouthful in.*

That much I recognised from the familiar version: Lizzie is careful to eat nothing. But the next line went off on another level altogether:

> *They spent their seed upon her face*
> *'Til it ran down off her chin,*
> *From her golden locks it dripped*
> *And spattered her pale breasts like curd.*

The violent bukkake imagery shocked me—and sent perverse heat burning through my flesh. My stiff, straight legs were starting to tremble with tension. Edmund must have felt it. He switched his right hand from my thigh to my pussy, sliding two fingers into the frictionless well of my cunt until his whole hand gripped my pubic mound. As he ground against my clit and flexed those fingers, his tongue switched tactics. Licking up the whole length of my split, he fastened his mouth over my asshole in a wet sucking kiss, and swirled his tongue right over that tight whorl.

"Oh!" I squealed.

It felt *extraordinary*. The most tender intimacy and the most intrusive invasion all at the same time. Dirty dirty dirty... yet the ultimate adoration. That wet and squirming tongue seemed to melt me as if I were made of chocolate. The poem was momentarily forgotten and I gasped a number of blasphemies that Christina Rossetti would most certainly not have approved of, as lightning shot up my spine. The circling swirl of his tongue stirred my whole body, then as Edmund made his hot tongue into a hard slick point that he inveigled right into my clench, the shock was altogether too much. I came. Like a thunderclap, like a monsoon. On his hand. On his tongue.

I'm not a quiet girl. And it was sheer luck I didn't tear the manuscript under my clutching hands.

The moment I had finished I pushed him off and turned, jamming my wet ass against the desk. Edmund knelt there, open-mouthed, staring up at me. At the long lines of my legs and the coppery flare of my muff. I put the toe of my shoe on his trouser crotch and felt the hard bulge straining under the cloth.

"Let's see that, Edmund," said I. My voice was husky.

He obeyed, and out popped a sweet, smooth cock from his open flies. It was satisfyingly stiff. *Not bad for a man of his age*, thought I. His pubic hair was silver-grey too, which made me blink. I hadn't realised that happened with age, though it made a kind of sense really.

Well, you live and learn, don't you?

Kicking off my shoes, I rubbed the ball of my foot against that hot column and Edmund closed his eyes with pleasure, grabbing my foot to furl my toes around his cock. My hold-ups were white but heavily patterned with William Morris roses; I wondered if he could feel the rasp of the weave on his stiffy.

"Very nice."

"My proud Hippolyta!" he groaned.

"Lick my pussy, Edmund. I haven't finished yet."

He moved between my thighs with alacrity, and I spread them wide for him. His mouth settled over my mons like a blessing, and I made audible noises of pleasure as he bestowed his kisses once more on my tingling clit. I could tell by the rhythmic shift of his shoulder that he was working his own tool too. From behind me I grabbed the manuscript, and as he ate me out I resumed my lines.

I was measured at first, almost stern in my diction, but that didn't last. Edmund was far too good and I was far too horny. One climax has never been enough for me: I like to come several times—and after the first I can take it pretty rough. Edmund seemed to understand my need for more stimulation. He nipped and nibbled this time, sucking hard on my puffy labia. As my arousal mounted toward a new peak I grabbed the back of his head and pulled him in, mashing his face into my pussy. I probably half-suffocated the poor man, but in all honesty he gave no signs of objecting.

Damn it. I meant to finish the poem, but I got no further than

> *"Did you miss me?*
> *Come and kiss me.*
> *Never mind my bruises,*
> *Hug me, kiss me, suck my juices"*

delivered in a breathless squeal that ended in a shriek of pleasure and an "Oh! Oh! Oh... Fuck yes!"

Spasming, I fell back across the desk. Edmund grabbed my ankles and I was vaguely aware that he was rubbing up against me. I heard him groan.

He soiled my lovely and rather expensive stockings with his jizz.

I liked that.

By the time I hoisted myself into a sitting position Edmund was resting his head against my thigh. His lips brushed my bare flesh just above the stocking edge.

"You are a very good girl, Tansy."

I giggled. "And you, Edmund, are a very dirty boy."

He smiled in acknowledgement, slightly shame-faced. His lips looked puffy.

"But very good too. You must have done that a lot."

He cleared his throat. "Would you like a cup of tea?"

I nearly laughed out loud. What a gentleman! "*Real* tea?"

"Yes. Ceylon blend."

Most of us had been drinking sage and chamomile for months. There are more important things to try and run the shipping gauntlet with than tea. I could only dream about a nice old-fashioned cuppa these days.

"God, yes. Thank you!"

He rose to his feet, tidying himself away. "Just a tick," he said, before departing for the inner recesses of the shop.

I watched him go, with a smile. Then I stood and stretched, glancing down at the desk. At the manuscript.

It took only a moment to stuff the papers into my handbag. I didn't stop to put my shoes on. I just grabbed them and my panties. Then, barefoot and bare-assed, I made a break for the front door.

Chapter Two

The Princess and the Frog

I didn't mean to steal the poem, I swear. I just wanted to copy it, and show it to a friend of mine at the university library who knows Victorian manuscripts. So she could tell me whether it was for real, you understand. There were details in the poem… It could be important. I didn't mean to get Edmund Blakey into trouble.

They call it TWOC-ing in legal circles, don't they? *Taking Without Owner's Consent.* Not theft. Theft means you don't plan to return it. I had no interest in the monetary value of the manuscript. And I had every intention of getting it back to Edmund Blakey before midnight, when the ogre returned.

Thanks to the long summer day I got everything done well before dark, in fact. Then I dropped in at home and lay down to sleep, setting my alarm for two hours later. I was *careful.* But I was also exhausted by this point—I'd been up all the previous night watching for a churchyard grim and I desperately needed a nap.

When I woke—five minutes before the alarm, as usual—my cousin Gail was busy shagging her boyfriend again. I could hear the rhythmic rattle of her headboard through my bedroom wall. I rose, showered, and dressed in slightly more practical clothes than I'd used for the Pulling of Edmund: black leggings, dove-grey mini-dress and black knee-high boots. Then I went online to report a probable ogre lair at the antiques shop on Hollness Road. We've still got cable and satellite links, thank goodness; it's the only real way we stay in touch with the outside world. And Them There have never been able to get to grips with the Internet.

When I'd done all that, Gail and Vince were still going at it—I could hear Gail's muffled squeals. Or maybe they'd had a break in the middle and had gone back to it; who knows. I rolled my eyes scathingly—but partly in envy of the fun they were having too, I admit—and went into the garage to get my car out.

It wasn't there. I stood with keys in hand, quite stupidly, trying to get my brain to work. The garage door was shut and locked. I'd picked the keys off the hook in the kitchen. I'd definitely driven the thing home. How had it vanished?

Gail. Bloody Gail. She borrows it sometimes. She's only supposed to do it in dire need, what with fuel rationing these days, but that doesn't seem to stop her.

There was a cold clench in my stomach as I raced back upstairs. I'd left the *Goblin Market* manuscript in the glove box. The Good Neighbours don't like iron, so a car is basically like a steel Faraday cage. They can't track or smell, or whatever it is they do, anything enclosed in iron. They can't touch it.

Usually.

"Gail!" I called, banging on her bedroom door. "Gail! Where's my car?"

In answer there was a low grumble of inaudible words from Vince and a feminine giggle.

"Gail!" My voice rose to a shout. "This is important! Get your ass out here!"

The giggle was accompanied by the resumption of the headboard rattle.

I lost my temper. Throwing open the door, I marched into the room. Vince was stretched out on the bed and Gail was riding him, cowgirl-style. Both were naked and the room stank of vigorous sex, but I ignored all that. Well, as best I could, anyway—it wasn't possible *not* to notice the way her little tits were bouncing up and down like two tennis balls, or the taut stretch of her thighs straddling his dark hips, or the sheen of sweat all over her slender body. But I did my best. I walked over, grabbed Gail's long hair right at the base of her scalp, and hauled her unceremoniously off her boyfriend. I caught a glimpse of his cock when I did it, all slick and bobbing, but that wasn't important right then. Gail yowled in protest as I dragged her out into the living room.

"Where's my car?" I repeated as I let go of her and spun her to face me.

Gail stuck her bottom lip out, wrinkled her nose mutinously, and then suddenly grinned a slow dirty grin. "Not telling."

Crap. I ran my hand over my face. "Gail, this isn't the time for games. Tell me where it is."

"Make me."

Oh great. She'd decided to play the brat. We'd been doing this for years. We'd grown up close, living in the same Warwickshire village and playing together and often sharing a room overnight. Very early on, Gail had discovered she liked to have her bottom spanked and, to be honest, I didn't mind obliging. I have powerful memories of her—back in the day when her hair was honey-brown and wavy, not blonde and straight—bending over in a corner of a remote field beneath the shelter of the willows, pulling up her skirt and displaying her teenaged bottom to me in the dappled light. *Go on Tansy,* she'd whisper: *Spank me. Please! I just need it!* I remember the sense of transgression, one that always brought a hot gush to my pussy, as I slapped her firm little ass. It had been our secret game. And yes, we still played at it sometimes, usually when Gail was between boyfriends.

She liked to initiate a session by acting the naughty girl. Something about rebellion and punishment clearly tripped her switches.

"I don't need this now! It's serious!"

"Make me," she repeated, eyes narrowing.

"Fine," I growled.

Seizing her hair again, I dropped her over one arm of the sofa with her ass in the air. For such a slim girl, she's got a nice round bottom. Planting my knee in a cushion, I pushed one hand down between her shoulder blades and aimed the other at that pretty target. Hard. Damn it, I usually make it a rule never to do this when I'm genuinely worked up about anything, but this time I was in a real fix. Gail squealed and kicked with her legs as I landed smack after smack on her ass-cheeks and thighs, but she was off-balance and couldn't get any purchase on the carpet. She rubbed her face in the seat cushions and clawed at the fabric and shrieked.

"Tell me!" I commanded grimly.

"Oww!" she howled, thrashing her thighs apart and giving me a distracting flash of her open pussy lips, pink and glistening from sex. She usually likes me to spank her pussy too, though rather more gently. But I wasn't playing nice today. I clapped my tingling hand down on her left cheek with almost the full weight of my arm, seeing the flesh jounce and hearing her scream.

"Jeez," said Vince: "Should you really be doing that?"

I looked up at him standing in the bedroom door, half-distracted from my mission. He was holding his jeans in front of his crotch to defend his modesty, but I could see the rest of his long, lean, mahogany-hued body all the way from his toes to the shaved fuzz of hair on top of his head. His brows were knitted in a frown, but his jaw was slack with surprise.

It must have been quite a sight from his standpoint, I guess. Tall redhead flatmate; little blonde girlfriend. Her legs were open and her ass was already scarlet, and her glistening snatch was pointed straight at him.

"Where's my car?" I demanded. When no one answered me, I shifted my hand and evened up the score on Gail's right cheek.

"AAAH!"

"Where's my car?"

Vince's mouth worked. "It's…" he mumbled, but ground to a halt. His eyes were wide, his gaze fixed on Gail's suffering rear.

I shook my head at their obstinacy. *Smack. Smack. Smack.* Swift and fierce, not giving her time to recover.

"Nooo!" she wailed.

I lifted my palm again, but held it aloft. "Where's my car?"

Gail, panting, twisted her face in my direction. "That hurts!"

The noise of my hand falling was like a shot going off.

"AH! It got clamped!"

I let go of her. "What?"

"It got clamped and towed," she sobbed. "We went out for pizza and when we got back they were taking it away on a truck."

I felt like hitting her again but I didn't. Never in real anger.

"You *stupid -*" I started to protest, but cut myself off. I had to stand up and pace around the room to vent my frustration. "You parked it on a double yellow line again?"

"Only for a few minutes!" Gail lifted herself on her elbows but made no attempt to rise from the spanking position. Maybe she was too sore to sit up. I don't know about her ass, but my hand was red hot and stinging.

"Where?" I demanded. "Where's it gone?"

"Here," said Vince: "We have the ticket here."

I shot him a hard look. So he'd known. He'd known enough to stop the pain, all along. He sort of sidled around us, his gaze sliding back and forth from Gail to me, until he reached the sideboard and found a piece of paper, all without turning to show me his bare butt. I suspected that under his crumpled jeans he was nursing an almighty hard-on. In fact, as he handed the ticket to me, I saw him squeeze his crotch through the denim. He and Gail were going to have to have some things to talk over real soon, I suspected. And probably more than talk.

But my main concern right now was with where they'd impounded my vehicle. I scanned the form anxiously.

"Croydon!" I felt like crying. I flung myself into an armchair, knotting my hand in my hair, and swore a blue streak. "That's miles away! Gail! For fuck's sake! Why'd you have to do it tonight? It's nearly dark! How am I supposed to get there before they close?"

"You can pick it up tomorrow," she said, reaching gingerly behind her to probe her red and swollen rump. She'd recovered quickly, as always, and seemed awed and pleased with the state of her bum-cheeks. "I'll pay the fine."

"No! I need it tonight!" I shook my head, aware that I was bleating in my distress. "This is serious, Gail!"

"Why?"

"I left the poem in the car, and I have to get it back!"

"The *poem?*" Vince asked, incredulous.

I tried to gather my wits. "An old, handwritten poem. I borrowed it from someone I know, and I have to get it back to him before midnight or he's going to be in serious trouble."

"Since when have you been into poetry?" sneered Gail.

I glared at her. "It's by Christina Rossetti. Heard of her?"

"Nope."

"She wrote *In the Bleak Midwinter.*"

Vince shook his head but Gail brightened. "The carol? Oh, yeah. A bit of a downer, isn't it?"

"Yeah. Well the rest of her work makes that look positively upbeat. She was the most miserable, whiny, self-loathing…" I ran out of adjectives. "She gave up playing chess when she realised she enjoyed winning. It was all about sacrificing her pleasure for a heavenly reward, as far as she was concerned."

"Sad cow."

"You might say that. *But*, right at the start of her career, she published a poem that wasn't anything like that at all. It was this big long story about a woman who gets seduced by goblins and saved by her sister. And really steamy, for the time. I thought… I thought it might have been based on something that really happened to Rossetti. There were a few of the Good People still around in her time, you know, even before the Return. I dunno—maybe it was that experience that turned her into such a religious fruitloop. And if she had anything useful to tell us about Them There… Well, I needed to check it out."

"Huh. What's the problem, then?" Vince asked. "Ring your friend. Tell him you'll bring it tomorrow."

"It's not his." That was the nub of the issue. It wasn't mine, sure, but it wasn't Edmund Blakey's either. "It belongs to an ogre, and she owns him. He should never have let me borrow it in the first place. When she finds it's missing… Do you understand? An actual pull-his-head-off-and-eat-his-brains-ogress."

"Oh."

"That's not good."

"No, it bloody isn't," I agreed with some heat. So now they understood. Or at least they understood the problem, if not my guilt. I'd been ever-so-slightly economical with the truth, so they didn't know what a massive bitch I'd been. I jerked my frame from the armchair and went over to where my handbag sat on the dining table. Swiftly, I started stuffing the contents into the pockets of my grey jacket.

"What are you doing?"

"Going out."

"Shall I call a taxi?" Vince asked. Considering he was standing there naked I might have found his chivalry funny, in other circumstances. I glanced at the window again. The rowan-twig cross dangling from the frame hung against a sky the colour of his jeans.

"It's too late. They won't be doing any pick-ups now it's dusk." I didn't need to add that the Tube would have stopped running an hour ago. Nobody wants to be caught underground as the Night People stir.

"Then how are you planning to get there?" Gail asked.

"I'll bike it."

"Tansy, no! That's not safe!"

I *knew* that. "Well I can't leave the guy out to dry, can I?"

They looked at me doubtfully. "Won't the impound yard be shut anyway?" Vince pointed out.

"Then I'll climb the fence."

"I'll ring them," he announced. "I'll ring them and tell them you're coming, and ask them to wait for you."

"You do that." I couldn't quite bring myself to thank the pair of them. This mess was their fault in the first place, wasn't it?

Well, no. It was mine. That was why I was going to do this damn fool thing. I scrawled the telephone number on a scrap of paper for Vince, pocketed the towing notice and headed back down to the garage.

Cars are safe at night, generally speaking, so long as you don't pick anyone up. Or stop if you hit something. Those steel cages protect you, at least till you reach your destination. So there was some traffic on the streets as I set off, though there were no other push-bikes in sight. An aluminium bicycle frame provides no security at all, and it looked like I was the only one in the whole of London fool enough to hit the peddles at dusk. Things would be different right in the centre of town, of course: one of the many oddities of the current situation is that there've been no attacks within the boundary lines of any medieval city walls, whether or not those walls are still standing. Them There wander in and out, but they don't mess with the people inside. The same goes for other old walled towns—Chester, York, Norwich, loads of them—and no one knows why. If we could replicate that in the modern cities as they stand now... well, we'd be winning.

That's the trouble, of course—we don't know nearly enough. We don't even know what triggered all this, though best guess is that it started in the West Country, down Exmoor way. We don't know why they came back, or where they'd been all these centuries. We know it's spreading, though. Lots of people got out when it started to look really weird, and some are still emigrating to continental Europe, but the rumours coming back from there and further afield suggest that the nightmares are awakening there too. Vodyonoi, bruxsas, vlkodlaks... and worse things. The USA, of course, has done what it always really wanted to, and sealed its borders to the rest of the world. They're getting on fine, if you believe what they say on Fox News, but there's no help coming from that direction.

Still, I wouldn't want to live inside the old City of London. It's packed with refugees from the countryside, destitute and paranoid. We do better further out here, I think. And I was glad that evening, ironically enough, of the nice clear roads that meant I could ride swiftly. Down the empty roads and dual carriageways I sped, past shops with locked down grilles and shuttered windows, and endless miles of houses curtained against the gloaming. Just looking, it was hard to tell what was abandoned from what still struggled on as normal, what was a nest of unnatural horror from what had simply fallen bankrupt in an economy gone to rat-shit.

Despite my complaint, it wasn't the distance to the impound yard that really worried me. I'm fit enough for a couple of hours' cycling, but the real vexation was how to avoid any bridges on the way. Canals, railway lines, overpasses at junctions… I suppose if I wanted to stick my folklore hat on I'd say they were urban examples of borders or liminal places, neither one thing nor another, where normal rules don't apply and the otherworld might intrude.

Mostly I say that trolls scare the crap out of me.

I had a close call early on. The road dipped down under a railway line and I was just thinking *It's still light really, it's probably okay*, when from the shadows under the girders something unfolded its long limbs and lowered itself down onto the tarmac. It was big enough to stop a bus dead. I glimpsed its rough human shape silhouetted against the still-luminous sky and I slewed to a halt in the centre of the road about fifty yards short, my face twisted into a scowl and my heart banging with nervousness. A truly inhuman head, with jaws the size of my torso, dipped into view a moment later and

I caught sight of the outline of a tumescent phallus jutting from its knobbly body.

"Damn," I said through clenched teeth.

Before the troll could emerge and begin its lumbering pursuit I jerked my bike round and threw my weight onto the forward pedal. Luckily the gradient was shallow and I got up speed before the thing could decide I was worth chasing down. But it took me another fifteen minutes to find a nice safe level crossing over that railway line.

See? Railways have steel tracks, and old railways bridges are cast iron or whatever. But that doesn't stop trolls from lurking beneath them. That's a good example of the way all the rules we've worked out seem to have exceptions. Really deadly exceptions, in some cases.

Thanks to the complexities of the urban transport network, it was properly dark well before I arrived at my destination. My phone screen with its street map app, socketed on my handlebars, glowed like a jewel. This wasn't a brightly-lit neighbourhood, or a very nice one either. A light industrial estate of some sort, it was all chain-link fences and grey warehouses—a plumbing depot, a discount tile warehouse, a tooling workshop. Everything was shut up and silent. Even in the absence of Them There, I'd have hesitated to hang round here at night.

Someone, somewhere, had a CD on. I could hear faint music. It was the only suggestion of life. I couldn't even hear any traffic.

The Citywide Secure Autolot was closed too. I pulled on the big metal gate in frustration but didn't manage to even rattle the hinges. Squinting through the bars I could see rows of parked cars and an ugly low building that was the office, but it didn't have any windows, so even if there was a light on and anyone waiting inside, I couldn't tell. I rang their reclaim number from the ticket in my pocket. The recorded voice told me they opened at 6 a.m. and closed at sunset. I walked round the perimeter fence and tried to imagine breaking in. Notices at regular intervals threatened guard dogs, but since my shouts and kicks hadn't brought any running yet, I doubted they were real. My chances of the police turning up to arrest me were reasonably slight, I reckoned, as they have enough on their plates most nights. The real problem was a purely practical one: fifteen-foot metal posts with sharp tips and coiled razor-wire. No chance. I wasn't Lara bloody Croft.

"Shit!" I protested unjustly, giving the gate another kick with my boot. I felt sick with frustration and, quite suddenly, there were hot tired tears burning in my eyes. "You stupid bastards!"

The music rose abruptly in volume, pushing its way into my consciousness. Cold clutched at my spine as I recognised the wailing timbre of a violin, just as I turned to locate the source.

On the opposite side of the road was a steep embankment that had probably once been grass and was now all sapling sycamores and blown litter. People are reluctant to cut trees nowadays, wisely so. Under the streetlight stood a man playing a fiddle.

I say *man*. He just looked like a man, that was all. I did not entertain for more than a moment the possibility that he was actually human—some poor lost busker. He was wearing a low, wide-brimmed hat and a long green coat, like the movie version of Fagin. Old-fashioned. Out of time. The only modern thing about him was a cigarette dangling from the corner of his mouth. Adaptability is not something the Gentry are noted for. In fact I'd go so far as to say they're not really that sharp, most of them.

But they don't have to be clever to be dangerous.

I stuck my hand in my pocket and clenched it around the iron nails.

He strolled across the junction toward me, his arm sweeping back and forth with the bow, his dancelike steps strongly suggesting a kind of playfulness. The music lanced through me to my core. I didn't run. I didn't grab my bike. I'm not sure I could have; there was something in that music that held me. Wild and passionate and unpredictable, it was just too beautiful to spurn in that way. Under the shadow of the hat I caught an impression of a youngish face and untidy fair hair. As he drew closer and circled me, the tone of his playing changed, gentling down to a sweet, plaintive sound that made my skin tingle and my nipples ache. I twisted my neck, keeping him in sight as he examined me from all angles.

Under the green coat his chest was bare. His trousers—I had to look, I was double-checking for a fly zip because that's a dead giveaway—appeared to be made of patchwork chamois leather and were almost unfeasibly snug. No zipper, just as I'd predicted: everything held together with little leather laces instead. Oh, and an impressive packet. I shouldn't have noticed that, but it was hard not to, given its size.

The nail points bit into my skin, until it was only the pain keeping me lucid.

He stopped abruptly and lowered fiddle and bow to his

sides. Then he dipped a small, mocking nod and flicked the cigarette away. I felt the absence of the music with a pang, but my head cleared too.

"You appear to be in distress. May I help?"

Yeah—sexy voice. I'd expected nothing less. Surprisingly deep from someone of his build though. Sexy voice, smooth athletic body, and ragged hair that even under his hat looked like tarnished gold. Yes, I know gold doesn't tarnish, but the phrase shot into my head and stuck. Dirty gold, if you want to be picky, then. Dirty eyes too. They looked like they might be grey or blue by daylight, with long black lashes—and they didn't so much undress me as tear my clothes off, fuck my brains out, drink my coffee and leave me tied to the bed unconscious and covered in spunk.

"It's very kind of you to offer. But no, thank you."

Oh God—his torso, sculpted by muscle, was golden brown and completely hairless except for a sun-blonded treasure-trail that ran down from his navel into the territory below. I shouldn't have looked. I really shouldn't.

I get turned on too quickly. That's my problem.

"What's your trouble?" he asked, as if guessing my thoughts.

Shit shit shit. Go away! "Really, thank you, but it's not…"

"Are you looking for something?"

I noticed, as he lifted his long hands to indicate the compound behind me, that he was no longer carrying violin or bow. He hadn't put them away anywhere; they just weren't there.

I cleared my throat. "My car's in there." Damn, did he even know what a car was? He didn't exactly look like he'd been keeping up with the times. "My, um, carriage."

"I know what a car is."

I actually blushed. "Sorry."

"You were crying. What is so important that it makes you weep?"

I'm screwed. I have to answer him. "It got locked up by mistake. If I don't get it back this evening... There's something inside it that I need back, tonight, or a friend of mine will be in terrible trouble."

"Then let me retrieve the thing for you."

"I'm not asking for help," I insisted.

He spread his hands magnanimously. "But I am offering."

There was a considerable pause then, as my mind tried to get into gear. Yes, he probably could solve my immediate problem. But I don't believe in free lunches. Especially when you're dining with Them There.

"You'd want something in exchange, I suppose?"

"Of course. But nothing you won't be willing to give."

"What?"

He reached out and, with a thoughtful air, pushed my open jacket back from my breasts. The dress beneath was not particularly low-cut, but it was smooth and clingy. It did nothing to hide the curves of bust and waist and hip. And I do have big tits, undeniably. It's difficult not to notice them. Big firm tits that looked up at him, their nipples already stiffening to hard points. He laid a single fingertip on my right nipple and circled the areola. It puckered, thrilling to his touch with the undignified eagerness of a puppy.

"Eight warm inches of your flesh, my sweet."

I shuddered, though I didn't pull away. He caught my

flash of fear and chuckled.

"Wrapped around eight inches of mine," he amended.

"I see." I should have been disgusted by his presumption. I should have been outraged by the way he was touching me without permission. But the reality was that my skin felt like it was running with little electric sparks from that nipple he was playing with, all over my breasts and down my belly, like he had a direct wire to my sex. And my knees were going wobbly. He wasn't wrong about me being willing, the bastard.

He inclined his head and bent to brush his lips, feather-light, across my cheek. It made all the hair stand up on my neck.

"You look perturbed. Is it an offence to desire such beauty as yours?" he breathed.

I made a little noise in my throat. I didn't think of myself as beautiful. Not in comparison to him.

"I promise you will enjoy it, and that I will not hurt you—unless," he added with a wicked grin, "that is your pleasure too."

Jeez. Oh, it would help if he wasn't so goddamn hot, if I wasn't creaming up at the sight of him, if I could just think straight past the surge of my sexual hormones. I wriggled out of his touch, and I think I deserve a medal for managing that much.

"Let's get this straight. One fuck, yes?"

He smiled. It was the sort of smile that made hearts explode. "Yes. Exactly."

"For how long?"

"How long do you want it to last?"

"I have to be at my friend's before midnight."

"As you wish."

"And I'll walk away freely afterwards?"

"You will be free to go. Whether you can walk straight…" He chuckled. "That depends on your resilience, my sweet."

"But you promise not to harm me?"

He drew himself up, amusement dancing in his eyes. "I will love you and leave you. You have my word that there will be no more between us than that. Forget me entirely, if you wish."

Okay, okay. That wasn't so bad. From what I knew, the Good Neighbours were people of their word. That's their great redeeming feature. They might toy with us, abduct us and kill us out of hand, but they can be held to a promise. I couldn't entirely shake my gut feeling that he looked like trouble, that there was just too much of a knowing twinkle in those beautiful eyes. But to be honest, I wasn't thinking with my gut right then. My gut and brain were both getting shouted down by my pussy.

Humans—we're not so smart we can't be relied on to risk everything for a hot fuck.

"Well then," I said, grudgingly. "Maybe."

"Maybe?" He took both of my hands in his and held them between us, as if wooing me in some old movie. His fingertips stroked the insides of my wrists, making my skin tingle. "What would it take to make you say *Yes*, my beautiful redheaded maiden? Shall I offer you a crown wrought of the sun, and dresses of starlight?"

"That's considered a little old-fashioned," I said dryly, trying to maintain some distance—and some dignity. "Most women these days will settle for wine and dinner."

He pulled my hands to him and pressed them flat against his breastbone, so that I could feel the warmth of his firm body. Blood rushed to my cheeks and drummed in my ears.

"Then what would it take," he asked, his voice dropping to a throaty whisper as he bent over me and smoothed my hands down his wonderful abs, "To make you say *Yes, oh fuck yes, now, I'm coming now?*"

Not much, I thought. I snatched my hands back just as they reached the low-slung waist of his trousers and I lost control altogether.

"Just keep your side of the deal," I gasped.

He grinned, his eyes holding mine. "We do have a deal, then?"

I nodded, swallowing hard. It was too late to back out. Well, maybe not quite too late. But too hard for me to say No, when my body was intent on betraying me.

"Good." His smile was like goddamn sunshine. What chance did I have? "Now, what is it that you wish me to retrieve for you?"

"Um, it's a poem. On paper. In the car glove box. It's an old Astra."

Seeing his expression of enquiry untroubled by any recognition, I added, "It's an old blue car," and told him the registration number.

"A moment then." Stepping back, he reached inside his coat, and from somewhere—he had definitely never put them away in there—pulled out the violin and the bow. Tucking the instrument under his chin, he played a phrase, high and merry. It smote me with the most peculiar feeling for a second, as if I were trembling and breathless and tiny, as if my whole body were one racing heart.

I had a bad feeling he could change people with that fiddle, at his whim. Change them into frogs or something like that, I mean.

"That should do it." He rested the violin, tilting his head as if listening to the vanished music.

"What's happening?"

"Wait and see."

I didn't have to wait long. I caught movement, low and swift, out of the corners of my eyes. Turning, I saw the first dark mote scurry across the road toward us, from the long weeds. At first I thought it was a big beetle, then as more joined it I realised they were mice. I'd never realised before how fast the little beggars could go, and I recoiled despite myself. They came out of the grass and the warehouse yards, and up from the rainwater gutters. Soon there were scores, then hundreds, flitting around our feet and leaping over each other.

"There," said the golden boy softly, waving his fingers toward the gate. They streamed off through the bars like iron filings drawn by a magnet, and in a few seconds there wasn't a sign of them.

"Oh," said I. "Wow."

"It'll take a little while," he warned. "They're many, but small. In the meantime... Shall we, my sweet?"

"Tansy," I mumbled. "It'll be done in time, won't it? It's just that I have a deadline, remember."

"You've nothing to worry about. This way, Tansy."

He laced his fingers in mine and led me across the road and up the overgrown embankment. I could smell the jack-by-the-hedge crushed under our feet. At the top was a long wall, painted black with tar, that might have been the back of some warehouse. There was a small door with blistered paintwork. He turned his back to the door and lifted the fiddle to his chin.

"Hold my belt, Tansy."

He didn't have a belt on. His low-slung trousers were held up by their own tightness. I slipped my fingers into the waistband of his garment, feeling the warm embrace of skin and leather and the roughness of pubic hair. He grinned.

One note was all he struck from the violin, before kicking the door open behind him and backing through, pulling me with him.

It got weird after that. Weirder, anyway. He took me through several doors, and several rooms. I'm pretty sure the rooms weren't all in the same place and certainly none of them were in a warehouse on that industrial estate. The first was the British Library Reading Room, which isn't like any other interior in the country and I recognised it straight off. As we walked through, one of librarians stared at us open mouthed, put down her pile of books and, without a word, followed us. The second was a strip-club—we picked up a pole-dancer in a spangly g-string there. Then what looked like a ballet school, all mirrored walls. Then a comedy club I think, where we provided a surreal interruption to the act on stage. There were others, but it was so swift and so confusing that my memory is blurred. We added to his entourage with each new location. There are, though, odd, sharp details—dog-headed things in the comedy audience lifting pointed muzzles to howl in protest, the lack of our own reflections in the floor-length ballet mirrors, the cobwebbed eye-sockets of a man poring over a volume in the library—that make me think we might not have been in real places at all. I just held to my companion, giggling in shock and with a giddy sense of recklessness.

I know we finished up in a restaurant. We were high up in a tall building by that point; I realised that because through the great glass picture-windows I could see city lights gleaming below us. It was a very posh restaurant, not the sort of place I'd ever have been able to afford to eat in. As we entered, several waiters turned and looked at us blankly. I'm guessing they weren't used to guests arriving through that big mirror. And we looked wildly out of place, me not least of all. The diners stirred, instinctively nervous. From the corner of my eye I saw one of the women who'd followed us go over to the pianist, lay a hand on his shoulder and whisper in his ear.

"Sir," said a waiter, approaching us. 'Do you have a reservation?"

"Do I need one?" he asked, showing too bright a smile and sweeping off his hat and flicking it into the air, where it turned into a crow and flew off to sit in a potted palm tree. The waiter flinched.

"No, of course not sir. Of course not. But I'm afraid there may be a short delay, as all our tables are full at the moment…"

Two couples at a table within earshot rose hurriedly to their feet. "We were just leaving, may we have the bill?"

"Sit down." My date's voice cracked like a silken whip. I was pleased to note that without the hat and under good light he was even more rakishly handsome. "Nobody think of leaving."

They sank back into their seats, backs stiff as ramrods. By now everyone was watching with wide, round eyes. I was pretty sure the diners were all human. Most looked ordinarily plain and middle-aged, despite their fine clothes, and they all looked nervous to varying degrees because it was obvious to everyone that my chaperone was one of Them There. I drew myself up taller, pleased despite myself by their reaction. Here were the fat cats sitting high and dry over the rest of us, and they were realising they were no more immune to the tide of chaos than any of the poor plebs down below.

"Hungry, Tansy?"

My date scooped up two fingerfuls of some terrine from a diner's plate and lifted to my lips; I felt obliged to open up and suck them. His manners lacked a certain delicacy, but I could hardly expect him to use the steel cutlery, could I? His fingers wriggled against my tongue and his eyes gleamed.

"Nice?"

Fish of some sort. "Uh-huh."

He led me between the tables, weaving back and forth, snatching up handfuls of food to taste himself, or pop into my mouth. Asparagus soused in butter and little rosettes of rare beef, wafers of bitter chocolate and wild twists of spun sugar. The diners bobbed and leaned, trying to keep out of our way. The waiters wrung their hands but did not dare interfere. The pianist struck up again, something ragtime and wild, as the strange woman leaned over his shoulders and nibbled his ear and the other women in our retinue draped themselves over the bar and various gentlemen, watching. Everyone was watching. My cheeks were burning and I felt horribly self-conscious, but it was liberating too. I couldn't help what was happening—I was under obligation to one of Them There and he would do what he liked, with me and with them. And I admit it felt good to cock a snook at the high and mighty.

My smugness wasn't to last.

"Well fed, my sweet?" he asked, slipping a buttery scallop between my lips and trailing slippery fingers down my throat.

With my mouth full I nodded.

"Good," said he, and turned to the three men in business suits sitting to my right. "Now undress her."

Whoa. I swallowed hard, uttering a "Mmph!" of protest.

"Sorry?" one mumbled. "You mean… *her?*"

He arched a brow, sweetly threatening. "Now, if you please."

The men, who looked as surprised as me, stood and clumsily pushed back their chairs, fumbling to catch at my clothes. For the tiniest moment I considered arguing, but a look at my date told me I'd only be goading him. He perched his fine ass on a table-edge and folded his arms to watch as the three tugged my jacket off, then awkwardly drew my short dress up over my shoulders and off. I felt the air caress my lace-cupped breasts. The man directly facing me forgot his nerves long enough to stare down at my cleavage.

"Sorry," he said hoarsely, then spoiled it by licking his lips.

I blushed all over, and on skin like mine that shows. I was used to being looked at, but not stripped and ogled in public. Not to being treated with such terrible disrespect. Shame made my skin prickle and my nipples tighten to hard points. It got worse as one man knelt to unzip my boots and the one before me hooked my leggings down over my hips and ass, baring my bottom. I could actually feel the kneeling guy's hot breath on the skin of my thigh. My hands fluttered, uncertain what they should be doing, trying instinctively but entirely in vain to shield my modesty.

My date must have been pleased. Little curled pats of butter from every table rose into the air as yellow butterflies and fluttered through the room. I was vaguely aware that cooked crayfish on a nearby seafood platter were scuttling off over the tablecloth, as stifled squeals of alarm sounded from all about the dining room.

For a moment I stood there in my underwear. Then the man standing behind me undid the catch of my bra and my tits bounced free. They felt momentous and hyper-visible displayed like that, as if they were shining like spotlights, as if they were heavy as suns and drawing every gaze into their gravity-well. I crossed my hands over my breastbone, helplessly. Off came my panties too. I was naked in a room full of people and the air was so thick with tension that I could barely inhale.

"Isn't she beautiful, ladies and gentlemen?" said the golden bad-boy. "So shy, yet so wanton a maid. Tell me she does not provoke a cockstand fit to rip a hole in every pair of trews."

"You're disgusting."

The speaker was a large woman in a flounced blouse seated at his table. Her face was drawn tight into lines of contempt, but you had to admire her courage. If not her sense.

He cast her an amused sideways glance and flicked out the tip of his bow, tapping her lightly on the bosom. Her blouse burst open, scattering pearls across the table and into her soup. As everyone stared at her enormous décolletage, she spasmed, her big breasts juddering. For a second I thought she was having convulsions, as she grabbed the table-edge and shrieked. Then I realised it was orgasm. No warning and no build-up—just the sucker-punch of orgasmic explosion.

Ouch! thought I.

His eyes were narrowed as he smiled at her. "Your blessings are not to be overlooked, either. But not so fine as my lady friend's, I think." He tapped her again.

"God no!" she cried as she launched off into another pitiless, humiliating climax. Her feet drummed the floor. Her male companion stared, aghast. Five times in all, until my date got bored and let her collapse backward in her chair, crimson-faced and heaving for breath, while he turned back to me.

Damn. Now I was really nervous. My throat tightened and I couldn't help averting my gaze. He circled behind me, took my wrists and drew them round to the small of my back, where he pinned them in one hand.

"Look," he murmured, grasping my throat with the other. I guess his fiddle and bow had done that disappearing trick again. "Is she not delicious?"

I didn't like that word at *all*, not when used by Them There, but there wasn't much I could do in the circumstances. Moreover, the touch of his skin had an actual physical effect on my flesh, as if pleasure oozed from his pores. It washed down my throat to my tingling breasts, and blossomed across the spread of my shoulder blades where my back brushed his bare chest. He pulled me up against him, lifting my chin, arching my spine so that my breasts thrust out, pouting. Feeling the hard press of his groin and thighs, I let my eyes half-close.

"Champagne," he ordered. "For my fair maiden. She must be wined as well as dined."

Ho. His idea of a joke then, following my flippant instructions. He circled, turning me on my heels so that everyone in the place could get a good look at my stretched, pinned body. Then his hand released my throat and descended in a long caress, stroking my breasts and tugging my erect nipples, tickling down my stomach to the soft down of my pubic hair. I giggled nervously just before he eased a finger into my split and ran it back and forth, stroking my ill-concealed clit and delving further back into my hot furrow.

They were all looking at me.

Damn and fuck it, I was wet. I didn't want to be, not in such an obvious way, and still giggling I writhed in genuine embarrassment—but only succeeded in wriggling my ass against his hard prod. He stirred me a moment before withdrawing that hand and licking his fingertips.

"She tastes so sweet," he remarked. The fingers descended once more and he spread the lips of my pussy. "See how aroused she is?"

They could see, alright. They could see the glisten of my juices and the engorged nubbin of my clit and the coral pink of my plumply flushed labia. Even those further away could see the way I leaned back against him, how my breasts quivered with each shallow heave of my chest. He was making a thorough exhibition of me.

I felt like a slave in a Roman auction. I felt like a pedigree bitch being shown in the ring at Crufts before being put to the stud dog.

"See," he observed, "what a sweet, willing slut she is."

Shame flowed through me in a hot, ecstatic wave and I closed my eyes in surrender to it.

"Sir. Your champagne."

"Shake it. I want her soaked, you understand?"

"Sir."

I heard the crackle of foil and then the pop of a cork. I held my breath, then let it out with a squeal when a cold squirt of spray caught me right between my breasts. I tried to get my hands free but my tormentor had them in a grip of iron; my desperate, instinctive wriggles were wholly in vain.

"Oh! Oh!" I must have sounded ridiculous. I tried to open my eyes but got a face full of spurting foam, through which I barely glimpsed the dark shape of the waiter shaking and spraying. He blasted my tits and my face and my belly, some going more by luck than judgement in my mouth, some undoubtedly going over my captor and the nearest spectators. My breasts bounced wildly. I was covered in the stuff, slick and shiny with it. And when the bottle was empty my tormentor spun me round to sit on the edge of a table and ordered another one.

"Pour it over her." He shrugged off his wet coat, which broke up into a thousand green butterflies that flew off to chase the golden ones. Then he crouched down and spread my thighs, and as the waiter tipped fizzing champagne over my breasts and down my belly he buried his face in my open pussy and began to lap, sparkling wine and sex juices mingling in his mouth and then splashing over his shoulders and chest.

I arched my back, gripping the edge of the table, kicking my legs apart. I couldn't help it—his mouth was as hot as the champagne was cold, and his tongue slithered over my clit and labia with demonic intent. My whole pussy felt like it was blossoming open, inviting him in. I swear I tried to hold on to some vestige of dignity. I tried not to look the diners around me in the eye as I jerked and heaved my hips, as the champagne rain splashed over me and the table, and piddled down onto the parquet floor. But I came all too quickly—with a forlorn cry, clutching at his hair—just like the willing slut he'd called me. My climax rose and burst like the gush of champagne, as golden as the squandered liquid.

But the bastard didn't let me stop. I need a rest after orgasm, a moment of respite at the very least, because just for a few seconds my clit is too sensitive to touch. I tried to push out of his mouth's embrace; but instead he tightened his arm round my thigh, mashed his head in closer and gave me a huge dirty lick. I protested; he ignored me. I thrashed and kicked, shoving at his head, but he was stronger and impervious to my struggles; he was intent on wrestling another climax from my flesh. Screaming blasphemous curses, I lost my grip on the table edge altogether in my throes, and fell back across the dinner laid behind me. Glasses tipped and fell. Cold desserts squashed beneath my bare back. I could see, blurred through tears and champagne, one foot kicking wildly and the shocked faces of the diners whose final course I was ruining. And then, despite my outrage, everything changed. The almost painful flare of my nerve endings became, miraculously, pleasure. I was flying like a kite, rising to the crest of a second orgasm.

My cries changed abruptly from "Oh fuck no stoppit please stoppit!" to simpler "Oh"s of need, no less wild and loud.

The waiter was still pouring champagne all over my supine

body as delight took me by force. I stopped being able to form words after that. Though my lover still didn't let me go, though he drove me through thickets of over-sensitised agony to a third and then a fourth orgasm, I no longer had the strength or the will to resist him. By the time he finally lifted his face from my pussy, I was whimpering and shaken.

No lover had ever dared do that to me. I doubt most of them would have been strong enough to pin my legs like that, to hold me down, to lash my clit with a tongue until I surrendered to the discomfort and the pleasure alike. I hadn't even known I was capable of such rapid response. And now my abused and swollen clit throbbed, wanting more.

He grinned wolfishly as if reading my thoughts, my fuck-juice glistening upon his lips and honey-stubbled chin.

"Don't fight me, my sweet slut." Rising to his full height, he surveyed my limp body with satisfaction. "I am master here, and you are naught but my adoring bitch."

I parted my lips to protest, and he slapped my open pussy in warning. Not hard—not hard enough to really hurt—but the sharp shock lanced through me, body and soul. I gasped out loud. And my hips tilted in the afterwash, begging for more.

He laughed and reached to his own clothes, tugging at the lacing of his trousers. No transformation of his garments this time; he undressed like a man. I think he liked handling himself. He jerked open his pants and hefted his cock and balls into view, preening them with lazy caresses.

"Is this what you want, my pretty little bitch?"

I didn't reply for a moment, too awestruck to speak. He was beautiful. Perfectly, impossibly, stupidly beautiful. No man I'd ever met had looked anything like that; artists would have killed for a chance to sketch him. His muscled abdomen narrowed down from hard shoulders to a sharply defined V, framed by his hips, that I'd only ever seen on classical statues —in fact he was just like a marble sculpture brought to life. There was no flab, no pelt of hair to hint at the coarse. His balls were bald and silken-skinned. His cock was perfectly smooth and stood perfectly straight, and it was just big enough to be delectably out of proportion to his body.

The piano jingled on, its rhythm feverish.

"Hmm? Want it?" His cock jerked under his stroking finger.

"Yes…" I admitted.

He bent over me, staring into my eyes. With one hand he scooped up the dessert from a bowl and then pressed it between my parted lips and over my tongue. It was Eton Mess, I think: cream and meringue and chopped strawberries, powerfully sweet. I sucked eagerly. He smeared it down my chin and throat and over my breasts. "Just delicious," he murmured, stooping to slurp at my nipples. Then he scooped more handfuls and crammed it into my pussy, slathering my hot flesh with the melting confection, filling me up. That first entry of his digits made my cunt tingle and flutter, sucking at him even as he drove deeper and spread me wider. I felt it all —hard knuckles, smooth cream, slippery lumps of fruit. His scissoring fingers opened me wide. My hips kicked and my besmeared breasts wobbled.

"Dirty little bitch," said he, setting his cock-head at my entrance and impaling me with consummate, unstoppable strokes.

I felt the dessert squelching up out of my cunt, all over his groin. I felt the kick of my half-painful, half-ecstatic yielding as his member stretched me. When he set his feet, grabbed my thighs and jerked me down the tabletop, bedding me onto his stake, I cried out without restraint.

What would be the point, after all, of holding my tongue? I was being fucked in public, before strangers. They would all remember every detail: my spread, split pussy; my big breasts wobbling back and forth with each thrust of his cock; my open mouth and stretched throat. My loud cries and moans and gasps could not degrade me further in their eyes, since I was already having my brains fucked out, to the musical accompaniment of a demented piano. Melted cream ran down into the crack of my ass. The faces hovering above me were flushed and tense—I was sure that the men were groping themselves under the table. I was vaguely aware that some people were on their feet, dancing, right in the periphery of my vision, but I was too busy coping with my lover's cock to pay that any attention.

His hands gripped my hips like he would break me.

And oh, he fucked me good and strong and hard. Not hurried though. He made sure that it counted each time he rammed me. He made sure to seek out every hidden corner and angle inside me in order to fill it to the brim with his cock. He bent and bit my breasts, he twisted my nipples, he slapped my thighs and pinched my clit. I felt like I would burst. I felt like I would shatter into a thousand pieces, like a rock under the relentless pounding of a hammer.

And then of course, I did. Loudly. Shamelessly. Screaming "Oh fuck yes!" and more, just the way he'd wanted me to.

He pulled out, grinning, not having even broken a sweat —assuming his kind ever sweat. He flipped me easily onto my stomach, face down into a selection of chocolate profiteroles, and slapped my ass merrily until I squealed in protest. Then he grabbed a handful of my hair, all matted with cream and chocolate sauce, and, pulling it back until my throat was taut with strain, held me steady as he drove his cock deep into my cunt once more.

"You like this, don't you, Tansy?" His voice was light and gloating and wicked. "You like this, my pretty little bitch." His hand descended on my bum with a crack that could have been heard in Paris. "Tell me," he hissed in my ear.

"Yes," I spat through bared teeth.

"You're such a beautiful slut."

"Ohh…"

"Such a good, eager slut that I should give you to every man in this room."

You dirty bastard. But my audible response came from my lips only as a wordless, bestial moan. *You dirty, brutish shit. Give me more.*

And he did—faster, this time. Still deep, each thrust discrete from the next, but more urgent now.

I stopped crying out with each thrust. It became one long ululating wail of dread and need and surrender—surrender not just to his cock but my own body's hunger for it. I could feel his thighs smacking off my ass and his balls bouncing on my pussy. I desperately wanted to touch my clit just so I could cope with it all, but he was riding me so hard against the table-edge that I couldn't get my hand under there.

Then I saw his hand go past my nose and plunge into a

crème brûlée. It vanished out of my field of vision as my sweaty hair veiled my eyes like a curtain of flame. But a moment later there was a wet kiss on my upturned asshole. It was cold and soft for a moment, and then his thumb slid into me on the slick of that cold softness, and he worked it back and forth in my anus. Suddenly I didn't need to play with my clit. Sensation showered through my nerve-endings like electric sparks falling from an angle-grinder. I was full of cream and shock, and my butt heaved, opening eagerly to him as orgasm ripped me apart.

On the tide of my throes his pounding redoubled. I clawed the tablecloth and screamed, my flailing arms knocking vases and dishes flying.

I heard his cry, a short, sharp "Hah!" as he let loose and blasted his spunk into my cunt. And I felt that too, for the first time ever—a white fire that filled my insides and made me come again, so hard that I all but blacked out.

The room span, faces and bodies swimming. My mouth was full of sugar and surrender. I could hear whimpers.

The music. That frantic, frenzied music had stopped at last.

I blinked my eyes open. Our audience was frozen, all too many of these formerly respectable diners caught in acts of deep depravity. Men and women, men on men, women on women. Tits out, cocks in hand or buried balls-deep in flesh. On their knees, sprawled over tables, pinned on either side by fellow gourmets. A young stud mounted on a busty middle-aged matron who was braced foursquare on hands and knees. A young blonde thrown across the laps of two men and held down, her bottom bared for a spanking. A waitress with her skirt hiked up to her hips straddling a guest and grinding her pussy down on her face. Lust had run through the assembly like wildfire, burning everyone in its path.

They stared, aghast and ashamed, their wits returning to them with the breaking of the enchantment.

He bent to brush his ear to my lips. "You were quite the inspiration, Tansy," said he.

Chapter Three

T.W.O.C.

Our pact fulfilled, now, by both parties." Standing back on the pavement before the closed gate of the Citywide Secure Autolot, I felt dizzy and uncomfortable, but floaty with sexual satisfaction. A dirty girl in every sense. My hair was soaked with champagne and matted to my head. Beneath my hastily re-donned clothes I was sticky with cream and sugar—and my pussy was so puffed up with use that my sex-soaked thong had slipped between my unfurled labia and was rubbing against my clit. I had to dig my nails into the palms of my hands in order to bring myself back into focus.

"Where's my…?"

"Here they are."

Out from between the metal palings scurried hundreds of mice, just like last time. Only this time, each one carried a tiny scrap of paper in its jaws.

"Oh no…" said I weakly.

"Hush."

My companion squatted down and spread his hands over the ground before him. The herd of mice boiled, each individual scrambling over every other in their eager attempt to rush beneath the shadow of those hands. They dropped their paper scraps there, and it formed a mound of confetti. He scooped up a double handful, flipped it, turned it over, shuffled the leaves. By the time he stood, he was holding a small sheaf of rectangular papers.

"Hm," he said, flicking through the pages. When he turned back to me he had one eyebrow crooked speculatively. "This is the manuscript you lost?"

I scanned the papers. They looked just as I remembered them, even down to an ink-blot on the second page. Definitely *Goblin Market*. Hastily I sought out one of the novel lines.

Goblin fingers, goblin lust

Yes, this was the right version—or the wrong version, depending on your point of view. I nodded.

"Excellent." Drawing a long brown ribbon from his coat pocket, he tied the bundle up deftly while I held it. "Now, you must agree I have kept my word to the letter, sweet Tansy."

"Yeah."

"You enjoyed it very much, didn't you?"

Yes, I'd enjoyed it—if you count being made into an exhibitionist slut and coming like a nuclear explosion enjoyable. I was still fizzing, still wanting to see more of that golden cock. But I had an intuition that once I came down from my sexual high, I might feel even more icky inside than my skin felt beneath my befouled underwear. He was insanely hot, but I didn't like him much. And he still made me feel uneasy.

"I guess," I said with shrug.

He put a single fingertip on my breastbone. His eyes shone. "Remember," he said. "I keep my promises. Every one of them." Then he turned away and walked up the street, his coat flapping about his heels, his bow arm lifted as he struck a faint pizzicato phrase from his fiddle.

Now why had that sounded like a threat?

I reached Edmund Blakey's shop at a quarter to midnight, blinkered with determination and still buzzing from sex and cycling, and I actually hit the doorbell before I came to my senses and thought maybe some more caution would be a good idea.

I took a step back onto the pavement and stared up at the shop. There were lights on inside, but faint and far back. Metal grilles were pulled down over the windows. It looked shut up for the night.

The seconds ticked by. I glanced at my phone to check the time.

"Come on, Edmund," I muttered under my breath. Had he run away? Had the ogress come home early? I breathed deep, but there was no warning scent of patchouli out here. I felt the first burn of indignation at how unfair it was, that I'd tried so hard to get here in time only to be frustrated. And yes, I realised how self-centred that was and it made me ashamed.

Biting my lip, I stepped up again and tried the door handle.

The door was unlocked.

Oh crap. That meant I had to go in. I knew it might already be too late for Edmund. But that didn't let me off the hook just yet. I had to know for sure, before I allowed myself the luxury of running for the hills.

From my jacket pocket I extracted a pepper-pot full of fern seed. I don't like to use the stuff, not just because it's a bugger to collect in quantity but because by all accounts it's not good for your lungs at all. As bad as a twenty-a-day habit, they say. But in the right place it's invaluable because fern seed renders you invisible—not to mortal eyes, but to the Good Neighbours.

I shook it all over my head and back and shoulders, trying not to breathe the damn stuff in. Then I pushed the door open and slipped into the shop. Here I inhaled furniture polish and old incense—but nothing fresh, thank goodness. Everything was shadowy. A few table lamps had been left burning, dotted about the interior, but from under their heavy shades they cast little illumination. The looming furniture was playing tricks on my eyes already, threatening to morph into a lurking ogre any moment.

"Edmund?" I whispered, just before deciding that wasn't clever. Fern seed didn't make me inaudible too.

His desk. He'd be at his desk, wouldn't he?

Slowly, trying to be as silent as a tall woman in boots in the dark can be, I sidled deeper into the shop.

His desk was lit, but he wasn't there. I stared at the heaps of paper, wondering briefly whether to dump the manuscript and leave. But only briefly. I knew I had to put it back.

Up the stairs then—the bare wooden stairs. I cursed

silently every time a tread creaked underfoot. There was a light on at the top too. I stepped into the ogre's bedchamber.

Edmund. There he was, sitting in an old chair, his head in his hands, the picture of despair. It took him a second to register my presence. When he looked up, his eyes were hollow with fear.

My stomach clenched. What right had I had to put him through this?

Reaching to my inside jacket pocket, I pulled out the rolled manuscript and thrust it toward him.

"I'm sorry, Edmund."

His eyes widened. I waited for him to explode. He just rose, took the pages from my hands and looked through them, sifting through the pages as if he didn't believe his eyes.

"Really sorry, Edmund. I didn't mean to…"

My words died. He opened his mouth to speak, and at that moment there was a noise in the shop below us—a scraping, heaving thump of something large moving across the wooden floorboards.

My bowels nearly turned to water.

"She's home," he whispered.

"Oh *shit!*" I lurched toward the sash window, remembering there was a fire escape out back there somewhere. My hands scrabbled at the painted woodwork, but there was no give to the frame. I was still yanking desperately at the lock when Edmund's hand closed on my arm.

I turned, balling my fist to punch him.

"Hide!" he gasped. "Quick! Over here!"

He dragged me across the room to a big, dark, unfashionable wardrobe that stood against the wall. Flinging open the door, he pushed me at the opening; for a second I resisted, then realised it was the lesser of two evils and let him bundle me inside. He closed me in darkness. Then his footfalls hurried away.

The goddamn door didn't shut properly. I realised that as I huddled there amidst the smell of old mothballs with my eyes fixed on the inch of lamplight still showing. I tried to grip the interior of the door with my fingertips, but the frame was warped or something and the door just bounced against it. I saw Edmund dash over to the bed and heave up the mattress. He must be restoring Rossetti's poem to its place in the nest, I realised dimly, even as my sweaty fingertips slipped and lost their grip repeatedly. My heart was trying to kick its way out of my ribcage and my hands felt like they were wearing lead mittens; it was like one of those nightmares where you know the monster is coming for you and you can't run and you can't hide and you wake up with a scream.

Except that the monsters are real now, and we can't wake up.

Then the ogress came into the room. I froze where I crouched, my eyes wide with panic—and surprise.

Surprise, because she was beautiful. Not in a Hollywood starlet way, of course. She was more of your BBW type: twelve feet tall, even stooping, and massively muscular, with the ponderous grace of a galleon under full sail. I was at the wrong angle to see the door, so I've no idea how she squeezed in, but it must have been one hell of a tight fit. She wore a loose skirt of ragged crimson knotted around her hips, and that was all. Her eight black-nippled breasts sprawled in their twin rows down the length of her torso, and her face was thrust out into a muzzle by the carnivore's teeth hidden behind her full lips. Those jaws were capable of crunching beef bones. Despite all that, I swear she was still beautiful. Her slanted eyes were large and liquid, like a cow's, her cheekbones were high and elegant, and her skin was as smooth and flawless as burnished leather. She was clearly proud of her appearance too, judging by the way her long black hair was braided with beads and by the collection of bright brass bangles ranging up her forearms. But the hooked claws on her fingertips served as a potent reminder of her predatory nature.

"Nasssty, isn't she?" said a low voice in my ear.

I nearly shot out of my skin, and only my fear of the ogress a few metres away stopped me yelping. Especially as the voice was accompanied by a hand grasping my bare wrist. It was a cold, narrow hand and it felt like it was made of wet sticks.

"Don't scream," said the voice. "You wouldn't want her to hear you."

I was swimming in cold sweat.

"Nor would you," I breathed, barely voicing the words. "I bet she'd gnaw your bones just as happily. Back off."

There was a hesitation, and a hiss, and then the hand was withdrawn. I heard the words, "Fey lass, why should you care?" almost inaudibly, and then a brief scratchy scuttling over my head.

Ogres eat people. That's their defining characteristic in what we used to call fairy stories, before we stopped using that word. Them There don't like the f-word at all, for some reason, and it's not wise to give offence. Not to something that'll cheerfully crack your thighbones and suck out the marrow.

Edmund Blakely, standing with head bowed before her, looked like a child in comparison to her stature.

"Petling," said she, gesturing at a tabletop before slinging a knotted cloth bundle into a corner. Her voice was deep and resonant, like a bronze bell, and made the wardrobe door vibrate on its hinges. I saw for the first time that there were two green gin bottles standing on the table. When Edmund dutifully fetched one for her, she bit off the neck of the bottle and spat it casually across the room before emptying the entire contents down her throat.

I took those few moments' respite from immediate threat to slip my hands into my pockets. I grabbed the iron nail cross and a lump of rock salt—it immediately stuck to my sweaty palm—though I didn't have much faith in either as repellents in this case. According to all the old stories, the best solution to ogre problems is a man with a great big sword.

Smacking her lips, the ogress lobbed the empty bottle in the direction of the door. I heard it smash. Then she wagged a finger.

"Peel," said she.

Edmund's step back took him out of the line of my sight. I watched the ogress watching him, gathering up the thin tight braids of her hair in her left hand and running them over her right palm. Her hair was long enough to be wielded as a flail, and that was exactly her intention. Her wrist snapped and the cords of hair whipped out with a hiss.

"Closer, Mund."

He moved back into the field of my view, only now he was naked. For a man his age he was in good shape—spare and pale, his chest fuzzed with grey hair. I was impressed despite myself to see that he was sporting a game semi. I guess you just can't keep a real gentleman down, even in the most trying of circumstances.

Slowly the ogress hunkered down until she was almost on the man's level. The flail of her bound hair swung back and forth, idly at first and then, without warning, like the strike of a snake. A dozen snakes, their heads heavy with glass and gold beads. The lashes wrapped stingingly around his flank and ass.

Edmund gasped and arched his back a little, and his hands flashed instinctively to shield his genitals as a pink flush bloomed where she'd scored him.

"Naughty naughty," she growled. "Wide."

Obedient, he spread his arms like he was being crucified. I saw his cock jerk, bobbing stiffly and already swelling bigger.

You kinky sod, Edmund, I thought.

"Apologies, mistress mine," said he.

Her smile was terrifying. The whip caught him down the centre of his torso, rocking him on his heels. "Good."

He whimpered softly.

"Good, yes?" she demanded.

"Yes!" he gasped as she struck across his upper legs. "Yes!"

Over and over she whipped him with her hair, on his ass and thighs and chest—and groin too, which made him jump and quiver and his erection thrash from side to side. Each blow seemed to quell it, but only for a moment. It bounced back with enthusiasm every time, belying the look of agonised dread on Edmund's face. She gave him a thorough scourging, front and back, making him turn on the rug to offer every inch of his body as a canvas to the pain. Her more enthusiastic strikes gave him little welts where the beads bruised the skin.

By the time she had finished he was running with sweat and gasping with every breath.

"Sweet petling. Missed me, I think. All alone without his scrumptious."

I couldn't hear Edmund's reply but I saw him duck his head. The ogress reached out and mussed up his hair, a gesture that looked fond but probably felt not dissimilar to being battered by an automated car-wash.

"Loves me, petling?"

He nodded. The jutting eagerness of his love was only too apparent.

"Happy, petling?"

Again he nodded.

"Petling needs a tail to wag."

I couldn't miss the look of fear that shot across Edmund's face, and nor did she. When she laughed I saw a mouth loaded with brutal canines.

"I gets a tail, sweet. Pretty tail for pretty petling. Knees."

She glanced around the room and I held my breath, willing her not to notice the wardrobe. There was a lot less furniture in here than in the lower rooms, thanks largely to the nest of books, but there were a couple of Welsh dressers filled with plates and clutter. As Edmund sank to all fours on the rug she rose and plucked from a shelf a glass candlestick, discarded the candle, and turned upon him.

My gut clenched. It wasn't a huge candlestick as these things go, but even so it made my eyes water. It was definitely knobbly, and Edmund's ass looked suddenly narrow and vulnerable.

The ogress sucked the candlestick, lubricating it with her

large and agile tongue as she patted his behind.

"Open for scrumptious, petling."

I clenched in fear, too shocked to do anything but stare. There's something about the territory of a man's spread ass that I find disconcerting. Like it's the only chink in his armour of masculinity. I heard Edmund groan as she licked a long, wet slick between his splayed cheeks then pressed the glass to the hole between. His thighs quivered. His ass bucked. I could see the sheen of sweat on his skin. Then I saw him shift one hand between his legs to tug at his cock and I realised he'd done this sort of thing before. And the makeshift dildo went in, lump by lump. The monster was almost delicate, taking her time as she worked it into his yielding ass.

Lump by lump, inch by inch… until the thick stem and round flared base were all that protruded from his anus. Edmund's groans moved me in unaccustomed ways. Nor had it escaped me that he'd positioned himself so that I could see it all. Deliberate? I guessed so.

The ogress sat back with a big pleased grin.

"Petling! Wag his tail! Wag it for me!"

Edmund, his face and chest pressed to the carpet, moaned and twitched his behind. It didn't wag—the glass was too heavy. The pressure inside him must be overwhelming, I thought, and then realised that in my consternation I had dropped the nail cross on my lap and was clutching myself between the legs for comfort.

Oh dear God. Was that the extent of my empathy? Was it really turning me on, watching a man being violated by a monster?

My clit throbbed under my fingers, and the monster

laughed. One of her long clawed fingers prodded the base of the candlestick, jiggling it inside him. Edmund cried out hoarsely.

"Is good? Is what petling wants, then?"

"Oh God, please… please…"

"Is big enough? Is tight and bright and bitter ticklish, merry Mund? Is filling every nook and cranny? Or does we needs bigger?"

"No! Just… please don't stop, mistress mine!"

I had a finger either side of my clit, pressing and rocking through my leggings. Despite my precarious position I was only too aware of how juicy my sex was.

She stopped, of course. Leaving him splayed and aching on the rug, she rose and sat herself on the mattress, thighs spread, and smirked down at him. I had to shift inside the cupboard to keep her in view. Only then did I realise that her eight nipples were all pierced with crescent slivers of what looked like bone.

"First, petling must eat his dinner."

"Oh…" he groaned.

"Eat it all up."

She lifted her skirts, revealing the great smooth pillars of her thighs, and then between them, opening like a dark flower as she spread them, a hairless vulva whose lips already pouted, plump and glistening. Now I understood Edmund's eagerness to worship my own cleft earlier in the day—though in all honesty my little ginger pussy must have seemed a miniature toy compared to the awesome proportions of the one he was used to. As he swept his tongue over my clit he must have compared it like a pea to the rosy plum the ogress presented now. As for my narrow cunt he'd had his fingers in—well, I suspected he'd be able to shove his whole head into *hers*.

She reached out a bare foot and hooked it under his pelvis to hoist him from his kneeling position—almost a kick but not quite. He scrambled into the embrace of her thighs and dropped, burrowing his face between those twin rows of teats, tugging at the bone pegs with both hands until she laughed and arched. Then she grabbed his head in a hand big enough to crush his skull and shoved him back down her body, mashing his face to her pussy.

"Hungry. Hungry little man," she growled with approval, as he fastened his open mouth on her flesh.

My own clit was burning in sympathy. I wanted to stick my hand down my leggings and moisten it with my sex juices, but I was afraid to move too much so I just scratched my nails over the hidden, tingling point, feeling shivers running through my cramped limbs. I couldn't see all that much. Just the back of Edmund's head bobbing over the ogre woman's pubic mound. Just the jut and glint of the candlestick dildo wedged firmly up his rear. But I knew what the feel of his tongue was like as it lapped a pussy. I knew his dedication and skill, and I knew what it must feel like for her, as he ate furiously at her cunt.

She kept her head at first. She stayed in control enough to gather up the ends of her hair again and whip him as he sucked and guzzled, aiming with a slow heavy beat at his trembling buttocks and the implement protruding from between them. Even muffled in her wet flesh, every one of those blows made him cry out and writhe.

But as he slurped even she succumbed. Her strikes became

less accurate. Her eyes rolled back in her head. She lost focus on her task altogether in the end, arching back instead and using one hand to grind his face into a pussy as wet and dark and ripe as a huge tropical flower. Her feet hit the floor, rucking the rug and lifting her pelvis off the bed, and all eight of her black-tipped dugs shook and bounced. Then she came with a roar of triumph, her huge canine teeth exposed as her lips writhed back.

My ears rang with the assault. My fingers ached as they rasped my clit.

Three, four, five times she climaxed—I could count them, for each orgasm was signalled by a vocal explosion, though the last one was a grunt so deep it was almost subsonic. And in all that time I don't think she let Edmund up for air once. Certainly, when she finally released him, he fell back with a huge gasp.

Slowly the ogress subsided onto the velvet mattress, caressing her breasts and belly in satisfaction. Edmund seemed almost forgotten.

"Mistress mine," he groaned. "Please!"

"Hah!" she coughed. Sitting up suddenly, she pulled him onto her enormous lap, draping him belly-down and ass-up over her thighs. With one broad hand she aimed a thunderous slap at his rear, catching him just under the jutting glass dildo. I know Edmund finally came at that point, because I heard his cries. They went on and on.

Orgasm jumped me at that moment too, in the midst of my fear. I'd been witness to something so dirty that I couldn't defend myself from the electric charge that burned through my whole body.

And that was the problem. My clit is a magic button: toggle it properly and it takes away all fear and pain. Unfortunately it takes away all caution too. My spasming legs juddered up against the inside of the wardrobe, and the nail cross slid off my body and hit the wooden floor with a bang.

The ogress was up and on her feet in a trice, dropping Edmund. The enormous face that had been racked with pleasure was sharp now with enquiry.

"What?" she grumbled, and came straight at me.

I had little time to react, even if my brain hadn't been fried by my own orgasm. I stiffened like a hare under the nose of a hound, my shoulders pressed to the wardrobe back as if in hope of retreating all the way to Narnia. I've never felt so helpless in my life.

She flung the door wide and looked in at me. I was hit by an overpowering waft of patchouli before I forgot how to breath, and for a moment it seemed quite likely that I was going to empty my bladder. That was the least of my worries, in all honesty. I saw her eyes look right at me, saw the curl of her lip and the glint of an exposed canine like a tiger's.

There were no two ways about it. She was predator. I was prey. My body gave up looking for any other possibility.

"Mice," she growled, searching the corners of the wardrobe with her gaze.

The door slammed and bounced as she turned away in disgust. I shut my eyes, willing myself not to pass out. When I opened them again the inch-wide crack of light was restored, and the ogress was lying herself down upon the bed.

Thank fuck for fern seed. I'll never go out without it again.

"Traps," she told Edmund. "Likes mice, I does. Tickles as

they go down."

She turned her head, frowning, like a woman discovering an irritating wrinkle in her bottom bed-sheet. Reaching under the edge of the mattress, she extracted a slim sheaf of papers that I knew only too well, tied in a brown ribbon.

"Upsy-downside," she complained. 'Don't make sense that way."

"Apologies, mistress mine," said Edmund faintly. "I made the bed this morning."

"Hh." She accepted the explanation, but turned the manuscript over before replacing it and then settling herself back down. Edmund didn't have to be told to go fetch her the second bottle of gin.

I stopped watching at that point. I was too focused on trying to restore my equilibrium. My pulse was racing so hard that I felt sick. The last undercurrent of sexual climax was still coursing through my veins, but it was horribly curdled by the adrenaline of terror. I couldn't believe I'd been so carried away by watching the two of them and their sex games. I couldn't believe I had survived the experience.

I hugged myself, feeling the shudders deep in my bones despite the uncomfortable lingering heat of arousal.

It was the sound of snoring that brought me back to myself. Boy did she fall asleep fast. I looked up just as the inch of visible room was blocked by a dark form. Edmund. He opened the wardrobe door.

"Mice, eh?" he said softly, then held his hand out to help me up. Ever the gentleman.

He was still naked, and though he'd mopped himself up he reeked of incense like a hippie's kaftan. I guess I'd found out the ogre-patchouli connection: it's the smell of ogress pussy.

I let him draw me out and I only glanced once at the snoozing ogress as I sneaked out of the room. The curve of her hip was beautiful, like an ocean wave. We didn't say anything as we descended the stairs; I don't think either of us wanted to discuss anything that had happened. I noticed that his ass was no longer decorated with the candlestick, though.

As we reached the lower floor I happened to glance down at my own wrist. There, where the cold hand had touched me in the dark, were four red-brown streaks of corroded blood. Though the blood wasn't mine. Turning my arm over, I saw the thumb-mark on the underside.

"You've got a Raw-Head-and-Bloody-Bones in that wardrobe," I said.

"What?"

"A Raw-Head-and-Bloody-Bones." I kept my voice low. "You have to destroy the wardrobe, Edmund. Cut it up with an axe and burn it all before sunset."

He stopped and stared at me, his handsome face pinched with disbelief as he re-evaluated his minxy ginger thief yet again.

"Really. It's dangerous," I added.

"You know about this stuff, do you, Tansy?" Then he answered his own question. "A lot more than you let on to me, when we first met."

"Look," I said, defensively. Why should he listen to me, after what I'd done? "You can't sell it on. They eat children."

He blinked and dropped his gaze, his mouth so tight his lips had all but disappeared. "Plenty of things eat children."

"Just… please, Edmund."

"Yes. Fine."

I nodded, grateful, wanting to touch his arm in comfort but not daring.

He led me through the front room. "Goodbye, Tansy," he said, distant and dignified.

I stepped out into the night, feeling withered by my own foolishness and churned up by emotions I couldn't even name. Then as the door snapped shut behind me, my foot came down on something with an unpleasant rubbery texture, and I stumbled aside. Glancing down, I saw that someone had accidentally dropped one of those antique doll babies on the doorstep. Its stuffed limbs were all askew and its porcelain face looked particularly ugly and livid under the moonlight.

I looked again. It wasn't a doll. I had a good idea now what was in the badly-tied bundle the ogress had brought home.

I made it round the corner before I hurled.

Chapter Four

Fey

I was woken out of a particularly dirty dream by the ringing of church bells. For a moment I lay there face down, trying to plunge back into sleep—I'd been lying on a tropical beach and Gavin, having covered me in sunblock, had been fucking my ass, slow and slippery, while everyone standing around waved their beach towels and cheered—but the noise was too insistent. I tried pulling the pillow over my head, but by then it was too late and I rolled over with a groan of defeat. Gavin was long lost to me, never mind the prospect of any beach holiday more exotic than Blackpool Sands. Arousal and loss clung to my skin like sunscreen and salt.

Well, I said to myself, *you've done it now Tansy, haven't you?* I'd entered the ranks of the real perverts last night—my first fuck with one of Them There. Well, first if you didn't count the house-hob who used to creep into my bed and lick my pussy when I fell asleep. *Everyone* has one of those sooner or later, and besides I never saw that one—it was nothing more than a furry lump wriggling beneath the duvet. Plus, I got rid of it when I started going out with Gavin, so it definitely didn't count.

But there was no excuse now. "Giving comfort to the enemy" was what they'd have called it, back in the days when occupation was something human armies did. I'd stepped right beyond the bounds of common decency.

I stroked my pussy, testing for bruising. It felt a little puffy still, but not unpleasantly so. I decided not to think about last night. It was easier just to lie quietly and keep my mind blank as I caressed myself.

But the bells clamoured on and on. There's a popular belief that the noise keeps Them There away—and maybe it does work in some cases, though that churchyard grim last week was proof that some of the Good Neighbours weren't afraid of the sacred. Whatever the truth, lots of people have scuttled back to the protection of the Church, in the hope that there's some supernatural power bigger and more amenable than all the elves and ghosts and goblins. Conversely, the Northern towns of Bradford and Oldham have taken the decision to impose sharia law.

Personally, given the choice, I'd rather take my chances with Them There. Funny how religion always boils down to punishing us for having sex, don't you think?

With that grumpy thought I rolled out of bed and into my dressing gown, testing my body gingerly for bruises and abrasions. I felt fine—better than I had any right to. A bit trippy, in fact, as if I'd eaten a lunch of cake and was having a sugar-high. Only my calves and thighs ached from being tensed for orgasm last night, and I couldn't help grinning as I rubbed them. The whole scene had been funny, in its way, hadn't it?

Although I'd bathed when I returned home last night, I thought another shower might clear my head. But by the time I got under the water, I was properly horny, my clit a burning button that needed to be pushed. Sudsing myself down, I fingered myself to climax twice, pressing my breasts against the cool bathroom tiles.

I was still in my dressing gown when I went through to the kitchen to rustle up some breakfast. Maybe I was bit careless about tying it demurely closed. I do know that when Vince ambled in, rubbing his scalp like he was rumpling invisible bed-hair, he stopped dead at the sight of the cleavage on display.

"Oops," I said, sitting up straighter over my cereal bowl and tugging the red silk back over my twin mounds. "Sorry."

"Christ, don't apologise," he said. "They're…" He grinned suddenly. "Well, that's one way to get a man up on a morning."

"Hah," said I scathingly. My relationship with Vince had always been one of polite disinterest. I was too busy with my own work to invest much attention in Gail's boyfriends. Vince was okay, as far as I knew. He was cute and seemed quite taken with Gail, and he was training to be a pharmacist. Standing, I went over to the sink to empty out my bowl. Normally I start the day with toast, but today even cereal seemed too much.

"Is Gail still in bed?"

"Still asleep. We had a late night last night," he answered

merrily.

"You didn't have to wait up for me, you know."

"Of course we did. But I meant, after that. We were… trying some new stuff out."

I glanced over my shoulder and smirked at him. He shifted from one foot to the other, his grin half-smug and half-goofy. He was wearing only a pair of loose, dark blue boxers and I was pleasantly aware of how near his long, fit body was to naked.

"Well, it didn't keep me awake. I was out like a light."

"You can hear us, usually, can you?"

"You're pretty loud most of the time."

"Sorry."

"No worries. It doesn't bother me."

As I slotted my bowl into the drying rack he moved in up to my shoulder. "Look… You and Gail are close, aren't you? Really close."

Some might say *too* close. But Vince didn't seem to mind our parlour games yesterday afternoon.

"I suppose so," I admitted.

"You know all about… This stuff." He illustrated his words with a pat on my bottom that made me jump in my skin—not because it was sharp but because of the electric flash of arousal that shot through my whole body. I forced myself not to show anything. Or at least, I think I managed to stifle the response. I froze in place against the sink, staring at the window, feeling the hot and bubbling ache in my cunt.

"Uh-huh," I gulped.

"I wanted to ask you something." Vince sounded odd; tense and a little nervous. "Some advice, you know."

"Go on." I could see our faint reflections in the glass. His dark face over my shoulder, the glowing pale V of my cleavage.

His voice dropped to a conspiratorial murmur. "I love ass. I mean, really love it. That spanking thing—yeah, I could really get into that."

"Good. That'll keep her happy."

"Yeah." He hesitated. "But, you see, what I really want to do is… um… plug her asshole. More than anything."

An unforgivably politically-incorrect vision of Vince's big black cock plunging into my cousin's stretched and oiled asshole flashed up in my inner sight, and I clenched my hands on the sink as my knees threatened to fold.

"You okay with that, Tansy?"

Oh fuck. "Yeah. I'm okay."

"So how should I persuade her?"

Oh God, my pussy was melting like warm butter. "Is she… uh… dead against it?"

"She's nervous."

I got that. I really enjoy anal—it just feels so good—but you need to be able to trust the guy.

"Well," I said hoarsely, aware that fuck-juice was actually slicking my inner thighs. "It's probably insecurity. Make sure you shower together before sex. Get her well soaped. That way she won't be so worried about you finding her dirty… in the wrong way."

"Right. I get you."

"And you've got to show her you love that bit of her too. Stroke her bum. Kiss it. Get your face down and kiss her there. You've got to let her know you're not scared of it. When you're having sex some other way, and you can tell she's about to come, finger her ass too, but keep it smooth. She'll get to like the feeling of a bit of pressure there."

"You sound like you know how it feels," he said softly, putting his hand back on my bum and squeezing.

"Oh. Yeah." My face was flushed and my skin was burning all over. "I love it."

There was a shiver in his voice as he said, "You love taking cock up your ass, girl?"

And I hate being called *girl*—but when Vince said it, it turned me on. I took a deep breath.

"Uh-huh. You've got to be careful though. If you push it too fast it hurts like nothing else on earth, and she'll never do it again. Start with your fingers and use lube. Use a *gallon* of lube. And a rubber, of course. Be slow and gentle. Don't ever get impatient. It's worth the wait."

"Oh fuck, yes," he groaned. His hand moved across the silk, caressing my bum-cheeks. "I can be patient. I can…" His voice broke.

I felt something else join the pressure of his hand against my rump. The warm, urgent prod of an erect cock.

"Jesus, Tansy," he said, almost sobbing. "Your ass is fucking beautiful, girl. I mean, Gail's is nice, but yours is *magnificent*. I see you walking round the house in those leggings and all I want to do is bend you over, girl, and fuck that big round ass. Is that wrong? I can't help it!"

It was wrong, but I couldn't help it either. The way he was pressing his hard-on against me and talking dirty in that hushed voice, his lips to my ear—it made me shake, and I let out a low moan.

"Oh, Tansy." His hands snaked round and cupped my

breasts through a dressing gown that felt like an increasingly flimsy excuse for decency. "Those titties too! I want to get my face in there and suck those big tits till you come, girl! I want to stick my cock between them and…"

With a sudden burst of decision I pushed him off and turned to face him. Vince took a step back. He knew he'd crossed the line.

"Sorry," he muttered.

The cock that had been rubbing up against me was still hidden, though it was tenting his boxers like the pole of the Big Top.

Damn and fuck it. I had to see. I reached to his waistband and tugged the pants down past his hips, making his dick bob and spring back up. *Oh*, thought I, enchanted. *Lucky, lucky Gail.* There it stood like a goddamn tree, the colour of Tudor oak and all glossy, rippled with veins. It really was a beautiful cock, and below it were slung a pair of big balls that must have been working like bejeesus last night, yet still bulged with creamy goodness. The sight literally made my mouth water.

Vince licked his lips. He didn't know where this was going.

I didn't say anything. I just shrugged the dressing gown from my shoulders to let it fall to my waist, baring those breasts he'd been fantasising about. My nipples stood out like bullets. I don't know if they lived up to expectations, but his cock twitched so hard it nearly slapped his flat stomach.

"Uh…" said he. "Wow."

I sank to my knees on the kitchen floor. My hands looked pale as plaster on his thighs. First I kissed his balls, breathing the musk of his body and feeling the smooth plums roll in their wrinkled pouch as my tongue caressed them. Then I licked my way right up the underside of his cock, mile after mile of it, all the way to the tip. His glans was moist already, a tear of pre-cum oozing from the eye in anticipation as I reached it. I tasted the evidence of his desire, probing the tiny slit with the very tip of my tongue, then teased his frenulum until he caught my hair up in his hands and crushed it, half caressing and half tugging. He wanted me to take his cock in my mouth, but he didn't want to ruin things with impatience. And I was enjoying myself.

I looked up at his face from my low angle, holding the blunt cockhead on my tongue, framing it with my open lips. Vince was watching too, but his expression was glazed. Returning my concentration to the job in hand, I swirled my tongue over and around his glans. Then I let him have what he wanted, sucking him all the way into the back of my mouth and opening my throat to him.

Oh, he liked that. I could tell by the rocking judder of his hips. And I liked it too. I love giving head. I love cock. Human cock, and—apparently—Gentry cock too. I thought of the specimen from last night, the one I'd never got the chance to suck. I contrasted its remembered smoothness to the rugged texture of the one in my mouth right now. As my bobbing head ministered to Vince's need I couldn't help imagining how my golden fiddler would have felt sliding over my tongue, pushing into my throat, cutting off my breath with every thrust of his hips. I bet he'd have been rough and forceful.

But this was good enough. This was real man, salty and hot and meaty. He wanted to fuck my mouth and my ass and my tits. He didn't want to play with me or put me on display or fuck with my head. He just wanted to fuck *me*.

I remembered Gail's words as I stumbled to bed last night: *Oh God, Tansy, what were you thinking of? That's so dangerous!*

Gail.

With a gasp I pulled back off Vince's cock.

"Girl…"

"Christ, Vince—what the fuck are we doing?"

He was still staring, open-mouthed, as I ran out of the kitchen and slammed my bedroom door shut.

What the hell had got into me? Seriously—what had I been thinking of? I paced my bedroom then threw myself on the bed. Gail wasn't just my cousin, she was my best friend, and her boyfriend was *way* off limits. I never made a play for her men! How had I ended up kneeling on the kitchen lino with Vince's cock down my throat, tits out and gobbling his rod like a sex-starved slut?

I stared at the picture on my bedside table, the only photo I had of Gavin, without really seeing it. It wasn't as if I even fancied Vince. I mean, he was cute, but that was it. When had "cute" turned into "hot"?

Except that I did fancy him now. Even right now, red with embarrassment and self-blame, I could feel the aching pull of disappointment. I still burned with regret that I hadn't tasted his cum blasting down my throat, that he hadn't sat me on the sink and stuffed me full of his cock, that I hadn't held his dark head against my creamy tits and had him suckle there…

It was as if I'd suddenly seen the hot concealed in the cute. And now I couldn't stop seeing it.

Gavin looked out at me from the photo. I'd taken it in the pub on our first date, he and I leaning in together as I held the cell phone out at arm's length. He looked so happy, his face creased in a grin. I remembered the way he'd put his arm around me as he walked me home, then pulled me up against him to kiss me—gently, yes, but with unconcealed hunger. I didn't fuck on a first date, not back then, but I hadn't hesitated for Gavin. I'd wanted him too much.

We'd fucked all night long. All night, drifting in and out of sleep toward the end, but too eager for each other to let go, to stop touching and kissing and pressing together.

Hell. I shook myself out of my reverie, confused. What was I doing, fantasising about Vince and Gavin in almost the same breath? I looked down and saw that my hand was pressed hard against my pubic mound, grinding my swollen clit. My body had recovered from last night's hammering and—obviously over-stimulated—was now ready for more.

I really needed to come. Again. Okay, *another* wank, then.

No, I realised with a sickening lurch, as at that moment the bathroom door slammed shut. What I really needed was to get out of the house before I had to face Gail.

Throwing on my T-shirt and skirt and a pair of sandals, I was out of the front door before she emerged from the shower. My plan was to go fetch my impounded car from Croydon, and on a Saturday morning that meant taking the Underground, so I set out walking to the station.

It was just a bit unfortunate that I'd headed off before I had any chance to cool down. Even as I walked, I was uncomfortably aware of the heat and emptiness of my sex, and the way my panties felt as if they were rubbing in all the wrong places. I suppose everyone gets that sensation sometime—the random hard-on, the crazy gotta-frig-now itch. Well, I had it bad that morning. It made nearly every man I passed a sudden source of interest. Furtively I eyed them up—the delivery guy dropping off crates of tinned food at the corner store, the two youths smoking on the bench outside the Tube entrance, the busker at the bottom of the escalator—wondering what they looked like naked, how big their tools were, what they'd feel like fucking me good and hard.

God, *every man* had a cock. It sounds stupid, but it was like the revelation of a great secret. Every one of them was capable of fucking me. Think of the potential.

My feet felt clumsy, tripping me up. An unfocused excitement made my blood run quickly. I shook my head at myself, bemused and irritated... yet enjoying it too.

Then the next Northern Line train arrived, and things got worse.

It was a Saturday in the middle of summer so of course the ventilation had broken down. And a big chunk of the Underground wasn't operating because of weekend maintenance work and a breakthrough of aggressive duergar into the Circle Line tunnel, so by the time I got to the middle of town every train, platform and stairwell was packed out. It was sweaty and hot, and inside the carriages we were pressed together, standing room only. I stared into space, pretending not to notice the hot young Spanish student-types I was crammed in against, my breasts bumping softly against the back of the taller one as the train swayed. The stuffy air in here was making me feel a bit dizzy. I hung my weight from the hand-strap overhead, feeling the tick of my pulse in my engorged clit and wishing I could touch it just to get some relief. Wishing I could lick that student's beautiful neck and feel the stir of his nape hair under my tongue.

That's when it happened. Someone behind me—unseen and anonymous—cupped my ass briefly with one hand.

Hey, it's not like it's the first time I've been groped on public transport. Normally I make damn sure I protest and embarrass the hell out of them. But this time, I just stood there. The weight of my own churning appetite seemed to pin me in place. When I didn't react, the hand took the opportunity for another pass, squeezing the full curve of my bum-cheek a little more boldly.

A hot bubble of arousal burst in my sex, releasing a trickle that flooded my knicker gusset.

Tansy, I admonished myself. *You dirty cow. Stop this now.* But my body wasn't listening.

Surreptitiously, moving with the sway of the train, my unseen admirer shifted in a tiny bit closer. It was definitely a man: I could smell his aftershave and his skin, and feel his bulk at my back. But I had no idea what he looked like. I licked my dry lips and blinked at the advert over the door, aware now that my nipples, despite the heat of the day, had hardened to points that were poking the Spanish guy quite insistently. I wondered how he didn't notice, but he was deep in conversation with his friend. I wondered what was happening to me, that I should respond to this molestation so submissively. It wasn't like me to be shy or fearful.

But then this wasn't shyness or fear. It was dirty, thrilling pleasure.

The hand moved, sliding all over my right cheek. The

flower-print skirt I was wearing was really quite short and those fingers found the edge easily. I wasn't wearing tights. Warm fingertips brushed my bare skin. Oh God... that felt *good*.

Involuntarily, I let out a tiny moan, and the eyes of Spanish guy's friend flicked to me. I flushed, then switched to gazing at the shadowy pipework flashing past the window. My ass was being bumped now, quite gently, by a hard knot of trouser-clad flesh. *Shit*, thought I. *He has a hard-on.*

The train gave a sudden lurch around a curve and everyone staggered a little. The man behind me took the opportunity to grasp my hip and pull my ass into his crotch. I didn't resist. I could feel his erection fighting against his clothes, pressing against my bum.

A stranger's rubbing his dick against me. And I'm letting him.

I could feel his hot wet breath on my ear.

Then we reached my station and the door slid open before me. Londoner's instinct took over and I pushed out onto the platform before the incoming tide could cram into the train. I didn't look back. I didn't so much as glance over my shoulder to see who had been taking such disgraceful advantage of the crowd. I just went with the flow, hurrying toward the Up stairs.

I should have felt sick and angry and violated. But my panty-gusset was awash and it would have been very difficult to pretend to be outraged. What I actually felt was a trembling exhilaration, as if I'd just got away with something. I didn't understand why. But that was the way it was.

I caught the train from Victoria to Croydon. Trains have

one advantage over the Tube: the carriages have toilets. I locked myself into the tiny, creaking chamber and braced myself against the wall to strum off. I had to: I was desperate. My pussy was a slippery, open gash, aching to be plundered. I rubbed my clit, picturing the cock I'd never seen pressing into my ass, the frotteur getting off on the friction of my firm bum-cheeks. My inner heat swelled, lifting me. Then my imagination went further, beyond reality, picturing what it would have felt like had he slipped his cock from his fly and pressed it against me under the pelmet of my skirt, inveigling it hot and bare between my thighs. Picturing the two Spanish lads exchanging knowing looks and twisting about to casually grip my arms and pin me, holding me in place as my unseen admirer pushed into my hot tight slot, watching my face as the helplessness dawned in it despite all my attempts to look casual —and everything slow and sneaky and furtive, trying desperately not to draw attention to ourselves. Fucking with infinite stealth, in a train full of people. I came three times. After that I washed my hands and looked at my shamed-faced expression in the mirror, as I tried to cool my burning cheeks by patting them with tepid water. But that shame was visibly tempered by a sly and secretive satisfaction. I could imagine that dirty perv on the Underground looking just the same way.

He must have thought I was a real slut, letting him do that.

My pussy clenched at the thought and I turned quickly to shove the door open before the temptation to stick my fingers back in my panties just one more time became overwhelming. I had that much self-control.

Still, my naughty little fiddle took the edge off my hunger. Temporarily. Enough to get me to Croydon, where I caught a taxi to the industrial estate.

It wasn't a comfortable ride. I watched as the driver tilted his rear-view mirror so he could get a good look at my tits in their tight pink T-shirt. That just made me more self-conscious. I half-wished I'd chosen my clothes more wisely this morning: a tee that didn't actually strain across my rack, for a start, or a skirt that wasn't so short that I could feel the seat fabric under my bare buttocks. But I also felt excited by his attention. How could he not look, after all, when my body was radiating sexuality like this? I didn't dare glance down at myself, but I knew that my nipples were stiff enough to be outlined through the soft fabric. My breasts felt heavy and I wanted to touch and squeeze them. How *could* the cab-driver not want the same thing?

If he hadn't been such a scary-looking bloke I might have said something. As it was, I spilled out onto the pavement in front of the Citywide Secure Autolot torn between my physical urges and real nervousness. Glad to see him drive off, but roiling with heat, and more than a bit appalled at myself.

Something wasn't right here at all, I thought. For the second time inside twenty-four hours, I faced those metal palings nearly in tears of frustration. *I need to get this done and go home*, was the most sensible thought that rose above the storm of conflicting impulses in my head. *I need to get home and...*

This time the place was open. Luckily the person taking the tickets and accepting payments in their dingy office was a woman—though I caught myself staring with fascination down her deep, satiny cleavage as she leaned over the machine printing out my receipt. She scowled a little at me as she handed the piece of paper over; I hadn't managed to wrench my gaze away from her boobs in time to go unnoticed.

What the hell's up with me?

"Take this to the guys round the back," she told me. "They'll find your car for you."

I walked out again, following the painted signs round the building and behind the rows of vehicles. There was a big open-fronted garage behind the office buildings, and several bright yellow tow-trucks parked outside. In the shadows behind the big metal doors I could see three or four men in blue overalls doing engine-repair type stuff to a truck. I wasn't really interested in what they were doing. I was, to be honest, in a real state of dithering misery and confusion. My body seemed to have taken over from my brain, and I couldn't think clearly. I just knew I was looking for some comfort for this itch.

Feeling almost dizzy with longing, I walked straight into the cavernous workshop area. The place smelled of oil and scorched metal. I approached the nearest mechanic. He was a big burly man with a shaved head. I liked that. I couldn't help myself. Uncomplicated and vigorous—that was what I craved. He looked tough, like you'd see him on the football terraces shouting abuse at the rival fans, but when he spoke he was polite.

"Can I help, love?" He couldn't keep his eyes from flicking over my tight T-shirt though.

"Um," I said, my cheeks blazing. Tension was making me quiver. I knew what I wanted to ask, but it was a question of whether I could bring myself to take that leap. The silence stretched.

"Yes?"

I licked my lips. "I was thinking, maybe…"

He lifted an eyebrow. "You okay, love?"

No I wasn't. But it was now or never. "Are you closing for lunch?"

"Open all day Saturday, love—Why?"

"Because," I said, taking a deep breath, "I really need cock right now."

The other blokes all looked over.

"What did you say?" His eyes narrowed.

"I need cock." Hell yeah, it wasn't exactly sophisticated. Top-shelf magazine stuff, really. But I wasn't trying to charm the guy with my sparkling personality, I was trying to get laid. *Speak the language they understand*, I reckoned. To make my point clearer I pulled up my top and bra in one motion, sticking my tits out like a model from one of the defunct lads' magazines. I think I was far enough into the shadow of the building not to be too visible from outside, but to be honest by this point I didn't care. I just wanted someone to touch me.

His eyes nearly bulged out of his head.

"Fuckin' hell!" said one of the other mechanics with enthusiasm. "Look at those!"

I think that was the point when I really lost it. *One man good, several men better*, said the demon possessing my pussy.

"Don't just look," said I, squeezing my boobs between my upper arms and then jiggling them up and down. "Come on guys. I need you."

They were closing in, drawn closer, staring.

"Is this something to do with your Eighteenth, Rick?"

"Is this the stripper, like?"

"Happy Birthday, Rick," said I. He was a gangly sharp-eyed youth. "Come and celebrate, everyone."

"Are they real, love?"

"Touch them and find out," I suggested. The speaker did, running his hand across his greasy blond hair in an oddly deferential manner before giving my tits a thorough groping. My nipples were so stiff they nearly twanged as he thumbed them. "They're real all right!" he announced with a huge grin, pinching my left bud and giving it a disbelieving tug. I wriggled like a fish on a hook, gasping with gratitude.

"Kin' hell. Look at her!"

"You sure about this, love?" said the first man, roughly.

"Oh yes."

"Then close the doors, Jakub," he ordered.

Jakub was a raw-boned guy with a shock of black hair. He was from Latvia or Poland or somesuch, I think, though I didn't work that out till later. While he hurried to shut the big garage doors, Boss Man dug into his pocket for coins.

"Rick, go get some condoms from the machine in the bog."

"Yeah," said the fifth man: "We don't know where she's been, do we?"

Fair point of course, but I shot him an irritated look, because he was the sort I wouldn't ordinarily have deigned to let buy me a drink. A stubby man with a face like a potato.

"Hey! No need to be rude," said Boss Man. "She's just a posh bird with a need for some hot action, aren't you love? Like a bit of rough, don't you?"

Well, I didn't think I merited being called a Posh Bird, but I couldn't deny the rest. Actually I'd never had anyone who looked as rough as the men in this lot—but my pussy was already running wet with anticipation.

"Mm-hmm. Yes please."

He laughed. "See how nicely she asks, lads?"

He helped me off with my top and bra and I shook my tits out, enjoying their freedom. Several hands grabbed, patting and squeezing. They weren't brutal, but their fingers were callused and there was oil ingrained into their knuckles and wedged under the fingernails of even the cleanest. I whimpered with pleasure. It seemed so easy, so natural, to surrender to their coarse hands, as if everything soft and tender and feminine about my body demanded acknowledgement by what was hard and dirty and masculine about theirs.

"Ask nicely for my cock," suggested Blond.

I dragged myself obligingly out of the others' grasps and furled my arms around his neck, looking deep into his eyes. "Please, I want your cock," I said. It might have sounded like I was teasing but I was completely sincere. I wanted every one of their cocks. I licked my lips. My voice was husky. "I want your big, hard tool inside me. I need it."

"Fucking hell," he whispered, pulling me up against him until my breasts squashed against his overalls. His erection was already keen enough to bruise me. But a hand —Jakub's— caught my hair and pulled until I was arching backward in Blond's arms, feeling his hips and cock grind against me even as Jakub bent to mouth my tits. Stubble rasped my skin and the workshop air felt chill where his tongue wet me. Then another hand tugged impatiently at the elastic waistband of my skirt.

"Come on—let's see what we're getting into."

Stubby got his wish. My skirt was whisked away, revealing the hot pink thong I wore beneath.

"Holy fuck…"

"Get a load of that."

Much was made of my bum at this point. A hand ventured a slap just hard enough to sting and I gave a little shriek, more in excitement than anything else. They clustered around in a circle, turning me and pushing me between them, patting my ass and tweaking my tits. They stretched the elastic of my narrow panties to perilous lengths, sawing it up between my labia and snapping it against my anus. I was fenced in by their grinning faces, a prisoner in a tiny corral—but one more than happy to be there. My little whimpers and squeals were all delight. Then Boss Man yanked my panties down.

"Well, the collar and cuffs match," Stubby laughed.

"Check out the ginger minge!"

"Do you reckon it's true redheads are dirtier than other girls?"

My pubic hair seemed to glow under the workshop striplights. When she was younger and crueller Gail used to describe my hair as "Orange," and I still have a weird lingering self-consciousness about my colouration, bred of many years being teased in the playground. Little boys used to say horrible things about my red hair.

Big boys seem to appreciate it a bit more nowadays.

That was when Rick arrived back with the packs of condoms.

They welcomed him into the circle. "Hey, what do you think of this?"

Rick grinned. "Not bad," he said hoarsely, putting on a

little swagger.

I didn't know if he was as blasé as he was pretending to be —who can tell with teenagers?—but I didn't care. I got my hands on the front of his coveralls and popped the studs all the way down to his crotch. Underneath he wore a plain black T-shirt and what looked like plaid boxer shorts. No jeans on a day this warm. Pushing the overalls off his shoulders, I sank to my haunches, my thighs splayed, and went straight for his crotch. His cock, as lanky and enthusiastic as its owner, bounced out from the confusion of fabric so hard that it nearly poked me in the nose. I laughed as I opened wide and wrapped my lips and tongue around that spanner. Over my head the others hooted and crowed with appreciation. I think it was only then that they really believed I was giving it away. Holding onto his thighs for balance, I deep-throated him until his pubic hair tickled my nose. He trembled like a horse about to shy and grabbed my hair.

"Mmmm!" I groaned, bobbing eagerly.

They let me eat Rick's length for only a minute or so before they got impatient.

"Fucking hell!" he complained as someone pulled me off him, leaving his cock waving about all slick with my saliva.

"Wait your turn, kid," Boss Man ordered, turning my head to his own groin. "You're the apprentice here, remember."

His overalls were already hanging off his hips and he had his cock out in his other hand, pumping it. He slapped my face with it playfully.

"You prefer man-meat to boy's, don't you, girl?"

Wordlessly I gobbled him down—all seven inches of thick,

musky-tasting goodness. He rewarded my greed by grinding all the way into me, filling my throat until I couldn't breathe.

"There's a good girl," he grunted, jerking his hips and jabbing me until I threatened to choke.

Then from behind, someone touched me. They'd knelt down unseen and now they patted my splayed pussy, rubbing my wet gash. Like a miracle, my throat opened to the invading cock. I suddenly found I didn't need to breathe; I just needed to come. And I did, my screams muffled by his solid flesh—though he must have felt them right the way through his body.

I came very close to blacking out, I think. I don't remember how I escaped his cock, but when I came to I was kneeling with my face buried in his thigh, and ropes of saliva hanging off my chin. I wiped my face, full of shame.

"Fuck. You're a horny little bit, aren't you love?"

"I have a German Shepherd like her once," Jakub mused. "When she is in season she let every dog in the village mount her."

"This bitch is definitely in heat," Stubby sniggered.

"Well you ain't doing it on the floor here, love," said Boss Man roughly, ignoring his own erection for the moment, in a manner almost heroic. "You'll fuck your knees up. Come on—hup."

He was right; the rough concrete was already hurting. He hoicked me to my feet and led me to the back of the workshop, where they dragged out a Formica-topped bench from somewhere and sat me astride it. The plastic felt cold against my burning pussy.

"Thank you," I mumbled, reaching out for them as they gathered round.

Two men either side and one standing over the bench, all five with their cocks out now. I sucked each one in turn; Blond's strop, curved like a banana; Jakub's big Polish sausage; Stubby's cock, which lived up to the rest of him but made up in girth what it lacked in length; Rick's slim cigar; Boss Man's now-familiar shaft. They stood over me, not so vocal now, watching intently, only the occasional jocular comment uttered as I turned from one to another, my slurping loud in that echoey workshop. And all the time my clit burned against the cool bench top like a live coal melting the plastic.

Second time round, Rick couldn't hold back any longer; he yanked out of my mouth and unloaded a great jet of cum all over my tits. I stared at the milky spill splashed over my freckled breastbone.

The guys guffawed and slapped his shoulders. His cheeks burned crimson.

"Couldn't wait, could you, kid?"

"Got somewhere to be going early?"

I stroked his spunk with tender fingertips, greasing my nipples with it.

"Hey—girl—can you suck those big tits?" This last one from Stubby.

I glanced at his leering face then hefted my orbs in both hands and bent obligingly. It's not about size; it's about flexibility. I could just about tongue my nipples, but I could lap plenty of Rick's jism off my skin. It tasted good—sweeter than I'd anticipated, and flavoured almost like grass. I craved more.

"Fuck," said Stubby. "I want a tit-wank off those."

He took my shoulders and laid me on my back along the

bench, then straddled me and hunkered down to slap his cock on my breastbone. Grabbing my tits with either hand, he squashed them together, making a tight sleeve for his shaft. My nipples bulged out between his spread fingers as he thrust and withdrew, slapping my mounds together with a pleased grunt each time and squeezing them like he was moulding dough. He was using Rick's spunk as lube, but I don't think he cared in the least.

"Uh!!" I cried, finding that mauling of my tits on the brink of painful—and disconcertingly exciting. But I was to find myself distracted from that. I was almost pulled out of Stubby's grasp for a second, as someone seized me under the armpits and dragged me further up the bench.

"Oi!" protested Stubby, resheathing himself in my tit-holster. My head was hanging off the bench now and my world was upside down. I comprehended nothing but a close-up of dark-haired thighs.

"You waste the good stuff," said Jakub, crouching to stuff his cock into my mouth. I shut my eyes then, as his hairy scrotum mashed up against my face. His cock went deep from that angle, and met much less resistance. He cupped my head in his hands and fucked my throat while Stubby fucked my tits. And then someone else sat on the far end of the bench—I felt rough thighs pressing up against me, my legs being lifted in the air and draped over arms, the push of something thick and hard and fleshy into my pussy, opening me wide—pounding out its own rhythm. I was only grateful that Stubby wasn't sitting on me with his full weight, because then I'd have been unable to breathe at all. I couldn't see and I couldn't hear—their voices were muffled by the hands over my ears—and all my consciousness was shrunk down to the awareness that I was being thoroughly fucked, three ways at once, my body used as a sex-toy by these men, without any solicitation or enquiry as to my own preferences.

And that it was *so* good.

Stubby reached his climax first—he must have shoved Jakub away to dislodge him, because the first I knew about it was the withdrawal of the cock from my throat and a sudden inrush of oxygen as my head flopped back. Then Stubby grabbed the hair on the top of my head, hauled my face up again, then lurched forward over my tits to stick his turgid cock in my open mouth and blast off. He got it mostly on target, but some up my nose and over my cheeks too. I gobbled frantically at his cock and he jammed me hard down on his stiffy to swallow the last dregs, and while I was still held in that position the guy fucking my pussy slammed in, so hard I thought the bench might tip, and came inside me.

"Jesus fuck!" I heard him gasp.

Stubby released my head with a sigh and stepped off me sideways. I had only a moment's respite before Jakub came back to finish what he'd started, cock down my throat again. The guys at the far end changed over too: I felt hands grasp my splayed ankles and lift them right up to my shoulders. My snatch must have been displayed like a split melon. The unseen man came down heavy on top of me, still gripping my ankles, pounding in like a jack-hammer into a hole already stretched open for him. I was crushed and choked all at once.

I nearly drowned in the glory of it. My orgasm flared and unfurled deep inside me, like a slow-motion explosion, and as it opened up so did my throat. I sucked Jakub deeper in, needing his mass to fill me at that end too. I howled and thrashed as I came. I don't know if anybody could hear me with all that cock in my throat, but they sure knew what was happening because Jakub spilled the briny contents of that heavy scrotum straight away, and the guy on top let go of my ankles and grabbed my tits hard and shot his load with a roar. I could feel the drops of sweat raining down on me. I choked down as much of Jakub's cum as I could, and the rest spilled out over my cheeks.

As suddenly as it had begun, it was over. I was left, gasping for breath, all loose-limbed and empty like a rag doll thrown down on the bench. They stood, they laughed, they scratched and tugged their clothes back on.

"I don't mind working Saturdays if we get that every week."

"Fuck… I'll do free overtime for that."

I blinked, taken aback—though I shouldn't have been—by how quickly it's all finished with for men. Me, I might be sore and a little dazed, but I still burned with need.

Boss Man—it had been him who'd taken me last, who'd nearly broken me folding me in two like that—lifted me up.

"You can wash at the sink," he said.

I could barely straighten up. My legs wobbled under me as he led me to the big stainless steel sink against the wall. There were rough green paper towels and slivers of grimy soap, but there was lots of water, hot and cold. I bent and slurped my fill, thinking I could drink a gallon. There was spunk all over my chest and neck and face. There was sweat and oil smeared over the rest of me. I was still wiping myself down with a wet paper towel when slim hands grabbed my hips. There was a collective roar of laughter.

He was in me before I could react, poking his cock between my bum-cheeks and into my swollen, open cunt. I looked round to see that it was Rick, teeth clenched, determined to acquit himself more heroically on a second showing. I just grabbed the sink edge and held on as he humped me, like a rabbit on speed, until I thought my teeth were rattling loose from my head. He wasn't big enough, not after two other grown men, to cause me any discomfort. It was just a question of letting him build up enough speed to achieve escape velocity.

His fellow workers cheered him on loudly: "Come on Rick!" "You go for it, my boy!"

Even so it took him a good few minutes—by which time I had my hand down between my thighs, coaxing my clit, itching for my own release. I think my gasps and jerks as I came one more time were what lit his touchpaper for him.

"You're bloody insatiable, love," was Boss Man's comment as he handed me my bra, shaking his head.

When they let me out into the car lot again, blinking in the daylight, I was still walking like a drunk. I felt a bit high too. Stubby went and fetched my car for me, presenting the keys with a flourish and a grin. I got a "Thanks darling," and some pats on the ass and a general invitation to come back any time I felt like it.

I giggled to myself, slightly hysterical, as I drove out. It was hard to believe I'd done something that crazy and I felt an urge to shout it out of the open window: *Look at me! I just fucked five guys!*

I was still buzzing as I drove home, but luckily I managed

it safely. Not all the way home—I decided to park up behind the high street near my place and do some browsing among the stalls of second-hand stuff in the street market. Realising from the big clock over the bank that it was well past noon now, I blew some cash on a sandwich and a fruit smoothie and sat down by the dried-up fountain to eat it. It was only when I took my first bite that my trippy mood vanished.

My teeth refused to close on the sandwich. It sat against my tongue like sawdust wrapped in grease. My mouth simply refused to recognise it as food.

I took a closer look. Chicken salad baguette with extra mayo. Perfectly normal. But when I tried again to take a bite my throat closed up. The first inkling that something was badly wrong trickled across the skin of my shoulders like cold water. I love food; I'm a woman of healthy appetites. I don't think the words "I'm not hungry" have ever crossed my lips, except in the sense of: "I'd love to eat it but I'd better not, it's like a billion calories, oh this is so unfair, it looks great." But this morning I'd thrown out my breakfast cereal and now my stomach recoiled at the prospect of a perfectly good crusty baguette.

I twisted off the lid of the fruit drink and put it to my lips. The cold smoothie struck the back of my throat; I could feel my body welcoming the liquid but not the taste. The strong fruit flavours felt like *too much*, somehow, and I grappled with nausea as soon as I swallowed. Oh, this was all wrong. My lack of appetite was as profound as if I'd just spent three hours at an all-you-can-eat buffet—not that those exist anymore, nobody wastes food like that these days, but I remember them with nostalgia.

I was still thirsty, fine, but it was as if I'd forgotten what hunger was.

I bit my lip then, trying to picture just what it was I did want to eat. If there was anything at all that would tempt my taste buds.

Cock. That was what rose to my mind. Big stiff cocks. Lots of them. There were no faces associated with these imaginary erections: they jutted up out of the shadows, stiff and throbbing with arousal. And my mouth watered at the thought of sucking down spurt upon spurt of creamy ejaculate.

I'd just been gang-banged by five men and I wanted more.

At long last the rational, critical part of my mind managed to kick its way through the door it had been locked behind all morning, to crash out into the daylight. And that voice of reason was pretty pissed off. I heard it scream at me, much as Gail had wailed the night before: *Tansy—what the fuck were you thinking of!? You stupid, stupid idiot!*

Quietly I crossed my legs and put my hand over my mouth, as if I could now, somehow, stop the brazen cocks that had been thrust into me. The warmth of my sexual elation went cold and clammy. I'd fucked five total strangers. Five sweaty, dirty men about whom I knew nothing at all—charmless, unwashed, not even terribly good-looking. Already it felt like some wildly implausible story from a low-end Readers' Wives page. What was my excuse? Had I been out of my mind? And how come, even now, I ached for more?

Shit shit shit. What if they told everyone? What if it had all gone wrong? They could have turned out to be real bastards. They could have been psychos. What if they'd decided to keep me locked up in there and just use me as a fuck-toy and never let me go?

The thought of that—chained up, kept in the dark, watered from a hose and brought out only to suck and take cock, servicing my captors with desperate gratitude—sent a plume of heat through me and made my pussy clench hungrily. And that scared me more than anything.

I'm not stupid. I'm horny and, yes, I love sex. But that doesn't mean I have a death-wish. I can tell the difference between safe and suicidal. Or I can normally.

Something was so wrong. I was not my usual self. I had woken up this morning… a nympho from a dirty joke.

Finally it clicked.

"Oh no," I said out loud, with epic British understatement. I followed it up with a soft, "You bastard."

Golden boy. Frog prince. My white knight, riding to my rescue. It'd been nothing of the sort.

And now the thought of his tautly muscled body and his mocking, merry face—the imagery I'd been pushing to the back of my mind all day—came back like a slap and left me quivering. The dirty, evil bastard. He'd tricked me. He'd kept his word—but he'd betrayed me. As if I should ever have trusted one of his sort. Oh, I'd messed this one up right royally. I'd thought that my golden boy was all right—just one of the Gentry amusing his aristocratic self harmlessly with a piece of human rough. I'd been lured into complacency by his good looks.

Because that's what Them There did, of course. Weren't there a hundred stories to warn me of that? They make an innocent-sounding bargain that turns out to be calamitous for the mortal. *I ask only… The first living thing to greet you on your return home. Nicht Naught Nothing. The contents of your cooking-pot. What you have under your apron.*

I should have known not to trust him. *I will love you and leave you*, he'd said.

It took me less than five minutes even on my phone's crappy search engine, to find what I was looking for on the Internet. There it was in black and white: *He haunts lonely places and isolated valleys, and is always smoking a small pipe when met. He searches out shepherdesses and milkmaids to seduce. Afterwards he abandons them and, having tasted the delights of fairy love, they pine to death.*

The Ganconer. The Love-Talker. He'd switched from pipe-smoking to hand-rolled smokes, that was all. Even Them There can adapt a bit.

"Shit," I whispered softly to myself, remembering.

The Raw-Head-and-Bloody-Bones in the wardrobe had called me a "fey lass." He hadn't meant I was acting like some whimsical stoner. He'd meant *fey* in an older sense. I was under a death-curse.

Chapter Five

And Leave You

S pare any change?"
 I was nudged out of my reverie by the figure standing in front of me, holding out a hand like a dried monkey-paw laden with terrible wishes. There are a lot of beggars around nowadays, of course, but this wasn't one of the ones I could pretend not to notice—if only because she smelled worse than a dead badger. From under a filthy headscarf and an even filthier nest of hair, rheumy eyes stared at me.

"Um," I said. "You can have my sandwich if you want."

Maybe it wasn't very polite of me—I had already mouthed one end of it after all—but I wasn't really thinking straight, and anyway it didn't look like hygiene was this woman's top priority. She took it from my hand, opened it and squinted at the contents. "What's the white stuff?"

"Mayo."

"Mayo, Sligo, Galway, Clare, Limerick. There once was a young man from… Kerry. Cork. Put a cork in it."

"Mayonnaise the condiment; not Mayo the county."

"Do I like it?"

"Well, I don't know." I was clammy with sweat and I just wanted her to go away. I needed space to get to grips with what I'd just realised. I was in deep, deep shit. The Ganconer had me locked in his enchantment. Pine to death for love of him, my ass. But if my raging hormones didn't push me into a lethal situation first, would I just starve? Starve to death? I couldn't picture that. But I couldn't go on pretending there was nothing wrong.

"Wassit made of?"

"Eggs, I think. Yeah. Eggs and oil."

"I likes eggs. Brown ones, not white. Brown ones got all the goodness. Brown bread. How now, brown cow. Are they brown eggs?"

"Definitely," I said, trying not to breathe through my nose. "Enjoy."

She turned away, holding the baguette to her face in both hands. "Kind o' ye." As she glanced back at me her eyes flashed like an owl's.

I ran my hands through my hair, distracted from my train of thought. The Ganconer had said I'd never see him again. He knew. He knew what would happen to me—didn't he? Maybe it was just an unintended consequence. Maybe he'd disenchant me if I asked. Oh, I needed to find him. Right now. There had to be a cure, didn't there? Maybe a second fuck? Like Lizzie and her goblin fruit? How was I to find a cure if I couldn't speak to him? Who else was there to turn to?

Who the hell doesn't know what mayonnaise is, but can name the old counties of Ireland?

Eyes that flashed yellow. Not human.

I shot to my feet, dropping the juice bottle. She was almost out of sight, hidden among the Saturday shoppers. Only the fact that people were giving her a wide berth allowed me to spot her.

"Excuse me!"

I hurried after her. She was munching the sandwich and still talking to herself as I caught up with her stooped, bony little frame.

"Puts 'em in boxes in sheds. Stinks it does. Wouldn't want to stand downwind. Where's the joy in that?"

"Please…" I didn't want to touch her, but I elbowed a passer-by aside to hover at her shoulder, racking my brains for a polite form of address. "Madam? Do you know where the Ganconer is?"

She ducked her head lower. 'Don't know what you're talking about. Sheds. No moon, no sun."

"I need to talk to him!" I was feeling stupid and desperate, but if there was one good thing about my addled emotional state it was that it seemed to have burned off any residual shyness.

"Not to me, then."

"Please… I'm in trouble."

"Boy trouble?" She paused in her hobbling walk and shot me a narrow glance. "What'd you want to be doing something that daft for?"

"I know, I know."

"He won't want to see you. They never do."

I nodded. "Where can I find him—the Ganconer?"

"Him? Hm." She crooked a finger, urging me to stoop lower. "You sure?"

"I've got no choice."

"Always got a choice."

Sticking her finger into her mouth, she popped it—wet with saliva and mayo and chewed bread—into my right ear, without any warning. It was utterly disgusting and I nearly screamed, which is ironic if you think what I'd willingly accepted in other orifices that day.

"There," she announced as I recoiled. "He won't want to see you, but you'll be able to hear where he's at."

Then she turned and hurried off.

Hey. Little old beggar-women always know the way, in stories.

"Thank you," I said uncertainly, and so faintly I doubt anyone could have heard. It creeped me out that she raised a hand in acknowledgement, just as if I'd shouted the words across the street. I waited until she was well out of sight before I spoke again, and all I said then was, "Okay. Okay, what now?"

Hear where he's at? I looked around me, at all the people walking and talking and selling and buying. At the store fronts and the *Commercial Premises To Let* signs on the boarded windows. At the kids skateboarding in the dry fountain basin and the busker with his battered guitar. I didn't think I had much chance of hearing anything here. Maybe somewhere quieter?

I wandered off toward a side-street, fighting the strong desire to wipe my wet ear. A scaffolder was climbing up onto a high perch and I caught myself staring at his ass in its baggy jeans, thinking *I bet he's good and rough*—before looking away, furious with myself.

The park. The park would be quiet. No one goes to the park anymore. They're scared of the trees and the open spaces… and the pond most of all. No one risks their little kids in a park. Personally I think they're being over-paranoid, but then I'm not a mother.

The park gates were chained and locked, but the fence was more decorative than anything else and I climbed up onto the low wall and rolled over the railings without any real effort. The lawns beyond were unkempt, gone to docks and thistles and long grasses now in seed. Under the bright sun the trees cast blocks of green shadow that threatened to hide all sorts of ravenous spindle-limbed bogies and supple-breasted, needle-toothed dryads.

I wanted a may tree, I decided. Hawthorn is the fai— the Gentry Tree. Stand under its canopy on the night of Midsummer Eve and you can see all sorts of things it would be wiser not to, so they say. Well it was early afternoon and not yet the solstice, but I was up for it. More than up for it, really. I was becoming aware that there was a tightness under my ribs again, a quickness to my breath, a jumpiness in my nerves. Just as if I was on my way to meet a human lover. All the familiar symptoms. I was undeniably excited by the possibility of seeing the Ganconer again. The heavy feeling of my breasts and pussy were proof of an unasked-for anticipation.

There—a hawthorn, low and unassuming, its white blossom now over and its unripe berries still green. Beyond it stood two other trees, much larger. One rounded and dense and the other ragged and expansive.

Oak and Ash and Thorn: a magical triad where Them There were likely to be seen, according to the old lore. Better and better. No wonder the park had been closed. Well, I'd better hope for the Ganconer being around, because there was a pretty good chance of catching the attention of something else in this location.

"Ganconer!" I tried to make my voice enticing, and not the screech of wronged woman. "Ganconer!"

There was no response. I waded through the long grass into the triangle described by the three trees and turned slowly, searching the shrubbery.

"Ganconer!"

Nothing moved except that the air quivered with a little heat haze. I didn't shout again. I'd called three times, so he knew I was there. If he wasn't showing up that was his choice. *You'll hear him*, the old woman had said. I shut my eyes, concentrating. Birdsong and distant traffic. The buzz of insects in the grass. Sun on my skin. The ache of my hungry cunt.

I wanted him. I wanted sex, any sex, but the thought of his beautiful body sliding over and into mine was the most alluring of all. I wanted those balls bouncing in their halo of golden hair. I wanted his big smooth cock. I wanted him to slap my pussy again like he had last night, and then throw me down flat and shaft me 'til I screamed.

A bee buzzed past my ear and I flinched, turning my head.

There! There it was! The faint sound of a fiddle playing behind me and to my left. Without opening my eyes I spun to face it, cocking my head from side to side to pinpoint the right direction. Then I stepped out toward it, my lids still screwed shut.

There was grass under my feet at first, of course. I was in the middle of a meadow, after all. I could feel it tickling my shins as I walked, like a thousand tiny fingertips. There was the smell of green in my nostrils and the melody in my ears— no, in one ear—and I followed it with my heart hammering, as if it were a single-stranded thread that was guiding me through a maze, a thread so thin that it might snap at any moment. The sound seemed to wander about, now on my left, now on my right or behind me. It led me back and forth, from side to side, from sun to shade. I put my hands out in front of me, worried about walking into a low branch and trying hard not to worry about walking into something worse.

And slowly all the other sounds died away and the fiddle strain grew stronger, until there was only that and the hollow sound of my footfalls. *Hollow?* I hesitated. Wooden boards beneath my feet now, and dust not flowers in the still air, and the plaintive, querulous music rising before me. I opened my eyes.

I was in an attic. At least, I thought it was an attic because it was so crowded; hanging on every wall surface and stacked against every beam and pillar were pictures: old-fashioned ones in ornate gilt frames and modern ones on stretched canvas. It was impossible to guess how big the space was, or even to see the ceiling. More beams, more pictures, in every direction. Stray shafts of sunlight lanced across the gloom, pale with dust. Dim bulbs hung in random corners. I was unable to stop myself glancing behind me. Directly at my back was a sub-Constable eighteenth century landscape showing a nondescript bit of parkland and a may-tree in flower.

Still the music played on, so I followed it. It gave me a nasty turn when I saw one of the 'light-bulbs' move. In fact it scuttled across my path, and I realised those plump glowing objects were really spiders, each as big as my fist. That first one scurried up a pillar and hurled itself into a picture of two Edwardian children playing on a swing, vanishing into the canvas as if into a pool of still water.

Yiee! I thought, biting my lip, but I pressed on, keeping a cautious eye out for more spiders. I felt like I was walking through the mind of some antiquarian art collector, watching his memories flit about.

A huge canvas blocked my way forward. It depicted a scene of mountains exploding and tiny human figures panicking beneath a blood-red, lightning-lashed sky, and I certainly didn't want to fall into that. Stepping with some caution around the cataclysmic scene, I saw the Ganconer just as he laid down his bow and violin. He was sprawled across an old-fashioned chaise, draped only in a sheet, and the sight made my pussy flutter. There were other people there too: a nude woman posed before an easel to have her picture painted by another woman in stockings and suspenders; a young blonde knelt before his couch sucking his toes; and others stood about watching. But my eyes were only on him.

"Violet," he said, his expression mildly quizzical. "I wasn't expecting to see you again."

"It's Tansy. And we need to talk."

He lifted an eyebrow. "We? I don't believe *I* do."

I took another step. Instantly one of his entourage interposed herself between me and him, and gave me a warning push on the shoulder so that I nearly stepped backward into two more women who had materialised behind me.

Whoa—territorial, much? thought I. She was shorter than me, with purple hair and beautiful butterfly tattoos on her shoulders. But she had no intention of letting me get one step closer. I restrained myself from pushing her back. Instead I locked eyes with him over her shoulder.

"You've not played fair with me, have you, Ganconer?" I wanted to sound firm and rational, but I don't think I was fooling anyone. I couldn't keep my eyes off that body of his, haloed by a judicious beam of light and almost luminous in its beauty.

"Haven't I?" He chuckled and, as I watched, his hand strayed to his crotch, lazily stroking the white fabric and outlining what was clearly a solid erection beneath. The cloth was so fine it barely disguised the shape of his cock.

I wrenched my gaze away. There were at least half a dozen people… no, more in fact… all watching us, drifting in closer. They were all women. Actually I recognised one as the librarian we'd picked up on our way to the restaurant last night. And the one posing for her portrait was the pole-dancer with the dyed platinum-blonde hair. She glared at me, no doubt annoyed at the interruption to whatever sort of kinky craft workshop was taking place.

"You promised me no harm," I said, gritting my teeth.

"And I did you none."

"I can't eat."

"Did I cut your throat? Did I pluck out your teeth?"

"I have no appetite. You know that."

"Really?" He caressed himself through the sheet, and I

stared at his shrouded shaft as it jerked and lifted. "I'd bet you could eat this, Tansy."

My pulse quickened. Yes, I'd love to eat his cock. His beautiful, luscious cock. I bit the inside of my lip in frustration.

"No," I said softly, but I think he could read my expression. Disengaging his foot from the oral embrace of the small blonde—*Sorry, Polly,* he mouthed—he stood, tucking the sheet about his hips to prevent it falling. His veiled cock tented the fabric, and every step made it sway provocatively. As he closed upon me, Alt-Girl slipped to the side to hover at my shoulder and the women behind me laid gently warning hands on my elbows, as if they expected me to strike him then and there. He loomed in over me, his breath warm with smoke.

"It seems to me that your appetite is quite healthy. Would you rather eat this or ride it, though?"

Both. Oh God, both. Over and over. My nipples scraped the inside of my bra, so sensitised by arousal that they hurt.

"I…" I shook my head. "That's not why I came here."

"Really. So you came to tell me off, instead?"

I clenched my teeth. "I came to ask you a favour, respectfully."

"Go on then. Ask." His lips were so close that I could hardly focus on his face. "Beg me."

"Please… Take the enchantment off me."

"Oh come. That's not what you really want."

The words shot from my lips before I had time to think better of them. "Don't you tell me what I want!"

The Ganconer's eyebrows arched in pointed disbelief at

my rudeness, and Alt-Girl grabbed a handful of my hair and gave it a sideways yank that made me gasp. I found myself pinned, not just by her hand at my nape but also by the threat of pain. It sent a perverse thrill shooting up from my pussy, like a distress flare.

"Don't dissemble. You came here to beg me for another fuck, Tansy." His voice was still warmly serene. "Once isn't enough for a wanton like you."

"I'm not after a fuck!"

He laughed. "Liar." Touching a finger to my throat, he ran it down my T-shirt and over my belly and right across my pubic mound. My hips twisted hungrily, proving him right against all my wishes. "How many men have you had since I left you, Tansy?"

"Five," I admitted, trembling inside with shame and arousal. Then, remembering Vince, "Six."

"I thought you looked… dishevelled. It's not enough, is it though? You want more. Now."

"Yes," I said faintly. "Do you call that no harm?"

He quirked an eyebrow. "I do. You seem to be enjoying yourself immensely. And if you are too heated to eat, well… I did not design the mortal body."

Okay, so he had a point. I'd been gleeful in my debauchery, for sure. I tried again. "But I'm not right! This isn't the real me—you've changed me!"

He squeezed my mons gently through my skirt, and it was like he had a grip on my soul. He could have carried me off to heaven or hell in an instant. My panties were sodden.

"Did I?" he mused. "How careless of me. Shall I stop it?"

"Yes," I whispered. My whole body was on fire with desire.

"Beg me."

"Please stop it."

He took his hand away and I lurched in the girl's grasp and nearly screamed with frustration, my intent flipping through a one-eighty turn.

"Beg me," he repeated.

"Please... please touch me." I hated myself as I said it, but my need was stronger than my pride.

"Go on."

"I want you to fuck me." Each word was an admission of weakness. "I'm so wet for you." Each was like the surrender of hard-won territory. "Please... I want your cock. I... need your cock. I need to be fucked, you bastard!"

He smiled, forgiving my impoliteness.

"Good girl. But sadly I can't, sweet Tansy," he said, suddenly flippant. "My girls would get so jealous." He turned idly on his heel. "But perhaps they can scratch your itch for you. Kiss her, Mel."

I was still rejecting the notion that he was in any way bound to his harem's will, when Alt-Girl grabbed my jaw, turned my face and kissed me, smearing my lips with her tongue. That was too much. He might be Gentry but she looked entirely human to me, as did all the other women in the room. I could make out the true colour of her hair at her roots, and I could taste the toothpaste on her mouth. I got my hand on her jaw and gave her a good hard shove off. In answer she slapped me across the face. I blinked, open-mouthed, and lifted my hands to retaliate, only to have them grabbed by the women behind me.

"Get the hell off me!" My cheek burned from the slap. The

other women were closing in.

"Now, ladies." The Ganconer was clearly amused by all this. "Don't fight. Someone will get hurt. Don't your people say "Make love, not war"?"

"Fifty years ago, maybe, they did," I snapped, more than willing to smack him one. And his bevy of creepy concubines.

"Is that a long time?"

"Uh-huh!"

"Then let us say it once more. Fair ladies, she needs your love. Make her happy."

Someone grabbed at my T-shirt, pulling it up to bare my back.

"No!" I shouted, twisting. "Get off!"

For that first moment my strength and determination held out. I was taller than any of them. I shoved and slapped angrily at their invasive hands, and almost broke free. But there were eight or nine of them, and only one of me. As they grabbed again, I suddenly found that I was having to fight with all my strength—and then that all my strength wasn't good enough. They could get two women on each arm and hold me fast. I kicked then, barging forward. In answer someone grabbed my left ankle and hauled it off the floor. All thought of fighting fair flew out of the window and I sank my teeth into flesh. That got me slapped across the face again, and this time so hard it knocked me silly. I opened my eyes to find myself spread-eagled flat on my back, all my limbs locked down, surrounded by greedy faces. They were pulling at my clothes and manhandling me without mercy. My T-shirt got yanked off with painful roughness over my head and my bra followed. Then my skirt disappeared down my thighs and the librarian, her blouse straining over her pillowy tits and her glasses already steaming up, fished about inside the gusset of my thong, her blunt fingers raking my wet pussy before she closed her fist and jerked my knickers off so ferociously that the elastic snapped.

I think it was then that I really understood what was happening and I started to scream, my rage now mingled with panic. This lot were nothing like my genial garage mechanics. They didn't joke or haggle for position or even tell me what they wanted. They didn't say a damn word. They were too focused for that. Just ordinary if pretty women, but there was a flat look to their eyes as if there was nothing behind them but black steel. They worked as a team, spreading my legs. A curvy woman in a sari knelt on my hair, pinning me to the boards more effectively than any bonds. I could feel the dry, dusty wood beneath my bare flesh. The stripper and an elegant woman in an opera dress dropped to their knees, and each took one of my nipples into her mouth, sucking hard.

"No!" I screamed, straining to see the Ganconer. "No! Don't you fucking dare!"

That was when the girl with the butterfly tattoos went down beneath my splayed thighs. Despite everything they'd done to pin me, I still managed to get my feet on the floor and buck my ass right off the ground, arching my back and thrashing my hips away from her mouth. Much good it did me. They slammed me back down and Alt-Girl Mel's mouth took my pussy, her pierced tongue lashing my clit.

After that I was lost. I kept on screaming protest, but my "No!"s became "Oh!"s all too fast. It took a pitiful handful of seconds—*seconds*—for my outrage and my rebellion to drown in a rush of arousal, as all my body's physical responses kicked in. I swore like a trooper and blasphemed like a Satanist, but it was all sound and fury, like Hamlet said: signifying nothing. My will was nothing. My pride was nothing. There was only the stretched star of my body and the bitches above sucking my tits and the bitch below licking my pussy and hammering on my clit. Then there was only me… coming.

With a last couple of lingering, possessive laps of her tongue, Mel moved away and switched places with a friend, leaving me open for the next of my violators. They took it in turns with me. Kisses like fluttering butterflies, kisses like blows. The one in the opera dress bit me. The one in the sari sawed her fingers inside me. Sweet little Polly ate me like an ice cream, giggling. Stripper Blonde slapped my pubis between sucks, like she was trying to nail my clit into me. It didn't matter; I came for all of them in turn. Nine of them, until all the fight was sucked out of me and the screaming was nothing but broken moans and I was on the edge of passing out, awash in a dark orgasmic sea. Only then did they let me go.

I opened my eyes when my head was lifted and my hair carefully, almost caressingly, gathered. The Ganconer, kneeling behind my head, looked down into my face.

"Now, will you lie to me and deny that they gave you pleasure?" he cooed.

I sobbed, exhausted. Tears trickled down the sides of my head.

"Say it. Say how it felt."

"It made me come," I moaned. "It felt good."

"Good girl. Good slut." He stroked my heaving breasts, comfortingly. "See what I have done for you? Are you not grateful?"

I swallowed. "No. It's not me."

"Ah. Do you still want my cock, pretty slut?"

"Yes." My voice was hoarse from all the screaming. His cock was still erect but still veiled. He drew my neck up, tilting my head backward, and rubbed that cloth-covered shaft over my face, pressing it down with his hand so that I could feel its unyielding hardness against my lips. I kissed his balls through the cotton, dampening it with my moisture.

"Isn't this the real you?" he asked softly. "Haven't you ever wanted to be used, truly used? Like an animal? Like a simple object? Haven't you ever wanted to be fucked by all sorts of men, by anyone, by the whole world? Treated as a thing purely desirable, with no will or say of your own? Have you never wanted to be seen only as a body, made to receive cock and fingers and tongue? To be nothing, and *everything*?"

I opened my mouth to deny it all, then thought better of lying. Better to kiss his shaft. Better to admit what he already knew.

But he laid me down again and sat back. His erect cock was held teasingly just beyond the reach of my lips.

"Well?" he asked, fending off my reaching fingers.

I recalled the question, and a spark of defiance. "Maybe, for a moment—when I'm frigging myself, when I'm ready to come. Before the rest of my brain starts working again."

"See? It's all you. Not me. The blame does not lie at my door, when at most I am guilty of freeing you. These are your desires, Tansy."

"But that's all just fantasising! It's not real!"

"Oh, it's all real now, Tansy. Everything is real now."

I couldn't argue ontology. "Please! Just fuck me!"

"No."

"Then cure me."

He chuckled. "No. You're far more entertaining this way."

"It's a joke to you, then?"

"Amusing, certainly."

I shook my head, despairing. "I will die. If I can't eat, I'll die. Don't you understand that?"

"Oh yes, I understand." He stroked his upper lip. "But there are always more of you, your kind. A never-ending variety, like snowflakes. You melt and go away. There are always more."

I was too wasted by my orgasms to be as angry as I ought to be. I just bit my lip and watched as he raised himself and turned away to his couch. The women had already melted away into the shadows, as if they were figments of his fantasy. As he conjured up a ciggie and flicked a match, I sat up.

"There's a way out," I told him softly.

"Hm?" He puffed the first cloud of smoke and glanced sideways at me. His left hand caressed his erection still.

"There's always a way out. That's the rule, isn't it?" I was sure of my ground, folklore-wise. Well, almost sure. "There's an escape-clause to every contract and every curse. Tell me what I must do."

For a moment he stared, and the light of amusement left his eye for the first time since we'd met. Then it came back, as if I'd only imagined its loss, as if a tiny cloud had momentarily shaded the sun in the Sahara, and now everything was restored to blistering, deadly sunlight.

"Very well," he said. "Tell me my name."

"Your name?"

Ganconer was just descriptive, I reminded myself. It simply meant *Love-Talker* in Gaelic.

"Tell me, to my face. I know you have ways of... writing lists on your machines. That will not do. Tell me, and I will... *pffft*." He made a contemptuous noise and blew out smoke. "Cure you."

"How many guesses do I have?"

He shrugged. "As many as you like."

"Is it Rumplestiltskin?"

Hey, it was cheeky, but worth a try. Never overlook the obvious. But he took a deep drag and shook his head, smiling.

"How long do I have?"

He waved the cigarette. "Take your time, Tansy. Take the rest of your life."

Oh, the bastard. Just how long was that likely to be?

They ejected me, not back into the park but onto an urban road. It was night, under a full moon, and in my skimpy clothes I was suddenly chilly. Recognising a faded old advertising hoarding that hadn't changed in a year, a sliver of lawn where Canada geese used to graze the short grass by day, and the canal that went under the road bridge, I realised I wasn't even that far from home, though this wasn't the way I'd set off that morning.

I had to cross the bridge first though.

I was in one hell of a mood, I admit. I was dressed again, except for my ruined knickers, but I felt grubby and shaky and frustrated. Frustrated above all, in fact. The Ganconer had teased me with his cock but refused to fuck me. He'd countered my demand for restitution with an impossible demand of his own. He'd cast me adrift, at the mercy of my rioting sexual appetite. I was thoroughly pissed off with the nasty piece of work.

Being angry helped me feel less scared.

Smug fucker, I said to myself. *I hope his dick gets eaten by slugs in the night. I hope an eighty-foot wyrm uses him a condom.* But I didn't so much as mouth the words. I still had some sense of self-preservation, and there was always a chance he was watching me.

Really, it would serve him right if I found out his name. True names can give you power over Them There. I would march in and call him by name and make the bastard crawl, I told myself. Although how the hell I was going to manage the finding-out bit, I didn't know. I tugged my skirt down over my thighs angrily. I'd start with the Internet of course. Them There didn't control the flow of information.

Maybe it was because of my overheated imaginings that, when I saw the huge, lumpen shape squatting in the shadows next to the bridge, I didn't turn and run. It was crunching intently on something—I hope it was a goose—and it didn't seem to have seen me, so I had my chance. But I didn't take it. I watched it bend over the bank and suck canal water, its back humped like a great boulder.

"Hey there," I said, slyly. "Trip trap trip trap."

The troll unfolded limbs like girders and, turning, vaulted up onto the road. The sodium street-lights highlighted it orange, but I think it would probably have been slate-grey under natural illumination. It was naked, and male. I mean, really *really* male. Its scrotum swung low between its thighs, like a drawstring sports bag.

God help me, but that sight made me cream.

"What folk been ye?" it rumbled, thrusting its head forward to sniff in my direction. Trolls are old, and half-blind, and dim. The English they speak is centuries out of date. "Foo?"

"Friend," I said.

A rumbling laugh answered that. Already its pizzle was stiffening and waving at me. *Now* that's *cock*, I thought, fascinated despite the dread in my belly.

"You want a hand with that?" I asked.

That actually stopped it dead for a second. I don't think it had ever met a human woman who didn't scream and run. It wasn't well-equipped for looking confused, but it tilted its head.

"I mean, two hands at least," I added, with a nervous giggle. "A stiffy that big must be quite uncomfortable for you. Can I help?"

With one huge hand it reached out and scooped me up, bringing me close to its flaring nostrils to breath my scent. I heard my purse hit the road as rubbery digits clenched about my torso. Its own odour was muddy and dank, like riverweed, and that snaggle-toothed maw was horrifying. Don't think I was completely insensible to the danger, as I hung there like Fay Wray with my legs dangling, but it was more a thrilling terror than real fear that made my heart hammer. It was... anticipation.

"Ganconer," it said, with a voice like a rockslide. I could imagine there was a hint of contempt in the rumbling tones. It hooked a serrated claw in the cleavage of my T-shirt and pulled, slicing through the cotton cloth and the taut bra beneath. I felt the cold curve of its nail and then the rush of the night air on my nipples as my breasts bounced free. Then it did it again to my skirt, and that fell off entirely. It must have been trying quite hard not to cut me in passing, I realised dimly.

"Yes," I gasped, my breath constricted by the long fingers around my rib-cage. "What's the Ganconer's true name?"

It snorted, taken aback again, and shook its head. Its breath was as cold as the air under a bridge. "I noot."

"Then who does know?"

"Ask the fissh," it said, lifting one of my thighs and dipping its muzzle to the point where they met. "The saumon fissh is alther-eldoste. The saumon woot alle names."

Then it licked me, and its tongue was cold too, an enormous muscular thing coated in saliva as thick and slippery as frog-spawn, that slid along the slit of my open pussy right to my asshole. I squealed in shock—at the temperature—and in delight at the sensation.

"Uuhh," it grunted, so that I felt the low note shake my bones like the bass speaker at a rock gig, as its tongue twisted and pushed against all my soft spaces. Then it withdrew and licked the rest of my torso, a slithering caress that encompassed my pussy and stomach and breasts. Goodness knows what it made of my pubic fuzz, since its own body was completely hairless. But I couldn't help wriggling and I think it liked that; it licked me more, sliming me all over. Then with a lurch it sank back onto its butt on the tarmac, and dropped me into its lap.

"Oh!" I said, finding myself sitting astride the cushion of

its huge bollocks, face to face with its erect cock. "Oh my, what a big dick you have!"

And I do mean *big*. It was easily the length and thickness of my own arm, and as stoutly erect as a stake. It swayed before my eyes.

Curling almost double, the troll licked its own prick, coating it in a layer of clear slime. It was an accomplishment that I couldn't help but admire.

"Mak plesaunce!" it boomed.

"Me?"

There was certainly no way any human woman could take that lot in any orifice. What else could I do? I enfolded it in an embrace, snuggling it between my slippery breasts and pulling upward. Slick troll-skin swept beneath my palms. His shaft was silky on the underside but callused into ridges on the upper and I massaged the lumps eagerly. I could imagine female trolls going for that rippled effect.

"Do you like this?" I asked.

"Goode! Goode!"

I'd wanted more cock, and now I was getting it in excess. I'd been subject to one tit-wank already that day, but I was going to have to put a lot more effort into this one. But, then again, I had a much bigger canvas to work on. I could get both hands on, spread wide, and use all the strength in my fingers. I could plant my knees in his thighs and bounce up and down, sliding my whole torso along the glorious length of that humongous cock. Its cleft head bobbed against mine and I thrust my face into the open slit and licked the cold briny seep within. The troll made an *uhuhuhuh* noise which certainly sounded like approval.

Damn, how I appreciated that. Far too many men just lie there and give no feedback until they finally blow, leaving me to guess if they're in heaven or are just falling asleep. I like a bit of reaction. I like some encouraging noises. Well, the troll gave me that. It grunted and mumbled and petted my back with knobble-knuckled hands. My breasts cuddled its thick branch, bouncing as I rose and fell. And hell yeah, I was loving it. This was fun, of the dirtiest, most outrageous sort. I'd always loved cock and, now that that love had been distorted into need, this was a big cock fantasy taken to the max. My lips polished the great fat fist of its glans, and I felt the surge in the pizzle's girth.

"Come on, big boy," I gasped. "Let's see your jizz. Give me a pearl necklace I'll never forget."

With a groan the troll sank back, half-recumbent. But the change in position gave it new ideas for me too. It snatched me from my perch on its ball-sack and swung me round onto its piebald belly. I found that from that angle it could lick my ass as I worked its cock. Its tongue flickered between my thighs, making me quiver and almost distracting me from my monster task. That tongue-tip—surprisingly pointed and dexterous, which was a good thing, considering—speared my open cunt first, and then the tighter orifice between my splayed cheeks. I writhed my ass against the cold and slippery invader. And yes, it did occur to me that with one snap of those jaws he could bite me in half. But the danger didn't seem real. My sense of peril was numbed by the Ganconer's gift of arousal. I was slicked now inside as well as out, its slime mingling with my own sex-juices, my labouring muscles cramping into a red blur of heat and force as I pummelled that monstrous, wonderful prod.

I was vaguely aware of the sound of a growling engine behind his grunts, but I hardly noticed. His scrotum contracted, quite suddenly and quite visibly. Then he erupted. I shrieked as his spunk got me in the face, in the mouth, up my nose, and all over my throat. I knelt up, the force of the gooey jets making me raise my hands in surprise, and still it came, all over my tits in surge after surge of white troll-cream. Pints of the stuff.

Goddamn. It tasted like cold miso soup.

Lights came on, blinding white, straight in my face. I screamed. The troll rolled onto his side, spilling me across the road, and scrambled away, a blur of reptilian skin and shadow vanishing over the parapet of the bridge. I was bloody lucky he didn't stand on me, in his eagerness to flee. They hate bright light, do trolls.

"Are you okay, miss?"

Voices coming from behind the light. I held my hand over my eyes as they came to get me. Two men. I couldn't see anything but their black trouser legs and their boots, but they could undoubtedly see every detail of me: my nakedness, except for that ripped-open T-shirt; my open thighs and grazed knees, skinned by my fall; my bare skin glistening with a slick of pearlescent semen; my face twisted into a peculiar expression of both shock and awe.

"Are you okay? Can you hear me, miss? Can you talk to me? Are you hurt? Do I need to call an ambulance?" Too many questions, repeated over and over.

"I'm okay," I managed to impress upon them eventually.

"Can you stand?"

I nodded. They took my elbows gingerly and helped me to my feet. Cum was dripping off my breasts.

"We'll get you to the hospital. Come on—just into the patrol car."

"I'm fine. I'm not hurt. My purse—it's on the road there."

"Don't worry, we'll get it."

As soon as we were out of the direct glare of the car headlamps, I could see the yellow and blue flashing of a police vehicle, and the uniforms of the men helping me. They wore stab-jackets and carried Tasers. They looked burly and butch and angry.

"Honestly…" I protested.

"You're in shock. You need a doctor to look at you."

"I'm alright!" My legs were like overcooked spaghetti and I wobbled in their grip.

"We saw what he was doing to you, the bastard. Don't worry. You're safe now."

"We'll get a task group down here by daylight and wipe that piece of shit out," growled the other.

"There's no need…"

"You don't have anything to worry about." They'd got the back door of the car open. One of them reached inside, pulled out a high-visibility waistcoat and held it out to me, to cover up my shame I suppose. I could see him trying to look away from my filthy, dishevelled body.

"I wasn't worried." The devil inside me, the one that sat burning in my cunt, made me speak. I'd had orgasms without cock and a cock without orgasm. I was half-wild with aching desperation. All sense of self-preservation was in shreds now. I knew, as I opened my mouth for the next sentence, just how badly they would take what I had to say. "I was enjoying it."

There was a silence—and then: "What?"

The word was a stone dropped into an ice-crusted pond.

"I went to him. I wanted it."

"You're a troll-fucker?" His voice was cold, cold, cold. "Now I've seen everything."

"Are you high?" the other demanded. "Pills? Coke? Crystal?"

"No!" I squeaked, indignant. But they grabbed my arms and spun me round to flop face-down over the boot of the car.

"Hands behind you," said the officer, slapping a handcuff around my left wrist before I had a chance to react to his command.

He forced my hand roughly to the small of my back, and locked the other wrist to it. I stared into the white paintwork of the car, an inch from my nose, feeling the banging of my heart magnified by the hollow metal beneath me. My bare ass was exposed and completely vulnerable. My feet barely had purchase on the ground, with my weight forward like that and a policeman pinning me with his hand between my shoulder blades.

"Now," he said, breathing hard. "I've come across pervs who like to fuck the pretty kinds of Gentry, and let me tell you we don't take kindly to their sort. But you tell me this: what sort of a dirty cunt goes looking for a *troll?*"

"This sort, officer," I answered humbly, working my ankles apart. The opening of my ass cleft displayed everything that lay between. I knew they were looking, and I heard an intake of breath and a rasping contemptuous laugh.

"You dirty fucking whore…" he growled, but he touched

me and that was what I wanted. He sank his fingers into the puffy wetness of my pussy and I moaned with relief.

"Reckon we can have her on a charge of Bestiality, Andy?" asked the other cop.

"I reckon we can have her any way we want," he answered, ramming a couple of fingers into my cunt. Despite my gasp of shock there was no resistance—I was as wet and open as I'd ever been in my life. "Right now though, this looks like a serious attempt to Pervert the Course of Justice, don't you think?"

I moaned again, half in gratitude and half in humiliation.

Cop Two uttered a harsh snigger as Andy demonstrated, by pumping his fingers, just how wet I was. I could actually hear his hand in my juices.

"Look at that: she's begging for it, the dirty bitch."

"Yes," I groaned.

"Is that right?" His voice was grimly taunting. "Are you a pervert, bitch? Are you a troll-whore?"

I felt the shame of the words strike me like blows and I didn't answer. He punished me by withdrawing his fingers and slapping my pussy hard with his open hand. Pain surged through me like lightning and a yell burst from my lips.

"You've no right to silence, bitch. I want a confession. Tell me how you plead."

Oh God, my pussy was on fire. The sting and burn of the blow seemed to light up my whole body. "Yes!" I moaned, panting. The humiliation was horrible. I'd never submitted to force before today. Never. Yet this was the second time in an hour.

"Yes what? Guilty or Not Guilty, bitch?"

I hesitated a moment too long. The second blow caught me full-on across my wet cunt and swollen clit.

I whined like an angry cat, and the word "Guilty!" erupted from me. I don't know how to explain that. It wasn't the pain. I was afraid of the pain, but that wasn't what broke me. It was nothing that calculated. It was just something about being spanked there, right on my pussy. My surrender was an instinctive response and it was accompanied by a gush of sex-juices.

He laughed and slapped me again, but less brutally this time, then squeezed my mons, and that made the breath boil out of my lungs in sobs.

"Do they pay you, whore? Do they pay you gold for jerking their big diseased dicks, or are you just a pervert who likes the taste of troll-cum?"

"I'm a pervert," I answered humbly.

He leaned in over me, his weight on my ass and back, to bring his lips closer to my ear. "Call me Sir. I want to hear some fucking respect."

"I'm a dirty pervert, sir." I could feel his belt and his night-stick and his excited cock grinding into me. Part of me wondered in horror—Were they true, the words he'd coerced from me? Had I really sunk that low, to crawl in lust after that which was inhuman?

Another part of me simply did not care.

"What sort? What sort of a slut are you, troll-whore?"

"I'm a cock-slut, sir. I just wanted his big cock." I wriggled my bottom against him.

"You stupid bitch. You've got a big fucking ass, but even you couldn't take that. If he'd stuck his cock in here"—he jabbed my cunt again—"Or even here"—two thumbs invaded my anus and pulled, spreading me into a gape—"You'd be dead, whore. Split like a fucking fish."

He was perfectly right. "Yes, sir," I sobbed, pushing down on his thumbs.

"Pete," he said, pulling away so that he could unbuckle his belt. "Keep an eye out. I think we need to reclaim this dumb bitch for humanity."

"Christ yes. Cunt or ass?" Pete asked roughly.

"Either. Both. Whatever you fucking want. Just make sure nothing creeps up on us while I get started."

Pete obeyed. With my head twisted to the side I could see him turn away, reluctantly it seemed, to watch the perimeter. Then I felt Andy's cock slap against me, first against the cold curve of my rump—where it felt red hot—and then into the split of my pussy, jabbing against my open sex. I couldn't help gasping as he pummelled the soft folds of flesh there. He felt as hard as rock.

"Got any complaints, bitch?" he asked, grabbing my hair and hauling my head back.

"Ohhh… gah!" I wailed, as his cock found the angle at last and bored into me.

"What was that you said? Something about police misconduct? Is that an official complaint you're making, troll-whore?"

I wasn't complaining at all, in fact. This was what I'd been aching for since the Ganconer refused me. This was what I wanted. Officer Andy's cock was thick enough to stretch me, but my cunt yielded with no resistance to his invasion and he plunged in to the hilt, ramming home with enough vigour to force another couple of yelps from my throat.

"Pretty tight for a whore."

"Oh God! Ohh…!" My repartee was admittedly limited.

"Heh. You like that, don't you?"

But he was only using my pussy for the lube. He pulled out as decisively as he'd entered and sought the shocked pucker of my other hole instead. It was a good thing the troll's tongue had been there already. It was a good thing I was all greased up with spittle, and the clench of my sphincter was already loosened by slippery invasion. Even so, he was so unrelenting as he forced entry that it should have hurt like hell —and the fact that it didn't, that my asshole opened up to that hard shaft like a latex glove stretching over a fist, told me that the Ganconer's gift was more than mere psychology. The sweat of terror oozed from my pores, but the inner ring of my ass-muscles expanded like elastic to accommodate every centimetre of his considerable girth. And then the familiar, wonderful wrongness of taking it in through the out door filled my head like hard liquor.

"Fuck," he grunted under his breath as he screwed himself in all the way to his nuts. "Fuck yes."

Yes, oh God, at last! This was what I craved so badly. This is what the Ganconer had denied me: the pleasure of being rammed—stuffed—filled to the utmost limit. Pressed inside and out.

Pinned down—like some deviant vampire getting staked —against the back bumper of the police vehicle, I wailed helplessly, jerking my wrists against the cuffs and thrashing my hips, but officer Andy just grabbed my ass and shafted me hard, his thighs hammering against me. And the knowledge of being scorned and used like that, of being nothing more in my violator's eyes than an orifice for him to fuck—and the filthiest, most degraded of orifices at that—combined with the slick rubbing of his cock in and out of my ass into an orgasm that rolled over me in a great, dark, slow-motion wave.

I tried to hide it. I tried not to cry out in my eagerness. But I failed.

"You dirty fucking whore!" he gasped, yanking back on my hair. His thighs thundered against my ass and then I felt the swell and shudder as he unloaded inside me. His orgasm seemed to go on forever.

Then in a moment he was out, leaving me empty and splayed.

"Here you go, Pete," he growled. "I've loosened her up nicely for you."

Pete took over at once, jamming his hands down on my ass-cheeks and spreading them wide to open me up.

"Heh. Look at the gape on that."

I could feel the night air on my most secret flesh. I could feel, I realised with creeping horror, the trickle of officer Andy's semen from the flexing whorl of my asshole, oozing down in a slow drool right into the furrow of my pussy. I mashed my flushed face against the cold metal and let all my humiliation out in a low wail, as my body shook.

Then Pete took his turn in my anus.

I'll let you into a secret: my asshole is actually even more sensitive to pleasure than my cunt is. The sensation of him filling me was no less disorienting and transgressive than on the previous occasion. But it was a pure hungry excitement that pealed though my nerve-endings, and I came again just as the fucker entered me. I think I made a better job of disguising my cry of climax as protest though, this time round. His cock was slimmer than Andy's but it seemed to be about a mile long as it sank into my depths. And he took real satisfaction in that entry. Instead of embedding himself and giving me a pounding like officer Andy had, Pete played around, pulling right out and then impaling me again all the way—repeatedly. Each forced entry made my asshole sing with sensation. Each act of penetration made me groan and cry out. Pretty soon officer Andy—who was supposed to be on lookout—got fed up of my helpless undignified grunts and squeals and he wrenched my head to the side and stuffed his leather-gloved fingers into my mouth as a gag.

"Shut up and take it, troll-whore."

After that I quit pretending not to enjoy it. I quit thinking at all, or anticipating what would happen to me next, or worrying about what the Ganconer had done. Half-choked and full of cock, I fell into a dark and simple Now where there was nothing but the sensation of my ass being fucked wide open and orgasm expanding from that stretched ring like a tangible blast-radius. I screamed around those thrusting fingers and humped my hips and buttocks up and down. I think I probably came four or five times. There was no way of counting.

Eventually officer Pete shot his sticky wad into my ass, then pulled out altogether and dragged me by my hair until I slithered to my knees on the road, where he pushed my face to the tarmac. There I knelt, in sandals and handcuffs, with my ass pointing at the sky.

"Kiss our fucking boots, bitch."

Groaning, I obeyed, reaching with my lips to the hard black leather of his toe-caps and tasting polish and grit. It wasn't fear of punishment that made me compliant. It wasn't even a desire to submit. Oh, that would have been just too simple. But like I said, a little shame can trip my switches. I'd flirted with humiliation before, letting it brush against my libido like some muscular, dangerous beast, all threat and thrill. But it seized me now without ambiguity and, for the first time, I felt the true power of its jaws and the heat of its breath. For the first time I saw it in all its terror and might.

The beast caught me up and took me into a world in which there was nothing but me and those boots; me and those angry, scornful men ordering me to do something unforgivably wretched and dirty. My mind might have been riven by conflict, but my body's response was unambiguous.

"Thank us for rescuing you."

"Thank you, sirs." My voice shook. My ass burned, uncomfortably empty. Cum was running out into my open pussy. My asshole felt so open and pliable after its shafting that it almost seemed I could take a troll-cock after all. When officer Andy tilted his boot up to my lips I did my best to wrap my mouth around the toe-end, which made him laugh.

"I think we've done our bit for mankind here, Pete."

"So where do you live, bitch?"

I told them. There was no fight left in me and I wasn't capable of walking. So they drove me home. I lay on my belly across the leather seat in the back of the car, my hands still cuffed behind me, my face in officer Andy's crotch, cleaning his cock and balls with my mouth as he stroked my hair.

When the car stopped, officer Pete walked round, opened

the door behind me and pulled me out onto the pavement using the handcuffs as a grip, while his comrade made himself presentable again. I swayed against him and he pushed me off contemptuously.

"Tsk. Look at the mess she's made of the car." Officer Andy was pointing at the back seat. I saw a wet stain where their spunk and my sex-juices, all mingled with troll-spittle, had drizzled down from my crack to make a long slick on the black leather.

"Clean it up," snarled officer Pete.

So I did, crawling back in to lick the seat clean, tasting the sharp and briny concoction, while they idly poked and played with my cunt and asshole to hurry me up. I wondered if any of the neighbours were watching through their curtains.

Then they marched me up the path to the front door.

"This your place?"

"Yes, sir."

Officer Andy pushed me against the paintwork to unlock the cuffs, then turned me to face him. "You learned your lesson?"

"Yes, s— uh... uh..." I stuttered as he caught my nipple in a hard pinch, tugging me toward him and down. I understood and folded to my knees again, nuzzling up against the bulges in their pants, kissing their hidden cocks worshipfully.

"Those fuck-holes of yours belong to men, not to monsters. And don't you forget it."

"Yes! Yes sir!" And I meant it. At least, when I said it.

"Good," he purred. "Now we know where you live, bitch, we might drop in every now and then to make sure the lesson's taken. Call it community policing."

"Thank you," I groaned hoarsely, mouthing his bulge. What else could I say? The thing was, they could turn up tomorrow night and I'd welcome them. They could bring along a van-load of their friends, if they liked. The Ganconer's curse would ensure I received them all with open arms—and legs. I might be exhausted now, but I could still feel the burn of my appetite deep inside, like unquenched embers. I might have had sufficient, but I would never have enough.

"There's a good girl." Officer Andy tugged at his fly and prised out his semi.

I was momentarily confused—he'd only just put his cock away and I didn't think he'd be up for a repeat show so quickly at his age. But I understood when he gripped my jaw in his other hand.

"You know how we mark territory against monsters, don't you?"

"Oh—no!" I tried to wail, but his fingers were biting into my cheeks and they stopped me shaping the words. I struggled feebly. Catching Andy's meaning, officer Pete was going for his pecker too.

"We've got to get rid of that stink of troll somehow, haven't we?" he leered.

"Come on." Officer Andy's voice dropped to a conspiratorial caress. "You know you have to."

My wide and rounded eyes met his. I think he saw something in me then, something I could not hide, because I caught his malicious flash of recognition.

He understood how much this degradation excited me.

"Good girl."

So they emptied their bladders. On me. They pissed on me, there on my own doorstep. On my face and tits and belly, splashing down between my spread thighs. On my night-chilled skin those bright streams felt scalding hot. I started to weep from humiliation and awe. And they groaned with relief.

"That's right. You let it all out, darling," said officer Andy in a horrible pastiche of solicitude. "You'll feel better now."

They both made me suck the last acrid drops from their fleshy tips. Then they dropped my purse and walked away to their car, whistling. My pussy throbbed, battening upon my shame like a leech, fat and hot and filled with blood once more.

It took me a long time to gather the will to find my key and open the door. I could have tried ringing the bell, but no one answers their door after dark. Especially when a cop car drives off with lights flashing.

When I staggered inside, Gail was waiting in the hall and Vince was standing behind her. They stared at me and the state I was in—naked, wet and bruised—with wide eyes, and Gail rushed forward with her arms out.

"Don't touch me!" I barked, throwing out my hands.

Gail halted, shocked.

"Just…" I said, more gently, "just don't touch me. I need a shower. Right now."

They shrank against the wall as I headed past them toward the stairs.

"What happened?" wailed Gail. "Tansy… what happened? It's been three weeks!"

BOOK TWO

COUNTRY

Chapter Six

Go West

"Wales?" complained Gail, watching as I stuffed spare socks into the pocket of my rucksack. "You can't go to Wales! Are you *crazy?*"

Vince, standing behind her with his arms folded over his chest, said nothing.

"I might not have to," I said, backtracking. She had a point—half the refugee population of London is Welsh. Their country is considered uninhabitable now. "I just need to find the River Severn. Its source is in Wales but the river-mouth's around Bristol. I'll start down the bottom."

"But that's the West Country—it's nearly as bad!"

"Gail," I growled, avoiding eye contact and reaching past her for the jacket hanging on the back of my door. "Don't exaggerate. It's not that dangerous. Where do you think the food comes from? Plenty of people still live in the countryside."

"Yeah—and they've gone all Wicker Man! They're on Them There's side! They make offerings!"

I'd heard that too. "Doesn't matter. I've got to get to the Severn."

"Why?"

I let out a deep sigh. "The fish. *The fish is the oldest one of all*—that's what the troll said. The oldest, wisest creature in Britain, according to legend, was the Salmon of Llyn Llyw. It was the one beast that knew where the boy Mabon was being held prisoner, so King Arthur could free him."

"What? What are you talking about?"

"If anything knows the Ganconer's true name, it'll be that salmon. So… I'm going to find it and ask it."

"You're going to find a talking fish?" Gail's voice sounded sour.

I glared at her. "Yes. I'm going to find a talking fish, because otherwise the *fairy curse* is going to kill me."

She went pale, and couldn't stop herself glancing around. "Don't say that word, Tansy!" she hissed through clenched teeth. "It's not safe!"

"Oh really?" I put my hands on my hips. "What does "safe" look like, anyway, Gail? I've forgotten."

She shook her head, silenced for a moment, and I turned back to packing. I heard Vince murmur something in her ear, but didn't catch what.

"Couldn't you …?" she asked.

"Couldn't I what?"

"Couldn't you just… manage, the way things are? I mean, you can drink soup, can't you? It's only solids. And you can… I dunno…"

I could've got defensive and mad, but I just felt crushed. I'd spared Gail most of the worst details about what I'd got up to. She understood the general problem, just not the extremes to which it was driving me. Even here, today, still covered in scrapes and bruises from my sexual spree, I could feel the manic urge building anew within me. My clit burned inside my jeans like the tip of a lit cigarette.

"No," I said, with precision. "I can't manage with things this way. I have to go."

"I don't want you to go out there!" She sounded like a little girl, scared that her mommy was going to leave her.

"I'm sorry, Gail."

"Are you sure you can find this... fish?" asked Vince—the first time he'd entered the conversation. He'd hardly said a word to me since I'd got home. I wondered how much, if anything, he'd told Gail about our attack of kitchen madness. "And that it'll help you?" he added.

No, of course I wasn't sure. I didn't even know if the Salmon of Llyn Llyw was still in the Severn, much less how to engage it in conversation. Maybe it didn't speak English—I sure as hell didn't speak Welsh. But I looked Vince in the eye and nodded.

"Then we're coming with you," said Gail.

"Yeah," said Vince.

"If we can't talk you out of going, then you need us along too."

"No," I answered. "That's not a good idea. It's not safe out West. Like you said. Besides, I don't know how long I'm going to be away. Time gets a bit unhinged when you get close to Them There—you saw that. I thought I was one afternoon with the Ganconer, and it turned out to be weeks. I could be away… ages."

"Then you definitely can't go on your own," said Vince calmly.

"You've got to have someone to look out for you, Tansy. If you're getting all… worked up."

"And if there's three of us, someone can sit watch while the others sleep."

"We've talked it over. There's more safety in numbers."

"Gail—I can't have you getting into danger too!" I protested.

"I'm not a kid any more, Tansy." She grinned. "You're only seven months older than me, remember."

I sagged. It was true, I still felt like I was responsible for her safety, as if we were still little girls and seven months made a difference. Tears pricked at the back of my eyes. Their determination to stick by me moved me beyond words.

"Thanks, guys," I said, managing a wobbly smile. "Okay."

"You sure now? That this is what you've got to do?"

"Yeah."

Gail came forward and gave me a big hug. I sort of wished she hadn't, because I was just too aware of the squash of her breasts against mine, and the sweet warm scent of her skin. Somewhere inside I felt a surging desire to grab that round little ass and sink my fingers into those firm cheeks. My hand was on the small of her back before I knew it—and it was only Vince's gaze on us that brought me back to myself.

"There's one good thing," I said, detaching myself from her embrace with some reluctance.

"What's that?"

"At least nobody's going to pick any of *us* out as virgin sacrifices."

❦ ❦ ❦

We drove due west down the M4, switched at the end to the M48 and came off straight away at Junction One to catch our first glimpse of the Severn Estuary, north of Bristol. It wasn't prepossessing—a great expanse of flat brown mud, and flat brown water that *looked* like mud. The Welsh coast on the far side was another brown strip, blurred by drizzle. Even the great sweep of the Severn Bridge away to our left looked dismal. On the water's edge a jumble of sticks lay lapped by the retreating tide. It all smelled of dead weed. I wrapped my jacket tightly around me and stared at a skein of seagulls flying upriver.

"Llyn Llyw!" I called, three times. But nothing moved on the caramel water except the regular eddies.

The journey had been uneventful. I'd made sure to fill my car's tank full before we set off, so as not to have to stop for fuel. But the petrol stations we passed, though fewer in number, had looked perfectly normal. It was the rest of the countryside that had changed in the past few years. The hedgerows were overgrown, the motorway verges a riot of unchecked saplings. We passed a few villages that were obviously palisaded with steel fencing, and quite a few burned-out or derelict buildings. Abandoned vehicles could be seen scattered every mile or so down the length of the motorway hard shoulder. I understand there's not much law enforced outside the cities these days, and no one bothers to clean up such things. What had happened to their drivers after breaking down or stopping for a desperate pee, I didn't like to imagine.

But grass still looked like grass and cows like cows, the sun still shone and traffic still roared onward. If you didn't look too close it might seem nothing had changed.

We'd left the car where the minor road dead-ended at a field gate, climbed over and crossed on foot down to the estuary foreshore. The weed-grown remnants of a broad path ran along the top of the bank—the Severn Way Long Distance Footpath, I guessed. It was a pity we couldn't drive the car along that, because no road paralleled the river. Using the Astra, we'd have to zigzag up a network of minor lanes, detouring to the water's edge where the roads allowed, then turn away again to seek out the route north.

"This is going to take days," Gail said quietly.

Biting back the response *Why did you insist on coming, if you're going to complain?* I rammed my hands deeper into my pockets. I badly wanted to get at least one of those hands inside my panties instead, and the physical frustration was making me prickly. Also, the more often I glanced at those sticks by the water's edge, the more unpleasantly they resembled loosely-articulated bones.

"Where are we going to stay overnight?" Vince asked.

"I was planning to sleep in the car," I admitted, trying to get a good look at the sticks without drawing attention to them. "It's relatively safe."

Dead bodies wouldn't be that unlikely out here. Abandoned victims of misfortune. The remnants of something's dinner. Bait. I didn't intend to investigate. It was always possible they were something that wasn't really dead yet —but just looked that way.

"Only from Them There. Not from your regular human

weirdo types."

"And it's bit too snug for three," observed Gail.

"Yeah." I was dreading it already. My condition demanded privacy. I couldn't presume to make Gail and Vince part of my madness.

"There might be pubs." Vince sounded doubtful. "Hotels."

"Mm." I nodded. Was I imagining that carrion aroma under the briny estuary smell?

"But we should really find something before it gets dark."

I glanced reflexively at my phone display. We had a good few hours yet. But he was right. And I didn't want to hang around here.

"Come on," I said. "Let's get back to the car."

We'd trudged in silence through the long grass of the field for several minutes, keeping the overgrown hedge on our right hand, before Vince grumbled, "Where the hell's the gate?"

I snapped to attention, looking up and down the hedge-line. The gate had been set back among hawthorn sprays, but perfectly obvious when we climbed it.

"Have we passed it?" Gail wondered. "I thought it was at the bottom of a dip."

We looked back. The grey sky seemed to press in over the top of the field. Nothing was visible over any of the hedges.

"It was next to a tree, wasn't it?" Vince said. "Is it that one back there?"

The field looked bigger than I remembered, with several dips and folds in the ground, though to be honest I hadn't paid it much attention on the way through. Now a cold feeling was settling between my shoulder blades.

"Let's go back a bit," I agreed.

We went back as far as the tree. There was no gate.

"I don't remember that fallen branch," Gail complained. "Have we come too far down from the river?"

"Maybe."

We carried on toward the river again—and blundered into a patch of brambles none of us recalled. I got my bare legs scratched.

"This is stupid," Vince said angrily. "You can't get lost following a straight line. All we need to do is back-track right to the river, then turn round and come back. The gate is in this hedge somewhere."

But before we reached the river, the hedge jinked abruptly into a right angle, opening the field out into an L-shape we'd never seen before.

"What the hell?" Vince muttered, rubbing at a bramble-score across his left arm.

There was a bull grazing around that corner, some way off. It lifted its head and looked at us, and I felt a palpable wave of dread.

"Shit!" I muttered and we scrambled back around the corner out of its line of sight.

The creature bellowed. The sound made sweat break out across my skin.

"Oh fuck!"

We started to run back along the hedgeline. Gail and I had grown up in a little village and we knew that lone bulls were bad news. And there was something about that big, grey, angular beast that had struck me as deeply wrong.

"Where's the gate?" Gail squealed, panting.

"Take your top off!" I shouted. "Both of you!" I slowed, throwing off my jacket and pulling my white T-shirt off over my head. "Take them off!"

They half-turned, staring, still trying to run. I waved the shirt at them frantically. My tits were bouncing merrily in their bra but I didn't care.

"Turn them inside out!" I yelled, terrified that any second I would hear the thunder of hooves. I flipped my shirt and, still jogging, yanked it on again over my head. In my panic I got the armholes all tangled up and I nearly stumbled.

"Turn them!" I bellowed.

There was an answering, bestial bellow from behind me.

I got my head and one arm through a hole, grabbed Gail's arm, and fled, tugging the cloth frantically down over my breasts. Burrs tore at my ankles. Inside a dozen paces I saw the gate in the hedge, and my car parked on the roadside.

"Here!" I screamed, letting go of Gail and leaping for the bars.

We threw ourselves over and fell onto the weed-cracked tarmac of the road. Vince brought up the rear and barely made it in time. I turned to see a huge grey shape hurtle past, angling a horn at him and barely missing. Its hooves drummed on the hard-packed earth. I stared, open-mouthed, hardly able to believe we'd escaped—just as Gail hauled me out of the way as a speeding van roared past at my back, missing me by inches.

The bull turned and trotted back again, tossing its head and snorting, before disappearing behind the tall hedge. Gail was clutching Vince, who looked grey.

"What was that about?" he asked, wrapping his arm

around her. His T-shirt was half-on too. "The clothes?"

"Pixy-led," I muttered, my mouth dry. "We were being pixy-led. That's how you break it."

"What sort of an idiot," raged Gail, "puts a bull in field with a footpath across it? We could have been gored! Idiot farmers! That's really dangerous!"

I didn't answer. I'd been the only one to get a good look at the bull as it closed on us. Its head had been almost all bone under a cowl of dried-up hide, and it had had no eyes.

"Let's go," I said, shaken. "I need a drink."

I let Gail drive this time. I was in too dark a mood to do it myself. I sat in the back seat scanning the map apps on my phone, and didn't even look up until she pulled in sharply into a car park.

"What's going on?" I asked.

"Pub. We need food, and the sign says they have rooms."

I saw a long, low stone building with a Virginia creeper growing up over the door. It looked okay. As we got out of the car, a family with two small children pushed the door open and walked in ahead of us. The kids were carrying balloons. *Family pub,* I thought. *It can't be that bad, can it? Not unless they still have one of those jungle-gym things and it's full of screaming kids. That would be really bad.*

It wasn't full of screaming anything. The front bar was comfortably busy, but they were all adults. There was a slight lull in the conversation as we walked in, and eyes automatically lifted to us, but the volume quickly returned to normal.

"Well," I said. "Let's get a table."

We found seats and I ordered drinks and took the bar

menu over for the other two to read. The barman smiled politely at me, but everyone standing at the bar—mostly middle-aged men with flushed, weather-beaten faces—looked me up and down. I'm not sure if it was the way I dressed or just the fact I was a stranger with the wrong accent. I kept expecting someone to fix me with a beady eye and say meaningfully, "You're not from *round* here, are you?" I imagine it must have felt worse for Vince.

"They're doing oxtail soup," said Gail brightly. "That's okay for you, isn't it?"

"Yeah. Okay." The thought of beef broth wasn't that enticing, but I needed to get some calories into me.

While the others chose what food they were going to order, I went through to the toilets beyond the bar to relieve myself—in more ways than one. Sitting on the loo in a candy-pink cubicle, I slipped my fingers into the plump folds of my sex and fingered myself to a frantic but silent climax. Just enough pressure released to stop me exploding, I told myself. My blood was still racing and my cheeks flushed as I washed my hands, looking into the mirror over the sink.

When I came out of the ladies' I should have headed straight back to our table, but I paused to look out of the big window. I was right at the back of the building. There was some sort of children's party going on in the pub garden, with balloons and flags and tables laden with food on paper plates, and lots of kids running around. The focus of the garden seemed to be a big bush laden with panicles of white flowers, and the children were taking it in turns to go up and pick a low flower.

Someone stepped up behind me.

"What are they doing?" I said aloud.

"Making wishes," said a male voice, in that West Country accent that sounded faintly comical to my London-trained ears.

"On an *elder* tree?"

The flowers made it easy to identify even at this distance. Elder trees are not wishing trees, generally. They are bad news in folklore. Witch trees, malevolent and vengeful.

"It's Bour Tree Day. That's the Bour Tree. Like on the pub sign."

I hadn't seen what the pub was named as we arrived. I'd been too engrossed in my web surfing. I turned to look sharply at my informant, and with that my brain emptied of common sense so fast that there was practically a plughole gurgle. He was young and, though he looked weathered too, it sat very well with his tousled curly hair, his bright blue eyes, and his insouciant grin as he looked me up and down. I'm guessing my tight white T-shirt and denim miniskirt and boots were to his liking.

I grinned back. The admiration was entirely mutual.

"I'm Aaron."

"Tansy. Nice to meet you, Aaron."

"Do you want to see the Bour Tree?"

I hesitated, running my tongue-tip across my lip. "Okay. But I thought elder trees were bad luck."

"Not this 'un. She's a good 'un."

He led me out into the garden. This was where all the women were, I realised: watching indulgently as their kids ran riot. Aaron took me over to the bush, which had three big trunks and a host of lesser ones. Hanging from the twigs was a glittering array of kids' tat: plastic key-rings and fuzzy little animals, transforming robots, a toy aeroplane, a necklace made of sweets.

"See?" said Aaron. "You make her a present and she gives you a wish."

I could hear some of the kids chanting as they skipped rope on the grass nearby:

> *Bour tree, bour tree: crooked wrong*
> *Never straight and never strong*
> *Always bush and never tree*
> *Since the Christ was hanged on thee.*

A Christian gloss on a much older warning, I thought.

"Hmm," I said, noncommittally. I didn't want to offend the man. Or the tree.

"Go on," he said.

A lock of my hair swung down across my face as he reached up without warning to my temple, pulled out the hairclip there and snapped it over a twig. My mouth fell open.

Aaron grinned. "Make a wish."

The hairclip was a cheap one with a white fabric flower on it. Even if it had been silk and diamonds, I wasn't sure it would have been wise to snatch it back. Gifts to the Fair Folk should never be rescinded.

I made myself relax again. "I don't need to. Mine's already come true," I said, letting him know I could be just as cheeky and forward as he was.

His eyes held mine, dancing. "Take a flower then."

I lifted an eyebrow and sought out one of the white clusters with my hand. "*Give me of your wood, old girl,*" I said softly. There are traditional formulae for turning aside an elder's malice, and that's one of them. "*And I'll give you mine when I grows into a tree.*"

"Ah," he said, eyes narrowing. "You're a smart 'un."

He took the flower from my hand, blew on it to remove any stray insects, and tucked it gently into the V of my shirt neck. His fingertips brushed my bare skin, setting it off in electric sparkles.

"I should take you to meet my gaffer," he said.

"Is he as cute as you?"

Aaron drew himself up, laughing. "No one's as cute as me. Do you play pool?"

"Yeah. Sometimes."

"Come on then." He walked me round to another door at the back of the inn, and as we crossed the grass he put his hand casually on the swell of my ass and kept it there. I didn't object. Once inside the door, in the corridor within, he drew me up against him and kissed me. It was a slow, soft and deeply dirty kiss, his tongue teasing its way past my lips and one hand drifting to squeeze my left breast and tweak my nipple. I responded to that in a manner far from ladylike— pressing up against him with eager, breathy mews of pleasure and sucking his tongue deeper into my mouth. I wanted him to push me up against the wall and ram his cock into me, there and then. The knot of flesh in his trousers grew hard as I ground myself against it, and his other hand tightened on my ass even as his mouth deserted mine.

"Oh, you're hot," he growled under his breath. He rubbed my nipple between finger and thumb, pinching it until my knees nearly gave way. "I bet you're a real goer."

"You won't know till you try," I whispered, running the

tip of my tongue over his lips.

"Hh." His eyes glittered with secretive speculation. "Be patient. Come on through."

With one hand around my wrist he drew me through another door. The smell of beer and cigarettes rolled over me, a sweet pubby aroma I found very pleasant. This was another bar room. The space was dominated by a pool table and it was full of men standing about with pint glasses in their hands— they seemed to have a real gender segregation thing going on here—and everyone stopped and stared as we entered.

"Look what I found," said Aaron, putting his arm around my shoulders and giving me a squeeze. It might have been meant to be reassuring. Or it might have meant something else altogether, like preventing me from turning tail and running. "She's real friendly, like."

There was no way I was leaving. I looked around and grinned, understanding very well. The men here were of all ages from eighteen up, dressed casually or in country style with flat tweed caps. Not an urban metrosexual sophisticate among them, and they were all openly ogling me. Someone whistled. I could feel their gazes like so many groping caresses on my tits and thighs, and it filled me with heat. I thrust my breasts out a little further, revelling in the attention and feeling my nipples swell to hard points.

"Come and meet the Gaffer." Aaron let go long enough to pat my ass, then steered me round the table. The Gaffer was one of the guys in the tweed caps, big and middle-aged and paunchy. He stood surrounded by a little knot of men who looked like they'd been hanging on his every word. He might not have had prepossessing looks, but it was clear he had status, and that I was being presented for inspection. His pale blue gaze slid over me.

"This is Tansy," said Aaron, running one finger down my spine, making me gyrate and squirm.

"A pleasure to meet you, Tansy." The Gaffer lifted his gaze from an unabashed consideration of my boobs and looked me in the eye. Without blinking, he added. "You've done well for yourself there boy. She's pretty. Magnificent knockers."

It was a test, of sorts. A calculated slap in the face, to see how I would react. I flushed and giggled, dropping my gaze with a strange instinctive coyness. I could feel my pussy swelling at the compliment. Because it was a compliment—degrading and crude and offensive, it was still an acknowledgement of my desirability by the most important man in the room. I got it. In times of trouble, scared people look for leaders. It just so happens that the sort of bloke who wants to be a leader is usually a tool of the first order, but that doesn't matter to most folk. Even if he chooses to impose some sort of weird elder-tree cult it doesn't matter, as long as he *leads*. I knew that with a single word from this man I could be on my knees in this back bar, tugging open his flies and sucking his cock while he sipped his pint with a complacent smirk and everyone looked on.

I wet my lips.

The Gaffer snorted a little laugh down his nose, then glanced away toward the bar counter. "White wine for the lady, Richard."

The barman from the main room had appeared from around some corner behind the optics and was leaning on his elbows watching us. His smile had been polite the first time

I'd approached him, but he had a real leer on his face now. He knew what was happening. Nodding, he reached under the counter.

"Want to play pool?" said Aaron, recognising that we'd been dismissed for the moment.

I shook myself from my sexual sub-space and nodded. I'd played a lot of pool at college. I was pretty good.

So they racked us up a new frame on the blue baize and someone handed me a cue. It was all part of the display, of course. The first time I bent over to take a shot there was a collective murmur, half jeer and half whoop. My denim skirt was very short and the motion exposed both the curve of my ass-cheeks and my panties. I paused and glanced over my shoulder. A couple of the guys had casually affected a low lean, for no other reason than to get a good view up my skirt. My knickers were, I recalled, a silky and inappropriate virginal white that day, and there was every chance that the moist stain of my sex juices was visible on the gusset. I wiggled my ass cheekily, then sank the first ball with a loud crack.

Laughter exploded around the room. I think they finally realised then that I was playing along willingly with their conspiracy. And as the game progressed I teased them more and more wilfully. Those standing opposite me, as I leaned over, got a fine view down my heavy cleavage, and those standing behind cheered each glimpse of my ass. There were even some difficult shots where I had to cock one thigh up on the table edge. I loved it. I loved their attention. I loved their lecherous, predatory adulation. I loved the way some of them had a hand in a trouser pocket and were playing their own game of pocket-pool as they devoured me with their eyes. I loved the way every man in that room, from the strutting grinning Aaron to his narrow-eyed Gaffer, was looking at me and imagining sticking a cock into me—my cunt, my mouth, my ass—and fucking my brains out on the stained blue baize.

Every time he crossed round behind me, Aaron made sure to grope my ass, to general appreciation. I had no objection at all, but I wondered what he'd do if I didn't present. So after the fifth or sixth time I turned and faced him. And with a grin he showed me. He took the cube of cue chalk and carefully, lingeringly, blued both my nipples where they stood out big and hard through my white cotton top. His arrogance took my breath away. I had to wrench myself out of a daze to take my next shot.

As the points ratcheted up, Aaron presented me with a glass of wine. I'd have put money on it being spiked.

"I don't need that to get where I'm going," I smirked, handing it off to a spectator so I could carry on whupping him.

Aaron took losing to me in good humour, even as we approached the endgame. He wasn't above cheating though. Just as I was about to sink the eight-ball, I felt something very hard press with great accuracy right into the softest, juiciest part of my pussy—almost accurately enough to enter me, were it not for the flimsy barricade of my panties. I jumped and the shot went wild. There were howls of laughter from the assembly.

Twisting to look over my shoulder, I saw Aaron crowing at his own joke, his pool cue reversed in his hand so that the thicker, blunter end was pointed right at my sex.

"Playing dirty, are you? Well, I like a good hard shaft," I

remarked.

"Whoo!" went the men appreciatively.

"How much wood can you take?" leered Aaron.

I looked at the cue end, considering its girth. "Oh," I said, licking my lips, "you'd be amazed."

They loved that. The chortles were deep and dirty. Aaron nodded, his nostrils flared, his mouth compressed to a narrow line of intent. "Let's see, then."

Stepping forward, he put a hand on the small of my back, and obediently I folded over across the table edge, bracing my hands on the cloth. Then he pulled my skirt right up to bare my ass cheeks. A natural showman, he slapped first one then the other, lifting his hand high and letting it fall with a loud clap, so that I felt the sting and the burn flood through my body. All the sass evaporated from me in an instant as I uttered a whimper of tremulous need.

He pulled my panties down slowly, making the most of the reveal. Instantly every man in the room scrambled to get behind me for a good view. Shame and pride swept through me in a poisonous curdled tide. I knew they were all looking at my pink and glistening snatch—at my exposed asshole and my knickers stretched slutily across my open thighs, hiding nothing. I felt my cunt flutter and my sex lips swell in readiness. Aaron's fingers probed me, spreading my inner labia, wetting themselves in my juices.

"Shall I pocket the pink then?"

I didn't answer, because the question wasn't aimed at me. His friends roared encouragement.

"Oh, I dunno lads," he said. "She looks a bit tight."

"I can fix that," said a big man with a bushy ginger-blond

beard, grabbing his crotch through his worn corduroy trousers and giving himself a squeeze. I looked at him wide-eyed, hoping his cock would live up to the promise of his frame. Others were just as eager to offer a solution. But Aaron laughed them off.

"Here we go."

And I felt the tip of the cue, hard and blunt, push up against my cunt-mouth. For a moment the ring of muscle held against it, but then the wood opened me up and slid past. After that there was no stopping it—in and in and in, inhumanly smooth and cool. I moaned as it butted up against my cervix. Aaron circled it around a little, found another inch or so of inner space, tested for give and then nodded, satisfied. He shifted his grip a little further back along the shaft, so as everyone could get a clear view. Several people clapped. He tapped the cue shaft with his fingers and I felt the vibration right through the wood and my core, making me pant and moan.

"Like that, do you Tansy?"

"Look at that, will you?"

"Fucking hell. You could get lost in there, lads."

"Someone pass me that magic marker."

I heard the pop of the cap. Then I felt the press of his knuckles as he leaned in to draw a mark on the cue shaft. But that wasn't all he had in mind. He wrote on my inner thighs too, on either side. Then he pulled the cue out and held it up for everyone to see, and they cheered like their football team had just scored a winning goal.

I was aware that the cue was being passed round from hand to hand, but more aware of the uncomfortable emptiness inside me. I shifted my hips, scratching at the baize.

Someone waggled the cue end in front of my nose: "What do you think of that, girl?"

There was my mark, inked in at a good handspan down the shaft. There was neat handwriting on the wood too: *Tansy*, and then the date. The varnish glistened with my honey. I stuck out my tongue-tip to lick it.

"No you don't." The cue was whipped away out of my reach. "That's staying like that. So's folk'll have something to remember you by."

I started to rise from the tabletop, but a hand descended firmly. Aaron. He pushed his thumb against the pucker of my asshole, pinning me in place. "Gaffer?" he asked, loudly.

Everyone, including me, looked to the Gaffer. He smiled benignly. "Go on, lad," he said. "You go first."

First. The word made my pussy clench and dilate. I moaned with anticipation as I felt Aaron crowd up behind my ass, unzipping. He slapped his hot cock twice against my bare bum-cheeks, and then rubbed rudely up and down the split of my butt and nuzzled it into my pussy.

That was the moment the door opened and Vince walked into the room. His eyes were narrowed with fury but he didn't say a word. Unlike Gail, who from behind his shoulder shrieked, "Tansy!"

Everyone froze. Vince had a blade in his hand. I recognised it as the folding saw I keep in my car glove-pocket for cutting protective rowan staves, but in his hand it looked jagged and nasty. It looked like business.

Aaron shrank back from me. I suppose that even out here in the sticks they'd seen plenty of rap videos. How were they to know Vince was a pharmacist and not a gangsta?

And at that moment he did something that shocked me—he stuck the blade between his teeth, snatched a pool cue from the rack next to the door and, without even glancing at it, snapped it across his knee, then flipped the heavy end up to brandish it above his shoulder, like a club. Every yokel in the room took a step backwards.

"Tansy, get the fuck over here." He didn't have to raise his voice. The force in it needed no extra volume. I stumbled across to him, pulling clumsily at my half-mast knickers, and he shoved me behind him, out into the corridor. I didn't look up as they pulled me out through the front bar room and into the car park. I was pink with shame. Vince's grip on my upper arm was so tight it hurt.

"Where'd you learn that move with the cue?" Gail asked breathlessly as we hurried to the car.

"Jackie Chan DVDs."

He whirled me round and slapped me up against the passenger door.

"Tansy, what the fuck do you think you were doing! D'you go looking for trouble? Shit, girl... You could have been... " He left the sentence hanging, as if it were too horrible to voice.

I looked up at him, utterly contrite and yet seething with frustrated lust. He'd put the knife away but still had hold of the pool cue. He looked angry and dangerous, and I loved it. I didn't care that we were standing in a pub car park. I didn't care that Gail was with us, watching. I just wanted him to shove me up against the car and fuck my brains out, my tits bouncing and my boots kicking the empty air. Shrugging off all thought, I caught his free hand and pressed it to my pubic mound.

He grabbed hold, instinctively, squeezing my pussy through my skirt and panties. I gasped and jerked, mashing my sex into his palm.

"Jesus, girl," he said, wide-eyed. "You're *dangerous*."

Oh, I knew that already.

"We should get in the car!" Gail lunged suddenly for the driver's door and I was distracted enough to look across and see the pub door open, several men starting to spill out.

"Oi! You fucker!" They looked riled.

"Shit," said Vince. He practically threw me into the back seat, then jumped in at the front next to Gail, dropping his cue. She gunned the engine even before we got the doors closed and we sped out of the car park leaving black streaks of tyre rubber on the cracked tarmac.

"I guess I'm not getting my ploughman's lunch," he laughed, shakily, as the pub vanished in the rear-view mirror.

"Tansy nearly got the ploughman," snapped Gail. "And the cow-herd and the combine harvester driver and the milk truck guy too."

"I'm sorry!" I wailed. "I told you this was going to happen!"

They didn't answer. I think it was finally sinking in, what sort of a mess the Ganconer had dumped me into. We shot down the narrow country lanes, zigzagging left and right at random, just trying to make distance. I gritted my teeth and rammed my hand hard between my legs, desperate to numb the burning ache there. My eyes blurred as my mind painted vivid pictures of the fate I'd been rescued from. I couldn't help it—imagining Aaron finishing what he'd started and fucking me in front of all his friends. Grabbing my wobbling ass as he pounded me, and giving me a sharp smack on either bum-cheek to remember him by as he left. Then the Gaffer—he'd be next, wouldn't he, given his status? Or would he just stand and watch with a patriarchal smirk as the others all had their turn? Oh God, the thought of them lining up to bang me… Fat cocks, thin cocks, long and short, all shooting their loads in me… on me… over me. The guy with the ginger beard—he'd have a huge one, I bet. Salacious older men. Husky young lads. All crowing and sniggering and congratulating themselves as they fucked the city slut until she screamed and came and begged for more. There were over twenty men in that room… would it be enough for me, at last? Enough to sate me? Enough to make me sob *Stop! Please! No more!* If I did, would they listen? I doubted it. I think they would fuck me until they were all done, until their jizz was running down my legs and drooling out of my split to puddle on their nasty beer-stained linoleum. Until my crack and ass cheeks were sticky and shiny with cum. Yes, some of them would've whipped out to hose me with their spunk. That was how the Gaffer would take his. He'd save my ass for himself, after all his men had ransacked my pussy. For the finale he'd fuck my puckered asshole, using their ejaculate for lube.

That image was the last straw. I couldn't stop myself. I could feel my sex clenching with hunger and it hurt too much to say *No*. Pulling up my skirt, I thrust my fingers in at the side of my panties. The touch of my own hand on my clit was enough to tear a moan of relief from my throat.

Vince heard. He looked over his shoulder from the front

seat and his eyes widened.

"I'm sorry!" I sobbed, but I didn't stop.

I was sitting in the back of the car frigging myself in public, and I couldn't stop. I was red with shame—at my exhibitionism, at my helplessness, with the humiliation of what had happened and what I'd fantasised about—but my need was only made stronger by my shame. And Vince seemed unable to look away. He was in danger of twisting his neck off his shoulders, the way he was turning in his seat to stare. I spread my thighs and pulled my panties aside to give him a good view of my fingers at play in my glistening pink slit.

"Oh shit," he said in a strangled voice.

The car slewed suddenly over to the left and shuddered to a halt. Without my seatbelt on I was tipped hard against the driver's seat. I hardly had enough sense to care.

"You!" said Gail to Vince. "You're driving!" Then she bundled herself right over the seats into the back with me.

"I'm sorry!" I repeated, hands out of my pants now and raised to beg mercy. "I'm really sorry, Gail!"

"Shush!" she scolded. She reached between my legs. "I said we'd take care of you, Tansy. I meant it." Leaning forward, she kissed my lips.

Gently, she eased my panties over my bum and down. I let out a feverish groan as her cool little hand slid into my pussy, and tears of relief ran down my face. For long, long moments I was completely lost in her kiss, feeling all the dread and loneliness wash out of me on a great wave of pleasure. Then she pulled back.

"Drive!" she urged her boyfriend, sliding two fingers inside me and making me writhe. "What if they're following us?"

"Okay!" Vince shifted the windscreen mirror.

He wasn't actually insured for my car, but that was the least of my concerns now. I pulled my top down as the car lurched forward, and scooped my breasts out of their lace bra cups.

"Gail… please… bite my tits, will you?"

She grinned. "Of course."

She looked so pretty crouching there, one hand in my pussy, her cheeks flushed and her lips shiny with gloss. So blonde and feminine and fragrant and sweet. Her hand was gentle too, but she knew exactly what she was doing with it. As she stooped to catch my left nipple in her teeth and nip, I arched my back and squealed with pleasure.

I guess Vince thought the view of Gail and me was fairly engaging too. I was aware of the car weaving from side to side as he tried to switch his attention between the driving and the scene in his rear-view mirror. I couldn't blame him. It wasn't every day he got to see his girlfriend finger-fucking her nympho cousin and sucking her tits until she came. Loudly. Several times. We were probably lucky he didn't crash, thinking about it now.

I was juddering out of my seventh or eighth orgasm, I guess, when I noticed something blur past us through the window. "Stop the car!" I moaned.

We slithered to a stop on a patch of gravel.

"What? What is it?"

"Back there! That house. The one with the rowans in the garden!"

Chapter Seven

Hob

It had been a farmhouse, I guess, once upon a time. Isolated now in a sea of unmown grass, it was boarded up and abandoned, like so many other houses, and its white paintwork was peeling. We hid the car behind a barn and approached the house from the rear, cautiously. It was the mountain ash trees out the front that had caught my eye. Protection from lightning and fire and witchcraft—that's rowan's virtue. Protection from the malice of Them There. Maybe it hadn't been enough for the family who used to live here. Maybe they'd been just too vulnerable out in their fields, or maybe they'd craved the huddled companionship of the towns. Whatever, with dusk approaching and a bunch of pissed-off locals behind us, it was too good a haven for us to pass by.

We prised off a sheet of hardboard and climbed in through the kitchen window. Then we explored the rooms by flashlight. The place smelled musty but was mostly dry. There was no electricity, of course, but we'd brought in the little camping stove from the car. Whoever had lived here had packed up most stuff but had abandoned a lot of furniture. We found odds and ends of crockery in the cupboard, and stripped-down beds when we went upstairs.

"That's not bad. We can sleep here," Vince said, pressing on the striped ticking of a mattress to check that there wasn't a nest of rats buried inside.

"No," said I. "Better stay downstairs."

"Why?"

"Bedrooms are where people sleep and fuck, and get born and die. That's the sort of thing Them There home in on. We're too vulnerable up here."

He looked disbelieving. "You're saying we can't sleep or fuck, now?" He had enough delicacy to not cite the recent shenanigans in the back of the car, but I blushed even as I shook my head.

"Right—like that's going to work. No, I just think it's just better we stay downstairs, in a room with a fire. Fireplaces have positive associations. And we want to be near the exit in case we have to evacuate."

We dragged a couple of mattresses down the narrow stairs into the front room. Vince and Gail were about to flop one down in front of the empty fireplace when I stopped them.

"Just a minute."

I went out into the hall and came back with a sweeping brush I'd noticed earlier.

"You could go look for a stop-cock," I suggested, starting to sweep the bare floorboards. "We could do with running water. Get that toilet flushing."

I'd been creeped-out by the dry toilet bowl and the sight of the open U-bend gaping down into the depths. There's nothing that says more plainly than a dry toilet: *This is the end of civilisation.*

"What are you doing?" Gail asked. "It's not that dirty in here."

"I'm trying to get on the good side of the house-hob."

"What?" She looked over her shoulder, as if expecting to see it leering at her. "You reckon there's one here? But you said the trees keep them out!"

"Well, there's a theory that Them There belong to two factions," I told her. "The Seelie and the Unseelie Courts—the good and helpful guys versus the bad and scary bastards. And rowans ward off members of the Unseelie Court."

"In *theory*?"

I pulled a face. "I'm not sure I really buy that. It's too neat. And it smells of wishful thinking. But rowans keep… the unfriendly ones away. And hobs are friendly. Mostly."

"Oh *great*."

"Be polite," I reminded her.

Gail made corned-beef-and-baked-bean hash for the two of them from tins we'd brought with us, while I swept the entire ground floor and Vince brought in firewood from the stack on the porch—luckily we didn't have to go outdoors again to fetch any. The place was pretty comfortable by the time we'd settled all our stuff in and lit the fire and they'd eaten.

I found a saucer in a cupboard and poured evaporated milk into it for the hob, setting it down in a corner of the kitchen. It wasn't fresh cream, which is what they're supposed to prefer, but it was the best I could do in the circumstances. I drank the rest of the milk and made up a pint of the protein shake I'd brought out of London. That was my dinner. When I came back in, Gail was unrolling the sleeping bags. I picked mine up and headed for the door.

"Hey. I thought we had to sleep near the fire."

"I'll be okay out here. Kitchens are good too."

"But aren't we better sticking together?"

I could feel the burn between my legs, already uncomfortable.

"I don't want to play gooseberry to you two," I muttered. "And I'm not likely to be able to sleep… for a while. You know."

"Again?" Her eyes widened.

"It doesn't stop, Gail. It doesn't let up. I'm…" I pulled a face. How was I supposed to explain that all the while they'd been eating, I'd been forcing myself not to stare at her boyfriend—and that I quivered every time he brushed past me? "I'm bad news," I finished.

The look she exchanged with Vince was laden with meaning. I was pretty sure I read *Told You So* in the glance.

"Well…" he said.

"Tansy…"

"I'm sorry. Goodnight guys."

"Tansy, don't go. We want you to sleep with us."

I gritted my teeth. Kneeling there in the firelight with those huge soft eyes, she looked impossible to refuse.

"You'll be fine without me," I promised.

"You don't get it, do you?" She giggled, which seemed

inappropriate in the circumstances. "We're here to look after you. So, if you need to fuck Vince... well... it's okay. You can do that."

I swallowed, looking from one to the other. Vince was trying to maintain an expression of benign sincerity, but I was pretty sure a grin was trying to break out from beneath it. "You mean that?" I asked.

"Yes!"

"You're both sure about this?" My voice rasped a little. My heart was starting to pound. "I mean, it's not going to mess things up between you?"

"I gather," said Vince, "that you two... Well, you've played together before, haven't you?"

I shrugged. "Yeah. A bit." It wasn't something I'd admit to, normally. Not because I was ashamed—it was just something we did occasionally for fun. And it'd been going on so long I'd forgotten to feel embarrassed. But it was private. Other people might not understand.

"How long have you been doing that, then?"

"A long time," Gail said, biting her lip and looking at me. We were both pink now.

"Have you ever shared a guy before?"

We shook our heads. That was true—we hadn't.

"Sweet." Vince's grin was beyond disguising now.

He pulled his shirt off over his head, revealing an athletic, nearly hairless torso that gleamed in the firelight as if polished. His hand brushed his abs and down over his belt to the bulge of the erection already tenting his jeans. I guess he could be forgiven for that hard-on, considering what he'd had to witness earlier.

"You want some of this, girls?" he asked.

"Oh *yes*," I answered gratefully, dropping my sleeping bag. Gail stood up and kissed my cheek.

Oh thank you, thank you, god of horny Tansys! thought I. *Thank you for broad-minded cousins and dirty-minded boyfriends!*

"Then let me see you kissing, girls. I want to see that."

We swapped a smile—an odd mixture of playful kink and shyness—and moved into an embrace. Gail's lips were soft beneath mine, her hips narrow, her little breasts achingly soft and sweet, her skin fragrant. I always feel that handling her is like handling a kitten. She feels so small and delicate compared to the men I'm used to, like I'll hurt her if I'm not careful. But I also know she's quite capable of whipping out her claws. I admit we put on a bit of a show for Vince, knowing how much he was appreciating what he saw. We got a kick out of arousing him, let's face it. We sighed and giggled and murmured as we slipped buttons and tugged down zips and slid each other out of our clothes. The firelight lit a warm glow on our bare flesh, painting it rosy as if we were blushing coyly. We made sure he got a good eyeful of our bottoms and thighs and boobs as they bounced into view, and of the caresses we bestowed on all those parts. I smacked Gail's ass, delighting in the sound it made, and she squealed with pleasure and wriggled up against me in a way that sent a fresh surge of arousal through my already melting body. Our breasts nestled together, soft upon soft. I sank my fingers into her bum-cheeks and bit her lower lip.

"Kiss her titties," Vince said hoarsely. "Kiss those big, beautiful tits, Gail."

Obediently, she grabbed an overflowing double handful and pulled them right up so she could fasten her mouth on them. Her tongue left my skin glistening.

"Oh, that's hot!" he groaned.

Her kitten teeth were sharp and her tongue an unmerciful tease; the pain was exquisitely judged. I could feel my legs growing weak. I gasped and arched my back to ease the strain on my flesh, as she pressed my orbs together hard and caught both my nipples in her mouth at once, nipping me till I squealed, "Oh fuck, Gail!"

"Poor Tansy," she crooned, licking those swollen points roughly. I could feel myself about to fall. My wide eyes met Vince's over her head.

"Come here, girls," he ordered, tugging at his belt buckle.

She let go of me with a show of reluctance, but we were both more than happy to try a new game with the body he offered us. Smirking and utterly naked, we crossed to where he stood on the mattress and snuggled up to him, our breasts rubbing against his bare chest. I heard the sharp intake of his breath, and then he kissed Gail tenderly, slipping an arm around each of us and pulling us close. His skin was warm and firm and the masculine smell of him was intoxicating. His palm cupped my butt. I licked the lobe of his ear as I awaited my turn. Then he kissed me, and his hand snuck into the crack of my ass, one fingertip playing with the pucker of my hole.

A reminder of our kitchen conversation, I thought, as his tongue poured over mine. My head swam.

"Yo, bitches," he teased, grinning, as he came up for air and surveyed us both.

"Yo, dawg," we laughed back, but I was at least half in earnest. I was more than willing to be his dirty bitch if he'd be my big stud dog and mount me. My pussy was already ripe for the taking. We kissed him, nuzzling against his bristly cheek, licking at his throat, sliding our hands over his chest and his stomach, plucking at his jeans buttons, stroking his cock through the denim. That member of his was as solid as tyre rubber.

Please fuck me with that, I prayed.

But it was Gail who took the lead. And it was only polite to let her. I followed, falling to my knees with her as she wrenched open the last fly button and released the beast. It sprang out proud from its cage, just as magnificent as I remembered from our illicit fooling around, weeks before. In unison we moved to pay homage with our mouths—lapping eagerly at his balls, kissing that shaft, licking its beautiful length all the way up to the tip. Our tongues entwined as we fought for the privilege of sucking on his turgid bell-end, both of us hungry for his meat, our kisses half-competitive and half-loving.

Vince put a hand on each of our heads, his fingers raking though our hair. I guess it must have been quite a sight from his angle: the blonde and the redhead kneeling before him, peeling off his clothes and mouthing passionately at his erect cock. Our pale skin and wet lips and half-closed eyes.

"Halle-fuckin-lujah," said he hoarsely, as if he'd seen the light. Holding us in place, he slipped his cock first into Gail's mouth and then into mine, pushing right to the backs of our throats as if testing the fit. I sucked joyfully. I'd never met a cock so stiff.

Gail lifted her lips from his scrotum. "Do you like my boyfriend's cock?" she asked me in a sweet voice.

I licked it from root to crown, making it bounce and weep salty drops upon my tongue.

"I *love* your boyfriend's cock," I assured her.

"Think you're ready to take it all inside your pussy?" she wondered.

I swallowed eagerly. "I'm ready to try."

"Then you'd better get a rubber on him."

I couldn't blame Gail for being careful. And in one of my lucid moments I'd actually packed condoms and lube—*lots* of condoms and lube—in the pocket of my rucksack. I left Gail to keep Vince warm while I went on a frantic hunt, scattering boxes and bottles over the mattress.

When I returned I had to take a moment, though, to admire her deep-throating her man. I mean, she's not a big girl —I've no idea where she was putting all of that cock. But she was taking him right down to the root.

She gave way graciously to me though, drawing back from his slick and glistening shaft with an elegant swoop. I tore open the wrapper and popped the latex cap, then used my mouth to unroll it down his shaft, demonstrating my own oral capability. Gail, chuckling, swung round behind me and slipped her arms round me as I knelt to work. She pinched my nipples first, rolling them cruelly between her fingers until I moaned in feverish acknowledgement. Then she slipped one hand between my open thighs and delved into my hot sex.

"You're all wet, you dirty bitch," she chided me, pushing her fingers into my cunt and working them.

"Ungh…" I answered, my throat full and my eyes

watering.

She stood up and presented two glistening fingers to Vince. I watched as he caught her wrist and licked my pussy juice from her hand.

"Think she's ready for you?" she asked.

He nodded, grunting deep in his chest. "Ready as she'll ever be."

"Good."

As soon as she'd said it, she snagged my hair in one hand and jerked my head back, stretching my throat. My open lips demonstrated both the shape of Vince's cock that had so recently filled it, and my genuine surprise. Honestly, Gail's not normally like that. She's usually a bratty little sub when she's with me. Yes, she likes to kick and scratch, but she isn't dominant. But I guess she was finding a whole new sort of thrill in this situation.

"Lie down," she told me, tugging at my hair.

I sank back on the mattress with my arms over my head and my thighs open. Planting my feet, I lifted my hips in invitation to Vince. He didn't need a "Please." He waded forward on his knees, lifting my ass right up onto his hard thighs. Then he stopped. I saw a frown cross his face as he ran his thumbs across the creases between my bum-cheeks and my legs.

"What?" I gasped.

"Someone wrote on you."

"Oh." I remembered Aaron and his marker pen. "What does it say?"

"*Fuck here.* With arrows."

I laughed, a dirty chuckle. "Go on, then!"

Vince's face broke out in a grin. Supporting the arch of my spine, he hitched forward and plunged his cock into my open portal. At that angle it was pushing right up against my most sensitive tissues. It felt like the angels storming heaven.

"Yes!" I groaned in welcome. "Yes… oh God—that is soooo what I need!"

"Good—'Cos it's what you're getting, girl," he said, thrusting deep.

I saw Gail coming around to kneel behind my head. As Vince started to move that big cock in and out of me, she caught my nipples between fingers and thumbs and began to tug them, rolling them cruelly in just that way she knew I liked, adding the fire of perfectly-judged pain to the exquisite pounding my cunt was taking at the other end. I couldn't take it for long. I began to wail. My thighs and my belly and my whole body went taut, my back arching like a bow, my vision filling with flame. I came screaming.

The relief was indescribable. I'd been days without cock and it had nearly killed me. Now I was getting what I truly needed. I think I was nearly sobbing as I came down from that orgasm. Vince ran a warm hand over my quivering stomach.

"Don't stop," Gail told him. "She'll come again if you keep fucking her."

"Greedy girl," he said, shaking his head. But he shifted his hips to surge into me once more. I proved Gail right in only a few moments, going into meltdown in his grip twice more in quick succession. Sweat lacquered his torso and dripped from his forehead to kiss my body. He rammed deep into me and went still.

"Just… need a moment," he said under his breath.

His cock was like iron inside me. Gail abandoned my tits and knelt up over me to run her hands across his chest and kiss him. I couldn't see that, but in compensation I got the most perfect view of her parted thighs and pouting pussy. I couldn't resist working one hand up and into that peachy blonde fuzz, and I wasn't exactly surprised to find her all swollen and juicy, her labia open in readiness.

She'd been so mean to me with the hair-pulling and the nipple-tweaking that I wanted revenge in turn. I smacked her wet sex with my open hand and she jumped, squeaking. She clung even more tightly to Vince then, and her thighs slid wider open. *Who's the dirty bitch here, eh?* I wanted to ask. I wasn't able to get much of a swing on my spanking, in that tight triangle between her legs—though I did the best I could, slapping her pussy until the honey drizzled down on me and she thrashed her ass from side to side. In the end she needed too much. She sank lower and lower until finally she mashed her pussy into my face, and only then was I able to bite her swollen, rosy clit and send her over the edge into orgasm.

She nearly drowned me. I lost all air as she slithered over my face, pressing herself into my open mouth, and it was that —combined with the insistent pressure of the great shaft filling my own sex—that, even without further movement on Vince's behalf, sent me into another heaving, frantic climax. Dimly I heard Gail shriek, though my ears were muffled by her thighs and the roaring of blood in my head. I tore my face aside, gasping into the inch of space afforded me by her sweat-slicked skin.

"Oh… oh… ooh!" Gail was still mewing. I felt Vince withdraw from me, slipping out of our grasp, but I didn't let

Gail go. I pulled her down on top of me instead, cradling her in my arms as I cushioned her slender body with mine. Her head lolled on my hip. I could see her sweet little asshole winking like a star above me, as the aftershocks of orgasm ran through her.

Vince's face popped into view, a look of slight consternation upon it.

"You okay?" he mouthed.

Grinning, I hooked one hand over Gail's ass and pressed my thumb against her rear hole, feeling the ready give of the muscle.

"You got round to fucking this pretty little ass yet?" I asked.

Gail moaned protestingly.

"Shush," I admonished, stroking the small of her back with the other hand. "Lick my pussy, you dirty little thing."

Obedient, she hitched down to bury her face between my thighs and I couldn't help a sigh of pleasure. But my concentration was on Vince. I cast him a significant glance aimed at her splayed ass-crack.

"Lube," I whispered.

He found it, after delving about on the mattress for the discarded bottle. His hand quivered as he directed a stream of gel at her ass-cleft, and I enjoyed the way it drooled down into the pucker of her anus. I enjoyed the movement of his fingers too, glistening as they worked the lube over her pale skin and stole inside her, one at a time. I could see he'd been trying out my advice. There was no resistance to these gentle caresses and, when he popped a broad thumb into that forbidden entrance, she even made a little noise of appreciative pleasure and sucked me harder.

But a thumb is not the same as a big blunt cock. As he knelt up in breathless silence and set his shaft to her ass, I knew we were asking a lot of her. A huge amount—looking at that thick, hard club, shiny with latex and my sex juices. Gail looked impossibly tiny and tight in comparison. He bobbed down a little and I reached up to kiss his dangling balls, licking at them until he made dark noises under his breath. I ran my hands all over Gail's back, firm and soothing, and murmured "Good girl," as he pressed into her.

"Tansy!" she gasped, her head jerking up in instinctive flare of panic.

"It's okay," I promised. "I'm here. I won't let him hurt you."

I could see the way her flesh yielded to the pressure—the stretching of her puckered hole, the flush of her open pussy. It was an utterly bewitching sight, as glorious as the collision of galaxies. But I couldn't afford to just witness it. I lifted my head to her pussy, wrapped my mouth over her clit, and began to lick.

She took his cock. She took it all, slowly, deep in her tight virgin ass, because I was there to hold her and comfort her and kiss the pain away. I felt each spasm through her body on mine. The moments when she tensed; the wet, slack spasms of surrender; the terror and the eagerness and the dawning realisation of pleasure. I couldn't see so much, just the shadowy beam of Vince's cock against the pale ceiling and the growing shadow as he pushed closer and closer upon her. Inch by great, thick, beautiful inch. Then nothing at all, as he eclipsed the light. But I felt it when he was fully within her, and then he could move freely, back and forth, caressing her inside and out.

"Oh!" she cried. "Oh *God*... that's good!"

I felt it when she came, twice, her body writhing on mine, her chin grinding my pussy. But I was too busy concentrating on her pleasure to take my own.

Vince orgasmed too, at last, finally allowing himself what he'd been striving to put off for so long. He announced it: "AhfuckI'mcumming!" all in a rush. As he lifted his hips I glimpsed his balls clenched up so hard they nearly retreated inside his body. He held on for a long moment inside her, then pulled out quite suddenly. His hand skinned off the rubber so fast that it was a blur. He was still ejaculating as he pressed his cock down to me, and the very last spurt of his thick creamy jizz slopped on my face before he buried the shaft in my open mouth.

Dirty, dirty boy. Ass to mouth.

That made me climax.

Oh, that wasn't the last of it. But the rest of that evening is blurred in my memory. I know Vince and I both paddled Gail's ass until she screamed. I know there was fucking and sucking and a number of unlikely positions tried out, with varying degrees of success —Internet porn has a lot to answer for. I remember lapping at Gail's pussy while she yanked unmercifully at my ginger hair and Vince finger-fucked us simultaneously, right up to his top knuckles. But I was so jazzed with arousal and repeated orgasms that I can't remember in what order it came, or what anyone said, or how it all ended. I just know we collapsed into sleep at last, Gail sandwiched between us, the scent of her pussy juices all over my face and hands, and my own sex sticky with repletion.

❦ ❦ ❦

When I awoke it was almost pitch dark. That didn't mean it was still night—the boarded-over windows kept any hint of light out of the room—but the firelight had dwindled to nothing more than the faintest of red glows. I could just make out the darker silhouette of one of my sleeping partners against it.

It was the sudden press of Gail's knee against my leg that had woken me, I realised, and the whimper she'd uttered in her sleep. I just wasn't used to sharing my bed with another restless body anymore. I looked up at the unseen ceiling over my head and waited for her to settle down again.

She whimpered once more—a throaty, liquid croon that sounded utterly sensual. I turned my head, smirking, wondering if Vince was quietly feeling her up in the bed next to me. Her leg shifted, rubbing up against mine as she spread her thighs. Her breath was coming swift and shallow and her hot skin was damp. The sleeping bags spread over us shifted, letting in a small draft.

Just as I realised that there was something under the bedclothes with us, Gail spasmed and groaned, her leg jerking. I recognised the sound of her sexual climax. Immediately, her breath settled to a calm sigh.

A house-hob, I thought—as I felt a small hand transfer to my hip. If I hadn't worked that out, I'd have jumped out of my skin. But as it was, I held still. Its touch was light and warm and dry, almost insubstantial. There was very little pressure as it transferred from between Gail's open thighs to mine. Its delicate little hands and feet—or maybe they were paws, because I had no idea what the thing looked like—gripped me so carefully that if I'd been asleep I wouldn't have felt a thing. I got the impression that it was about the size of a monkey.

I felt a soft warmth caress my pussy, and gently insinuate itself into the split of my sex. A tongue. A long and very dexterous tongue. It delved the whole length of my slash, and began to gently lap.

Oh good grief, that was welcome. I hadn't even been aware that I'd woken up horny, but that pussy-licking was pure heaven. I allowed my thighs to open wider under its ministrations, pretending to sigh in my sleep. Hobs are house-goblins, the most intimate and domestic and common of the Good Neighbours. Even before Them There came back, there was supposed to be many a lucky farmstead that was tenanted by a hob. They did housework at night and looked after the animals and brought all kinds of luck and prosperity. And they were particularly associated with female servants. They liked their girls neat and tidy and hardworking, and were sure to punish slatterns. Folklore was coy about the relationship, mentioning only that the creatures were partial to a drink of cream left out for them at night. The reality had turned out to be more earthy. I envisaged a sort of Tess-of-the-D"Urbervilles fantasy with a whole row of milkmaids asleep in the hayloft, the house-hob working his way from girl to girl, licking each pussy to orgasm, dozens of young women gasping and smiling in their sleep and waking next morning awash with bliss.

I wasn't far off that myself. It was a very long tongue at work down there—soft and flexible and warm, easily able to lick from my ass crack all the way up my pussy to the burning button of my clit. Long enough, too, to slip right inside me and stroke every inner inch and lick at the gate of my cervix—an extraordinary sensation. With great care it drank from me, supping at my juices as if I were a nectar-heavy flower, making me flow with honey. I felt my barriers dissolve, my orgasm waking and muscling forward. My hips worked, quivering. The bedclothes were suddenly too hot but I didn't dare fling them off in case that betrayed the fact I was awake. I was sweating and panting, liquid trickling down my thighs, my limbs locked with tension. That tongue was inexorable and untiring and eventually I couldn't take it any longer. I started to buck as orgasm unfolded within me, leaf after leaf. I gave no conscious direction to my hands. It was simple instinct that made me reach down and grab at the thing between my legs to grind it closer against me.

I felt something solid and fuzzy under my fingers. Then that was snatched away. The bedclothes billowed as the hob wrenched from my grasp and shot away across the floor with a patter of feet on wooden boards. Reeling, I scrabbled for the torch I'd left by the mattress. I flicked it on just in time to see something dark and low vanish around the door.

Slipping out of bed, I stumbled in the wake of that glimpse. The torch beam was dim, sending wild shadows dancing across the unfamiliar angles of wall and roof. I found myself in the kitchen, open-mouthed, listening to a frantic but muted clatter as the unseen hob moved from cupboard to cupboard, like a rook that had fallen down a chimney and become trapped in a room.

At last I managed to switch my brain on, and the torch off.

"Hob!" I whispered. "It's alright! I'm not going to hunt

you!"

Groping for the formica table, I laid the flashlight on it and bent over, resting my breasts on the cold top.

"Look!" I wheedled.

The clattering stopped.

"Look, Hob," I breathed, reaching behind me to part my ass-cheeks with my hands. "Aren't you hungry? It must have been so long! You must be so hungry…"

For a moment there was no response and I held my breath. Then came the bump of a cupboard door. I had the wit not to move. It was like waiting for a wild animal to come out of hiding. I held myself almost motionless, face down and ass up, my hands holding my cheeks open, my naked pussy splayed and pulsing with heat. I assumed the hob could see in the dark, after all. Gently I shifted my ass back and forth, hoping to entice it.

The lino was chilly under my feet.

"Are you a good girl?" said a voice, as faint and whispery as dry leaves.

"Me? Yes, I'm a good girl." My breath was condensing on the cold tabletop. "I swept the floor and made up the fire before bed. I washed up."

"What's your name, good girl?"

"Tansy."

"Are you clean, Tansy? Are you careful? Not lazy, not silly, not dishonest?"

By most standards I reckoned I counted as deeply dirty and reckless, to be honest, but that wasn't the answer the hob was looking for. And at least I don't think I could be described as workshy.

"Yes," I lied. "I'm a good girl. A good, sweet girl. Take a look." Then I tried wheedling. "I've got cream for you, Hob. Lovely warm cream."

With the lightest of thumps it landed on the table next to me, and I tried not to flinch. Then it hopped onto the small of my back. I thought again of spider monkeys, as long, satiny limbs wrapped around my ass. Tiny hands spread my labia. The sigh of a long exhalation of breath reached my ears.

Then the tongue. Wet and slick, slipping down my ass-crack from hole to hole.

"Oh!" I gasped involuntarily, my body turning inside-out with delight. "Oh yes, Hob!"

"Hungry…" it muttered.

"You eat up," I urged, following the words with a strangled "Oh! Yes!" as it began to feast in earnest.

So intense was the pleasure, I nearly forgot that I'd had an ulterior motive for waylaying this hob. But before I could ask the creature anything, the growing, swelling insistence of orgasm became all-consuming. My legs straightened, straining. For a while there was no sound in the kitchen except a muffled slurping and the faint rattle of the table legs on the uneven floor. Then I came, biting my lip to stop myself crying out. In the aftermath I remembered to breathe again, and to speak.

"Hob?"

It speared my cunt with its ten-inch tongue and fireworks went off behind my eyeballs.

"Hob… oh God… Hob, please… where is the Salmon of Llyn Llyw?"

It withdrew its tongue and sniffed.

"Llyn Llyw is a great and beautiful lake. I seen it once," it said wistfully, which didn't really please me because there are no lakes on the Severn, not even little ones. But the hob hadn't finished. "Last I heard, the lake is below Bevere Island, most often. Though the Brenin fears the Pendragon may seek the *bradan feasa*, they say, and perhaps he'll take it away himself. But you don't want to go up there, anyway."

Whoah whoah whoah… Who the hell's the Brenin, for a start? I struggled with the sudden glut of information, stuffing the names away in my memory to consider later, when I had net access. *Bevere Island?* I racked my brains trying to remember the roadmap, but in truth my brain wasn't really working that night. I fastened on the hob's last statement.

"Why not?"

"Not safe for good girls. The Wild Hunt is abroad."

"How can I—Oh!"

The hob had decided our conversation was at an end.

For the rest of the night it ate my pussy. And I came. I lost all track of time and thought and self. I was just a string of orgasmic stars, blazing in the dark. Only when Vince got up and started to bump around in the living room did the hob let me go and scuttle off behind the skirting board.

When Vince came into the kitchen, naked and cradling his morning glory, I hadn't had the energy to move. My legs were so locked they'd set and I was still doubled over face-down on the table, my glistening pussy pointed straight at him.

"Shit, Tansy…" he breathed.

I screwed up my eyes against his torchlight, which seemed far too bright.

"It's okay," I mumbled, trying to get my elbows under me. "Just give me a moment… Ah!"

He gave me rather more than a moment. I guess even the nicest guy is liable to lose sight of the common courtesies when confronted with that sort of opportunity. Two big fingers slipped into the hot sink of my cunt, and I groaned in new surrender.

I'm just a girl who can't say No.

And that was when Vince finally got his wish, and fucked my big beautiful ass.

Halle-fuckin-lujah, as the man said.

Chapter Eight

The Elder Tree Witch

B evere Island, it turned out, was a tiny nub of land sited where the Severn skirted the town of Worcester. This wasn't bad news. It put us clear of the Welsh border at least. Once across Offa's Dyke, that's when you're really into dangerous territory. I still flinch when I remember the early Youtube footage of that afanc attack on the family at Bala Lake. We'd all watched it, unable to believe it could be anything but viral marketing for some horror film—but it had turned out to be real, all right.

Here be dragons, once more.

The hob's tip was the best lead we had, whatever our anxieties. And yes, I was chewing over its mention of the Brenin and the Pendragon, though I didn't know what it was referring to in either case. I mean, yes: I knew who the Pendragon *used* to be, obviously—King Arthur—just not what the name signified nowadays. *Bradan feasa* just means *Salmon of Knowledge.* And *Brenin* is a Welsh word meaning *King.* But there wasn't much choice, so we headed north, upriver.

One big problem we had was fuel. There were petrol stations, but they were jealously guarded and we wasted a lot of time and mileage trailing from market town to market town trying to find someone who would sell diesel off the ration card. They all turned us away; sometimes politely, sometimes with cold blank stares. I was getting really anxious by the time we resorted to stopping at a farm and trying outright bribery.

We sent Gail in to do the negotiating, figuring her to be the best out of the three of us at tugging on the heartstrings. We watched across the muddy farmyard, the smell of silage and cow manure sharp and sweet in our nostrils, as she chatted up the farmer in the blue coveralls, waving her hands pleadingly.

He shook his head. I couldn't stay out of it and plunged forward.

"Really? Not even a couple of gallons?" I heard Gail say.

"I'll give you a blowjob," I offered. They both stared at me.

He was sure he'd misheard. "What's that, now?"

I put my hands on my hips. "I'll give you a blowjob. The best head you've ever had, I promise."

He looked me up and down. He was tall and lean and looked like he'd never cracked a smile in his life, but his thick eyebrows rose as interest awoke in his expression.

"Tansy!" protested Vince, at my shoulder. "For God's sake, you don't have to do that!"

"No, it's fine. I want to." I looked the farmer in the eye. "I really want to."

"You'll have to swallow," he stipulated.

I grinned. "No problem." He'd no idea that the prospect of a warm, salty, gooey load down my throat was making me salivate.

"Jesus, Tansy," Vince complained. Gail shook her head in dismay.

"It's okay, honestly." It was more than okay; I could feel an ache that was the nearest thing I could recall to hunger, as well as a flutter and clench in my pussy.

So Gail and Vince went off to pump agricultural diesel from the farmyard tank, while I faced up to Old McDonald.

"Where shall we go, then?" I asked.

"This'll do, here."

Here was an open yard with a big stinky byre full of cows watching us.

"It's not very comfortable."

"It'll do fine."

His glance pointed me at the ground. I looked down at the concrete under my feet, painted in a thin slurry of cow-shit, and the indignity struck me like a slap. I met his eyes one last time, just to make sure of his challenging, merciless gaze. He was making the most of his trump hand, the bastard, and making sure I knew it. That realisation brought a gush of wet heat to my treacherous pussy.

Without another word, I went down on my bare knees before him, in the cow-shit slick.

"Get those tits out," he told me.

Submissively, I pulled down my top and hefted my breasts out into view. My nipples were stiffly perky and I was dizzy with humiliation and arousal.

"That's nice," said he, blandly.

So I popped the press-studs of his overalls and sought within. His cock was already erect and waving like a flag of victory. I gobbled him down, revelling in the taste of his thick musky meat, and he didn't make any more demands after that, just let me lose myself in the art of giving him head. He took *forever* to come though—in the end I had to be almost brutal with him, just to save my aching knees. But he rewarded my efforts with a flood of spunk that almost choked me, and a grunt of satisfaction.

As I found my feet and he tidied himself away, he remarked, "I heard you lot were around."

"What?" I mumbled, wiping semen from my lips.

"A pimp out of London and his two whores—ginger and blonde. He's a rubbish pimp though, to my way of thinking. You had to do all the work yourself."

I goggled, thinking that if Vince had heard, then this dickhead was just about to get his nose broken. "Who told you that?" I asked, appalled.

"The Gaffer. He said to keep a look out for you."

Shit. We were a good thirty miles and more away from the Bour Tree pub. I'd never have guessed the Gaffer's reach would be so long or vindictive. Vince must have really put his nose out of joint, showing him up like that in front of his toadies.

"You going to tell him we came this way?" I asked faintly.

"Oh, I reckon I have to."

I turned on my heel and walked away, stuffing my boobs back into my bra. Vince dropped into the driving seat as I reached the car.

"Let's go," I said grimly, fishing a pack of baby-wipes out of the glove box and starting to clean up my knees and boots. "We've got trouble."

"You're trouble all on your own, girl." He gunned the engine.

"You don't know the half of it. That lot from the pub are still looking for us."

Vince shot me a hard, angry glance. "You're joking?"

"I wish," I said, with feeling. "That's all we need, isn't it?" I swabbed moodily at my legs as we zigzagged down the twisty lanes. I felt scared and wired and guilty at the danger I was getting my friends into, and the combination didn't sit well with me. As I tried to knot up the plastic bag I'd stuffed the dirty wipes into, it split and I lost my temper.

"Shit!" I shouted, flinging it all down.

Vince pulled the car over into a field gate and stopped the engine, glaring at me. I glared back—and then became aware that I'd rammed my hand between my thighs and was grinding it against my pubic mound in frustration.

"Get the fuck out of the car," said Vince softly.

I was so surprised I obeyed. He came round onto the verge side where I stood, and shut my door for me with a decisive clunk. His eyes bored into mine.

"Turn around. Face the car."

All the air went out of my lungs. As I turned, he tugged up my skirt, swatted my bum-cheeks and then reached down to grab my pussy, mashing it hard in his hand. I let out a strangled squeal as the burn flamed through my flesh.

"This is what you need, isn't it?" he growled in my ear. "You're just gagging to open wide for every man we meet, aren't you?"

"Yes!" I moaned.

"I don't know why you bother putting knickers on in the morning, girl. Unless it's to keep your knees warm." He demonstrated by pulling the garment in question right down and exposing my cunt. "Spread them."

I did what I was told, stretching my panties across my open thighs and thrusting my ass out in presentation. He smacked my sex with his open palm and I heard the wet splat.

"Damn!" he said appreciatively. "You're just fucking insatiable. Your pussy's like a black hole, girl—you're going to swallow the whole damn world. Well, put me at the top of the queue."

Action was matched to promise as his cock suddenly butted up against my pussy and—without preamble or foreplay—bulled straight into that tight hole, making me cry out.

"Is there a problem?" he asked, grabbing my hips and making space for his cock inside me with a few firm thrusts.

"God, you're hard!" I yelped, awed. I couldn't believe he was fucking me in broad daylight at the side of a public road. Where anyone could see us.

"That's watching you blow that farmer," he grunted, through gritted teeth. "You, going down on your knees in the shit for that big ugly mother. With your tits out, wobbling. That's the dirtiest thing I ever saw. You're the dirtiest girl I ever met, Tansy. Sex on a fucking *stick*, girl! Sure, my cock wants some of that."

And I wanted to give him everything his cock would take. With the whole world watching. Bracing against the car, I moved my hips to meet his every savage thrust. He was hard as iron and he moved like a machine built for fucking. I didn't think it could get any better—until Gail wound down the window from inside, pulled out my tits from their straining bra and bit them, chewing on my nipples until I came—screaming, "Yes! Oh Christ yes... yes! Fuck me! FUCK ME!" up and down the Queen's highway.

Yeah. Vince was right. That *was* what I needed.

We rejoined the River Severn at Grimley and walked down past Bevere Island. There was no lake, just a weir, and no answer when I called, so we kept on going southward, toward Worcester. Even though we were heading into the suburbs, we couldn't see much sign of urban blight from where we were on the long-distance footpath. The trees and hedgerows here had run riot. Every wall and fence was swamped in woodbine and bindweed, and the overhanging branches were laden with plums and ripening apples. Weeds pushed through the crazed gaps in crumbling tarmac. Nobody was at work in those gardens, and the windows we glimpsed were cracked, or broken and gaping. There was no traffic, and no pedestrians in sight. Nothing disturbed the eerie rural silence but the birds—wood pigeons crooning sleepily overhead and crashing about in their clumsy mating scuffles, songbirds peeping and fluting. A scrawny dog looked at us, ears pricked, down the length of a lane, and then bolted away.

The day had turned warm and sunny. But there was something in the generous golden caress of that summer air that felt even more creepy than the grey clamminess of the estuary mouth. We picked our way in silence up the desperately overgrown track, looking about us as we pushed through the pungent banks of cow parsley and climbed over fallen willow branches. I kept one eye on the smooth green shine of the river for any glimpse of a big fish, wondering whether I'd walked right past it under some shaded bank.

"Bradan Feasa," I called softly, using the title the hob had told me. But there was no answer. Insects danced in the nets of dappled sunlight, their wings a golden blur.

Then Vince put a hand out and the three of us stopped dead. Looking up the path ahead, I saw a man standing there. He was spinning stones idly into the water, trying to make them skip. Just the sort of thing a guy might do to kill time, while waiting for someone. Nothing threatening about it at all. Except that this was a big man with a bushy ginger-blond beard who looked all too familiar.

We froze. All I could think was that any second he would glance our way, and then we were really buggered. Maybe literally. I wondered if there were any more of them out there. My question was answered when another man strolled into view across the footbridge. We heard his voice, faintly, as he hailed Beardy.

I grabbed Gail's sleeve and tugged her off the path, behind a tree and through a gap in the hedge beyond. I was glad when Vince didn't have to be told to follow. We scraped through the hawthorns, covering ourselves in scratches, to find ourselves in some sort of green lane that ran behind a row of large detached houses. I took the lead and headed straight for the first gate, opening it on what looked like it had once been an orchard garden. Little apple trees stood at regular intervals in the knee-high grass, their branches bowed to the ground under the weight of glistening green apples, though scrub elder and cow parsley were growing up in the sunny spots between them now.

Beckoning the others through, I shut the garden gate behind us and we scurried up the nearest row of trees until we were tucked out of sight.

"How did they find us?" Gail mouthed resentfully.

"Probably spotted where we parked the car," Vince whispered. "Then sent men on to the next road bridges, and left someone to wait for us too."

"That means we can't go back," I muttered, straining to catch any glimpse of movement down by the bottom hedge.

"No."

"Crap."

"What's his problem!" Gail hissed.

"I guess they just don't like tourists around here," I answered, wondering what the hell we were going to do if it wasn't safe to go back to the car. Wondering whether to lie low and sneak back to the river later, or cut out through the front garden of this house and take another road altogether. Wondering whether the house was actually empty, or inhabited by yet more irritable, territorial countryfolk. If it was the latter, we were trespassing and they'd probably be royally pissed off.

I could smell the damp patches forming dark rings under the armpits of Vince's T-shirt, and it was terribly distracting. Sweat and trampled grass, turned earth, and the cat-piss smell of elderflower. I moved a few feet away, just to get a clear head. I dragged my boots free of the long grass that clung to them, accidentally kicking over a puffball fungus in the process.

"Tansy!" squeaked Gail.

I turned just in time to see her pitch flat on her face. I was still wondering how she'd tripped over from a standing start when I saw her hauled backward several metres through the weeds, clutching vainly at the long stems, her mouth wide with shock.

I tried to lunge after her, but my feet wouldn't move and I tipped forward onto my hands and knees. A glance at my ankle told me the worst—there was a ropey grey *thing* coiled around my boot. Both boots. It flexed visibly. I just had time to phrase the word *tentacle* when another thrust out of the ground and whipped around my right forearm.

Where it touched, sensation blossomed under the skin, like flowers bursting open.

"Tansy!" Gail wailed, far too loudly.

"What the -?" Vince yelped, his arms flailing.

"Shush!" I moaned, but that was the last moment I wasted worrying about the Gaffer's crew hearing us. Because, all around us through the grass, great grey-green ropes were rising like shoots reaching for the light. There was a wet glisten to them that was more fungal than floral, though, and they were as slippery as eels. I've no idea if they were all limbs of one great underground creature or many small separate ones. I don't suppose it matters. In moments the three of us were caught and bound by several tentacles each. They slithered bonelessly up my thighs and arms, feeling their way along the skin and under my clothes, to furl around my torso. They were, I discovered as I thrashed in vain, trying to tear myself free, horribly flexible—and far, far too strong.

They hoisted Gail. I saw her lifted high above the grass, on her back but held aloft by a dozen tendrils. One gripped each of her legs to haul her thighs apart. An appendage as thick as a python emerged obscenely from the waistband of her jeans and flexed. With a sharp ripping sound the cloth gave way and shredded. Her bright pink panties lasted less than a second— and I just had time to think *That's deliberate!* before a tapered tentacle oozed up between her thighs right into her splayed sex.

"No!" squealed Gail, sounding outraged.

"No!" roared Vince.

He was still on his feet but faring no better, his clothes literally torn off him as I watched. Then I stopped looking, stopped paying attention to anything going on elsewhere, because I felt the first slippery invader probing from behind me, up between my own sex lips and muscling into my cunt. It was neither warm like a mammal nor cold like the squid it resembled most, but tepid and slippery and full of purpose. In seconds it filled me and I felt it flexing. For a moment I struggled wildly, in blind terror. It did me no good at all. All my thrashing did was open the iris of my ass to another questing tendril.

"No! Oh fuck no!" Gail's scream was less outrage now and more hysterical panic, and I knew just how she felt.

I nearly dislocated my wrists wrenching at my living bonds. Looking down between my thighs I saw a great muscular ripple run up the tentacle that violated me. And then I felt it—the bulge forcing its way into my sex, opening me up then filling me. Another bulge, another pulse. Meanwhile, the one insinuating itself into my anus slipped past the portal of clenched muscle and filled my ass.

The slime tingled on my inner membranes, like arousal in alchemical form.

I felt myself hoisted off the ground, face down and legs spread wide, my ass and pussy stuffed with writhing, oozing appendages like the trunks of elephants. They weren't just filling me—they were fucking me, their waves of stretching and contracting muscle working me like I was a sex doll. And, of course, my body responded. I felt myself opening in welcome, felt my own hot juices mingling with the creatures' tepid slime. I started to pant and squeal, my fear turning to excitement, my excitement becoming an overwhelming imperative.

"Stop this!" Vince cried. "How do we stop th—AAH!"

That's what the men saw when they burst through the orchard gate: the three of us stark naked, trapped and bound and despoiled. Gail was stretched out on her back, her tits barely visible between the coils wrapped around her chest, her pussy impaled by something resembling an anaconda. I didn't even get that much dignity. My ass was in the air, my legs wide apart, and I was suffering a full-on double penetration. Vince was held with his toes off the floor, like a chrome hood ornament, his spine bent like a bow and a tentacle rummaging around in his back passage. I don't know if he'd ever taken it up the rear before, but his eyes were wide and there were little explosive grunts bursting out of his throat—*uh-uh-uh-uh*. His cock stuck out from his torso at full erection, a whip-thin tendril wrapped tight around it, stroking and milking it with rhythmic squeezes.

I reckon that was the sight that stopped the men of the

Bour Tree coming any closer.

To be honest, I barely registered that we had an audience, I was so busy wrestling with my orgasm. I came first, of course. I was already fired up before the ravishing started, and I screamed as I climaxed, half in release and half in terror. But from the sounds Gail was making, she was on her way too. I tossed my head, my hair flailing in my eyes. As I blinked myself back into lucidity my gaze fell on the puffball I'd kicked through the grass. Its empty sockets stared up at me.

It wasn't a fungus at all. It was a skull. Human. The implications fought their way through my mind even as the relentless plunging between my legs caused my body to gather toward another orgasm.

"Aah!" cried Vince, and I looked up in time to see him ejaculate heavily, white spurts arcing from his cock and splashing onto the writhing grey ropes.

Would it be quick or slow? I wondered. Would they hold us here, fucking us, until we died of exhaustion? Or kill us swiftly, and feed off our bodies just as eagerly?

A tentacle coiled up around Vince's straining throat.

Quick, I thought, dazed.

"Tansy!" he yelled, his voice already strangled. "Do something!"

I had no idea what to do. I'd never heard of any Good Neighbour like this. But as a slick tongue of living tendril lapped at my face, searching out any orifice to penetrate, my blurred gaze finally registered the blobs of white flowers on the elder scrub.

And I remembered that somebody owed me.

"Bour Tree!" I screamed. "Elder Lady! You gave me a wish!

Save us! Save-"

Then the tentacle spilled in over my lips and silenced me. I couldn't stop coming even then. That thick member filled my throat like a cock, and though it cut off my airway its touch was pure bliss. I was still spasming as I blacked out.

There was a piece of straw sticking up into my left nostril. That trivial but intense irritation was what finally woke me up. When I lifted my head, blinking, dried grass was stuck to my right cheek. It smelled of dust and summer. Beyond the straw were thick wooden bars.

"I can't do this!" Gail wailed.

I tried to sit up. I tried to call out. That was when I discovered that my hands were tied behind my back and that my mouth was gagged with a stick as thick as two fingers. Curling my legs under me, I flopped about and struggled desperately into a sitting position.

I was in a wooden cage. Vince, wearing only a pair of baggy drawstring trousers, lay next to me on the straw. Beyond the bars was a room—it looked like the interior of a medieval cottage, all wooden beams and brick fireplace, copper pots and bunches of herbs—and sitting on a stool in the middle of the floor was Gail, with a small mountain of cabbage at her feet, a chopping board on her lap and a tiny knife in her hand. She was dressed—like me, in fact—in the skimpiest of slave's garments, nothing more than a thong around her hips from which hung a cloth flap front and rear, and a loop of fabric that came down from her neck to cross in an X over her breasts and tie behind her. Looming over her was the ugliest woman I'd ever seen in my life.

There was no confusion about what *she* was. She was so tall and so ugly that there was no mistaking her for human. And I'd seen pictures approximating to her since childhood—she was a Rackham nursery illustration of a witch, made flesh. Not muscular and broad like the ogress had been, but bent and skinny like a woman carved out of warped wood, her ancient skin seamed with wrinkles, and her nose and chin so prominent that they curved together like the two halves of a pair of coal-tongs. Wild, bristly black hair framed her head. Her hands were huge, as knobbly as sticks, and ended in ragged yellow nails, one of which was pointed threateningly at Gail's face.

"Chop these greens and make a stew, slattern, or it will be the worse for you," she said. Her voice was like the scrape of chalk on an old-fashioned blackboard. "Make our dinner or end up in it."

The Elder Tree Witch, I thought, panic turning my sluggish blood liquid again. I'd asked, she'd answered. *Out of the frying pan into the fire. Oh shit.*

White-faced, Gail picked up another cabbage and began to hack at it. The knife clearly wasn't very sharp, and Gail has never been particularly practical. As the witch turned away, humming to herself, my cousin stifled a sob.

I looked at Vince, lying at my feet. He seemed to be unconscious. He was gagged like me, and his hands were tied behind him with leather strips. I was sympathetic, but that didn't stop me giving him a kick to try and wake him. Gratifyingly, he groaned and started to stir. As the witch picked up a big book and began to leaf through it, I started to tug at my bonds. I could feel spit leaking out round my gag and I hated it. Though I didn't have any real idea what I thought I could do next, I did know I wanted my hands to be free.

As it turned out, I didn't get enough time. The cabbage skidded away from under the knife and fell on the rug. As the witch whipped around, Gail threw everything off her lap.

"I can't!" she shouted. "It's not possible!"

I recognised that voice. Gail was having a full-on bratty tantrum, and she couldn't have picked a worse place. But there was just no reasoning with her when she got into that mood. The only way I'd ever found to deal with my cousin when she got like that was to hand out a good spanking, because until she got that catharsis she'd just get wilder and wilder. Yanking wildly at my bonds, I tried to yell a warning but it came out as an idiot moan past the gag and no one heard. The witch stooped and seized Gail by the jaw, hauling her to her feet.

"Lazy trull," she snarled.

"Fuck you," Gail spat through clenched teeth. Full marks for ballsiness, no marks for common sense. Maybe that runs in the family.

The witch laughed. No, there's no other word for it—she cackled. It was a spiteful, gleeful sound. "You'll change your mind about that!"

Hauling Gail under the main roof beam, the witch uncinched her leather belt and used it to bind my cousin's wrists. Despite her crooked, clumsy-looking hands, she moved swiftly and with dexterity, and she was clearly immensely strong. Gail never got a chance to break away. The witch yanked her bound wrists up straight over her head and, lifting her clean off the floor, snagged the belt over a hook that stuck out from the beam. Gail was suddenly left hanging in mid-air, her bare toes a foot clear of the rag rug below. God, I couldn't help thinking she was beautiful like that; her rage and helpless frustration seemed to make her glow. She kicked out, vainly, trying to find purchase on the empty air. That appeared to amuse the witch too. Going over to the fireplace, she came back with a hearth-brush in her hand.

It was one of those old-fashioned birch-twig brushes. If the handle had been longer it could have sold as a witch's broom in a Hallowe'en display. As it was, the birch brush was just right for this witch to wield one-handed. With a cruel, almost disparaging flick of the wrist, she whipped it across Gail's ass.

Gail shrieked. I'm not surprised—those thin twigs were no joke. I could almost feel the sting as they contacted her soft flesh. Her tits bounced as her whole body spasmed. For a moment I froze in horror. The brush spun back and descended again, across Gail's thighs. Again, she screamed.

Vince shot up awake, roaring protest behind his gag. I hauled at my wrists and felt the leather stretch a fraction. The birch whip hissed again.

Gail didn't have any defence against this punishment. Her legs and torso were all but bare, and the branches scored her pale flesh with hundreds of tiny welts, raising the colour to her skin in a crimson flush. She screamed and kicked and thrashed, but it did her no good at all. The witch was merciless. Thighs and belly, back and breasts—whichever way the girl twisted she exposed another portion of her flesh to the lash.

Now, Gail can take pain. She can soak it up like a sponge when she's in one of her moods, but I found this terrifying. It didn't take long before she stopped swearing and just howled. Her defiance crumbled, first to bitter protest, then to dread, and then to helpless surrender. Her cries went up a notch too, when the witch tugged aside the girl's few clothes and made sure to lash her bare nipples and mons as well. Her back arched and her breasts shook wildly and her thighs scissored, casting wild shadows.

Vince threw himself against the bars, but bounced off. They might only be rough timber lashed together with hide, but they were tough enough to hold us.

"Please!" Gail screamed, at last. She'd held out an extraordinarily long time, it seemed to me, but she was all but broken now. Her hair hung down in sweaty strings and her cheeks were glazed with tears. Snotty sobs bubbled in her throat. "Please! Oh God!"

The witch paused, chuckling to herself. She didn't seem to have broken a sweat, and I knew she was only toying with Gail.

"No 'fuck you' now, then?" she mused, plunging a cruel hand between the girl's thighs and grabbing her pussy.

Well I knew, that that pussy would be running wet.

"Oh!" my cousin cried, her head jerking up. "Oh!"

"Sing, little bird." The witch's wrist worked. It was clear she was driving her bunched and knobbly fingers into Gail's cunt. "Sing your heart out. Will the cock-bird hear and come to you?"

Vince, sitting in the straw, kicked at the base of a bar and probably came close to breaking his bare foot. I heard his groan.

The witch suddenly released Gail. She turned away to the

fireplace again, and in that moment of respite I realised that the bonds around my wrists would never break. But they had stretched to an extent such that I might be able to wriggle my ass between my hands. I stopped pulling and curled up on my side, shuffling backward.

The witch returned, carrying something she'd plucked from the mantle. It looked like a leather harness of some kind. I realised its purpose when I saw that the other component was a great thick wooden phallus, double-ended and cunningly curved, which the leering witch showed to Gail. It was smooth and dark as if well-oiled and much-handled—and the larger head was almost twice as big as Vince's cock.

"Will this make you sing, my sweet bird?" she asked mockingly.

Vince moaned behind his gag. Gail started to sob—but I saw the flash of fire in her eyes. She was burning all over, inside and out, with pain and exhaustion and broken rebellion. I knew only too well how terribly horny such ill-treatment made her. When she'd been slapped into submission, that was when she needed to orgasm most of all. It was what made everything all right again. I knew that. I knew from experience the taste and the smell and the heat of her lust—oh, so well. I just didn't know if she'd be able to take that monstrous cock.

Lifting the skirts of the ragged dress that hung, sack-like, on her frame, the witch slotted the smaller, curved end of the strap-on up between her own thighs and cinched the straps about her hips. The dildo stuck out, jiggling, from her pelvis, and she gave it an obscene caress as if it were living flesh. Then she spun Gail round to aim at her from behind. Gripping one thigh in each enormous hand, she spread them and pulled back, swinging the slender younger woman until her pussy was a glistening bull's-eye, open and unprotected. She angled the wooden weapon right at that fleshy target, cackling with delight. The sight—that foul sadistic old hag, the tender and brutalised girl—made my heart pound and my blood boil. It was wrong, wrong, wrong... and God help me, there was a core of dark excitement under my burning outrage.

With a final heave I managed to force my ass through the circle of arm and leather, nearly dislocating my shoulders to do it.

"Sing, pretty sparrow," said the witch, and pushed the phallus into Gail's open split. The girl cried out as the oiled wood squeezed into her tender pussy.

I pulled my feet through the loop and grabbed at my gag.

"Sing, little bird." The cock emerged a few inches, streaked with Gail's honey, then surged forward again remorselessly.

"Oh! Oh! Oh!!"

"Stop it!" I screamed, wrenching the wooden bit painfully out of my mouth and grabbing at the bars of the cage. "Stop it! I asked you to save us!"

The witch paused, swinging her awful face in my direction, her tiny dark eyes glittering.

"I saved you," she said mildly. "One wish only stretches so far. Rather like a slattern's cunny."

Gail was sobbing and panting and drooling.

"Let her go," I said, switching tack. "I'll do the work instead. She's an awful cook. I mean, really crap—you'd have to be starving to death to sit down to one of her dinners. I've seen her burn a boiled egg. Seriously. Now, I can cook."

I knew I was gabbling, but I had to hold the witch's

attention and stop her ramming that thing home.

"I'll make a great cabbage stew for you. I need some root veg to go in it too, of course. Have you got carrots? And garlic? You can't make a really good soup without garlic. Onions, of course. Butter for frying. Or, get me some other ingredients and I'll do you a fantastic spaghetti bolognese. Or a fish pie. I do the best fish pie in England, I swear. Garlic bread. Roast chicken with a honey glaze. Chocolate brownie fudge cake. Just… let Gail go. Let's swap. Her in here, me out there."

The fact is, I'd say or do pretty much anything to protect my cousin.

And the truth is, I craved that monster dildo in *my* hungry snatch.

The witch's eyes narrowed. "Cabbage stew," she said, with emphasis.

"Right. Cabbage stew it is. Rich, savoury… little croutons on top."

She considered, her cold gaze roaming idly over Gail's suspended body, still impaled on the bulbous tip of the dildo.

"I had thought to keep this one as my house-servant. But I suppose it will work as well the other way round."

"Better," I said with manic confidence. "I'm stronger than her—look at us. And I can reach the high shelves."

"Hah. Mouthy, too. I don't like a girl who talks back, you know."

I bit my lip. "I'm sorry."

"Better. Strumpets must know their place. You wouldn't want me to have to punish you, as well?"

I flushed. "No, madam."

The prospect of a whipping like that terrified me. I'm no

pain-slut like Gail. But that strap-on… that was a different matter. My cunt, so recently stuffed and stretched by a monstrous tentacle, felt empty and hollow now, longing to be filled.

"You must learn obedience."

"Yes, madam."

"Let's see."

With a grunt, she pulled out of Gail's snatch and dropped her so that she swung back down to vertical. I could hear my cousin's shuddering breath and I let my own out with a sigh of relief. But she didn't release Gail from her bonds immediately. Instead she crossed to the cage and stared down at me. The wooden phallus still jutted from her hips, glistening as if varnished. The witch stood so close, and the implement was so long, that it rapped against the bars.

Without pausing for thought I slid to my knees and kissed the fake cock, bathing the carved dome in my mouth and licking the elegant shaft. I could taste Gail's pussy juices, tangy and laden with familiar musk, and under that the subtler bitterness of oiled wood. It made my own sex run moist.

"Heh," she said, her eyes narrowing as she watched me work. "You'll take this for the little lassie, will you?"

Oh yes! I lifted my pouting lips from her cock-head and nodded.

"Show me."

Standing, I turned and thrust my rump against the bars, pulling up that pathetic excuse of a skirt and baring my sex. Bending at the waist, I gripped the bars behind and to either side of me. My pussy was framed by the rough boles and perfectly presented. I saw Vince's eyes widen.

"Fuck me instead, please," I said, my voice shaking.

She made no reply, but reached through the bars to grip my hips. Her hands were hard. Not nearly as hard as that wooden cock she wielded, though. Even the most tumescent flesh has some degree of give to it. This had none. It slid into my pussy like a stake, and she thrust like she intended to impale me through the heart. Now, as the guys in the pool room had discovered, I have a deep cunt. I can take a big, big cock—but this one made me wail. If I hadn't been so aroused I don't think I could have borne it. Even so, I howled and howled as she swung in and out of me.

I never let go of the bars. I never tried to pull away. I howled all the way to orgasm, while Vince sprawled at my feet and stared, aghast.

The Elder Witch screeched as she came, like a bird of prey.

Afterwards, she forgot me, momentarily at least, and I slumped to my knees. She crossed to a high shelf on which sat a row of earthenware pots with pasted labels, selected one and brought it back to the centre of the room, popping the thick cork bung.

Gail still hung from the roof-hook, eyes closed, looking all but unconscious. Her skin was fiery pink and flecked all over with welts. Her garments hung askew, and her breasts were still exposed. Scooping a fingerful of white gunk from within the pot, the witch slopped it onto the girl's right nipple. That poor pink bud was swollen and inflamed, and I hoped the salve was cool.

Gail's eyes shot open and she whimpered. I winced as I caught a waft of something gingery, imagining the sting should it be applied to my own bruised flesh. But the witch was relatively gentle as she rubbed the salve into Gail's skin, all over one breast first and then the other. Thoroughly. Nowhere else on her body.

That worried me. But I thought I'd pushed my luck already, as far as challenging our captor. I was still getting my breath back from that thorough pounding she'd given me. I didn't even dare take Vince's gag off, though he glared at me and mumbled, heaving against his bonds. I just shook my head and signed for him to be patient.

On a twisted leather thong round her scrawny neck, the witch wore a bronze key that fitted the barrel-lock on our cage door. Lifting Gail down with a single hand—that made me wince, I can tell you—she hauled the girl over to us and stuffed her unceremoniously onto the straw. Gail fell into my arms and grabbed me. Her whole body was trembling and slippery with sweat. But I saw the burning ache of need in her eyes as she gazed up at me through her tears, and I knew that not even that harsh treatment had quenched Gail's flame. Hell, she'd probably sulk at me for having stolen the fuck, knowing her.

"Out you come," said the Elder Witch to me.

I tipped Gail against Vince and she wrapped her arms about his neck like a shipwrecked sailor clinging to a bollard.

"That's right, deary," said the hag cheerfully. "You make the most of him while you've got him."

I clambered out of the cage and straightened up, and she clanged the lock back into place. I know I'm tall, but she was two feet taller, even hunched over as she was. I made the mistake of meeting her gaze. She slapped me across the face and sent me staggering.

"Oww!" I cried.

"Proud airs butter no parsnips, deary."

Shock and rage clawed at each other in my breast, but I knew better than to retaliate, after the example she'd made of Gail. She grinned at me, her widely-spaced teeth as grey as slate and sharp as awls. There was nothing aggressive or even stern about her manner. She was simply teaching me my place.

"Yes... madam," I said haltingly, lowering my gaze.

"That's better. Now, you have cabbage to chop. I want that cauldron there filled." She nodded at the big bronze pot hanging on chains over the fire.

Dismay must have shown on my face.

"Is that a problem, deary?"

"No. Not at all, madam." I didn't want another slap. "That's a *lot* of stew."

"There's me, and you three." Her ratty little eyes flicked to the cage. "*Milk and meat.*" She looked back at me. "*And cunny sweet.* We have to fatten up your boy, there. And my three strong sons will be home to eat tonight—each of them bigger and more handsome and more hungry than the last. So off you go and start chopping."

I shut my sagging jaw, feeling dizzy. Catering quantities were suddenly the least of my worries. *Fatten him up? Oh no.* Suddenly I knew which fairytale this was. I crossed over to the heap of cabbage and looked at it in despair.

"Now, you wouldn't be the sort of girl who'd think about sticking that little knife into me, would you deary?"

It was a very small knife, with a leaf-shaped bronze blade. It probably wouldn't even reach her heart. Assuming she had one. I licked my lips. *No, I'm intending to push you into the gingerbread oven,* I said to myself.

"Of course not, madam," I told her.

"Nor will you run away, will you deary?"

I shook my head. I wasn't going anywhere without Gail and Vince.

"That's a good lass. Well, I must go out to pick those onions you asked for. But just to make sure, I think I will have you on a lead, deary. Kneel upon that stool there."

I balanced nervously upon the stool where Gail had sat. The witch stalked around the kitchen—another pot from the shelf, though a different label this time; another visit to the mantelpiece. She removed her phallus, this time, to my disappointment. Oh, how my empty cunt craved that big dildo again. My pussy was literally dripping fuck-honey, but I was doomed to frustration. The new toy she took down was wooden too, but substantially smaller—and a distinctive domed shape, with a narrow neck. Narrow enough to be gripped by an anal sphincter. *Oh!* I gasped silently, my eyes already watering.

It seemed to be attached to a long cord of braided rawhide. She secured one end of the leash to the base of the roof-pillar. Then she smeared the plug with salve.

"Head down," she ordered me.

Gritting my teeth, I grasped the stool in front of my knees. She flipped up my loincloth and spread my ass cheeks.

Cold. Slippery. It was almost enough to distract me from the sight before my eyes. There we both were, reflected in the polished copper base of a great pan that hung against a wall. Me kneeling precariously on the three-legged stool, with my breasts threatening to fall out of their meagre sling. The Elder

Witch standing behind me. Only… in the reflection she was no crooked and gangly hag. She was slim and straight and young, with a heart-shaped face and a great fell of golden hair in which stars sparkled. Her fine clothes glittered with dark gemstones.

I had no idea what to make of that, and my reflected face with its open O-shaped mouth revealed the confusion and dread I was feeling.

"Smaller," she said.

I didn't even have time to wonder what she meant, before something solid, the size of finger, slid smoothly into the clench of my ass and settled there, its flanged end protruding. I could feel the leather cord hanging down against my bare thigh.

"Bigger," she added.

And it grew inside me. I uttered a moan of fear as it swelled, filling and stretching my inner space. In a matter of seconds it was large enough to make it very obvious that there'd be no tugging this thing out. There'd be no forgetting it was there either. It filled my ass and my awareness. I was tethered, squirming, on my butt-plug.

"Shush, deary," she admonished. "You'll be glad of it soon enough."

I whimpered as my empty sex clenched in envy of its neighbouring passage, but I didn't dare complain. Gingerly I found my feet again, straightening up around the invader embedded within me. My lower lip trembled as I faced my captor. She cackled again and patted my breasts, almost fondly, before tickling my mons with her savage nails.

"Sit," she ordered.

"I can't," I whispered.

She didn't waste breath on me the second time. With one hand on either shoulder, she pushed my butt down onto the stool. The greased wooden plug sank deep into my hole, impaling me fully and finally. Shock slammed through my whole body like a tsunami and I screamed.

"There," she said. "Now, chop cabbage, deary. I will not be long."

Chapter Nine

Greedy Girl

"Tansy!" whispered Vince hoarsely. "Cut me free!" I blinked the tears from my eyes, feeling them run down over my cheeks, and looked over at the cage. Gail had pulled Vince's gag off and was curled up on his thighs, her arms around him. Still bound, he could not reciprocate her embrace.

I glanced at the cottage door through which the witch had vanished, but there was nothing but a ruddy light under the frame to suggest who or what was beyond. With infinite care, I eased myself to my feet. My whole body was glazed with sweat. The butt-plug felt like a fist in my ass, and every move I made inflicted fresh pangs of discomfort. The humiliation was exquisite too—worse, if possible, than the physical distress. There can be no dignity in having your asshole crammed to bursting. Especially if that's the tether holding you prisoner.

I approached the cage at a hobble, trailing my leash behind

me, just as Gail unfurled herself from Vince's lap and reached through the bars to me. I saw my tears mirrored in her glistening eyes as she caught my face and drew me to her lips, her kisses feverish. As I brushed her waist with my fingertips she shivered and whimpered against my tongue. I knew that every inch of her flesh must be burning from the birching. But the touch of her lips and her skin was sweet beyond words. I wanted so badly to hold her. I wanted to comfort, and be comforted.

"It's all right," I told her, in the face of all the evidence. "It's okay."

"Open the lock!" Vince hissed.

"The key's around her neck," I said, shaking my head. I didn't name the witch. She'd have heard that.

"Then cut these!" He shuffled himself so his bound wrists faced the bars, and I knelt with the bronze knife and sliced them free, laboriously slowly. I was afraid all the time that the Elder Witch would walk back through the door and find her housemaid slacking off from work, but for once my anxieties did not prove true. As soon as he could move, Vince reached out to Gail and caught her in his embrace. They kissed tenderly, his hands feathering over her scarred flanks with fear and eagerness.

I watched, aching, and moved even in my envy. I was on the outside of the cage, but I was less free than they were.

"What's going to happen to us?" Gail gasped into Vince's chest.

It was impossible to tell which of us she was addressing, and I didn't answer. *Fatten him up*. I knew Vince's intended fate. He looked round at me, hot-eyed.

"We're going to escape, aren't we?" he said. "Tansy, you know all about these things, don't you? Tansy will find a way, Gail. Don't you worry."

I nodded. What else could I do?

"Just don't eat anything she gives you," I warned them. My voice was ragged. "Throw it in the slop-bucket."

"Why not?"

"If you eat their food, you fall under their power. You might not make it home for hundreds of years."

Or ever...

I went back to my stool before they could question me further, and made myself sit down. It wasn't as bad second time around. While I chopped cabbage, Vince kissed Gail's hurting skin better—every inch, all over. It might sound like a strange reaction to their predicament, but I knew how much she craved his comfort, and how persuasive her hunger could be. She sighed and wriggled and shuddered against him, urging his hands into her wet places and his mouth to her bruised flesh until, by the time the Elder Witch returned, they were cuddled up on the straw together in an embrace so close and gentle, so absorbed in their intimacy, that I doubt they even noticed the witch's arrival.

She, in turn, merely glanced at them and sniggered. She dropped the contents of her skirt into the apron spread over my lap—onions and garlic, leeks and pea-shoots—and then, crushing one onion in her leathery fingers, grabbed me by the hair and rubbed them across my eyes. "Did I tell you to cut his hands loose, deary?" she asked. "No, I did not."

Having punished me that much, though, she seemed to lose interest in the subject.

So, streaming tears from my burning eyes, I chopped all the cabbage, made a cauldron full of stew, and set it on to boil. The hag sat herself down in a rocking chair next to the fire and took up her knitting—a shapeless grey thing that frankly looked like it was made out of hair acquired from roadkill—and while the food cooked and the other two lay helpless in a post-coital doze, she set me on to sweeping the floor and scouring the table and laying three places for dinner.

The places weren't for any of us. As soon as the soup was ready the Elder Witch dished herself up a bowlful and ate it in her rocking chair, smacking her lips and eyeing me.

"Tasty," she announced. "Would be even better with a little meat in it, but that will have to wait till we butcher at Samhain. Then we will have blood-sausage and chitterlings, deary."

I gritted my teeth and averted my gaze. Well, at least I knew that Vince had a few months. Samhain is the old name for Hallowe'en.

She offered me a wooden dishful of soup too, but I shook my head. I wasn't hungry, of course. Thirsty, yes. I wondered where she fetched the water from, and if that counted as enchanted.

"Suit yourself," she said and carried two bowls over to the cage, pushing them through the gap under the locked door, following them up with slabs of bread and cold dripping. "Eat up, dearies!" she urged.

I shook my head at them vehemently from behind her back and they took the dishes but didn't lift them to their lips. As the witch turned away I saw Gail tip hers into the shadows at the back of the cage.

Just then, as the last light faded from the chinks under the eaves, the cottage door was flung open and in marched three men. I say "men" only because they were naked and their rubbery cocks and balls swung about between their legs in such a blatant manner that it was hard not to stare. They were in no other way human in appearance. So much for the witch's description of her three sons as "each more handsome than the last." In fact, they were all astonishingly ugly. Their grey, lumpy flesh looked as if it were melting or rotting off their misshapen bones. One lacked a nose altogether and bore gaping holes in its face, the next had a nose that hung down to its chin, the third had a snout like a pig's. Tusks and horns sprouted in painful profusion. Web-footed, hunch-backed, sag-bellied, boss-eyed, hardly any two body parts symmetrical —they made trolls look decently natural.

I couldn't begin to guess what had fathered any of these mutated creatures upon the Elder Witch, but I was glad I'd never seen him. I slid back into the shadow of the fireplace angle, trying not to attract their notice.

"A fair evening, Mother!" the first cried in a rough, slurred voice.

"Welcome home to you!" she answered.

"The stars are out," said the second, drool bubbling from between its jagged fangs.

"The fire is lit," said she.

"Our bellies are empty," the third announced, each word accompanied by a wheezing whistle.

"The kettle boils," she told him, "and supper is ready."

The first was carrying a cluster of speckled fish roped together with twine through their gills. He handed this to his mother and the three lads limped and flopped onto the benches by the table.

"Quick, deary," she ordered me. "Fetch down the fish pan and the lard and fry these."

I had to come out into the firelight. The three sons stared and stamped their bare feet and made burbling noises.

"She's has a pretty mouth."

"She has pretty bubs."

"She has pretty hams."

"Wait, wait," the witch cackled. "First things first, my fine boys."

Averting my gaze, I set to frying the trout, glad they'd already been gutted. While I laid them out on the skillet, the Elder Witch served up huge steaming bowls of the cabbage soup to her children, and they fell to eating with an enthusiasm which might have been gratifying if the slurping and snorting and belching hadn't turned my stomach. I did my best not to watch. The fish went into the melting fat and I made myself busy poking them about with a wooden spoon. It made me jump when first one, then another trout opened its dead mouth and began to sing—a liquid warbling like the plaint of a blackbird. Soon all the fish were singing, and I could hear words:

> *Milk and meat*
> *And cunny sweet:*
> *One to suck,*
> *One pot-luck,*
> *One to fuck.*
> *What does the morrow bring?*
> *Fair winds, damsons ripe, the boar runs west -*

This we sing.

I tried smacking the fish on their nasty little heads, but it didn't make any difference. The song only stopped when they were thoroughly fried. By that time, the three pugly sons had eaten every scrap of the enormous stew.

"Serve them forth, deary," said the witch, who had gone back to her rocking chair and her knitting.

Gingerly, I heaved the big skillet from the fire onto the table boards. I was relieved that the boys were so greedy for the fish that they all but ignored me, merely pawing my ass a little as I came within reach, before snatching the trout hot from the pan. I retreated to the fireside.

"Bigger," said the witch in an undertone. Inside me, the butt-plug swelled, and I stifled a groan. I tried shifting my stance, but there was no relief and all I managed was a vain and ungainly wriggle which I couldn't hide.

"Smaller," she muttered, smiling to herself.

My chest heaved as relief swept over me.

"Bigger."

My eyes watered as I stifled a squeal.

So she carried on playing slyly with me, as the three lads sucked the flesh off the fish bones and watched my unwilling gyrations curiously. Oh, it was torture of the most peculiar sort. The expansion and contraction in my ass became like a dark wave rolling through me, or the pulse of a great, strange heart driving my blood. Its effect on the other parts of my body was not entirely unpredictable; and as my pussy woke and swelled, both the discomfort and the relief afterwards morphed into other sensations. I could feel the burning flush in my face, the sweat speckling my breastbone, the secret leak of dew onto my thighs. I clenched my fists, wanting to hold on to something but not able to grab anything. The lamplit room swam before my gaze. My breasts felt swollen and heavy and my clit burned.

At last they pushed the skillet aside and all three gave me their full attention. They had tiny, dark, soulless eyes just like their mother's.

"Is she ripe?"

"Is she ready?"

"Is she eager?"

"So, deary," she said, giving me a moment's respite. "Which of my fine sons do you think the most handsome?"

I bit the inside of my cheek. "How can I say?" I answered huskily. "They're equally good looking."

This caused the witch to nod sagely. "Which of my fine sons will you wed, deary? Which will you bear children to, and make of me a grandmother?"

I might not be able to think straight, but that was too horrible to contemplate.

"None. I can't choose between them," I said firmly. "I can't."

She nodded again, seeming to find my indecision perfectly natural. "Then tonight you should get to know them all better." And she gave me a push in the small of the back, sending me into the arms of the nearest.

He pulled me into his lap, facing outward. I didn't resist, but I shut my eyes for a moment just so I didn't have to see their leering faces. His thighs were hot and dry, more muscular beneath mine than I'd anticipated, and his hands surprised me by managing to bare my breasts without tearing me with those ragged nails. Eagerly he pawed at them, squeezing my flesh and hefting each orb before letting it drop, just for the pleasure of feeling them bounce. That didn't feel bad to me. My breasts ached for contact just as much as the rest of my body. When he plucked at my nipples I couldn't help wriggling in his lap, arching my back to follow his pull. Beneath me his cock swelled, jumping up to slap my open pussy. I looked down and saw his flushed knob end jutting out between my thighs, shiny and turgid, crowning a venous, inelegant length.

The two other brothers leaned in across the table. They couldn't reach my sex from where they sat, but they could lick and nuzzle at my breasts. God, that was foul. I didn't really want to see that bifurcated tongue coiling around my nipple, or those snaggley tusks threatening the swells of my flesh, so I pushed them feebly away, moaning in disgust. That only caused the first brother, the one in whose lap I sat, to grab my wrists and hold my hands up and out of the way, giving his siblings better access to my tits. I shut my eyes again.

I didn't have to see, but I couldn't help feeling—the slick wet slither of flesh, alternating between hot and cold with their breath; and the response of my nipples, swelling and hardening until they stood like glistening pink switches, flashing signals of pleasure through my body with each pass of a rasping tongue.

I tried to stifle my moans, but I couldn't.

"Bigger," said the witch. Once again the butt-plug swelled within me, but this time it wasn't remotely uncomfortable. My ass seemed to welcome the prodigious girth, sucking it in deeper, squeezing the hard contours in a grip like greased velvet. My gasp became a high keen of need and I jerked wildly.

"What's this?" the first brother asked, probing between my ass cheeks with his lumpy fingers to find the source of my distress. "Is she filled already?"

"Is she burning?"

"Is she ready to spend?"

"I prepared her for you, my fine boy," said the witch. "She had to be stretched."

He gripped the leather right up next to the butt-plug and gave the thing an experimental wiggle. It was too much for me —that implacable bulk in my anus, and the two mouths sucking wetly on my breasts. Orgasm ignited in my ass and flared outward like a corona of fire, consuming me from bottom to top. My shriek would have woken the dead. The boys drew back from my scratched and throbbing tits.

"Smaller," said the witch. And as I hung limply from one of his meaty paws, her lad drew the plug out of my ass. I felt the lack of it like a terrible loss, as my sphincter spasmed in pulses, clenching vainly around the O of empty air left behind. But not for long. With a heave and a push, the witch-child positioned his erect cock at my gape and filled me again.

She was right. I felt a keen pang of gratitude at that moment to the Bour Lady, who'd stretched my ass so inexorably and greased me up to hell and back. Otherwise that gnarled and twisted member would never had slid into its sheath with such ease. I'd never have welcomed the violation so warmly. The challenge was still considerable, but I'd never have groaned "Yes!" as he took me by the hips and began to jog me up and down in his broad lap, impaling me deeper with every thrust, if I hadn't been made ready for him.

The other two stood and came round the table, staring. I looked up into their grotesque faces, tears of disgust and gratitude running down my own, and they stroked my wet cheeks curiously before patting my breasts. Their own cocks, as twisted as driftwood, stood erect over their bulging ball-sacs, and they took my hands and tried to get me to grip and stroke those misshapen members, but honestly, I had no strength left. I only fumbled feebly as they pressed my palms to their stiff tools. I couldn't even look at them properly, because every particle of my will was bent to dealing with the invasion of my ass. Their brother grunted and huffed in my ear, paying no more respect to their wishes than he did to mine. Clearly they'd have to wait until he was done with me.

But they didn't wait. They were too impatient for that. With a growl of irritation, they moved simultaneously to push his shoulders and tip him backward from the bench onto the floor. He sounded like a sack of potatoes falling—but he hardly seemed to notice. He kept on jerking his hips, working his cock in my butt. As for me, landing on top of him, my fall was comfortably cushioned by the monster's belly and chest behind me. The monster's cock deep in my asshole was more than enough to worry about.

Or so I thought, until one of the other brothers took my ankles and spread my legs up and apart, lifting my knees to my chest and opening my pussy like a split oyster. As he leaned over, drool ran out of his nightmare of a mouth and splashed onto my tits, and I sobbed.

God knows, I hadn't shown much sense of pickiness in my sexual partners recently. I hadn't cared what they looked like or how they acted, so long as they had cock to fill my ravenous holes. I'd fucked a troll, for heaven's sake. But a troll is only reptilian. Not truly ugly, just bestial. Lying there with one twisted cock up my ass and another angling toward my cunt, I was acutely aware that these three were worse than inhuman. They were grotesque mockeries of men. In their repulsive grip I could see myself in a contrast so extreme it was offensive. My sweet, fragile flesh under the clutch of their leprous-looking hands, and overwhelmed by their massive, shapeless bulks. My smooth curves abraded by their rough and callused hides. My soft vulnerability beneath those savage teeth and yellowed claws. It was wrong, it was wrong, it was wrong. And as the second brother pushed into my cunt and the third squatted over my face—his dripping, knobbly prick pressing into my open mouth and his hairless balls flopping down and filling my eye-sockets to blind me—I felt the sheer obscenity of it take possession of my soul and pitch me into an orgasm like a whirling darkness.

And I kept coming. Whilst they fucked; all three of them clustered around me, humping, like a ball of toads at spawning time. I kept coming. The friction of those two huge cocks squeezing into my ass and cunt, sliding over each other, sent me crazy. The pressure of a dick surging down my throat, making me fight for each breath; the heat and the constraint and the horror of it, and the awareness of my own beauty and defilement at the core of it all, the *cause* of it all—it made me spark off like chain lightning.

All the time, the Elder Witch sat there rocking and nodding happily and clicking away at her knitting.

And when they came, squirting their glutinous spunk deep into my ass and pussy and mouth and filling me until it overflowed and gushed out, I swallowed as much as I could and choked and thrashed and came again. Ashamed. Defiled. And loving it.

Even as they left me, sobbing and soaked in jizz, on that rag rug, I still loved it.

❧ ❧ ❧

I don't know how long we were in the house of the Elder Tree Witch. The days there seemed to melt into one another. Every morning I'd rise and do my chores: sweep the ashes from the fire, clean the straw from the cage, and take the quilts from the Bour Lady's bed outside to beat and hang over branches to air. I drew water from the well—thank goodness there was something safe for me to drink—and chopped kindling and scrubbed the dishes and made another vat of cabbage soup. She never wanted any other recipe. I fed the hens and the cocks. The work was long and physically demanding. The muscles on my arms grew hard, and I could see them moving under the freckles of my forearms.

Every morning, without fail, the Elder Witch would find me as I worked outdoors, and she'd bend me face down over the kerb of the well and fuck me with the wooden strap-on. Braced across the gap with my arms trembling with strain, staring into the darkness below and the shimmering circle of reflected water, I got to feel like I was looking into my own cunt—always wet, always yawning open. My cries would echo up out of the shaft in a wild and mournful clamour.

Every day the witch would anoint Gail's breasts with more of that salve, then sit and comb out the frightful thicket of her own hair with her long nails, whilst gazing into a silver hand-mirror and muttering to herself. Then she'd go out for a few hours. I think she saw things in that mirror. Far away things. I managed to walk behind her and get a peek once or twice, but all I glimpsed was her inexplicably altered reflection—as beautiful in the glass as she was ugly in person.

Every evening the three sons would arrive just as the sun set, bearing their fishes. And every evening they'd fuck me into trembling, limbless ruination before leaving again, to go who knows where. There was almost no change to the pattern. Their greeting to their mother, the conversation, the singing fish—all of it was repeated exactly as the day before. I've known human beings who like their routine and repeat the same old stories again and again, but this was on another scale altogether. Them There are not the same as us.

The only real variation came in the song of the frying fishes. That one line, where they predicted what the morrow would bring, changed with the weather and the creep of the season. And the sex varied too, but that was because I was involved and, I guess, humans are agents of chaos in this otherworldly realm. It always ended up the same way, though: with me broken and sobbing and ecstatic.

So after the first few days it became harder to differentiate my memories. Although I remember clearly our second day in cottage. That was when something very strange happened to Gail.

I was woken in the morning by the sound of Gail's voice, calling my name softly and fearfully. I crawled out of my bed —I'd been given a blanket on the rug before the fire, as if I were a dog—and rose dizzily, feeling my way to the cage through the shadowy room. The dim light creeping under the door and eaves told me that it was morning, and the sound of the witch snoring in her bed up the rickety staircase overhead told me that it was early. Gail crouched against the bars, reaching through to me. I grabbed her hands and kissed her hot lips, tasting salt on them. Her face was wet with tears.

"Tansy! What's happening to me?" she whispered, clutching at my face.

I had no idea what she meant. I looked for Vince, but he was lying asleep, a dark bulk against the straw. I was still trying to collect myself from my ordeal the night before. I'd fallen asleep almost immediately after my ravishing and I was still crusted with dried cum, and thick-headed with confusion. I knew Gail and Vince had watched, helpless, as I'd been forced to take those three cocks simultaneously. I knew they'd witnessed my shame, and my eager submission to that vile degradation.

"What's wrong?" I whispered, stroking her arms. "Gail?"

"They hurt!" It came out as a sob.

She drew my hands down and I found the source of her torment. Her breasts—her beautiful little breasts, so soft and tantalising and delicate normally—were burning hot and swollen to twice their normal size, standing out from her ribs like over-ripe fruit. I ran my hands over her nipples and found them thick and turgid, as if they'd been stung by some venomous creature.

My first thought was that the birch-whip scratches had become infected overnight. But her skin was unmarked, as flawless now as it had been before the whipping started—just as my own flesh, come to think of it, was neither bruised nor abraded by the trials of the previous evening. My second thought was a horrible suspicion of the salve I'd seen the witch rub into my cousin's tender flesh.

"Oh! Your hands are so cool!" she breathed gratefully. "What's happened to me, Tansy!"

"Shush," I said, stroking her hot orbs as gently and soothingly as I could. "Oh, you poor thing!"

"They feel like—Oh!"

Her gasp nearly woke Vince; he jerked and grumbled in his sleep. I felt wet under my palm, a hot trickle spurting over my fingers. I lifted my hand to make sure it wasn't blood. It wasn't. White droplets.

"Oh fuck," I muttered. It was running down in tiny rivulets from her right nipple, pale against her flushed skin.

"What?" She caught at her breast and a jet actually spurted onto me. "What!"

"Milk," I said, feeling stunned. "The witch has made you start to give milk."

Gail made a noise that was a bit like a laugh but mostly hysteria.

"Look," I said. I didn't have any experience of the subject but I remembered stuff I'd read. "I think… if you draw it out it'll stop hurting. You're just full."

"Full!"

There was a wretched, incoherent, pointless exchange of words after that, but she took the advice in the end. I helped her, massaging her breasts until both were running and there was milk all over my hands, while she clung to the bars and wept quietly with confusion and embarrassment. But we stopped when we heard the heavy unmistakeable tread on the stairs. We both looked around, wide-eyed.

That was how the witch found us when she came down—

kneeling face to face through the cage bars, my hands cupping Gail's oozing tits.

"Started already, has she?" the witch asked, smiling broadly. "That's good, deary. Now I shall have posset for breakfast."

She went to a small barrel under the stairs and twisted a spigot to release a stream of brown liquid into a wooden bowl. When she brought it over, Gail and I both shrank back.

"Come here, deary," she told my cousin, fixing her with a gimlet eye. "Let's see those dugs of yours."

A yeasty, familiar scent rose from the bowl in her hand: home-brewed beer.

"Do what she says," I whispered, as Gail looked anxiously at me.

Reluctantly Gail came forward. The witch got her to stand with her breasts jutting out either side of a bar, and took one in a huge, firm hand. Gripping the nipple between thumb and finger she squeezed, drawing down the milk in a smooth jet that hissed into the beer bowl. Gail moaned, closing her eyes.

I felt her shame, and her surrender. I hated it, and hated more the strange sick way it aroused me.

"That's right, deary. That's what you need, isn't it? You'll feel much better when I've done."

In a very few minutes, she expertly milked both of Gail's breasts dry. The two liquids made a disgusting-looking froth where they mixed, and the milk seemed to curdle in the beer. But the Elder Witch lifted the bowl to her mouth and drank it down, smacking her lips when she finished.

"Want the dregs, deary?" she asked me, holding out the bowl.

There was about a half-cup of slop left. I shook my head frantically.

"Then get you out the back door and draw water from the well. You've last night's pots to wash for a start."

That was how I discovered the back door to the cottage, tucked behind a partition half-wall, and the well in the clearing outside, and the wood pile and the chicken house. And the routine with the strap-on dildo, that was to be mine every morning.

That was when I discovered, too, that my leash had the miraculous property of being as long or as short as necessary, provided I didn't go more than fifty paces from the house. After that it locked tight, and swelled warningly in my ass. You can bet I tried the "smaller" command… but I just didn't have the witch's knack.

It was a tough start. Five hours later I was carrying the skillet—scoured now and ready for the evening—back indoors to hang up by the fireplace, when without warning my legs folded under me and I slid with a thump to the rug, the room spinning around me. My arms felt like lead. I'd had nothing to eat for at least a day, apart from several mouthfuls of cum, and my diet had been pretty inadequate before that. I wasn't hungry—I was never hungry anymore—but I was getting weaker. I shook my head, trying to clear it, suddenly scared.

"Tansy!" Gail called softly.

I looked around. The Elder Witch had gone out again, on whatever errand it was that witches might run. I crawled unsteadily over to the cage and forced myself to stand.

"Come here," she said, pressing herself to the bars and reaching for me.

I let myself lean against her, finding comfort in the embrace and the sweet milky scent of her skin. I was taken aback, though, when she pulled at my arms, urging me down again, lifting a breast in one cupped hand like an offering.

"You what?" I mumbled, my brain fogged with exhaustion.

"Go on. You have to have something… to eat."

"I…" My jaw dropped.

Conflicting emotions crashed in my chest. Disgust was one of them. This was my cousin whose body had been hijacked, who was being used as a milch-cow. It was appalling. Her body, so familiar to me, was only half-recognisable now. I knew her sweet, small breasts so well—like honey-coloured flowers, hardly a handful each. Not these fat, turgid globes, swaying under their own weight, her nipples dark and staring. It was horrible to see the change in her—but weirdly fascinating too. They were so sexualised, in a disturbing way; exaggerated caricatures of her pretty little tits. I couldn't keep my eyes off them. My hands itched to touch them, and my mouth burned to kiss and suck those big nipples.

"Come on," she urged, her eyes pleading.

Still I hesitated. She had to pull my head to her breast before I licked nervously at her nipple.

Beads of milk sprang up from the point of her tit. The sight took my breath and my sense away. Instinctively, I latched on to suck.

Oh, she tasted sweet. Sweet and creamy and warm. Far more delicious than my protein shakes, more comforting than semen. She filled my mouth with blissful richness, and as I nursed I felt her fingers stroke my hair and I heard her make soft, throaty noises of pleasure. I soon realised she was enjoying this intensely. I mean, like most women I love having my tits sucked, but for Gail now the sensation was clearly heightened by her condition. Off the scale, judging by undulation of her hips.

"Tansy, touch me," she whispered.

So I snuck a hand through the bars and cupped her soft little pussy, and she settled into my palm with a sigh. It didn't take my fingers more than a moment to discover how wet she was.

Our mutual bliss didn't last long, though—I felt her sex wrenched from my grasp and a jolt run through her frame. I pulled back, eyes flashing open, to see Vince standing behind her. My cheeks flared scarlet, as I realised how perverted the exchange he'd witnessed between the two of us must seem.

But Vince didn't seem to be upset at all. He was too busy tugging down his trousers and shoving his stiff cock into Gail, without preamble or foreplay.

"What the hell?" I croaked.

Wordlessly, balls-deep in his girlfriend's pussy, Vince gave me a dazed smile.

Gail looked over her shoulder at him. "I'm sorry, Tansy. He's been like this all day. Since he…"

"What?"

Gail exhaled, panting as she adjusting to his penetration.

"She gave us one of those fish to eat. While you were outside. I'm sorry," she repeated.

"I told you not to…"

"We're hungry! We're not like you—we can't just starve!"

My anger died, swallowed in despair.

"Did *you* eat any?" I asked, looking at the way her hips were gyrating and her flushed cheek was pressed against a bar. At her half-closed eyes and parted lips.

"Just a… little bit," she admitted, distracted by what Vince was doing to her from behind. "Oh God, yes. Oh… Oh… Please Tansy, suck my tits!"

There wasn't much else I could do. I had no heart to tell her off, and I think Vince was beyond hearing me. So I reverted to her breasts and captured the other stiff nipple between my lips and drank, while he circled his hips and fucked her, deep and slow and dreamy. Gail let go then and just dissolved into her joy. And I reached through the bars to stroke her pussy and cup his balls, feeling the unhurried slide of his cock in and out of her. All my churning agitation settled gradually. It might have been only resignation, but just for that moment it felt like peace.

She came with a beatific sigh.

"Gail," I said as she slid to the bottom of the cage, wrapped in Vince's arms. "Thank you."

She looked up at me and giggled. Her pupils were so dilated that her eyes looked black.

"I'll get us out of here," I promised.

She giggled again. "No worries."

No worries? I clenched my teeth. "Vince, look after her."

He nibbled at her ear lobe, and gave no sign he'd heard me at all.

Chapter Ten

The Wild Hunt

They both stopped talking altogether, over the next few days. I watched as the food took its effect, understanding fully for the first time the traditional dire warnings against eating and drinking while in the realm of the Fair Folk. For Gail and Vince, past and future vanished. For them there was nothing but a Now of appetite and urges, and fulfilment of those urges. They fucked and ate and slept, and that was all they seemed to want. I watched with a sense of increasing isolation as their mental fires shrank to a faint glow. To be sure, they seemed perfectly content. It was hard to feel sorry for them, as I witnessed their incessant giggling and rutting and caresses. They'd reverted to a state of animal contentment, doped on sex. I felt a bit jealous, to be honest.

And very lonely.

I should have been planning our escape, I know. My mind was still clear, or as clear as anyone living on cum and breast-milk and a curse can expect. I should have been caching weapons or searching the witch's spell-book—which was handwritten in Latin, by the way, which I can't translate—for one to use against her. But without Gail and Vince to talk to I felt adrift; responsible but powerless. I couldn't think where to start. The work and the sex kept me too busy to plot. I watched and waited, and that was all.

Okay, I'll admit it. Having that hard wooden bulb up my ass all day and night might have... made me more docile, somehow.

It was difficult to see where we might escape to, even if I could devise some means of breaking us out. There were no windows to the cottage, which was lit by oil-lamps, but there were two doors, front and back. When I went out the front door I could see that the house stood just above the barren beach of a huge river, or possibly some inlet of the sea. The sand was striped in shoals of rust and coal-dust, and a landscape of bare rock and burnt dead trees stretched up and down the shore. Overhead, the sky was racked with hurrying clouds that threatened thunderous downpours but never shed a drop. But worst of all was the water: bright red, and the banks clotted with black matter. I couldn't get close to the river, but it looked a lot like blood to me.

If this was some warped version of the River Severn, I didn't even know which side of it the cottage stood upon. The far shore looked miles away, far beyond reach.

Out here was what looked like a stone well, too, mirroring the one at the back of the cottage. But this one was capped by a heavy slab. Also, I don't know what a well would be doing on the top of a rise above a beach. I could sometimes hear scratching noises coming from the underside of the great stone, which meant I didn't want to investigate any more closely. There was a small wooden shack out the front too, a hen-house of sorts. But the hens were dead. I don't mean they weren't moving. They shuffled around, little bundles of bare bones and ragged staring feathers, their blind skulls cocked from side to side. I had to go out each morning and throw them handfuls of grit and ashes and bone chippings from a pot the witch kept behind the door. They pecked assiduously at this offering, though the lumps fell straight through their empty carcasses and onto the ground.

I've heard that headless chickens can run around for a little while, but that weirded the hell out of me. I didn't like the front door view much.

If I walked out of the back door, the scenery was completely different. From this side, the cottage stood in a pretty woodland glade, surrounded by gently rolling land that cut off any view except narrow glimpses of the sky. The weather changed from day to day, and the trees moved gradually from summer green to the first tints of autumn. This side looked natural. The well was just a wet hole in the ground. The hens were just hens.

The cocks however…

The cocks didn't live in the chicken hut. And they weren't the sort with feathers and beaks either. They were kept upstairs, indoors, in a long box under the Elder Witch's bed. One of my daily tasks was to get them out and feed them milk and milled oats. The first time I saw them I didn't even recognise what they were—I took them for a dozen enormous fat slugs in various shades of pink and dun and brown, all nestled down in their hay bedding. But when, under orders, I picked one up, I found it warm and dry and velvety. It certainly squirmed in my hand like a slug, but no slug ever had two hairy bollocks hanging from its back end.

I nearly flung it down, I was so shocked. Though I shouldn't have been surprised, really. Stealing penises and keeping them under the bed was *exactly* the sort of thing medieval witches were accused of by the more crazy priests.

Anyway, once I'd got used to them, I actually found the cocks sort of sweet. My initial worry was what they'd look like at their bases—the point of severance from the body, as it were —but the flesh was as smooth and seamless there as though they'd never been appendages, and had always been individual creatures in their own right. They wore little leather thongs looped around their shafts just before the scrotum, like miniature dog-leashes, and they slurped oat crumbs and milk through their tiny mouths, nuzzling my fingers for more. They dearly loved to be stroked. If I held them and petted them, they'd go still and start to swell up, stiffening—but do that too long and they'd spill their oats again, so I had to be careful as I played with them. I've got no idea what sort of sensory apparatus they had, but they moved like caterpillars, and if I put them down on the floor or my knee they'd make a bee-line straight for my pussy, humping along with a blind, dogged determination. If I snuggled them between my breasts they'd arch and slap themselves up and down like they were having some sort of ecstatic fit.

The leather thonging, I discovered, was there to pull them out of my cunt again once they'd squirmed inside. They *really* didn't want to leave. It was bizarre and kind of cute to see two or more of them wrestling for access, butting each other out of the way.

See—it wasn't all work.

So that was how I spent my days as scullion to the Elder Tree Witch. Until one night the fishes' song gave a prediction I'd never heard before:

What does the morrow bring?
Golden sun, blackberries ripen, the Brenin rides by -
This we sing.

Neither the witch nor her sons remarked on the forecast at the time, but the next day I was out at the front of the cottage, feeding the dead chickens and trying not to think about the filled molar I'd found in the pot of ashes, when I heard a bestial snort behind me and I looked round. And there he was.

I really don't see how he'd managed to sneak up on me, riding a big horse like that. It was a black stallion, with an arched neck and a mane like rough silk that was hung with tiny silver bells. The Brenin was dressed entirely in black too —a hodgepodge of fashion stolen from history. Mr. Darcy boots, a long Victorian riding coat, biker leathers on his legs and a belted medieval shirt embroidered down the front—all topped off with a black half-mask in the form of a skull. Behind the skull's eye-sockets his eyes glinted. His hair was a dead white and it hung down as far as his elbows, while his skin, where it showed, was the colour of long-buried bone. Frankly, he looked like a manga villain, and he should have been risible anywhere outside of a convention auditorium… but he wasn't. I could feel reality crinkling up around him, like cellophane exposed to heat.

As I stared, the horse reached down, snatched up one of

the chickens and ate it, dry bones and dusty feathers crunching in its teeth with a noise like a packet of crisps.

"Bour Lady," I said through dry lips. I didn't dare raise my voice. But I didn't have to. She stepped out from the cottage and strode toward the rider, wiping her hands on her apron.

"Oh, Brenin! Such an honour you pay me! Are you hunting today?"

He switched his attention to her, his thin lips twitching in a smile. "My Hounds rest at the moment, Grandmother. They've run hard this morning and we've already taken down two hinds. I thought I'd call in at the house of my favourite beldame and see how she is keeping."

I noted that the moment he opened his mouth, the rest of the chickens bolted back into their ruined hut, though there was nothing unpleasant about his voice that I could discern. It was a cool, dry, well-spoken voice, and it somehow made me think he was used to giving orders.

"Well! I am well!" she cackled merrily, practically dancing on the spot. "These old bones are still strong. You must stop a while and break bread with me."

"Willingly, Grandmother."

"Quick, skivvy!"

She signalled to me and I came nervously around the front of the horse to join her. The animal snorted at me in a disparaging way and pawed the rock with a silver-shod hoof, the bells strung in its mane making a shivery noise.

"On your elbows and knees," she commanded me, nodding at a spot below the Brenin's boot. "So that my lord may alight."

Nervous though I was, disobedience didn't even occur to

me. I was well-trained by this point. I put down my pot of grit and sank into position as a mounting block for him, bracing my back. His booted foot was hard and he didn't spare me his weight. I let out a little gasp of relief as his feet finally struck the dirt.

"Will you have beer, my Brenin? Wine? Milk?"

"Wine. But first I would relieve myself after the ride."

"Of course. Skivvy!"

I knelt up. At first I didn't realise what was expected of me. She signalled impatiently for me to face the Brenin, with his high boots and long legs. I noticed he wore a knife at his belt and the hollow horn of a ram, chased in gold, and that he had a riding crop with a thick stock thrust into his left boot. He was popping the crotch studs of his leathers.

"Open your mouth, girl!" the witch screeched.

A blowjob? That was no hardship, I thought. He was hot in his creepy way, and he'd make a welcome change from the three grotesque witch-spawn. As he revealed a smooth cock, full and curved but not yet erect, I licked my lips expectantly and set them in a welcoming pout.

"Open! You want him to piss all over your face?"

My eyes widened as realisation hit me. My heart clenched and blood rushed to my face, masking my freckles. After everything that had happened to me, everything I'd submitted to, I still found it hard to believe anyone could expect *this*. It made me feel dizzy. I felt a twinge between my legs too: shock manifesting as arousal. I looked up into his face, as he stepped in and I opened my mouth. He smelled of saffron, and rain upon dust, and his expression was unreadable. But he must have felt my involuntary tremble as, taking my jaw in his hand, he fed his elegant ivory cock between my lips and over my tongue, and set his legs a little apart.

I took his cock as far back in my mouth as I could, telling myself it was no different than necking a pint of beer, and the further back the less I would taste it. I was sort of right. Except it was hot. And not beer. In fact it tasted like honey—one of those strong, dark honeys collected from arid pine forests. As the flood commenced, tears brimmed in my eyes, making his form waver above me. I'd been pissed on by those two cops— long ago it seemed now—but never pissed *in*. Never reduced to such humiliation on such an intimate and primal level. I couldn't breathe, he filled my throat so. And my belly. I couldn't do anything but open my throat and swallow it all down, and it seemed to take him forever to empty his bladder. His fingers were cool where they held me, cool where they brushed the hair back from my face so he could watch my eyes. I couldn't hide from him the emotions that battered me —the revulsion, the abject submission, the desperate desire to perform well, my slowly growing panic as my air ran out. I was going to gag soon. I was going to choke and wrench away. I would end up with his hot spray all over my face, as he held my hair to keep me in place—and the thought set me burning.

At the very last moment, just before fear became reality, the Brenin pulled out. Not all the way, but enough for me to snatch a gasp of air. And to recognise part of the cause of my distress. His cock was no longer entirely soft and slender, but pumped fat with arousal. He used it in a thorough exploration of my mouth, making sure I tasted the dregs before he released me properly at last. I was crying properly now, salt tears running down and mixing with the bitter-sweet drops on my lips as I licked them.

I could no longer look up at his face.

"I like her." He stroked his cock idly and it bounced to full erection between his long fingers. "Those eyebrows—even her lashes—they're like flame. She's a rarity. And she's very receptive."

"Yes, she is. Try her cunny, my Brenin, if it pleases you. '

"I'll have her rear entrance, for preference."

"Of course. It will be quite ready for you." The witch's voice changed to one of command. "Smaller."

Grasping the long leather rope, she pulled the shrunken butt-plug from my anus with no effort at all.

He pulled the riding crop from his boot, wielding it in the hand that was not busy caressing his stiff shaft. The whip, roughly rounded in cross-section, was much thicker than a modern one, though it tapered to a springy point. I had a nasty feeling it was made from some sort of dried animal pizzle. Contemplatively, he poked and slapped at my breasts, the muted sting exciting my nipples to points.

"Face down," he said. "Grip your ankles."

I obeyed, lowering my face and shoulders to the ground and reaching behind me to grip my calves. My ass was exhibited upward, pointing into the air. The Brenin walked round behind me, flicked my skirt up with his whip and surveyed the view presented. I could feel my asshole, pliant and open, oozing grease where the butt-plug had been pulled from it. He set the narrow end of his crop across the hole, pressing slightly. My sphincter fluttered, dilating. He tapped it softly then with the very point of the crop, and I felt my anus spasm, ripples of pleasure flaring out across my ass.

"Very good," he breathed. Crouching down behind me, he fed the thick head of his cock into my waiting hole. "You may speak," he told me indulgently, as he impaled my ass.

I didn't speak. But I made plenty of uncouth noises as he rode me. The greased butt-plug had left me dilated, and slippery as hell, and in dire need of stimulation. He gave me that in abundance. His gave me a thorough rodding with that long cock of his, opening me up far deeper than the butt-plug had done, every thrust sending an aching wave of sensation right through my body until even my fingertips tingled. I didn't dare let go of my ankles and touch my clit, so I just had to ride out each internal spasm. But the discomfort of his bulk only enhanced my arousal. My groans were heartfelt and uninhibited. I felt every plunge of his cock inside my ass. I felt his balls slapping against me. I felt orgasm swelling in my bowels where it had no right to be. And I felt his fingertips on the small of my back, aggravatingly light—until the moment he dug his nails in, which is when I screeched like a cat getting fucked on the rooftop by her tom. His cock swelled then, stretching me further. I knew he was about to erupt. I couldn't stop from coming myself, my cheek grinding into the gritty rock and my ass bucking to meet him. All pain gone, all shame gone, all Tansy gone—nothing left of me but an open gaping ass, begging to be filled.

He did that.

Then he paused for breath, still rooted deep inside me. My anus clenched and spasmed around his shaft as my involuntary muscles danced. I could feel sand crusted on my open lips. I could feel my hips and knees cramping from contortion and strain.

"Good," he said, reaching out to grasp my hair and twist it round his fingers. "Go again."

One good hard tug, pulling my hair back, and I was off again up another gathering wave of arousal. He'd just ejaculated, but he was as hard and big as ever. His appetite was punishing, his stamina relentless. Again and again he sank his shaft into me, though my ass was already so full of his copious spunk that I felt it squirt out and splash over my spread cheeks.

This time I swore and cursed him and begged for mercy— and in truth I meant *Please don't stop. Please fuck my ass. Please make me come again.*

He showed me mercy. Then he pulled his cock out and hosed a second hot blast of his silky semen over my back and ass and pussy.

I didn't collapse. I wasn't actually capable of that much movement. Knelt there, bottom-up, I felt like I'd never shift again. The feel of his cream tickling down my bare skin made me whimper.

"She's a good fit," the Brenin said, standing.

"Well, my sons have been working her diligently, Brenin."

"Where did you get her?"

"She came to me. Three of them, together."

"Three women?"

"Two ewes, one tup. And a fine haunch of meat for winter salting, he is."

"Would you sell her to me?"

"Ah. My sons are each set upon marrying the girl, so fond are they of her. It would break their hearts, my Brenin. And she is no bad maidservant either."

"Then I will compensate you well for your loss."

"You are forever generous. Perhaps you'd like to see the other girl too? A pretty fair-haired little milkmaid... much to your taste, I imagine."

I pushed myself up on quivering arms, bracing my palms on the ground.

"That sounds intriguing, Grandmother."

"She's a real beauty. Perhaps you'll prefer her."

"Perhaps I'll want both. Let us discuss the price of this one."

"Skivvy," she said to me. "Go fetch the golden-hair and bring her out for my lord the Brenin." She took the key from about her neck and held it out.

I think my heart stopped beating.

"Hurry up!" she snapped.

Hauling my protesting body into an upright stance, I took the twined leather from her hand without a word and hurried away obediently toward the cottage door. Although I couldn't help looking back as I ducked under the lintel. It seemed that negotiations were already underway—and that even witches get careless when they're feeling horny. He had her face down over a rock, her skirts flung up over her back, and he was rooting the foul old baggage with some vigour.

Jeez, I sincerely hope that when he called her "Grandmother" it was just an honorific title. But then, I wouldn't put anything past them.

Once inside the house I nearly fell over the rug in my eagerness to get to the cage door. I had the key, and for the first time I was not tethered. This might be our only chance. I jiggled bronze against bronze, feeling the unseen teeth catch and give way, and then yanked the door open. Gail looked out at me with a woozy smile, from where she sat astride Vince's face. I could see his tongue-tip stirring the ruby of her swollen clit.

"Come on!" I hissed, grabbing her by the wrist and wrenching her out into my arms. "We have to go! Now! Out the back!"

Ignoring her squeaks of protest I pushed her toward the rear door of the cottage and turned back to the cage. Vince was on his feet, looking me up and down with a big dirty grin. I can say with some confidence that escape was not what was on his mind.

"Out you get, big boy," I whispered, beckoning. "If you want to come, you'll have to keep up."

Vince obeyed, his bobbing erection pointing the way. I paused en-route to snatch up the birch hearth-brush and the Bour Lady's hand-mirror, before hustling Gail out of the back door. Listen: I've read a lot of folk stories about fleeing from witches. I know how it goes. It's all there in Grimms' Tales. Right now we were up to our eyeballs in a story of the nastiest kind, and I could only hope I'd guessed correctly at the rules of the plot.

"Run," I told Gail as soon as we emerged into the woodland glade. "Run and don't stop."

Like she's ever obedient. She twisted in my grasp, looking back for Vince, who'd just emerged, blinking in the golden daylight. He swaggered up to us, buffing his erection through his loose pants. I brandished the birch bundle and flicked it warningly against his bare chest.

"Vince, if we don't run she's going to kill you. Real soon

266

now."

His smile faded to a look of puzzlement, as if I were speaking a foreign language he could only understand a few words of. He tilted his head. I couldn't wait any longer. Dragging Gail, I set off.

"Run!" I growled.

We ran. I'm not saying we were particularly fast—Vince and Gail hadn't been out of the cage in weeks and had had no exercise except for sex. And the three of us were barefoot. But I didn't let them stop. I towed Gail when she slowed down, and Vince—thank goodness he seemed to have some inkling that flight was more urgent than fucking—took his turn too. When the going got really difficult, I used the birch whip to drive her on. God, I'm a mean bitch when I have to be. She squealed in protest and resentment, but she got to her feet and kept moving.

The forest went on forever, it seemed. I had no idea which direction we were going or where we wanted to head, but away from that cottage seemed a good thing. The woods were fairly open but the ground rose and fell—mile after mile of undulating valleys and little streams and yellowing trees. Fantastic for an afternoon ramble, but not so great when you don't have a map and a thermos of hot chocolate and a car waiting at the end of the hike. There were no roads and no landmarks. Well, we saw a stone tower through the tree-tops once, but we cut away to avoid that. When has an ancient, windowless stone tower in a forest ever boded anything good?

When we couldn't run any more, we walked. On and on. Our legs scratched, our feet bruised and our stomachs empty.

Then I heard the witch scream with rage.

My blood went cold. The voice was faint and distant, but I didn't doubt it was hers. I pulled the heavy key from where it hung around my neck, and lobbed it behind us into the leaf litter. At the very least, I thought, she wouldn't be able to cage us again.

The key morphed and grew, its metal flowing. In moments it stretched clear across the valley behind us, right up the slopes and over the rises to either side—a featureless wall of dull bronze. It was so tall that it disappeared behind the tree tops. It was so broad that I couldn't see where it ended. It stood between us and pursuit.

See, a Masters in comparative folklore does have its uses.

We pressed on.

An hour later I heard the witch howl again. This time I threw down her hand-mirror. It became a huge silvery mere that stretched from horizon to horizon. Maybe she would drown as she tried to cross, I thought.

She didn't.

The third time—and by now we were so exhausted that Vince was holding Gail up on her feet—I threw away the hearth-brush. It became a thicket of wicked thorns, each as long as my hand. We didn't run any more when we saw that. If it wasn't enough to stop the Elder Witch, I figured we had no more chances. Three times is the charm.

She hit the thicket like a charging rhino. I heard the crash and the scream, and she kept screaming as she dragged herself deeper and deeper into the barbed-wire entanglement. She must have been beside herself with fury. Eventually we could actually see her pushing through the branches; a dense black mass emerging through the crackling, creaking thorns.

Then she stopped. She didn't fall. The thorns on which she was impaled held her up. She just let out a long breath, a faint wail dying on it, and hung there. There was no sound after that but the drip-drip of her blood on the leaves below.

I sat down then, for a long time.

🐦 🐦 🐦

"Tansy!"

The moan caused me to jerk my head up from my knees and the cradle of my arms, and I realised I'd actually dozed off. The light was ripening toward evening. The first thing I did was look over at the wall of thorns. The witch's body was still there—sort of. There wasn't much left of her big black bulk now but a tangle of dead twigs and cobwebs and withered leaves, like an old rooks' nest. Her flesh had reverted to the material of the woods.

"Tansy!"

I realised that it was Gail speaking, though she hadn't said my name in days or weeks. I looked round. She was standing with her back against a tree bole, her hands pressed beneath her breasts, and she was crying. As I scrambled to my feet I saw that her breasts were leaking—big dark stains spreading across the undyed cloth that covered them.

"It's okay," I said, sinking to one knee before her and pushing aside the fabric to bare her nipples.

She was hot and full to bursting once again.

"Don't worry, it's all right," I murmured, as Vince joined me.

Gently I took the tip of her right tit into my mouth and began to suck, just as Vince nuzzled up to her left, and I felt her hiccup of relief, followed by an animal whimper. She cupped both our heads in her hands, and held us to her breasts as we fed from her, side by side.

I don't know who moved first, him or me, but by the time my hand slid up her inner thigh into the moist heat of her pussy, his hand was there too, and we caressed her together. When I slipped a finger inside the wet clench of her sex, he pushed his bigger finger in beside mine, and they moved over and around each other in the silky slick of her juices. When she came, shuddering and jerking, we both felt the flutter and grip of her cunt and the gush that flooded our hands to the wrist.

As her milk calmed its constant flow, I weaned myself onto her pussy. And Vince knelt behind me and fucked me doggy-style, without haste. We were lost in the woods, but we had found each other.

We might have kept going until we fell asleep right there, but I broke it up.

"Come on," I said, wearily, tugging at Gail's hand. "The light's going. I'll find us a rowan."

I couldn't. We were deep into lowland forest here, and the best I could do before it got too dark to see anything at all was locate a wide-spreading holly, and even that didn't have any berries. It made for an uncomfortable night too. We tried to clear the ground below before we lay down. But any time anyone moved, a fallen leaf would stab them in some bare patch of skin.

The only good thing was that the temperature didn't drop with nightfall, and it stayed dry and balmy. If nothing else, that convinced me that wherever we'd found ourselves, it was in no natural corner of the Welsh borders. The stars came out in a glittering profusion so extravagant it was like the whole sky was lit up for Christmas. I lay there listening to Vince and Gail breathing, wondering whether to pick yet another annoying prickle out from under my shoulder-blade, as I watched the stars fill the sky. Then, miraculously, I watched them drift down and outline every branch and bush until the whole wood was alight. It was quite beautiful. When pale, shimmering forms began to flit in and out between the trunks I felt some unease, but they didn't seem to take any notice of us. Perhaps it was the protective holly, or perhaps we were not worth paying attention to. They passed like shreds of luminous mist, intent on their own journey. It was hard to be sure of their shapes, though the one I saw most clearly made me think of a stag, with its many-branched antlers. It was much easier just to lie there and watch, mesmerised by the delicate, flickering beauty of it all.

In the morning the whole forest was covered in a dew-beaded gossamer. I felt almost guilty rising and breaking through it when I wandered away to pee, leaving a dark trail in the silvered foliage. Mist wreathed faintly among the trunks, and there was no sound at all.

Except a humming—so low it was almost inaudible.

My curiosity piqued, I climbed a rise and saw before me perhaps the most beautiful, welcome sight that my eyes had ever fallen upon. Right there in front of me was a break in the trees and a steeply rising field of long grass. On the crest of that field was an enormous electricity pylon, like a metal giant striding across the skyline.

My heart leapt. Now that—that was something the Good Neighbours could do nothing with. They couldn't attack it or hide it or warp it. The thick lines were still intact, and still carrying their charge. They must go somewhere; somewhere people lived, and used machines, and turned on electric lights at night. I ran back along my tracks grinning like a loon.

"Gail! Vince! Get up!"

Vince sat up first, rubbing his hand over his stomach. "Tans?" he mumbled. "Hungrr…" It wasn't exactly articulate, but I could have kissed him for those words. Except that then we'd have started humping, and right now I was trying to keep my mind off that.

"See," I said, rubbing Gail's back as she stretched. "You're going to be okay, both of you. Now we're away from… her, and her awful food, you're both going to get back to normal. It's all going to be fine. Come on! Follow me!"

They followed, Gail dragging wearily at Vince's side. My heart ached to see her like that—we'd fed on her strength, and it was taking almost everything out of her. Personally I felt great; my muscles weren't even stiff after our chase yesterday and our night of discomfort. I was guessing my physical resilience was another effect of the Ganconer's curse. It wouldn't do for me to damage too easily and spoil his fun prematurely, would it? Or maybe it was just this land, this realm.

We reached the place where I'd first heard the humming and I held up my hand for silence. "Can you hear that?"

There it was, the furry growl of the electricity. But there was another sound too, now, and even before I identified it the hairs stood up on my neck in dismay. It was a high, light shivery sound and it made my skin crawl. It held some terrible connotation.

Bells. Tiny, tiny silver bells, plaited into the mane of a black horse.

"Oh shit!" said I. Then I was off, dragging them in my wake. "Look!" I cried as we laboured up the rise and the first strut of the pylon came into view against the sky. "See the pylon? See it?"

Vince nodded, confused.

"Run up there! Get between the legs! You're safe there. Keep by the pylon, whatever you do. Them There can't touch you. Then, if the coast is clear, follow the electricity lines. Go east if you've got the choice. But follow the lines, and don't step out from beneath them! Do you understand?"

Gail, looking bewildered, mumbled, "Okay..."

"Go!" I gave them both a shove. "Don't stop and don't look back! Vince—look after her!"

Thank goodness there was still enough enchanted food in her system to make her unable to argue. She did frown like she was trying to remember how, but Vince took her firmly in hand. They set off up the hill and, with one last glance, I turned away downhill—back toward where we'd spent the night. Back toward the sound of the bells. Tiny bells that shouldn't have been audible from more than a few feet away, but what need have Them There for the rules of physics? I knew what was closing in on us. And I knew he was after me.

When I heard the plaintive call of a hunting horn I remembered the ram's horn at his belt and knew he was close. I ran round in circles in the clearing, muddling our tracks. Whatever happened, I needed to give Gail and Vince enough time to get to their steel sanctuary. Then I belted off through the wet leaves, leaving a trail a blind man could follow—

heading away down the valley, in exactly the opposite direction.

This was it—the Wild Hunt the hob had warned me of. And I was its quarry. But better me than Gail.

I'm fast, when I need to be. I've got the long legs for it. At school I only gave up cross-country running when my tits got so big that *everyone* I passed stopped and stared at me. Now I ran through the still grey morning as if the devil himself were at my heels—which, let's face it, was probably close enough to the truth. The trees thinned out as the ground dropped. Yellow leaves spiralled down around me and one slapped my bare stomach with a wet kiss. The horn sounded again— louder, closer, an extended staccato tootle. "Doubling the horn"—I remembered that signal from my country childhood, when Gail and I used to watch the local hunt ride by through the fields. I stumbled over a branch, recovered my balance, and glanced back, expecting to see hunting dogs.

And I certainly saw something. They might have been Hounds, but they definitely weren't dogs. They were men. In that one blurred moment I saw three of them, descending the slope in my wake. They looked naked. Believe it or not, that put heart into me. I had a chance, running against other human beings; none whatsoever against dogs. So I ran and I ran. I've never run harder. I ran as if my life depended on it— or someone else's did. The air of that place seemed to bear me up, and the dead leaves hurtled by under my feet. My fear gave me wings.

But I couldn't win. I was the hunted. That meant every decision was mine. Which direction to take, which log to jump, which tree to dodge. I had no idea where I was heading,

I simply reacted to every obstacle in turn. And every decision cost me time, no matter how minute an amount. But the Hounds had no such concerns. All they had to do was hurl themselves after me. Even if they hadn't been bigger, stronger, better-fed, more experienced... No, I was never going to escape.

The lead Hound caught up with me as we ploughed through a drift of leaf-litter. I heard him at my shoulder, loud over the sounds of pursuit behind. I tried to jink left but he grabbed my arm and momentum spun us round. He swung me over and I fell, rolling in the damp leaves. He came down on top on me then, both of us gasping from the chase. All of a sudden my muscles felt like cotton wool; panic swept through my bloodstream like a sickness. I grabbed a handful of rotted leaves and smacked them into his face, aiming for his eyes. As he flinched I tried to scramble away, but his hand closed on my thigh with terrible force, digging into my muscle as he jerked me over on my back. I didn't have enough breath left to scream. I tried to kick at him—he was nearly naked, except for a rough leather harness—but he wrenched my legs apart and knelt up over me, grabbing at his crotch. He wore some sort of protective leather flap over his genitals. Yanking this down, he allowed his erect cock to spring out, like a weapon, into his hand. I looked up into his dirt-streaked, blank-eyed face.

And I knew him.

"Gavin!" I cried.

BOOK THREE

COURT

Chapter Eleven

The F-Word

Gavin hesitated. I stared up at him, at his heaving chest and his wild face, my mind in a spin. In that fateful moment one of the other Hounds ran in from the side, grabbed Gavin by a shoulder-strap and hauled him off me, trying to fling him away but ending up in a violent grapple. The two men fell over each other, punching and snarling, then broke to circle one another before slamming together again. Fists flew. Fingers gouged.

Abandoned for the moment, I rolled and pushed myself up onto my knees. Any plan I had to run off died as I looked about me; I was surrounded. More of the Hounds circled us. Lean, fit, scruffy-looking near-naked men in hob-nailed sandals and harness and leather greaves to the knee, like TV gladiators but without the steroids. They carried no weapons, but their arms were hard with muscle and their faces feral.

There were no catcalls, and they weren't even grinning. They were too focused. And the two scuffling men didn't speak a word as they fought. Just gasps and snarls and bared teeth—totally animalistic.

No, I definitely had no plan to run off. They'd caught me once, and they'd do it again. But there was more to it than that. Part of my mind saw all these things analytically, as if from a distance, but the rest had dropped all pretence of rational thought. Instinct had taken over. It told me that I had Gavin back, after all this time, and that whatever happened I mustn't leave him. So I just knelt there and watched him fight.

And oh God did that watching hit me like a freight train of hormones, despite all the pretensions of my better judgement. I'd never actually seen him battle anyone before—I certainly don't go out with the kind of dickhead who picks fights on a Saturday night. But now, in that woodland arena, it was different. Gavin stood tall and powerful, defying all challengers for the right to fuck me—wholly and magnificently masculine. So fast, so strong, and so savage that it took my breath away and made my pulse pound—not just in my chest, but right there in my groin.

And I knew that whatever happened, he mustn't lose.

When Gavin punched his opponent in the ribs and moved in to grab his neck and pound him, focused on knocking him down for good, a third man took the chance to close in from behind. I grabbed a dead branch from the fallen leaves and staggered up to smack that third Hound as hard as I could over the back of the shoulders. The rotten wood shattered into several pieces and I doubt it did any damage at all, but he whirled on me, hands raised.

"Fight fair!" I screamed at him, backing off. "One at a time!"

It wasn't exactly heroic, but it gave Gavin the chance to turn too, and spot the guy. This fight was over in seconds. A roar of rage and some hard shoving was all it took before the interloper caved in. The sight of Gavin standing there with arms raised triumphantly —glazed with sweat, his muscles pumped and his cock as glossy and proud as the Brenin's stallion—was almost more than I could deal with. I twisted on my heel, looking round at the glowering, poised circle of men for the next attacker. That was when Gavin seized me from behind.

I didn't struggle this time. I let him pull me against his torso and grab my breast and my hip, his hands rough on my skin and incredibly heavy, taking possession. I could feel his chest heaving against my back as he turned me, three-sixty, like a hostage-taker with a human shield, showing me to the whole circle of Hounds. Steam wreathed up from their flesh into the damp morning air. I saw stubbly faces and sweat-slick skin—and dark, dilated eyes. They glowered, shaking their heads and clenching their fists as they caught their breath. After such a chase they must have been horribly frustrated. They wanted their quarry. I could feel Gavin's triumph burgeoning with every shift of our bodies together.

So too could I feel the flood of my body's response. He'd hunted me through the forest, run me down and pinned me. He'd fought other men for me. He was the man I'd yearned for, for two years, and now he'd earned the right to reclaim me. The woman I used to be would have been so ashamed to admit it, but my sexual response was primal and unequivocal.

I knew what he was going to do even before he pushed me to hands and knees before him. I didn't resist. I didn't want to. My sex was slippery with anticipation of the claiming that was to come. I wanted him, desperately. I wanted those men to see him take me. It needed to be public, in front of all the world. My hands sank into the leaf-litter as he came down behind me, straddling my ass. He lifted my scullery rag. Then his cock slapped against the crease between my buttocks and I spread for him, arching my back to present the prize he demanded. It was achingly ready for him. His hands were heavy. His cock jabbed at my pussy, blind and brutal, rubbing up and down my split until the wet folds guided it to the mouth of my open, surrendered cunt. He impaled me with a long, victorious thrust that nearly turned me inside out.

"Ah!" I cried, my eyes flashing wide, the circle of watching men blurring momentarily before my gaze.

I was glad he was tired and, after all that running and fighting, he needed to take his time. He fucked me slowly, with enormous deliberation. Making things clear to his pack-mates. Staking his claim, as he staked my cunt. I rammed my hands deep into the leaf-litter to push back onto him, and the cold mulch beneath the fresh-fallen leaves squirted up between my fingers. I could hear him panting, just as I was panting.

"Gavin!" I groaned, over and over, as he took me; inch after unstoppable inch of that thick shaft I'd missed for so long, reclaiming its sovereign territory.

Every memory I had of him came back to me in a blur of images and sensation, in those glorious moments. The sound of his laughter and the taste of his sweat. The way he would press my tits together and bury his face in them as if he wanted to suffocate there. His unflagging appetite for eating my pussy, and the fierce lift of his brows as he watched my face from between my thighs. The way he'd lie over me and cover my mouth with his as I started to come beneath him, as if he could taste my orgasm. The throaty bark he sometimes emitted at his own climax. The way he'd slip his longest finger inside me and just cup my sex after it was all over, savouring the settling of my pulse and the long slow spasms of my cunt mouth as I relaxed into his embrace. And the wrecked, incredulous smile on his face after a blowjob, as if I'd just granted him the key to heaven in a gold-plated box.

Oh God, how I'd missed him—with all my heart and every inch of my body, inside and out. As he fucked me there, in front of all those men, without the least tenderness or recognition, tears welled up and ran down my mud-streaked cheeks. I shut my eyes, as low and incoherent moans escaped my lips.

The sound of hooves—a dull thud on the wet soil—made me open my eyes again. The black horse was pacing before us, mincing a little in dismay at the soft ground, while behind it an array of horses and their fabulously dressed riders descended into the dell. I lifted my eyes to the stallion's rider. The Brenin, white as bone and black as jet, his hair wreathing about him like mist, bore a faint dispassionate smile on his lips. He'd set his pack on me and hunted me down. Now he was watching me being ravished by his lead Hound, my forearms mashed in the dirt, my tits swinging against the torn leaves, my ass high. Hunting dogs, after all, deserved their reward. And Gavin, his thrusts quickening to a punishing judder, his thighs smacking against mine, was taking his prize right now. Over and over, faster and faster, his cock slammed deep inside me.

With my gaze fixed on the huntsman's, I came right then, just as Gavin filled me.

It wouldn't have mattered to me after that if the other Hounds had taken their turn. I rather expected it. But Gavin had other plans. As the first of his fellows shifted forward, already unhitching his erection from confinement, Gavin rounded on him, snarling. I felt the ripple of surprise sweep the pack. Several of them lumbered in and Gavin jerked to his feet, spilling me to the floor.

"Off!" the huntsman called, pulling the whip from his boot.

He sent his mount in, striking at the Hounds until they dodged away. I huddled up, trying to keep my limbs from under those huge, heavy hooves.

"Tie her!" he demanded, throwing down a coil of braided leather to Gavin who, despite his exhaustion, still stood in truculent defiance.

He must have had some higher mental functions left, because he picked up the plait and came to bind my crossed wrists before me, while the Brenin waited and the Hounds milled about in frustration.

"Gavin," I whispered desperately, running my hands across his sweaty chest, through the rough hair I remembered so achingly well, brushing unfamiliar new scars and flecks of leaf-litter and streaks of mud. "Gavin? Do you remember me? It's Tansy."

He raised his eyes to mine and frowned, faintly, as if confused. His face was more weathered than I recalled, and a little thinner. The life that had taken possession of him had left his musculature more exaggerated, his body leaner but heavier. Yet it was him. I recognised him as well as I knew myself. He just didn't know me.

His semen was running down the insides of my thighs.

"Gavin," I said again, without hope, and let my forehead fall against his shoulder. His sweat smelled strong and clean and masculine. For the briefest of moments his hand rested on my waist. Then the whip cracked and Gavin jerked with pain as the blow fell across his shoulders.

"Give her here!" The huntsman's command was sharp. With a soundless snarl Gavin pulled away from me and passed the rope-end to his master.

"No!" I protested, trying to turn back and grab at my stolen lover despite my crossed and tied wrists. But Gavin's response was only to his master, as he gripped my sides and boosted me up, dropping me belly-down over the horse's withers. It was incredibly uncomfortable—so much so that when the Brenin slapped my ass and shoved his fingers into my unprotected cunt, puddled them around and retrieved them to taste the mingled effluvia of Gavin and myself from his gloved hand, I kicked in shock but I registered the violation less keenly than I might have.

"You bastard!" I howled, all caution forgotten, blind with rage.

"Fall in," he called, and blew the horn. The horse swung uphill, each step jolting painfully through my stomach. I screamed out loud. The Brenin put a hand on the small of my back.

"Sleep," said he.

And that's the last I remember of that.

❧ ❧ ❧

Nothing wakes you up quite as effectively as a lubed finger sliding into your ass. Except maybe an unlubed one, I suppose. Whatever, I went from unconscious to wide-staring-awake in less than the split second it took me to wrench myself off the invasive digit and roll over, kicking like a horse. I heard a feminine chuckle, and looked up into a piquant, grinning face framed by electric blue dreadlocks.

"Who the fuck are you?" I blurted, before I had time to think better of it.

Despite the pointed delicacy of the face it was plastered over, the grin was wide enough to devour a small melon, and composed of many, *many* crocodile-sharp teeth.

"I'm Milkthistle," said she. "I'm in charge of the ewes. Time to eat."

She turned away and I took the chance to look quickly around me. It was pretty dark. We were indoors, in a very large room dimly lit by yellow lamps. The fact that the lights were moving about made it more confusing, because they cast constantly shifting shadows. The lights appeared to be shining golden birds, hopping around in a tangle of branched roots that poured down the walls and cascaded onto the floor. But that hardly troubled me, considering the events that had brought me here. I was already over the boundary of calm and normal and well into the territory of stunned panic.

There were other women here. Human-looking women, unlike the alarming Milkthistle. They were naked, and they stood or lolled about, tethered to the bare wood of the roots by cuffs at their ankles or wrists or throats. The first two I looked at were playing with their own pussies with that languidly mindless lasciviousness only too familiar from Vince and Gail. The sight made me look down at myself. I was cuffed and collared and naked too, though not tied to anything, just lying on the tanned hides that covered the floor. In fact, I was more than naked.

"What the hell?" I squeaked, clutching at myself.

In the light of my captivity, I shouldn't have been distracted by something quite so trivial. But shock overrode common sense for a moment when I realised my familiar ginger felt was gone. Not a hair remained. My entire body was as Hollywood-bare as a porn starlet's, my sex a sensitised open rose of silky petals that my hand found deeply shocking. I'd never gone bare before and the sensation was unnervingly alien, as if it weren't my pussy anymore. I actually grabbed my head next, terrified I'd been stripped bald there too—but I still had my eyebrows and my mop of curls on top, even if they were bound back from my face in a Mohican-style mane.

I don't know why the depilation should have freaked me out so, but adrenaline poured through my bloodstream, making the leather rugs slippery under my sweating thighs. Heat seemed to radiate from my skin. Hissing through bared teeth, I shuffled backward away from Milkthistle, trying to hold down my panic. She was untying some of the women. Not all of them—but the ones she did loose crawled on hands and knees to a huge wooden salver mounded with food in the middle of the floor. The freed women dug in to the provisions, tucking morsels into their mouths with their bare hands.

As the women bent and stretched for the food, I noticed that they wore dyed horsehair tails arching from their ass cracks.

Milkthistle was a lot smaller than the human women. But she was naked too, and just as lithe, though her skin wasn't smooth like ours. She was covered in long, mobile, fleshy extrusions, which flashed and flared little patches of ragged butterfly-bright skin every time they lifted. The golden light from the birds shone through that webbing as if through stained glass windows. When she'd released all the captives she intended to, she went back to the platter and picked out food herself, carrying it to the women who were still bound. Those seemed to be the ones too far gone in a masturbatory trance to feel hungry anyway. I watched as Milkthistle peeled a banana —When was the last time I'd seen a banana, for heaven's sake? —and thrust it between her thighs with a giggle, before presenting it, glazed in her fuck-honey, to a stoned-looking brunette.

"Eat up, pretty," she crooned, teasing it between the brunette's lips.

The girl took it, with a distracted air, and began to munch slowly. I thought of Gavin and his Hound comrades. Their overwhelming sexual hunger. Their dead-eyed faces, capable of expressing emotions no more complex than anger or lust. His utter lack of recall when he looked at me.

Pain ran through my breast like a knife cut.

Fuck that, I thought savagely, taking another look around me through the shadows — this time, for a way out. The walls of the room were painted red on the bottom half, cream above, and there was a row of columns down the long axis. I was close enough to one column to see that the painted plasterwork was peeling and decayed. There were no windows that I could see, but the roof was missing. Overhead I could make out stars, through the twisted branches. Double doors, probably wooden, stood at either end. It all looked naggingly familiar, though I couldn't quite place it. I rolled onto my knees, intending to make for one of the doors.

"You too. Go and eat." Milkthistle was standing beside me.

I jumped a little, then eyed her up. She was only about half my height and probably not even a third my weight, though her body was certainly adult. Her breasts stood out proudly, black-nippled against her bone-yellow skin. Her almond-shaped eyes had slit pupils, like a cat's, and they glowed where they caught the uncertain light of the golden birds.

She didn't appear to be armed, but I didn't take appearances on trust. Not here, and not with Them There.

Playing for time, I shuffled over on my knees to the platter. It was mounded with an insane hotchpotch of food: roasted fowl and wildly exotic looking fruit, steaming loaves of bread, blancmanges and quails' eggs, parsnips glazed in honey, sweet pastries and slabs of cheese. Other, crazier things too: whole roasted carcases of some unidentifiable rodent (Rat? Dormouse? Squirrel?), crispy-fried spiders as large as my fist, live fish still flopping about. It was as if they had no real idea what we ate, and just presented their best guess. Assuming any of it was real in the first place, of course, and not just wild mushrooms and forest berries under an illusory glamour, the way it was so often in stories. Where the hell would Them There be getting bananas and tarantulas from anyway?

Just for a moment, I considered trying to eat something. It

would be easy to give up and stop fighting. I'd lost Gail, and could only hope she and Vince were safe—somehow, somewhere. I'd found Gavin, out of the blue—but he didn't know me. He couldn't talk, and he was as much a prisoner as I was. My life was in the hands of a crew of psychopathic jesters. By any standards I was screwed. If I ate the food I would stop caring. If I ate, I'd be a happy fuck-puppet like all their other slaves, and probably wouldn't even notice if and when they killed me.

I actually put my hand out to a sunset-hued persimmon. Then my stomach heaved and my throat closed convulsively. The Ganconer hadn't even left me that way out.

"Eat up!"

"I'm not hungry," I growled.

"Eat, stupid mortal!"

I gave Milkthistle a cold glance. "I said I'm *not hungry*."

"You'll regret it." She gave me one of her carnivorous grins.

"Probably."

"Because it's time for you to wear this now." She brandished—not entirely to my surprise—a curved horse-tail the colour of my own fiery hair. It ended in a familiar butt-plug shape of hard leather. It would fit neatly into my ass and the tail would rise at a cocked position from between my cheeks, the hair switching behind me as I walked. I bit my lip as I felt a hungry spasm run up my rear.

Oh God, how my ass missed the Bour Lady's butt-tether. I'd worn it so long I felt empty without it.

Milkthistle misunderstood my expression. I knew that as I heard her chuckle.

"Don't be shy," she hissed. "It's the Brenhines' command that you all wear them. Turn round and give me your ass, mortal. I'll slip it in so sweet you'll hardly feel it."

I wanted that. My body, insatiable as ever, burned for it. But that pissed me off. It was almost like wanting to eat their cursed fruit.

"You can try," I said, getting to my feet and walking off.

I guess I just don't submit that easily to women. I need them to overthrow me physically first.

Well, Milkthistle certainly rose to the challenge. I'd hardly moved beyond the feeding circle when a bolt of pain struck me on the thigh, so unexpected and so fierce that I twisted and fell, screaming with shock and clutching my leg. I was convinced there'd be blood. I was sure there'd be a wound. But when I dared peek under my clutching fingers there was nothing—no scratch, no mark and, I realised belatedly, no more pain. It was gone as abruptly as it had hit.

I stared up at her as she swaggered over and looked down on me.

"Fuck!" I protested.

Grinning like a shark, she lifted a hand to her ropes of blue hair and pulled something from between the twists. It was too small for me to see it between her fingertips. A pin maybe, or an arrowhead. She waited until I knew she was going to do it, and then she threw it at me. The pain hit between my breasts and I thrashed wildly, too agonised this time to scream.

Elf-shot, said the analytical part of my mind. It didn't help any. What did help was knowing that it was only pain—not real harm. This time I didn't wait for it to leave me. I gathered my limbs and launched myself at the bitch, bundling her over onto the floor and snatching at her wrists before she had time to arm herself again. I had all the apparent advantages of size and weight—but good God she was strong; far stronger than any human her size would be. She fought with the twisting muscularity of a cat. She screeched like one too, and I was vaguely aware that all the birds overhead were screaming as well. It took all my effort to pin her face-down on the floor, her arms pinned to either side under my knees. I'd learned from the Ganconer's girl-gang too, and I used my feet in her hair to keep her in place. Her legs thrashed, scissoring. I ground down with my body weight and used one hand to hit her bare ass spitefully.

She howled, humping her ass and spreading her thighs

I'm not proud. I'm not fucking proud of what I did. But I was completely off my mental balance—despairing and horny, scared and angry and lost. Lost was worst of all. My judgement was completely shot. And I hated this vicious little bitch. I whacked her ass until my arm hurt and the smell of her sex was pungent. I slapped her pussy and felt her as wet as a swamp down there. She pushed right up into my kneading hand.

"You fucking like this, do you?" I snarled, bending to stick my head in there and biting hard at her bum.

She spread wider. I shoved fingers inside her cunt. It was like she had no bones. Despite her tiny frame she took all four fingers of my left hand in her hot wet grip and I suspect she could have taken more if I'd dared. I wasn't terribly gentle as it was. And the horse-tail plug she'd dropped only a moment before was within my reach.

Around the room the shadows flickered and thickened and

292

clustered, like spectators pushing in for a closer view.

"Come on then, bitch—you wear it if you like it so much," I told her, pushing the stitched leather plug between her cheeks. I saw the dark purse of her asshole open like a mouth to gobble at it, and I plunged it in hard. She was yelping rhythmically now, banging her pelvis up and down on the hides, her cunt sucking my hand.

"Not such a great top now, are you?" I spat. "You like this, don't you? You like this!"

This feeling of dominance was intoxicating. Lust and power bubbled up and overflowed within me—and I cannot presume what it would have made me do. As it happened, I wouldn't have a chance to find out. Fire cracked across my ass cheeks. The sudden, searing pain made me forget Milkthistle, and forget how angry and dirty and mean I was feeling. I forgot everything except the importance of getting away from the fire flaring over my flesh. I was yards away from her and piled up against one of the central pillars before I realised what the hell had happened.

The room was full of the Gentry. Foremost, and the focus of my dawning horror, was the Brenin and a woman who stood at his left. He, still wearing his death mask, was wrapped in a voluminous black toga like Virgil pictured at the bottom of the Inferno, and he carried his whip in his hand. I guessed that the woman would be his queen—the Brenhines. She was dressed in the style of a Classical goddess, all in drifting translucent white. Her slender body was perfectly visible through her draperies. Her hair was jet-black but crowned and wound with gold wire, and her golden carnival mask was composed of intricate petals, as if her face were an orchid.

Beneath a row of trembling gold beads, her lips were full and dark red, like blood-bruises.

I whimpered, touching the burning weals across my bum-cheeks.

The room was suddenly deathly silent. Not a bird shrieked, not a courtier shuffled. The captive women had shrunk as far away from the scene as possible. Even Milkthistle was quiet, though I could hear her panting.

"What," said the Brenin softly, "is cause of all this cacophony?"

"Oh, Brenin," squeaked Milkthistle, raising herself to hands and knees. "It was the maid. She would not eat. She would not wear the tail. Your commands… I tried to punish her…" The creature gulped. "But she rebelled."

"Really?" said the Brenhines dryly, her lips curving like rose petals ready to fall. "Rebellion? I'm sure that's not what it looked like."

The Brenin didn't smile. He walked toward me, and I shrank back against the pillar, not daring to try and stand. All my pretensions to dominance evaporated in his presence. My ass was burning—the abrupt pain of his whip now transmuted into a fierce warmth that encompassed my rear and my sex. My legs were quivering with shock and fear.

He stood over me as I crouched there, my eyes downcast. His expression remained inscrutable under that mask as he held the whip across both hands. I didn't dare blink. Without hurry, he reversed the crop so it was stock uppermost and angled at me from his groin. As I'd noted before, the handle was thicker than that of modern riding crops, bound in leather and delicate wire—and it was unmistakeably phallic now in the way he used it. Brushing it against my lips and cheekbones. Slapping it lightly against my face. I turned my mouth toward it instinctively, parting my lips, licking at the dark leather. I felt rather than saw him nod, as he eased it over my tongue. The trembling had spread to my whole body now, as I sucked in the phallic stock.

"Rebellious?" he said thoughtfully. "She looks beautifully submissive to me. Perhaps you need lessons, Milkthistle."

"My Brenin!"

I shut my eyes as he pushed the whip stock right to the back of my throat. Accepting it. I didn't gag. It wasn't food. It was a cock, and cock never made me gag now.

"Stand up," he whispered, taking me under the chin and withdrawing the shaft. "I'm going to whip you."

I let him draw me to my feet and turn me against the pillar. I put my hands on the column to brace myself, feeling the sweat of my palms soak into the cold plaster. I'm not Gail. I hate pain. I fucking hate it. I don't welcome it.

His first blow landed across the broadest part of my ass. I managed not to cry out, though my gasp was loud. I'd just worked out that he'd struck me with far less force than when he'd driven me off Milkthistle—when he got me again. Again I held on, didn't scream, didn't run, didn't collapse. The burn flowed down my legs and wrapped around my pelvis. I could feel my pussy throbbing, my labia swelling.

I hate pain, but it seems I like being made to take it.

After the sixth blow, he leaned in and licked the fear-sweat from my shoulders.

"Wear what you are told," he murmured, running the stock of the whip down my backbone.

I pushed my ass out, presenting to him as he parted my split from behind with the handle of his hateful whip and slipped it into the welcoming passage of my cunt. I knew my juices were running out onto his fingers as he worked me.

"Eat what you are told," he went on, transferring the lubed-up stock to the whorl of my asshole and pressing for entry. His breath was hot on my ear, his voice low and sublimely intimate. "You are mine to command."

The handle was slimmer than his cock had been and it slipped in easily. But the binding made it ridged and I felt every inch.

"My Brenin…"

"Master." He bit at my earlobe.

"Master." My arousal was soaring with every stroke. And my hope. Here at last was someone who pulled more rank and wielded more power than the Ganconer. "I can't," I explained. "Not *will not. Cannot.* I'm under a curse. I can't eat."

He drew the handle from my anus with one long, slow pull, leaving me gasping and empty.

"If you don't eat," he said, without audible concern, "you will not survive what is done to you in this place."

Then he turned away from me.

I dug my nails into the crumbling plaster. I wanted him to fuck me. At the very least I wanted—I expected—him to let me come on his whip handle. Frustration sent me into a mental spin. I'm a terrible sub, let's face it. He'd denied me orgasm, and I got mad and crazy.

"What? Being turned into some *fairy* fuck-toy?" I said, twisting, my voice curdling with defiance.

The lights went out. All of them, instantly. I whipped

round, seeing nothing but blackness. When my turning took me back to the pillar, I flinched. Without having moved, they were there behind me, the Brenin and the Brenhines, on either side of the column. They were visible because their skin fluoresced faintly in the dark, like decaying fungi. I could see her beautiful pale body through her robe, and the white fall of his hair framing a skull which shimmered eerily.

"Give her to me, my love," said the Brenhines in her warm, lush voice. "I will take pleasure in killing her."

"No." He didn't sound angry. His voice was the same as ever—cool and controlled. "She's proud, and she needs that knocking out of her. For her, I think, the Punishment of Rhiannon."

Unseen hands seized me, and dragged me away through the dark.

Rhiannon. Oh good God, I knew what that meant. I had a very good idea anyway. As I was hauled down unlit corridors, and through a flooded atrium of tumbled marble and black moon-shadows, the words *fairy fuck-toy* went round and round in my head like a death sentence. Or a curse I'd invoked on myself.

The story of Rhiannon is from the Welsh *Mabinogion*. Accused—quite wrongly—of infanticide, queen Rhiannon is condemned by her husband to be stationed by a riding block at the castle gate, every day for seven years. To everyone who passes through the gate, she must make an offer to carry him on her back all the way to the main door. I'd always had my suspicions about that story. It just seemed to me that being made to offer each and every man in the kingdom a "ride" had a far more obvious and humiliating meaning than any pointless piggyback.

They took me to an entrance portico. Great doors stood open, and beyond them I could see a sunlit woodland. Behind me, all was night and moonlight. The roof of the entrance hall was held up by a single pillar and they roped my hands to a ring set high on that. They set a pot of oil nearby and they greased my ass and my cunt well, as deeply as they could reach.

Then they fucked me. And every person who passed through the doors that day, in or out, took the time to stop off and fuck me. Some of them stayed for hours and made a party of it.

Understand, when I say "person" I don't mean *human*. Comparatively few of them looked human. Those that did tended to be willowy and masked, in the style of their king and queen, like Venetian carnival goers. The others… well, the good news was that most of them were human *sized*. Or thereabouts. Everything else was a lottery. Animal, vegetable or mineral. Mammalian, reptilian or avian. In any combination. All of them seemed to have cocks or cunts though, and a profound eagerness to put them to use on me.

I was Rhiannon. I was Laura with the goblin market-men. I was a fuck-toy for the whole of the Elven Court.

My awareness of the ordeal grew fairly hazy after a certain point, as my mind shut down to all but the basic autonomic responses—dilation, arousal, swallowing, breathing, orgasm—but I remember spindly apple-tree men and stout dwarves, serpents and goatish satyrs. Something headless with a single arm and a single foot, and a todger like a third limb. Pookas with human bodies but the heads and hooves and genitals of small ponies. Goblins by the dozen, from as small as my hand to as big as bears. Bears, yes—one at least, who spoke most politely. Stag-horned, bull-horned, fox-eared, doe-eyed, boar-tusked, winged. Furry, hairy, scaled, feathered and chitinous. Hooved or clawed or booted. A lizard-like humanoid wearing centurion's armour, blessed with two pricks it used in me simultaneously, fore and aft. And something that seemed to be made out of mud, that nearly suffocated me before others pulled it off.

My jaw and tongue ached with sucking. I begged for water and they brought it for me just so I could keep going. I choked and snorted cum. I licked it from every imaginable colour and shape of cock.

I remember the stink of fur and sweat, leather and perfume and musk. The overwhelming tastes of jism and pussy-juice. They fucked my ass and my mouth and my cunt. They took me singly or in clusters. They rolled me into a ball and swung me upside down and bounced me like a rag doll. They stretched me out between them and crushed me beneath their bodies. They spurted on my face, in my hair, all over my tits and ass, in every crevice and orifice and cranny. Three little mannikins in tiny leather aprons and workmen's belts even fucked me obsessively between the toes.

And I couldn't stop coming. I came for them all, big or small, foul or fair. I was the ultimate lay, the universal slut. When I couldn't even lift my arms anymore, or roll myself over, I could still orgasm.

Beyond the mighty doors of the portico, the day rolled on to evening and turned to night. With twilight came a rush of traffic, and I learned it was better to keep my eyes closed and just feel my way. Some of my night-time patrons had a look about them as if they had been dead some time. Something tomb-cold spooned up against me as if it would never leave, its cock wedged in my ass, trickling what felt like ice-water into my bowels.

I think that comprehensively disproved all that good-Seelie versus bad-Unseelie Court nonsense. Both parties came and went here.

When I thought I couldn't go on, they made me. When I thought one more orgasm would kill me, they proved me wrong. They rode me to my uttermost limit, and beyond. They made me choke and weep and beg for respite, even as my hips lifted and my pussy spread for more.

Then, at last, the first grey of approaching dawn started to show through the open gates. The last of the revellers left me and I found some relief. I lay on my side, discarded on the red tiles, my arms still bound though the rope lay slack across the floor. Every bit of me that wasn't numb from overuse ached with exertion. My lips were sore, my eyelashes gummed together with spunk, and my ass felt like it was inflamed to twice its normal size. All I wanted to do was sleep.

An irritating noise kept me on the edge of consciousness. A swish, like the sound of brushing.

"Tansy? Good girl Tansy?" The voice was faint and whiskery and self-deprecating. I recognised it, dimly.

"Hob?" I whispered, not opening my eyes.

"What has happened to you?" Small hands stroked my hip anxiously. "Are you well?"

I felt tears well in my throat and eyes. I'd been used so

thoroughly and for so long that it was hard to deal with sympathy. "I'm okay," I mumbled.

"Who is she?" said another voice, very similar. Several pairs of tiny paws were patting me now. "Is she hurt?"

"She is Tansy. She's a good girl. Very tidy. Very polite."

"We will help her."

Oh God—how I ached to be treated kindly just for once. To be petted and soothed and held. Then from behind me one of the hob voices rose in a shriek.

"She is *not* a good girl! She is dirty! Look at this!"

There was a scampering of feet. With some difficulty I wrenched my eyes open and looked round, but I knew what they'd seen. I'd peed on the floor at one point, to the loud derision and amusement of my audience. Their cruel mockery had stung bitterly at the time, but I hadn't had any choice. I'd tried to lie as far away from the puddle as possible, but there it was. And there *they* were: seven hobs. For the first time I saw what those shy Neighbours looked like, in all their grotesquery. Almost entirely head, dark grey, no visible body but spindly little legs, and arms that brandished small sweeping brushes.

"Dirty girl! She's a dirty girl!" they shrieked in horror.

The other thing you noticed about them straight away was their cocks. Big, rubbery cocks completely out of proportion to their overall stature, that hung down from beneath their chins and trailed along the tiles, getting in the way of their cleaning.

"Slattern! Lazy slut! Drab!" They dropped their brushes and rushed at me. "Punish her!"

Oh shit, thought I, as they rushed my body. They were

small, but I was too weak to resist. They rolled me right over on my back and pushed my legs up to expose my pussy. One crammed his semi-hard cock into my asshole, while another scrambled on top and pushed his into my open cunt. A third leapt onto my ribs and began to slap his tool wildly between my breasts with a flapping sound. For a moment the almost comic indignity of it all struck me. Here I was, a Snow White being frantically humped by a gang of house-proud dwarves. But that was the last flare of my pride, as it burnt up forever. As a forth hob climbed onto my face and worked his pliable cock into my mouth, and I felt the ones already pummelling me begin to stiffen, the familiar burn of my arousal woke and took possession of me once again.

Oh, those cocks were big. The one down my throat was cutting off my air. But I was so close to orgasm that I couldn't tell the difference between arousal and terror. I didn't need to breath. All I had to do was swallow, swallow, swallow. And be fucked… And come.

Chapter Twelve

You Live and Learn

The stinging slap of the crop on my open pussy jerked me wide awake.

"Tell me about this curse," said the Brenin, as if our conversation had never been interrupted by the trivial matter of my punishment.

I opened my mouth, but all I could do for a moment was gasp. Partly because of the burning shock still flaring through my clit. Partly because I was lying on my back with the Brenin's two feet on my pubic mound and breasts, and they were heavy enough to stifle my breathing. Partly because I was struggling to believe I was still alive. The last thing I remembered was passing out in the entrance hall with my throat blocked by hob cock. Now I was in a large chamber, looking up at a chair with the Brenin sitting on it, and above him a broken roof through which the full moon was gazing.

"Take your time," said the Brenin, tilting his head to look

down at me. His long hair was like a fall of snow. But my pussy sparked with pain and lit up again as he tapped it with the tip of his crop.

"Master!"

Okay… I was lying supine at his feet. He was sitting on a throne—quite a modest throne really, of carved wood, but up on a dais—and I was lying on the step below, being used as his footstool.

He smiled. Well, his mouth did. You never could see what his eyes were up to, behind that mask.

"The Ganconer," I said.

I was still covered in cum—I could feel it sticking my fingers together—but I wasn't aching anymore.

"That wastrel?" His lip curled.

"He did me a favour. That was his price. I had to fuck him. And now…"

"I hear his paramours pine away for love of him."

"Well. Not me."

"Interesting. You're made of resilient stuff, it seems." That sounded like a compliment, of sorts.

"I've managed. Master."

"But you can't eat?"

"Not solids. I can drink."

"I noticed." His lips moved into a thin smile again. "Piss. And semen. Lots of that. All bodily fluids?"

"Uh…"

"Blood?"

"I haven't tried," I said faintly, knowing that there was no point in asking him not to do that to me. If he wanted, he would.

"What about honey? Cream? Wine?"

He lifted a deep goblet in his left hand. It was made of glass, at a guess, in blue and white, moulded finely with little figures of maenads dancing. Like his toga and that ornate sandal on my breast, with the straps that went all the way up his calf, it looked Roman. So did the interior decoration, come to think of it. The atrium with its square pool, the painted walls… What was it with Them There and Romans?

"I don't know, Master." The prohibition on eating in their realm applied to drinking too. I'd generally stuck to water and Gail's breast milk.

Thoughtfully, he took a sip from the cup and ran the tip of his tongue across his lip.

"Open your mouth."

I obeyed. Not out of fear, but because he was the one to tell me. From the moment he'd found me in the Elder Lady's cadaverous garden, through his pursuit of me, and right down to my captivity and punishment, he'd been swaddling me in a grasp of ownership. And now that grasp had closed. No coercion was necessary to make me into an obedient slave who'd do anything he wanted of me. He'd tamed me. And I'd surrendered.

Besides, after what I'd been through, keeping my wits no longer had any appeal.

Filling his mouth with wine, the Brenin bent a little and let a thin red stream fall from his lips onto mine. I swallowed and gasped and licked, the wine splashing on my face, and then opened my mouth for more, like a baby bird. The liquid was sweet, and it hit my brain with a rush. It was long time since I'd had a proper drink.

"Such a greedy little bitch."

"Yes…" I gasped. "Oh fuck yes."

That seemed to please him. His eyes glinted behind the mask as he reached down, undid the thong that held his sandal on, tugged open the eyelets and slipped the shoe off. Returning his bare foot to my chest, he rubbed it luxuriously across my cushioning breasts, catching my nipples with his toes and playing with them. His smirk of satisfaction was almost broad.

I moaned a little, my breasts responding to the rough kneading with tingling pleasure. I could feel the warmth of the wine running down to my stomach and spreading through my insides. The tiers of teardrop-shaped oil-lamps in the candelabra nearby seemed to swim in my vision, their glow filling the room.

Tick—the tip of his crop flicked against my clit, making me gasp and arch. He used his feet to push me back into place.

"Do you like pain?"

"No—Oh!—Master!"

"I could teach you to like it," he promised, gazing into my eyes.

He laid his crop across his lap and reached into the wine goblet with his free hand. His hand emerged holding a lizard by the tail—a blue lizard, iridescent as a butterfly, that twisted and snapped in his indolent grip. With a flourish he lowered it to my left breast, sprinkling me with wine droplets. The creature's mouth clamped shut over my nipple, tight enough to make me jerk, and clung with its splayed body to the mound of my breast.

I whimpered under my breath.

He pulled another lizard from his glass. This second one was glittering green. He laid it upon my other breast, where it bit down on my right nipple. But the Brenin had to do something else with his foot then. He solved this by sliding it up from my breasts and over my face, pressing it in to my mouth. I seized his toes eagerly, sucking and licking at them— anything to take my mind off my painfully clamped nipples. He tasted of saffron and salt.

"Oh," he said softly. "How interesting. It's not pain is it? Not even submission. It's… something else."

The third lizard was ruby-bright and bigger than the other two. He showed it to me very deliberately, clearly enjoying the way my eyes widened, pleading and desperate over the arch of his foot, and my moans came out muffled. He dropped the lizard onto my bare mound.

Without the protection of my pubes, my nerve endings seemed to feel every scale and every claw.

"Open wide, little red bitch," he told me.

I did, though I cried with horror. The reptile scuttled down over my splayed vulva and shoved its broad head into my cunt.

"In you go," he told it gently.

In it went, shouldering through the narrow gap of my flesh and wriggling inside me. I would have shrieked, but the Brenin had the ball of his foot pressed hard to my mouth, and nothing escaped past that bung but fine spittle. I could feel myself opening up as the lizard twisted around inside me, over and over, rubbing against every inch of my inner walls, roiling around, never still. I started to buck.

"Yes," he murmured, rubbing the sole of his foot over my

face, tender and implacable as he desecrated me. I was humping now, my cries audible and climbing the scale. The lizards wouldn't leave me alone. The pain at my nipples ran in jagged ley-lines over my body. Soon I was coming—horribly, unforgivably, like a fucking nightmare, like a dark goddess.

No, it's not pain for me. I'm not Gail. But I'm a lot more like her than I thought. Both of us have this urge for sexual catharsis. For a ferocious struggle that takes us to the limits of what we can endure, that'll break us down and reduce us to flotsam and set us free of ourselves. For her it's pain. For me, it's more like... debasement, I suppose. The deepest shame.

The moment it was over, the lizards jumped ship and ran away across the floor. I was left wrecked at the Brenin's feet.

"I know," he told me, tracing the midline of my body with his fingertips, his eyes warm in their dead sockets. "I know what you need. That makes you *my* slut, twice over."

I couldn't answer. Luckily, perhaps, for me, at that moment a hollow knock sounded at the throne room door. The Brenin sat back, returning his foot to my breasts, and seemed to forget my existence. I turned my head the other way, to watch.

Three courtiers came in. Two were guards—hulking men, one with a stag's head and one with the head of a ram—and the one in the middle was a woman. She was very tall, and paper-white with horizontal striations across her skin that might have been scars or tattoos. A lot of that skin was visible, because she wore only a long skirt of bright green, low on her hips. The guards looked familiar to me from the night before, but the woman did not.

She went down on both knees, a little stiffly, before the

throne.

"Angharath, of the Isle of Apples, gives greeting to you, Brenin of the Cornovii." said she. "I was sent to you with news."

I lost track of the conversation after that. The wine had taken hold of my senses and I was floating in a warm golden haze, my conscious mind fading in and out. All I was really aware of was the bliss of my pussy and the warm weight of the Brenin's foot on my tits. I gathered that the news from Angharath was bad. I was vaguely aware that the Brenin sent a guard to summon the Brenhines. I woke up a bit more when she came in—perhaps because he got up and stepped over me to greet her. She was, I thought, the most beautiful woman I'd ever known. I mean, *ever*. I'd never seen anything like her. The long peplos she wore was unstitched at the side and just the sight of those delicious slices of pale gold skin, and the push of her pouting breasts against the fine silk, made my sex moisten anew.

He motioned her to sit on the throne he'd vacated. As she did so, she glanced down at me, with a slight curl of her lip. He remained standing on the stair below me.

"Why have you asked me to attend you?" she asked him.

"Because, my lady, I wish to ask you to convene the war council."

For a moment she came sharply into focus, even through my addled haze.

"What?"

"We've had confirmation from Afallach. The Pendragon has returned."

"Is there no doubt then?"

I faded out for while, half-aware that their voices were sharp with anxiety, then drifted back just as the Brenhines said bitterly, "It has been many years since the Unseelie Court of the Cornovii. I would not welcome its return."

"We have no choice, my lady. We must be ready to face him."

Stoned as a skunk, I put my hand out to touch his robe. They both went silent. Even I realised my interruption was probably unwelcome.

"Her hair is an ugly colour," said the Brenhines, with the cold voice of someone really talking about something else. "I don't like her."

"That's your prerogative, my love. Let me address the war council."

There was a pause.

"Samhain," she said, her voice gravelly with reluctance. "After the feast. Give me until then to prepare, at least."

He relaxed, exhaling, and bowed. "My gratitude, love. You've made the right decision."

"I hope so."

He looked down at me, blinked, then gestured to a servant. "You—get this one cleaned up and take her to the kennels. The Little Red Bitch might as well stay with the Hounds."

They led me out of the throne room. The envoy from the Isle of Apples waited outside, leaning against a pillar. As I passed, I realised then that her pale skin was actually birch bark. From behind she was completely hollow and inky black, like a rotted stump.

❦ ❦ ❦

They set me to bathe in the atrium pool. There were no lamps out here, and no golden birds. Only the moonlight pouring in through the shattered roof, and tiny glinting glows like fireflies that hovered over the water and the great half-sunken blocks of carved marble. I had to let my eyes adjust to the dim illumination.

The water, it turned out, was warm—like the old baths of Aquae Sulis. As I waded into the pool I remembered a weekend visit to the Bath museums, years ago, when I was still a little kid. There—that Roman thing again. This place was like a Roman palace that had been sunk thirty feet into the earth. Up there near the roof I could see huge trees growing, their branches outlined against the stars, their roots dangling down into the steam. The Fair Folk were always supposed to live underground, according to tradition.

Well, my head seemed to be clearing a bit.

I settled into the embrace of the water, watching a haze of semen detach from my skin and drift away in skeins, glowing like UV under a blacklight. The effect was rather pretty, I thought... if you didn't know what it was or how it had come about. It took ages to rinse out of my hair.

After that I lay back in the water and stared up at the stars, enjoying my languid weightlessness. My body felt remarkably good, to be honest. No aches. No ill effects from its sustained ordeal. Several of the fireflies came down and danced over my breasts, where they rose like pale and glistening islands above the water. When they brushed against my nipples I felt a cold tingle, not at all unpleasant, and my soft buds rose to points.

The moon drifted into view, distorted by the rising heat. It looked like a woman's body, white against the night sky. It was a shock when I recognised myself—my long pale legs, my big breasts, the darker drift of my hair. I was looking at my own reflection up there, as if the top of the room were a mirror. Me, swimming among the stars.

The mental gymnastics became unsupportable and I sat up abruptly, blowing water out of my nose. When I looked up again there was just a missing roof and the moon beyond, cool and serene and round.

When I waded out, the attendants dried and dressed me, in a sort of feminine version of the Hound harness, all crimson leather straps and collars. A version which left my pussy and ass uncovered, I noticed, but nicely framed. There were no mirrors for me to look in, but I could guess at the effect of the costume. My breasts were lifted from below to emphasise them even more, as if they needed that. My nipples themselves were concealed—sort of—behind a precarious and straining wisp of silk that tied under my arms on each side. I suspected that the function of the cloth was to make anybody looking at it think only of wrenching it off. My feet were still bare—no running away for me, then—but I had soft leather legging-type greaves that were slightly padded around the knees. That boded badly, thought I. Or well, depending on your point of view.

By the time I was ready, my head felt completely clear. Interesting... as the Brenin might say. Whatever stoner effect it was that the Gentry food had, I seemed to burn it off really quickly compared to other humans. Did I have the Ganconer to thank for that too?

My handler, Cuckoo—a short, ugly, immensely squat woman in an apron and lead-shod boots, and a great improvement on Milkthistle in my opinion—walked me from the bathing pool, right to the back of the underground palace, past the kitchens to the kennel block. By the time we got there I was wired with enough anticipation to set me trembling again. She used a big bronze key to open the door to a barrel-vaulted hall.

"There you go, deary," she said. "All you can eat."

The Hounds were lined up waiting for me, in two rows. They didn't have much choice about that, since two big slabs of wood like railway sleepers had been laid down, and the men were tethered out at regular intervals. The method of their restraint was novel—they stood with arms roped behind their backs, but what really stopped each one of them from moving was the soft thonging wrapped about his balls and cock and running taut down to a ring in the log beneath his feet. Half a step would be enough to castrate any one of them, so they stood stock-still, eight to a side, unable to touch each other, unable to escape.

They looked at me, and the noise they uttered made the hair stand up on my neck. No words of course, just a growling, throaty rasp of bestial need. Cocks twitched and jumped, swelling despite their bonds. And my cunt responded with a greedy spasm of its own. I looked up the lines for Gavin. Yes—there he was, right at the far end on the left side. Another stubbled, handsome, hot-eyed face among so many. Only I knew how special he was.

"Come on, deary." My chaperone patted my bare bottom encouragingly. "Got to get it done before we bed you down for the night. Otherwise they won't be letting you have *any* sleep." She chuckled to herself, then cast me a quizzical glance. "We normally let three or four of the girls do this, but the

Brenin says you can handle it on your own."

"Yes," I said proudly. "Oh yes."

Sixteen men. Sixteen cocks, rampant and jutting already. Sixteen ball-sacks full of lovely fresh jizz for me. The Brenin was right—I was such a greedy bitch.

I went down on my knees in front of the first man on the right. He had a rug of dark hair on his torso that merged with his pubic pelt and then became a ceaseless flow down his muscular legs. His cock was dark and thick and was wasting no time standing to attention, his congested glans peeking out from his foreskin. I bathed it with my breath and he tried to step forward and cram it into my face, but his bonds brought him up short, pulling cruelly on a scrotum that was carried high and looked full to bursting.

He let out an agonised growl of pure lust, and I almost felt sorry for him. At any rate, I was determined to make it up to him for his frustration. Placing my hands on his beautiful hairy thighs, I ran my tongue up the length of his shaft and enveloped it in the wet warm cave of my mouth.

Sixteen men. Sixteen cocks. I took them all. Cuckoo fetched me water between times, but aside from that I took no breaks and shirked not a single man. I tried to be unhurried, though they were so aroused it was impossible to stop them sometimes. Sixteen throat-loads of cum released and swallowed, licked from my lips and wiped from my tits into my mouth when it accidentally spilled. Sixteen mouthfuls of jizz, each subtly different in flavour and texture—sweet or bitter, thick or fine—and sixteen wonderful hard cocks, each one individual in its shape and length, its taste and its preferences. Some liked to be licked, some sucked, some pumped, some deep-throated. But they were all eager to be pleased. I knew I was only just learning the lexicon of the Hounds' oral needs, and the knowledge that this was to be my task every day made me buzz with delight. *Every day, and every day a little better at it*, I told myself, slurping noisily at number seven as he stood on his toes and jiggled ferociously up and down. Yeah, they all came in different ways too. Some loud, some silent, some writhing, some wringing with sweat. Every one of them delicious.

I went to Gavin last of all, saving the one I wanted above everyone else until the end. He'd watched every performance of service and now his rock-hard thighs were set astride and glistening with sweat, his big cock sticking out before him like a sundial gnomon reading blowjob-o'clock. His shoulders were pumped from where he'd strained against the ropes that kept his hands pinned back. I looked up into his familiar face with that blondish-brown stubble and those fairer, slightly unruly eyebrows. They were drawn now into a pleadingly quizzical frown, like he thought I might perversely choose to stop right here, before giving him what he wanted. I could see the glint of his teeth—not a grin as such, more a grimace of arousal so urgent it was nearly pain. There was a bead of perspiration running down his balls, and a sticky strand of pre-cum drooling from the mouth of his hugely engorged cock.

I wrapped my tongue lovingly around his glans and kissed away that precipitous seep. I felt him move against me with that familiar shudder of contentment, like a cold and exhausted man getting into a hot bath he'd been craving all day. In the past he'd often whispered my name at this point, and run his fingers through my hair. He couldn't do either now. But he uffed deep in his chest—a noise of gratitude and wonder.

I gave him everything I had. Every treat and every trick, everything he'd not been getting from me for two years. It felt to me like, if I could only get it right, then he just might recall earlier times. Lazy Sunday mornings in bed, the outside world forgotten. The 69 in our tent at the festival we went to that summer, insanely loud and not at all discreet, reviewed with whoops and catcalls by campers around us. That franticly naughty blowjob behind the house-plant poly-tunnel, in terror of any member of his staff walking in on us.

But mostly I just focused on sucking his cock because I loved it, every hard inch, and I loved the smell of his sweat and the feel of his skin and the bounce of his balls, and I craved his cum in my mouth, even though I had a belly full of the stuff already. I wanted his pleasure. It meant more to me than my own.

When he came—foaming and copious and nearly drowning me, so wildly did he buck in my throat—it had the tang of ripe avocado, just as I remembered.

I rested against his thigh after he was done, and cast an eye around the hall as I caught my breath. The other guys were sitting down, watching but looking relaxed. Gavin didn't sit. He stayed braced at the extreme end of his leash as Cuckoo came bustling up, handed me another cup of water and slapped his hard ass.

"Good lad," she said cheerily, just as if he were a horse. Then she crouched down and began to pull out the knots behind his scrotum that held his balls prisoner. His glistening, satisfied cock sprang free from its bonds, and Cuckoo moved to untie his hands.

As soon as they were free, he pulled me to my feet. I looked up into his face, smiling, though a little uncertain. He looked pleased with himself, not entirely to my surprise, but I wasn't sure what else was expected of me this evening. Gavin made that clear by putting his arm around me and steering me to one of the stalls at the side of the hall. It was heaped with hay and covered with a patchwork quilt. Picking me up, he laid me down on this and straddled me.

With my stomach full of cum, and after all my exertions, I was certainly willing to lie back. In fact I felt unusually languid. I gently stroked the long, spent curve of his cock as he looked me over, from head to thighs. His fingers lingered on my hip but his eyes kept returning, first to my face, then to my breasts. I lifted those a little, inviting him to take a closer look, and the red silk stretched across my boobs creaked with strain.

Maybe Gavin had some sense of humour left intact. He took so long tugging one of the knots free that I wondered if he was actually teasing. But the look on his face as his gaze swept over my bare breasts was quite serious. Warm too. Lowering his upper body over mine, he dipped his mouth to my right nipple and began to suck.

I was lost. Lost straight away. The other Hounds, the kennels, the whole palace—all of it vanished from my consciousness. There was only Gavin, licking and nuzzling and nipping at my tits until I moaned and wriggled with delight; lapping between my breasts, tickling his tongue down my belly to my navel, snuggling down between my raised thighs. I watched as he bowed his head as if in prayer over the soft folds of my open sex. His tongue made me believe in heaven again.

He licked me for—oh, it felt like hours. I came hard and I came soft, I came until I was just one whimpering, tender, animal mass. Then he rose up over me again and filled me with his cock, and as he ground his hips on mine and I lifted and stretched to one more orgasm, he covered my mouth with his and ate my cries.

The last thing I thought I heard as I curled up in his embrace and drifted off to sleep was his breath against my ear, and the soft groan of his voice: "Tansy."

So I became the only bitch in a kennel full of hounds. Gavin's bitch. And for what seemed like weeks and weeks, so far as I could tell, I was happy. Life was simple and all my needs were fulfilled. Often.

Don't think that I forgot what had brought me here, or what I was looking for. I remembered… Well, some of the time, I did. But there wasn't much I could do about finding the Salmon of Llyn Llyw here, was there? There was no prospect of escape, and even if I had been able to slip away I wasn't going to leave Gavin. I was a captive. A slave. And I accepted it.

I liked it.

It wasn't without its challenges, of course. One dirty slut and sixteen guys with near-constant hard-ons makes for a certain amount of trouble—though I'll admit that the stress was felt by Gavin rather than me. No one dared challenge him openly for fuck-rights to me, but there had to be a certain degree of give-and-take.

Every evening before they doused the lights it was my task to fellate the entire pack—my midnight feast, as I came to think of it. So it was established from the first day that my mouth was available for common use, if I was not engaged otherwise. Gavin, deeply possessive, liked to kneel up behind me, balls-deep in my cunt, whenever I took a throat-full of spunk from yet another horny man-dog. And when I introduced him to my ass for the first time, it made both of us deliriously happy.

I loved that. Spit-roast has to be my favourite form of cooking.

But Gavin wasn't any sort of undisputed alpha dog—I think the whole damn pack was made up of alphas, which is why they ran so hard and why all their backs were laced with whip-marks—and the others became adept at finding times when he was occupied elsewhere, getting groomed or taken out by one of Them There, and then they'd be all over me. Okay, so I didn't help much. All it took was one look and a slap on my well-padded ass from a sinewy, surly Hound, and I'd be bending over and showing him my wet pink welcome mat.

Poor Gavin. I was always contrite after straying, despite my utter inability to resist temptation. But the smell of another man's spunk on me drove him crazy, and he'd fuck me like he meant to die inside me. He was outraged by the prospect of having me taken away from him, but at the same time the sight of me getting shafted by some other male aroused him beyond description. So he'd flaunt me at the others, display me, tease them—and just occasionally turn his back long enough that he'd catch me at it and drive them off and fuck my brains out.

Maybe things aren't as simple as I thought they were, even

for Hounds.

Gavin only spoke my name late at night, after everything else was over. The tiny candle flame of hope he'd lit that first night guttered and went out. He was a Hound, neither more nor less sentient than the others. Trapped by his base animal instincts.

I wasn't the only tail anyone got in the kennels, of course. Them There of many kinds made visits, sometimes for a favoured pet, sometimes for the whole pack. And when all else failed the Hounds would fuck each other, as dogs will, though they played so rough it made me wince.

And there was the Wild Hunt, of course.

I wasn't taken out on the Hunt, for which I was deeply grateful. Instead, the Brenin set aside a special form of exercise for me. I suspect it was seen as quite an honour for me, to have so much of his attention. I was his special little bitch. He'd ride out alone and I would accompany him on foot, like a dog going out for walkies. I'd wear a scarlet leash attached to the collar around my neck, and scarlet boots to protect my feet from the mud and stones underfoot. But no coat, no cloak, just my soft leather harness. We'd walk through woods and along roads, and even into human villages. He always made sure I looked at my most beautiful before setting off, and that I'd had a sip of wine to take the edge off the cold. Not too much of an edge though, because that was our particular pleasure. The game was such that whosoever we first met on our perambulations, whether Fair Folk or mortal—well, that was who I had to fuck, while the Brenin watched with a detached smirk.

Sometimes I got lucky and it was a handsome Gentry lord

or beautiful lake-lady. Far more often it wasn't, and I suspect the Brenin loaded the odds somewhat. I pleasured hags and barghests and urisks, delivery drivers and tramps and squads of soldiers. The Brenin walked me into a crowded market place to offer me to the highest bidder as I stood with eyes meekly downcast, my legs trembling. He tied me face-down over a low branch by a footpath and watched from hiding as three separate passers-by had me one after another, furtively, and then scurried off without a word. He caused a queue of traffic a mile long by laying down the illusion of a felled tree on a busy road, all to present me to two farmers driving their prize ram to stud. It didn't matter if the humans were unwilling. He made them do it anyway. I recall with a shameful glow of delight the day we interrupted a Christian prayer-group held in a farmhouse. He sat on the table and grinned all the way through as they fucked me in turn, tears of outrage in their eyes. That lot were particularly rough and unkind, in comparison to others I'd been offered to. Several called me the Whore of Babylon as they sodomised me.

He didn't only trample my delicate sensibilities among anonymous strangers, of course. He liked to make use of me in Court—often as a footstool; two or three times as a lamp, trussed up with a candle clamped in my ass, forbidden under threat of the whip to move, even when the hot wax dripped on my pussy. He made me, blindfolded, suck the dick of a cockatrice, and only gave me the antidote to its poison when I vomited black froth. He invited the ambassadors of every Court and Realm to fuck any orifice of mine they preferred, as a genteel courtesy over canapés.

There were many of those visitors. Diplomacy was frantic.

Wherever I turned, Them There were muttering in corners about the Pendragon. He clearly worried the hell out of them. But no one ever explained why. Them There are not big on explanations.

Here's the thing—I loved the Brenin. Not as a human being loves another human being, you understand. Not the way I loved Gavin. But as a bitch loves her unpredictable master—with trembling devotion, desperate for the next caress, terrified of the next blow. I'd lie awake at night in dread and anticipation of what he would demand of me in the morning. I'd keep a supply of wine on hand just to be able to face him without losing control of my bladder. I loved him because he'd set himself to giving me the purest, filthiest, most debasing, and thereby the most emancipating sex imaginable. The Ganconer might have trapped me with his curse, but the Brenin had set me free. Or at least, that's what it felt like. Free from thought and responsibility and guilt. Free from the past, and the future.

The day it occurred to me to wonder why he put so much effort into me… Oh, that was a nasty shock.

I was on hands and knees in a bus-stop. The Brenin had invited a gang of youths—uncouth, charmless, small-town teenagers of the type I remembered only too well from my own teenage years—to make free use of me. Then, afterwards, he'd turned them all—whether from irritation or whimsy— into hedgehogs. I was gasping through tears as I wiped spunk from my eyes. My cunt and asshole stung from over-use.

He lifted my chin to look into my face.

"Strange," he said, wiping a blob of cum from my cheek and feeding it to me on his thumb. "You are moved so much more when I put you out to your own kind, than by the most unseelie wight. Why is that?"

What could I say? *Of course* it was more humiliating to be subjugated to a gang of spotty, foul-mouthed teenagers than a vast and terrifying troll. Getting fucked by a monster was one thing. But there was simply no excuse for taking it from a leery, sniggering pack of alcopop-swigging losers eager to try out every perverted thing they'd seen on the Internet. That's what made it so shameful. That was why I wept. And why I'd climax so hard—over and over again.

But as I sucked cold jizz off his hand it occurred to me that he should never, never have asked that question. It should never have occurred to him to wonder how I felt. I looked up, my wide eyes meeting his cool and level ones.

"You are a delight to me," he said softly, stroking my hair. The compliment was horribly uncharacteristic of him. "I shall miss you," he added.

My stomach dropped. "Miss me, Master?"

"The year dies. Samhain approaches. There will be no place for beauty such as yours when I raise the Host and we go to war."

He sounded positively pensive. It made my blood run cold. *The Host* is synonymous with the Unseelie Court. Traditionally it's considered deadly to humans who come into contact with it.

"Please," I said, not sure how I was even going to finish that sentence.

"Do not worry, my little red bitch," he said. "I will let no other kill you." He looked at me for a long time, until I felt dizzy, until the world seemed to fade away, and all I could see was that skull mask, as black as scorched wood. Then he did something truly terrible. He put his hand up to the mask, and took the rim between his fingers.

"No!" I gasped. "Please don't!"

He paused, and removed his hand.

"Time to go." Then he turned away.

I couldn't have told him what I dreaded. I barely recognised it myself. But the fact that he'd showed me any solicitude made me sick to my soul.

For years I'd heard all about the sort of shitty stuff Them There do to people. It's not like I didn't know what the Brenin and his kind got up to. I *knew*. Them There scared the crap out of me, just as they scared anyone with any sense. But I'd never had to hate them, yet. I honestly didn't think there was any point in blaming Them There for their actions, any more than you'd cite a tiger for murder or a dog for humping your leg. It's just what they do. They're not human. We're *not* fellow-travellers. They want food and sex, and to them we're nothing more than supplies of that. To blame them, you'd have to prove them *capable* of things like empathy and conscience. I hadn't ever seen any evidence for that.

Had I seen it now?

The conversation was over, anyway. Waylaying a crusty old shepherd who was walking his two collies back down through the high fields, the Brenin made sure I had other things to set my mind to.

Autumn drew on, crisp and cold that year. Outside, the days grew shorter. Inside the brugh, the balmy summer night was unending.

But my complacency had been shattered. The Brenin's hints had me badly worried now. Some huge change was on the way, something that threatened me and perhaps every human. My bucolic fuck-fest was not going to last forever, and I knew I needed to find a way out.

How do you escape from Faerieland?

While the Wild Hunt was out and the Brenin otherwise occupied, my first pre-occupation was to avoid the Brenhines, who'd never taken a shine to me and was in an increasingly foul temper as Samhain approached. I buried myself out of sight among the throngs in the kitchen and tried to keep from being underfoot. There, human slaves mingled with Good Neighbours of the more stolid and domesticated kind— lumpen humanoids like Cuckoo, who seemed to have no particular weirdness about them, and squabbling goblin types. It was chaos, but then every great kitchen is chaos. At least here real work seemed to be getting done, and every couple of hours great platters of food were taken out to various quarters, to feed members of the Court both high and low.

I made myself useful in small ways. Fetching pitchers of ale from the buttery, turning a spit while the under-cook nipped out to relieve himself, sawing huge loaves of bread into trencher-sized pieces. I just made damn sure never to examine the meat—lest it look a little too much like me.

If, during a slack moment, some servant fancied a quick tossing off, I was always willing.

Then the great autumnal feast of Samhain was upon us— the start of the dark half of the year. Chaos in the kitchen became a state of sustained panic, interspersed with bouts of anarchy. We were expecting guests from every Court, it seemed. From the Silures, the Atrebates, the Regni—even as far as the Calidones. Everything had to be ready for this one night. I hid under a table when a major brawl erupted and I saw the Cook, losing her temper, distend her jaw and swallow a spriggan whole.

"Wretches!" she howled, picking up a small goblin and banging him against a chopping block until he went limp. "Find that Yallery Brown and I'll gut the little turd! How am I supposed to prepare the Samhain Feast in these conditions, I ask you!!?"

"What's he done?" I asked Cuckoo, who was huddled next to me.

"Took a shit in the well, I hear," she giggled, rolling her eyes.

In the end they settled the Cook down without further casualties and sent the hobs down the well to clean it out. In the meantime Cuckoo fetched a pair of wooden milk pails and a yoke.

"Here," she said, dumping them at my feet. "You're a strapping lass. Trot you down to the river and fetch water, so I can get these eggs boiled."

I obeyed, stopping only to put my outdoor boots on. The buckets were heavy even when empty and they swung wildly about, so I wasn't looking forward to the walk back uphill, but it gave me an excuse to keep out of the way. I left through the main gate, glancing back to see the mounded earthwork that was all that was visible of the palace from the outside. My excursions with the Brenin had made me familiar with the route down to the bridge, so I made my way directly there. It was the very tail end of October, of course, so all the broadleaves were on the turn now, or already nude, with even the oaks starting to look sere. Only the moss that carpeted the rocky ground was still bright and green.

The bridge was a single immense slab of stone, Neolithic in appearance, with a central pier that raised it several metres above the narrow ravine. The guardian troll, Inkhorn, was away hewing logs for the ox-roast. I had to climb down the side of the bridge and follow a spidery path to reach the level of the water. Down here the river sounded more of a force to be reckoned with. There were deep pools and great craggy fern-patched boulders dislodged by past floods, and the water was dark and green and powerful. I glanced upstream, and saw a flash of silver—something scaled and shiny surfacing momentarily from the water.

Something inside me clenched with apprehension. I shucked the yoke from my shoulders and left the buckets where they sat, to edge my way up the bank to that next big pool.

It had been created artificially, I found. A wall of stone held the water back long enough to make a deep basin, shaded by hazel bushes. Above the pool the river gushed in over a shallow fall. I stood a little way back from the bank and held tight to a hazel branch, having learned to be cautious. Deep inland waters were places where Them There like Peg Powler and Nelly Long-Arms waited, hungry for human lives.

The dark surface of the water broke and I saw a fin, and a humped red back that flashed silver where it caught the light.

"Bradan Feasa," I whispered. There was an ache in my chest, as if my heart had stopped, and I could feel my hands shaking. This was it. This was the one I had sought.

A second pass and it rolled its head from the pool as if to look at me. I glimpsed a round staring eye, a downturned mouth and a hooked lower jaw. It was a great big fish—seven or eight feet long at a guess, and ugly as all get-out. It looked horrifically old, almost prehistoric. The jaw and the ruddy colour told me it was a spawning male salmon.

"Bradan Feasa," I repeated, my lips burning.

It dipped beneath the surface and rose again, shaking its head—and as it rose it changed shape. It metamorphosed like reformed plasticine into the shape of a man who waded to the pool edge. He was completely hairless and, despite his broad shoulders and extreme muscularity, barely less ugly than the fish. His bald head was yellowish in colour, his body flushed red and painted with purplish spots. He looked really ill, to be honest, and I remembered some nature documentary saying that salmon die straight after spawning, their bodies worn out by the trauma. Worst of all, though, his eyes weren't human. Rather, they were the eyes of a fish—round and still, lidless and empty.

When his hips emerged from the pool, I saw that he sported a huge, charged erection. I don't know why I was surprised. I still associated wisdom with continence, I suppose, somewhere deep inside. But I knew how to respond. My body knew. Letting go of my hold on the hazel, I came forward and knelt on a flat rock before him, thighs parted in submission.

"Bradan Feasa," I said for the third time.

He stepped from the pool, streaming water, and came straight to me, his cock pointing the way. I should have tried to talk to him, I suppose. I should have asked him for the Ganconer's true name, since that after all was the goal of my long quest. But I didn't. An erect cock trumped all other priorities as far as I was concerned. As he grasped my head in his icy hands I opened my mouth and swallowed his penis, glad to no longer have to look at those terrible eyes. He was cold there too. Every inch of him was cold and smooth and slippery. I did my best to warm him up, I took him as deeply into my throat as he could reach, embracing that clammy shaft willingly. But nothing mitigated the cold-blooded fish-chill of his flesh, even though he moved his hips and pushed in and pulled out, just as a real man might, sinking his fingers in my hair and holding me tight.

I've never known anyone so focused on coming. I don't even know if he felt any pleasure, though I hope he did. No sound escaped his lips as his balls contracted and his flood filled my mouth. That was cold too. It shouldn't have been a shock, but it was. I jerked back a little but he kept on gushing, and it squirted up my nose so that I choked. He pulled out, still jetting, splashing my face, hurling thick pennons of cream into my hair. It was an insane amount of cum for any man to produce. Orgasm wracked his body with spasm after impossible spasm. His hands tightened in my hair and I grabbed his thighs, frightened for him. He shoved back into my mouth but there was too much for me to take and it ran out from my open jaws almost as fast as he ejaculated, slopping down over my tits like a tide of cream.

Then I heard him sigh. And he stepped back away from me and collapsed back into the water, limp as a rag. As the waves settled I saw the huge fish floating there, belly-up and motionless.

I'd eaten the Salmon of Knowledge.

Killed him too.

Oh shit, thought I, appalled.

It wasn't exactly what I'd been expecting. Nor was the result. For a moment my mind was almost completely blank. Then all the doors in my head flew open, and suddenly I was thinking far, far too much—swamped with thought, absolutely overwhelmed with it. I grabbed my head, like I could rip the clamour from my skull, and I screamed.

It wasn't that he'd imparted any new knowledge to me. Instead, it was as if I remembered everything, all at once. *Everything* I'd ever watched on TV or read in a book or online, and suddenly I could make the connections. All of them, simultaneously, whether true or false, deep or trivial or utterly meaningless. Everyone I'd met, everything I'd done, the whole long journey here in all its craziness and pleasure and pain.

Look at you, Tansy (Bitter Buttons, Tanacetum vulgare, *and they certainly don't come much more vulgar than me), up the Severn (to the Romans, Sabrina… the witch; to the Welsh the Afon Hafren) without a paddle, looking for the Salmon of Knowledge (called Fintan in Ireland, but Finn MacCool ate that one, and at least he cooked his) in his spawning pool (Hazel trees for wisdom, grab them by the nuts). No clue (that's a ball of string, Ariadne gave Theseus a clue in the Labyrinth) what you're doing, pretending you're Arthur (Pendragon, The Once and Future King) rescuing young Mabon (Mabon ap Modron: Son of the Mother) from the dungeon (tower, a donjon is a tower not a cellar) of Gloucester (that's Caer Loyw). And you just had to fall in with every dirty phouka and thick spunkie around, hobgobbling your way up to Oh Brenin and titty Titania themselves. Getting Unseelie Caught by the Wild Cunt like that, and all for the Ganconner (he certainly conned you). That liar with the lyre, the cat with the (fanny-)fiddle, not to mention the mice (a mouse organ, why not, I've had every other type of organ) and the girl-gang(-bang) (nine of them, Mel and Polly, NINE OF THEM, Melpomene and Polyhymnia of fucking course, how a-muse-ing, and the MICE—HOW COULD I HAVE OVERLOOKED THE STUPID MICE?). Oh good God! (of course he is!) (I always wondered why no one wanted to risk fucking him if he was so hot)—but what's he doing here? He must have been here since Roman (in the gloamin') times. They all have, I guess. That's the reason for the atrium (chamber, four in the heart) and the sandals (caligae, gave the nickname to the mad bad emperor) and the toga parties (donning the toga: a sign of entry into manhood, along with getting rat-arsed and laid). It's probably the last thing they really remember from their previous outing in the mundane (by definition, surely: that's a tautology) world. Fay is from* fatae *(Have you got any Italian in you? Do you want some?). So I* was *looking for Mabon all along. Son of a (wolf) bitch! Son of the Mother: Mother Rome: Dea Roma.*

Oh, my *head!*

I took a deep breath, as the chaos swirling through my brain sank and swayed and settled back to some sort of manageable level. Tears were running down my face and I could hear myself laughing hysterically. But I could breathe again. I could see again.

And I knew the Ganconer's name.

Chapter Thirteen

Solstice Sunrise

Shock held me motionless for a while, semen dripping from my hair and tits and chin. When I moved at last, the first thing I did was go to the water's edge and, ignoring the chill, rinse myself off. It was important that the Salmon's milt returned to the water to fertilise what eggs lay down there among the stones. Come Spring, new salmon fry would hatch and make their way downriver to grow, carrying his legacy.

Then I went back up to the palace. I didn't bring the buckets. It was dark now, I'd lost hours somewhere along the way, and the eggs would already be boiled or forgotten. The doors stood wide open and lamplight streamed from within.

The first person I saw when I stepped inside the portico was the Elder Tree Witch.

I stopped dead, my heart climbing in my mouth. She was quite unmistakeable, despite the fact I'd only seen this incarnation of her reflected in mirrors or pots until now. Her long golden hair glittered with clear dew-drop gems and on her white gown hung deep amethysts of darkest purple, like berries. Her mask, as she turned to me, was made of many overlapping elder leaves.

"Hello, deary," she said. "You've done well for yourself."

I dropped to one knee. "You look especially beautiful tonight, Bour Lady." *Given that I killed you a month back.*

So, it seemed, they were immortal. Well, why should that surprise me, when they were tied so closely to the seasons and the cycles of nature? Death and Life in that realm always follow on from each other. Nothing ever really ends.

"You remember my sons." She gestured behind her, where three slender young men stood shaking off their travelling cloaks and handing them over to servants. One was blond, one dark, one had long hair of rich chestnut. They were all jaw-droppingly handsome, and although they were too busy and clearly of too high a rank to waste a greeting upon a human slave, they all cast me slyly interested glances.

They're dressed their best, for the feast, thought I, and wondered what their reflections would look like now, if there were any mirrors in this place. *Tonight they come in Seelie form. A last fling before Winter.* It made sense suddenly. Not two rival Courts, but two alternate forms. Not good and bad, but beautiful and ugly. Like the two faces of the Bour Lady's house. Both equally real.

"Are you well provided for?" she asked, her voice like satin.

"I am the Brenin's own bitch, lady." It wouldn't hurt to let her know.

"Ah. How fortunate for you." She flicked a fan at me and wandered away, ostentatiously disinterested.

Tonight was All Hallows' Eve, when all the powers of terror were released upon the world and the summer went into abeyance. Even back home in the urban sanctuary of London it was an occasion of genuine peril. And tomorrow—what would all these fine ladies and lords look like tomorrow? Especially if the War Council chose to mobilise, when they met tonight? If they were going to war, then it made sense that they would take on their Unseelie forms for that. War is an ugly business, after all. And it'd be more practical, wouldn't it? Ravening monsters, not fancy courtiers, to take on the enemy. Whoever the hell he was.

I didn't know what the Brenin would look like tomorrow, and I didn't want to know either. It would be very bad indeed, I suspected. I'd been lucky with him, so far. Lucky that he prized beauty and pleasure when in his Seelie form. Lucky that blood and torn flesh and terror and decay, all that was ugly—not evil or immoral, just ugly—belonged to the Unseelie.

My luck was about to change, I was increasingly sure. I leaned against the wall as I rose from kneeling, dizzy with foreboding.

"Girl!" It was Cuckoo, looking flustered. "Where have you been?"

"I'm sorry… I was waylaid."

"And laid on the way, I don't doubt! Well, get you into the Great Hall and join the other dogs under the tables."

I wasn't sure whether this was me being let off or me being downgraded, but I hurried to obey. My head was still spinning, connections being made and revelations popping in my mind like soap bubbles, making my skin tingle. I needed some nice, repetitive task to work at while I tamed these mnemonic fireworks, and this was ideal.

The Great Hall was a bit of a surprise though. Normally a frescoed room, this night it was seven or eight times larger than I'd ever seen it, and it looked like the interior of the most immense hollow tree. I stared up at the fluted buttresses of wood converging a mile over my head. Maybe this tree was Yggdrasil itself, I thought—the World Ash. The guests dined in concentric circles, with the highest-ranking of the Fair Folk in the central ring around an open space, reclining upon couches in Roman style. Further out, the more uncouth types sat upright like medieval banqueters, along great long tables. There were hundreds of them, and they were already eating and drinking and banging on the tables for more ale and throwing things at each other. Goblins ran up and down the tabletops, serving out more platters onto cloths already stained with spilt wine and mounded with dirty dishes and discarded bones. It looked like it was going to be a riotous night.

I decided to stay away from the limelight and I ducked under a table two rows back from the Brenin and Brenhines and their greatest guests. Down there among the knees and the boots, crawling through the dried leaves that carpeted the floor, my job was simple. I had room to make my way up between two rows of revellers. If I brushed against someone's knee and they opened their legs, gesturing at their crotches, it was my duty to wiggle in and pleasure them orally. They never saw me. They never knew whether I was male or female, even. I was just an open mouth providing a little more random entertainment for the evening.

I had sucked off an ettin, three satyrs, and a huge, foetid, hairy thing I couldn't identify, when I heard something that stopped me in my tracks. The strains of a violin, playing high and fast and wicked. Fiddle music to make your heart leap and your feet bleed. And I knew at once that it was an instrument I'd heard before.

Crawling out from under a bench, I stood to look at the centre of the room. In the open space before the royal couple stood a figure in a shabby green coat and broad-brimmed hat, playing up a storm. A troop of lithe goblin acrobats performed eye-watering and frankly impossible tricks around him—one, I saw, dove up into another's asshole and climbed out of its throat—but my attention was fixed on the musician. And I certainly did know him.

And now I also knew something about him that made me shake inside. Something that changed the whole game, if I was right. Something whose repercussions I couldn't begin to untangle.

If I'm right about what he is.

The musical piece, insanely proficient, came to a crescendo and ended. The goblins scurried off-stage. Bowing, the Ganconer swept off his hat and paced the inner circle, holding it out like a café busker. Some of the grand ladies and gentlemen in their glittering jewel-encrusted clothes tossed small objects into the hat. Most ignored him. Several laughed derisively.

It was so strange, seeing the Ganconer in this context. When we'd first met, he'd seemed a creature of unearthly beauty and potent threat. I'd had nothing to compare him to, then. Now, among the puissant and the glorious of all the domains, he looked tawdry and small. It was like seeing the object of a teenage crush after many years, and realising what a dull and average person he was.

I had to speak to him.

That was the problem. I was torn—I didn't want to butt in during the entertainment, but if I left it too long he might just flit away again. He didn't seem to be too well thought of here.

Shit. I was running out of time. This had to be done tonight. I had to make my move, or I might not live to get another chance.

I waited until he finished another reel and bowed low, flourishing his bow. When he straightened up, I was standing beside him.

"I know your name," I said, quietly.

The Ganconer frowned.

"Tansy. Fancy seeing you here. Don't interrupt while I'm playing."

He lifted his bow again. I don't know if my fish dinner had granted me some new-found insight, but I was suddenly struck by the conviction that he was nervous.

"Do you really want me to say it here, in front of everyone?" I asked, moving to look him straight in the eye.

A tic jumped in his cheek. All at once he didn't look at all like an insouciant strolling player. Fiddle and bow were both gone in a moment. He grabbed my harness at my shoulder.

"Outside. We'll talk in private."

He just about dragged me down the aisle toward the door. We were almost there when the Brenin spoke, his quiet cold voice cutting through the hubbub of the room and spreading a wash of hush.

"Ganconer."

An ogre guard stepped in front of the exit, barring our way. We came to an abrupt halt and the Ganconer wheeled us around to look back toward the Brenin.

"My lord?"

"Don't damage her." It was a calm voice that, somehow, suggested that the consequences of disobedience would be unthinkable.

The Ganconer, unblinking, nodded once and dipped a bow. This time our leave-taking was uninterrupted.

Outside the feast hall, the palace was all but empty. Wordlessly the Ganconer pushed me on through deserted passages, his footfalls echoing in hard snaps on the tiles, his grip harsh upon my arm. He shoved open a door and yanked me out into an open space. The stable courtyard—I remembered it well from one of the Brenin's shocking afternoon entertainments. There were no grooms or ostlers about now; everyone was at the feast. The Ganconer turned me and caught the ring at the front of my collar, holding me prisoner as he looked me up and down in the moonlight.

"My pretty little wanton looks well. I'm surprised you're still alive, frankly, but you seem to have found your niche here."

He caught my right nipple between thumb and forefinger, pinching it. My spasm made him grin.

"Giving you plenty of food and exercise, are they?"

The grip on my tit made me groan, all words superfluous.

"I thought so."

He pinched the other nipple to even up the score, tugging me close to him so his breath was on my face.

"It's all a slut like you wants, isn't it? Cock, and more

cock."

He wasn't entirely wrong. And his casual manhandling had brought a flood of warmth to my ever-eager pussy. Without even meaning to, I was rubbing up against his thighs. He chuckled.

"That's why you brought me out here, isn't it? You can't live without this, you dirty slut."

I shook my head helplessly, opening my lips to protest my serious intent, but he stopped my words by sliding his tongue into my mouth and kissing my breath away, while his fingers twisted and ground the buds of my tits. One part loving, one part cruel—the contradiction cut through all the rational parts of my mind to the hot red core of arousal, and made me whimper and press my sex up against his gathering hardness.

"Missed me, have you?" he growled, sliding a hand over my bare bum and squeezing the firm mound. "This is what this is all about, isn't it? You're just desperate for another ride of my horsey, aren't you, little girl?"

"I didn't… I mean…" I gabbled.

"Your wet little cunt is just aching for another stir of the Ganconer's cream-stick. Don't bother lying to me. I can smell your fuck-juices, you poor little whore."

"I know your name!" I gasped.

In a split-second everything changed, as he grabbed my throat in his hand and choked off my breath.

"Shut up!" he hissed.

Oh. He's terrified, I realised.

"You. I don't want to hear you talk." His voice was rasping, but there was a hint of unsteadiness beneath it. "You've got better things to do with that mouth, slut. So you don't say another word until I tell you to."

He kissed me again on the lips, as if to seal them. Then he slacked off his grip just enough to allow me to breathe, and licked my face all over, enjoying my gasps.

"Cat got your tongue?" he asked.

I tried to speak. I couldn't. He'd taken my voice. Literally, taken it. My eyes widened.

His teeth glinted as he grinned. Slowly he ran his hand down my body and cupped the mound of my sex, sliding fingers into my furrow. His long thumb ground into the flesh over my pubis, and when I winced in discomfort he didn't miss it. Yanking out his invasive fingers, he knuckled my belly directly over my bladder instead, and watched knowingly as I tried to squirm away from him.

"Can't you even scream?" he gloated. "That's a little unfortunate for you, isn't it?"

He transferred his grip from my throat to my hair and spun me round, then walloped my ass cheeks to prove his point. I tried to escape, but he had me pinned by my ginger locks. I tried to shriek in protest, but nothing came out of my empty throat but a hiss of breath. So I twisted and arched, dangling from his fist, unable to do anything about his heavy hand slapping my bottom so cruelly. It went on and on, terrible and inflaming. My excitement flared along with my panic. And all the while I was wondering *Why? Why does it make him angry? What's he worried about?*

Then the Ganconer turned a trick that left me no leisure to worry about motivation, or anything else. He dragged me sideways by my hair, to a rack where horse-tack hung. Snatching down a long rope—a lunge rein, I suppose—

he clipped it to my collar. His next acquisition was a whip. Not a short crop for riding, or even a longer lash for rounding up hunting dogs, but a seven foot training whip, as thin as a reed and as wicked as a jay's beak.

Oh shit, I thought. He had stolen my voice and I couldn't call for help.

"Here," he said, gruffly. I could see the swelling bulge of his erection, given a crisp black shadow by the full moon. "Here, you dirty little bitch. Let's put you through your paces, shall we?"

He let out enough slack on the leash, as he backed off, to put me right at the end of the tip of that whip, brandished in his left hand. I tried to retreat even further but he yanked at my neck, pulling me back into place. With a flick of his wrist he sent the narrow strands dancing across the skin of my hip. It might have floated like a butterfly, but it stung like a bee. If I could have, I'd have squealed. But I only managed to mime my protest.

"Good," he said. "Now run."

With another kiss of the lash he set me off running in circles around him, keeping me close enough with the taut rein, using the very tip of the whip to spur on my efforts. I stumbled and slid on the uneven cobbles. My tits bounced wildly, and my ass jounced in time with every skittish step. I couldn't find a comfortable pace—whenever I did he would strike at the front of my thighs, causing me to flinch and stagger. Each wicked kiss of the whip felt like the stab of a wasp's sting, like poison and lightning in one. It was extraordinary that such a tiny movement of his hand could produce such an effect in my flesh. He leaned back comfortably on his heels, controlling me with an arrogant economy of effort, while I felt the lead build in my limbs and the fire in my lungs. Burning lines laced my buttocks and the backs of my thighs. I couldn't see them, but in my mind's eyes they shone with a blue electric glow.

"I was hoping you'd show more stamina," he remarked, above the sound of my gasps. I was really staggering now, and even the lash couldn't hasten my stride. I skidded on a wet cobble and nearly pitched over, managing to catch my balance at the last moment.

"Stand!" he snapped, and I came to a halt, grateful to him despite myself. "Face me! Hands behind your head!"

I assumed the posture required, the ephemeral gratitude evaporating to be replaced by dread. The whole front of my body was open to him in this position. My chest heaved, my out-thrust breasts rising and falling. Twin targets, with visibly pointed bull's-eyes straining against their silk.

"Don't move," he warned. "Not a muscle."

Then he flicked the whip against my left nipple. He was very accurate. The tiny, concentrated pain went through me like a strike of lightning, from tit to core. I couldn't help it—I twisted and arched, but that only thrust my breasts out further, making them more vulnerable, and then he punished my other nipple for my inability to keep still. I could feel the sweat running down my body, tickling between my tits. I could see that the silk stretched over my poor boobs was wet and dark. Every sting brought another wash of heat and wet and terror. Between my legs, my sex was perversely inflamed. I felt dizzy. If he stuck to torturing my tits, I thought, I might be able to bear it. It was like a red-hot tongue licking me. It

342

was like the kisses of a demon. It was like evil pleasure.

Then he started down my body, slowly, a few inches at a time, and I knew I was wrong, and that I couldn't bear it after all. My fear must have shown in my face. When he reached my navel he paused.

"Open your legs," he ordered.

I obeyed. I writhed in dread but I set my thighs apart. I knew he could almost certainly see the swollen nubbin of my clit poking out between my unfurled labia. But my terror was greater even than my arousal. I knew something awful would happen if he whipped my pussy.

"Let it out, slut," he said, as if reading my mind. "Let it all out."

Then he struck again, and again—but not at my pussy. At the lowest part of my belly, directly above my naked pubic mound. Right over my bladder. It was agony. The fire stabbed right inside me and grew to a furnace. Suddenly my control collapsed and I found myself pissing right there, hard and hot in front of him, onto the cobbles—a gush of pure animal surrender.

He timed it so that the stream was just starting to slack, and then he flicked my clit. I came, still pissing, and only the taut leash and the broad collar stopped me tumbling over backward, nearly robbed of my senses, on the verge of blacking out. Nothing like that had ever happened to me before.

My cries and sobs were all but silent.

"Animal," he said, throwing down the whip. He strode forward, looping the rein around his fist to shorten it, and grabbed my wet pussy. "You're nothing but a nasty little mammal, you and all your kind—giving yourselves airs, whilst all the time you're nothing more than a clever type of pig that's been taught to walk on two legs."

He slapped my face with his piss-wet hand, ironically gentle, and wiped it over my mouth.

"Well, I'm going to put you back where you belong."

The Ganconer grabbed my hair and spun me across the yard, pushing me in front of him. I recognised the stable dungheap in front of me—a huge pile of sodden straw—and then he shoved me down on hands and knees in it. Horse-dung has never smelled particularly unpleasant to me, but that doesn't mean I want to be up to the wrists in it. I gasped and spat and shook my head.

"There. Down in the midden. Where you belong. Living in the dirt. Fucking in the dirt."

His grunted staccato words suddenly made sense as he finally released his cock from his pants and stuffed it into me from behind. My pussy was still clenching and dilating from my last orgasm, and despite his lack of gentility the push of penetration made me open eagerly, bracing myself against the midden as best I could to take him.

Oh God. I'm going to come again.

"You filthy little animal," he growled, shafting me hard and deep. "You dirty fucking beast. You love this, don't you? You fucking love it down here in the shit, with my cock up your bitch-hole!"

Every word struck like a blow. I was nearly torn apart by the spasms of my climax. I'd have screamed "Yes!" if I could have. As it was, I don't know whether he could feel the pulse and clench of my cunt, but he grabbed the straps of my harness and tripled his rhythm, juddering into me like a jackhammer. The bastard was just too aroused by the abuse and the whipping he'd given me to hold back.

"You fucking animal!" he snarled. "Oh, yes, there it is! Tell me what a dirty whore you are, bitch! Tell me how much you love this! Oh…! Oh…!… Yes!"

Hey. That *Tell Me* sounded like permission to me. After all, it's the letter of the thing that counts, when it comes to curses. As the Ganconer filled me with gush after gush of his cum, I opened my mouth and spoke, though his thrusts all but slammed the air from my lungs and it came out in grunts.

"MAPONUS! That's your name! Maponus Apollo!"

He pulled out in a rush, which to be honest probably saved my life. As it was, I felt a blast of heat on my backside and thighs, but I didn't notice the sunburn until later. I was too concerned by the agonising burst of light that flooded the yard, so bright that I screwed my eyes shut but could still see it through my lids.

"Oh!" shouted the Ganconer's voice. He yelled out words in languages I didn't understand—the first sounded like Welsh, the second was probably Latin—and he laughed.

As the light faded I opened one eye gingerly, trying to focus past the blue blobs dancing across my retina and the tears spilling out on my lashes. It wasn't night anymore. It was broad, brilliant daylight. As I watched, stunned, the dungheap under my hands put up slim green shoots and these burst into flower, a swathe of yellow winter-aconite and white snowdrops. In seconds the midden was completely invisible under a carpet of blossom. I looked around me, and saw no stableyard. I was out in the open, on grass, among trenches and mounds and what looked like ruined walls or the remains of some ancient building site, grown over and returning to nature. Small trees were colonising the tops of the walls.

Viroconium Cornoviorum, I thought. *That's where we are. The Roman town on the Severn. Of course it is. I've only been taken a few miles north.*

"Oh," he said, behind me. "Yes. Yes, you're right. I had forgotten. The Merlin devoured me, and I lay in darkness, and I forgot."

He'd forgotten who he was. He'd forgotten he was a god. Until I'd come along… frail, human, fallible Tansy; I had brought him back to himself. I'd set him free.

I risked turning to face him, but shielded my watering eyes. He was too bright to look upon.

"Tansy…"

"Please!" I said. "I can't see!"

His blistering personal illumination dimmed to a bearable level. Very cautiously, blinking and wiping away my tears, I looked up at the figure standing over me. The one who had been the Ganconer, but wasn't any more. He was naked except for a pair of baggy plaid trousers that sat low on his hips; his bare chest was a golden-tan, his hair the same tarnished gold mix of dark honey and blond, though longer now and more curly. He looked both younger and physically stronger. There was a sparkle in his beautiful eyes that was entirely new, and his smile lit up not just his face, but the whole world around him. He was recognisably the same Ganconer, but entirely unlike him. All that was peevish and sly and mean in him had been burned away. All that was tawdry and small-minded.

Don't get me wrong—I'm not saying he was nice now.

346

Gods aren't nice. But he was no longer burdened by weakness.

"Yes!" he cried suddenly, lifting his arms and turning to survey the land about us. "Yes!" He threw back his head and laughed for joy, and the tumbled walls echoed his wild exultation. Birds rose from distant treetops, calling excitedly. He looked like he could run the length of Britain without losing breath. He looked like he could wrestle a stag to its knees bare-handed. He looked like he could lay a hundred women in a night and bring delight to every one of them.

"Tansy," he said, remembering me again. Even his voice was deeper and richer; a voice made for shouting with joy. "You found me. Oh, you brave pilgrim." He shook his head. "But I have used you ill."

With a wave of his hand, the horse-shit and the red kiss-marks of the whip faded from my skin. The sexual glow remained.

"That's okay," I said weakly, shaking like a leaf. "No problem. Have you killed them? Have you destroyed them all?" I glanced around. It was easier to look at the landscape than at him.

"Not at all. The Court exists only by moonlight. Here it is day."

All the pent-up terror went out of me in a long breath.

"Now I will keep my word to you, and more." He stopped and took my hand, drawing me to my feet. "What will you ask of me?"

His arm slipped about my waist. I don't think I've ever felt so inadequate as when he held me, then. Despite my sudden cleansing, it seemed wrong to juxtapose my imperfect body with his. I struggled to meet his gaze.

"Uh. I don't know."

"I will lift the curse, as agreed. You will be a normal woman again."

"No!" The word shot out of my mouth before I could think about it, and panic followed after. "I mean, hold on… let me think about this. I'm not sure."

He lifted one perfect eyebrow. "Not sure?"

I gaped a bit, floundering as I sought the words. It may sound weird, but imagine someone offering to take your libido away, to make everything calm and rational and easy. Would you really go for that?

"I'm not sure it's a good idea," I said slowly. "If I change… what happens when I look back? At all the things I did, I mean, and all the things done to me. I wanted it all, at the time, but it'll appal me afterwards. Like getting drunk and happily doing something really *really* stupid and then remembering in the morning and wanting to die of embarrassment—only, way *way* worse. It'll make me… a victim. How on earth will I live with that?"

He nodded. "If you like, I can take away your memories of this time."

"No!" I shook my head. "Really. I don't want you to do that! It'd be like taking away a part of me. What we do, what we remember doing, is what makes us. This is me." I looked down at myself, at my degrading costume and my flushed skin. I acknowledged to myself that he'd been right about that, if nothing else, back in the picture gallery: that edgy desire always had been a part of me, even if I hadn't recognised it. "This stuff is me too. I didn't know it. But it is."

Maponus looked into my face, frowning a little. "Then…

do you wish me to leave you at this Court, after all?"

I shook my head again. "No. It's all about to hit the fan down there; they're about to march off to war against Arthur, or Aslan, or whoever the hell they think he is. No. I want out of there. And Gavin too. Will you save Gavin?" My voice rose, certainty flooding it. "I can't leave him behind!"

"My mercy extends as far as your love. If Gavin falls within that compass, then yes. I will take you both away, and home."

"What about Gail?" I asked. "Is she safe? Is she alive? Can you find them? And she loves Vince, I think, and he loves her. Save them all. The humans. Please."

He shrugged and nodded, laughing. "If it makes you happy."

"Yes."

"Is that what you really want, Tansy? To go home unchanged? To be the cunt to every cock? Were you not afraid of that?"

I bit my lip, trying to explain, to myself as much as to him. "It's like you told me ages ago: that *is* a part of what I want. I don't want to pick and choose. I don't want sex to be calculated, because I think it's too important for that. I want it to be bigger than me, something overwhelming, something I have no power over. Like love, or the stars, or the ocean." I swallowed. "For me, that's how the humiliating, crazy, slutty stuff works. It's like a doorway into something bigger than myself. And a mirror, that shows me myself walking through that door. Because I know it should be degrading, and that it's not what I should be doing, and that it goes against all the rules, and that everyone will look down on me for doing it—

and I still love it. It's like that's the moment I'm really taken over, possessed, by desire. I'm touching something vast. Now I totally, *totally,* get that that sort of thing is not for everyone. But that's how it works for me. I don't know why, but it just does." I shook my head. "Does that make me… messed up?"

Maponus smiled. "It makes you a priestess," he said.

"Okay…" I tried to wrap my head round that.

"And I will need a priestess in this new world."

My mouth made an O, but I had no words to fill that space. I wasn't even really sure what divine aspects Maponus embodied. No one was, any more. But the Romans had identified him with Apollo, so youth and light and prophecy of the future were likely candidates.

"But I can tell you this much, Tansy. If you find it too hard to live with sometimes, there is an answer of sorts. In the very poem you sought when we met."

"*Goblin Market?*"

"All along. The brave girl, almost as brave as you, who rescues her sister."

I frowned. "What? A second dose of fruit? That's not right —it's completely the wrong way round, in fact. The humans of the Court eat the food all the time, and it just makes them worse. What they need is to *stop* eating the stuff."

"It's not the fruit. Another kind of juice."

"Then…?" I felt the pieces shift and fall together in my mind, a jigsaw pattern completed at last. I thought of Laura licking the mashed fruit from Lizzie's body, lapping it from her sister's sex, and thus regaining her senses. I remembered late nights in the kennel of the Hounds. My tender lassitude in Gavin's arms, so unlike my frantic horniness of the day. His words breathed in my ear.

"Oh…! It's not the fruit. It's the person. Their cum. That's why Gavin remembered my name!"

"You love him. He loves you. It is in every mouthful you take of him. That is what draws the poison."

I covered my face with my hand, overwhelmed by the realisation of how closely Gavin and I were bound. And how much I needed his love now. *Literally* needed it. "Oh God."

"That is all you need, is it not? Let us depart, then, and reunite you with your paramour."

I looked around, taking in the bright, pale sunlight and the winter flowers, and the bare branches of the trees. "But it's too late, isn't it? We're way past Samhain. What if they've gone to war and he's dead already?"

"It's Midwinter, here and now. But if the Fay have the ability to move about in the river of time, then I am capable of far more. I am greater than they, Tansy."

Midwinter—of course. The start of the long journey into Summer. The natal day of every solar deity and of light. The Feast of the Unconquered Sun.

" Well then. Happy Birthday, lord," I said.

EPILOGUE

Deo Mapono Apollini

So now I'm the high priestess of Maponus Apollo, new god on the block. Or rather, a very old one reborn. It's not what I wanted when I got into this, but I have to admit I've got no one to blame but myself. Anyway, it certainly has its compensations. After all, I do get to have sex with a god every so often. That's… sublime.

And in between times there's Gavin. The man I love. He keeps me safe, and brings me back down to earth when I'm running wild across the rooftops. And he loves me. I've got actual physical proof of that, because it's only sucking his cock that keeps me from going as crazy as a Delphic prophetess.

Oh, yeah—that's another perk of the job. Maponus Apollo is a god of prophecy. I can see things about people now —auras, visions, glimpses of the tracks of Fate. And I'm in considerable demand. In some very high places.

We do okay out of that. More than okay, really.

Besides, with Them There at war, it surely helps humankind to have a god on its side.

I don't manage it the way the Delphic virgins did, though. All that breathing the sulphurous fumes of the Underworld— it's not exactly healthy, is it? I reach my trance my own way. On my knees, usually, with four or five men and women working relays to stoke my orgasms until my mind just lifts off —and *bang*, I'm flying, and I've got my god speaking through me. It's a hell of a hit. Gavin has to spend a lot of time gentling me afterwards.

What a way to serve the community, eh? Ventriloquist's doll for a Romano-Celtic deity. A tool of higher powers. His pet human. What a life.

Hey, I've got no cause for complaint. Though I will admit to feeling a bit ashamed sometimes.

But let's face it, I like that.

END

ABOUT THE AUTHOR

Janine has been seeing her books in print ever since 2000. She's also had numerous short stories published by Black Lace, Nexus, Cleis Press, Ravenous Romance, Harlequin Spice, Storm Moon, Xcite, Mischief Books, and Ellora's Cave among others. She is co-editor of the nerd erotica anthology 'Geek Love'.

Born in Wales, Janine now lives in the North of England with her husband and two rescued greyhounds. She has worked as a cleaner, library assistant, computer programmer, local government tree officer, and - for five years of muddy feet and shouting - as a full-time costumed Viking. Janine loves goatee beards, ancient ruins, minotaurs, trees, mummies, having her cake and eating it, and holidaying in countries with really bad public sewerage.

Her work has been described as:

"Hardcore and literate" (Madeline Moore) and "Vivid and tempestuous and dangerous, and bursting with sacrifice, death and love." (Portia Da Costa)

OTHER SINFUL PRESS TITLES

PEEPER by SJ Smith
BY MY CHOICE by Christine Blackthorn
SHOW ME, SIR by Sonni de Soto
THE HOUSE OF FOX by SJ Smith
A VARIETY OF CHAINS by Christine Blackthorn
IN BONDS OF THE EARTH by Janine Ashbless
THE LIBERTINE DIARIES by Isabella Delmonico
SINFUL PLEASURES - An Anthology of Erotic Tales

For more information about Sinful Press
please visit
www.sinfulpress.co.uk